Beast Master's Legacy

J.M. Sampson

Contents

Dedication

Dedicated to the memory of Andre Norton

Acknowledgments

Thanks to my Astro Navigator and wife, Teresa. Her input was crucial for the interstellar navigation involved in the story.

About the Author

J.M. Sampson enjoys creating interesting fiction across more than one genre. He has published fantasy books, a Christian redemption book, and is now imagining the realm of space, with science fiction tales. Life-long science fiction fan, he invites you to travel interstellar distances from within the pages of his mind.

Chapter 1

Cade Storm sat in a dark corner of the dingy barroom. Staring into his glass of Cygnus beer, he wondered how many people had drunk from the glass since it was last cleaned. Downing the last of the liquid, he contemplated whether his immunity vax was still protecting him. He settled the glass on the table and watched debris slide along the inner surface with the remnants of liquid, adding to the already blackened residue at the bottom.

Pulling a crumpled piece of paper from his pocket, he read it for the hundredth time. *Cade, your mother is in poor health. I believe she is grieving because she misses you. I know you aren't interested in working the ranch, but a visit would help put our minds at ease. Please consider coming home.* Absently folding the note, he wondered if his father was trying to coax him home, using a contrived illness.

Peripheral vision alerted him to someone approaching his table. Cramming the paper into his pocket, he eased his right hand to the grip of the stunner holstered at his side. He continued to stare at the liquid in the glass, but his mind, honed by combat experience, focused on the intruder.

"I've been told you're Cade Storm."

Looking up from his beer glass, he turned his head to see a Zacathian female looking down at him. Her neck frill was iridescent blue and green. He could not recall ever seeing a female of her species. She was slender and stood about five feet in height. "That's my name; what do you want with me?"

"My name is Zina. May I join you for a drink? I need to talk to you about a matter of great importance."

Her teeth were not pointed like the males he had met, and she didn't have the fangs normally visible at the corners of a Zacathian's mouth. If it weren't for iridescent highlights that gave the appearance of scales, and her neck frills, she could pass for a human female. Short, iridescent hair that varied in color from blue to green, framed her face and shimmered as she moved. "Why not? Have a seat, but you'll find the cleanliness of this establishment leaves a lot to the imagination."

She settled in the chair across from him, as a server with a dirty towel over his arm came to take her order. He watched as she ordered a beer and then leaned toward him with her right elbow resting on the table. "A close friend of mine is seeking the service of a Beast Master."

Suspicion arched his right brow, as he cocked his head to one side. "What would that search have to do with me? I'm not a Beast Master."

The server returned to set a glass of beer in front of her, on the table. She picked up the glass and took a drink. Lowering the glass to the table, she revolved it slowly in her hand, while gazing into his eyes. "You're not currently a Beast Master, but I knew your grandfather. A hundred years ago, when I was five, my family went to Arzor to conduct research in the ruins of a forerunner facility. Your grandfather, Hosteen Storm, settled there after Terra was burned off by the Xiks."

Storm signaled for another glass of beer. When the server handed it to him, he held it up and peered into the murkiness, suspecting he would find something swimming in the gritty liquid. The Zacathian's revelation that she knew his history, increased his wariness. "You've got me there. My grandfather was a Beast Master, but that has nothing to do with me. Something tells me you didn't come to this mud hole of a planet to rehash history. Did my father send you to find me, and persuade me to return home?"

She leaned back in her chair. "I'm not here at the behest of your family. My only interest is that you have the blood of your ancestors, coursing through your veins. You have the sight."

He downed half the liquid and set the glass on the table. "You sound a lot like my father when he's lecturing me, or trying to tell me who I should marry. It's been interesting talking about the past with you, but it's time for me to leave. I have an important meeting."

She smiled as she moved her left hand to rest on his. "You have nowhere to go. I spoke with your former captain before he lifted the ship this morning. He said you were a good man, but you seemed to be running from, or to, something." Pausing, she turned her head to look around the seedy barroom. "It's hard to believe this could be what you were running to. You requested to be discharged from your crew contract when you earthed here, on Cygnus 3. You're stranded here until some tramp freighter, or passenger ship, happens to make a visit and agrees to take you to other worlds. Your options are limited because there is less spacer traffic here than on a deserted island." Leaning forward, she lifted her hand from his, crossing her arms on the table in front of her. "I have the means to lift you from this mud-encrusted planet."

Cade leaned forward, both elbows on the table. He scratched his chin with his left index finger. "You have my attention. What do I have to do to catch a ride?"

"Come with me. It's not far to my captain's room, and time is of the essence." Cade motioned for the server to bring his bill. He pulled out credit chips and laid them in the server's outstretched hand. He rose from his chair, and followed Zina as she left the bar and stepped down onto the muddy, rutted pathway, that passed for a street. As she led him toward the small spaceport, situated about a mile outside of the mud brick town of Obsequy, Cade looked up and observed yellowish clouds drifting across an orange sky. The town's sole purpose for existence was to fleece as many credits as possible from the spacers who manned the ships visiting the port.

About a half mile before reaching the port, Zina left the mud road as she climbed two steps to the entrance of a dive that served as an inn. A sign above the door, written in Trade Universal, read, 'Spacers Paradise Inn.' Storm wondered what part of paradise was represented by the ramshackle building. He ducked under a warped board that infringed upon the top part of the doorway, and threatened the scalp of anyone who stood six feet or more in height. They entered the run-down lobby, and he followed the Zacathian up a broad stairway that was probably a very ornate feature in the building's distant past. Zina stopped in front of a door with the number 6 on its dirty surface.

Storm felt dizzy as he suddenly saw the inside of the room, without the door being opened. He had experienced the same disorientation the day he arrived on Cygnus. He reached out and steadied himself on the doorpost. "What's happening to me?" He shook his head. His mind and vision cleared, and he noticed Zina staring at him. Turning her attention to the lock, she pressed the keypad combination and opened the door.

The room was dark, but not too dark to see a figure laying on a bed. A big cat that looked to be a panther, sat by the bed, staring at its occupant. Storm shook his head as he felt the dizzy feeling return. In his mind, he could see the person in the bed. He realized, with amazement, that he was seeing through the eyes of the cat. The dizziness passed and he noticed the cat now redirected its gaze, looking intently at him. "Why did you bring me here, Zina?"

The man on the bed coughed, and said, "Come closer, Storm."

Cade warily approached the bed and stood next to the big cat, which seemed determined not to leave the spot where it was sitting. A ruffling of pinions drew his attention to look to his left, where an eagle roosted on the back of a heavy chair. He turned to look upon the face of the man lying on the bed. The face was gaunt and reflected pain. The man appeared to be well beyond middle age.

Zina went to the other side of the bed and gently rested her hand on the man's right shoulder. "I have brought him as you requested, Captain Sartre."

"I don't have much time left to me, Cade. I received a poisonous wound on the last world Zina, and I visited. I'm a Beast Master. Though not long-lived, like Zina, I've been around enough years to visit new worlds as first in scout. I never used my team's skills for the purpose of war, but for discovery. I have asked my team to go with you, and they have agreed. I want them to be set free in a world where they can live out their lives as they were created to do."

Cade Storm scratched at the stubble on his chin. "I thought a team wouldn't bond with another Beast Master. I've never worked with a team and wasn't aware that I had the ability to see through an animal's eyes until today."

"It's true that the creatures who join with a Beast Master, establish a bond with only that person." Sartre coughed, and a fleck of blood appeared on his lip. Zina used a cloth to wipe his mouth. His voice weakened. "In this case, I've asked my team to bond with you for one last mission. A mission to find them a new home."

Cade exhaled a deep breath as he grasped for an excuse. "I would like to help, but I currently don't have a way to get off this forsaken world."

"Death will enter to find me at any moment." His voice weakened further as his words came with difficulty. "I ask that you see to my body being rendered to ashes. You will also need to take my Zina away from here. Return her to her home world after you find a place for my team. Swear to this, and you will have what's left of my worldly goods, including my ship, Searcher."

Storm looked at the floor, reluctant to say what was haunting him. Years of family discontent flooded his thoughts. "I'm afraid you've come to the wrong man for help. Dependability is a trait I've never owned. My family is disappointed in the type of person I've become. I can swear to you that I will do as you ask, but I'm unreliable. You can't trust my oath." Cade felt as if something were moving through his brain, and the dizziness returned for a moment.

Sartre rallied in a last attempt to convince Cade. His voice was momentarily strong. "I've looked into your thoughts. I see the mind of a man who is honorable. The problem is that you do not trust or believe in yourself." The man's body was racked by a bout of coughing. "Promise me you will take care of my team. Your promise means something to me." His speech was growing weaker, and Cade could barely hear him.

Cade Storm's excuses began to evaporate as he realized a stranger believed him to be worthy of trust. He reached out his hand and laid it on the man's shoulder. "Captain Sartre, I will do my best to carry out the mission you have tasked me with."

Sartre moved his lips, but no sound came out as he mouthed, "Thank you." His body relaxed as death kept its appointment. The cat growled a low salute to its dead team leader as the Eagle shrieked a single time.

Zina used the room's com to call the desk. After terminating the call, she said, "Sartre made the arrangements several days ago." They waited about thirty minutes when a knock came at the door. Storm went out the window to the fire escape, and was followed by the cat and the eagle. The mortuary workers gathered the body to take it to the furnaces. When they had left, Cade reentered the room, and the team followed him.

Zina went to a drawer in the decrepit dresser and pulled out a pouch made of Yoris hide. She opened the flap to reveal a sheath of papers. "Captain Sartre transferred ownership of his ship to you the day we found out who you were." She reached out to hand him the pouch.

He didn't take the pouch from her. "How did you find out about me? I've only been planet-tied for two days, and I wasn't aware of having the ability to communicate with animals."

Zina lifted her reptilian head slightly and pointed with her chin toward the eagle. "The morning you arrived, while you were making your way toward the bar, you experienced a moment of dizziness, did you not? Flying high above you, Aeolus saw through your eyes, verifying you had the 'sight'."

He shook his head and pointed to the Yoris pouch. "You hold onto that for the time being. I'm going down to the mortuary to see that his wishes are met."

As he walked out, Zina said, "I'll stay with the team until you return."

When he reached the mortuary, he went inside and asked to witness the process. He stood and watched as the body was placed in the furnace. A flash of light signified the firing of the disintegrator ray. Within minutes, the ashes were placed in an urn and handed to Cade. He carried it back to the room.

Zina approached him and held out a pouch belt with a sheath holding a knife. "I wasn't as confident as the captain that you would return. He instructed me to give this to you. Besides the knife, it contains his credit repository access card." She watched him set aside the urn, while he strapped the belt about his waist. She handed him the Yoris pouch holding the ship's documents. "Our stay here is no longer necessary. It's time to make our way to the ship."

Cade lifted the urn, and they left the room. They settled the bill at the front desk before leaving the inn. Entering the narrow road, they slogged through the mud, making the short trek toward the spaceport. The big cat moved beside Zina and pushed her head under the reptilian alien's hand. Zina stroked behind the cat's ears. "Her name is Maska. She is the second and last feline to be teamed with Sartre." She pointed upward to the eagle soaring high above them. "She is Aeolus, descended from Baku, the African Eagle that was teamed with your grandfather." Zina paused. "Sartre had two meercats on the team until four years ago. He was not successful in finding another pair to replace them on the team."

They approached the gate to the spaceport, and Zina pulled a card from the pocket of her jumpsuit. She showed it to the guard, and he waved them through. They walked another ten minutes and

Zina pointed to a tall ship sitting on four fins, with its nose pointing skyward. "That's the Searcher."

Storm gaped as he looked in awe at the Searcher. "She's a heavy cruiser. I was the pilot for one just like her during the war. How did the captain obtain such a vessel?"

"Captain Sartre found the ship shortly after the military deemed her to be of no further use and decommissioned her. She is equipped with some of the newest technology because she wasn't in service of the military very long before the end of the ten-systems war." Zina fingered the wrist control she was wearing, sending a signal for the hatch to open, and the boarding ramp to deploy. As they approached the ramp, Aeolus flew in through the hatchway ahead of them, and Maska led them by gliding gracefully up the ramp. After they were aboard, Zina fingered her wrist control, retracting the ramp and closing the hatch. "The captain had the ship's stores replenished after we grounded here. The ship is ready to launch."

Cade looked around the cargo bay they had entered. There was a small stable with hay piled in a containment ring, but there weren't any horses. He noticed an enclosure that held a den large enough to house Maska. The big cat went to a spot just in front of the den and stretched before laying down. Fastened to a bulkhead, Aeolus had an aerie with a heavy perch that was located six feet above the deck.

The Zacathian waved her hand in a gesture indicating the animal shelters. "When we lift, the team settles into their cushioned habitats until we are in space. They stay in this area of the ship, cargo bay 3.

We used to have two horses, but they died, and it's difficult to find any of the old stock. Before the captain was bitten by a Juvian arachnid, he had planned on visiting Arzor to seek new mounts there."

Storm held out the captain's urn to Zina. "Place this in storage. We'll spread his ashes on a planet that will be suitable for him."

She accepted the urn and placed it in a nearby storage locker before leading him to the antigravity lift, where they rose to the next deck. "This is cargo bay 2. There is a large freezer that holds meat for Maska and Aeolus. If we run out of the frozen meat, our food dispensers on this deck can replicate a product that meets their needs."

They rose to the next deck, and Zina stepped away from the lift and took a few steps through a door. Cade followed her and discovered a scientific laboratory. She said sadly, "This part of the ship was mine. Like most of the males of my species, I thirst for knowledge. Females are expected to hold down the nest at home while the men pursue exploration. Ben Sartre understood and respected my desire to explore. I owe him everything."

Storm reached out and rested his left hand on her shoulder. "This is still your part of the ship, for as long as you want it."

She displayed a very human-like smile. "That is very kind of you, but I do not know if I can remain on the Searcher. It will seem empty without Ben." She sighed. "He and I were more than friends. We were bonded."

Cade was surprised. "I thought Zacathians and humans were incompatible for intimacy."

Sighing, she said, "You are correct about that. But we loved each other for our minds and our personalities. I believe it was a perfect love between the two of us. He would do anything to make me happy, and I was the same with him. I reminded him, when he offered to bond with me, that my life span was much longer than his. He said that he guessed it would be nice to be married to a young woman for the rest of his life." A tear escaped and ran down her cheek. "I promised him not to get emotional when he left." She led Storm back to the lift, and they rose to the crew deck. "Crew billets, two freshers, the galley and a small gym are on this deck. They rose to the last deck, the bridge and control room of the ship.

"It appears you and the captain were the only two crewmembers. It seems a ship this size would need an engineer."

"We did have one, but he signed off the crew roster two planets fall back." She opened an access panel on the pilot's side bulkhead and retrieved a wrist communicator. She handed it to Cade. "The captain's control and communicator device."

He strapped it on his left wrist. "I'm guessing you and Captain Sartre faced a lot of dangers on the worlds you visited."

"Yes, there are a lot of unknown dangers when visiting planets that were recently discovered. Ben's task was to identify dangers as a first-in scout, and my occupation was often dangerous because of the sites I studied."

"He moved over to the pilot's chair and seated himself as he looked over the control panel. He laughed as he pointed to initials scratched below the hyperdrive control. "This is the ship I piloted. I put my initials there when we made our first flight." He paused. "Since you were bond mates, why didn't the captain leave this ship to you?"

"I told him I didn't want it. I knew it would be hard to find a crew that would sign on, to travel the stars with a female Zacathian for captain. But the main reason is that I probably will not go into space again, once I return home. It wouldn't be the same. My thirst for exploration has been replaced with the emptiness of losing Ben."

Storm looked at the young Zacathian. "Did your captain have a particular planet in mind for his next stop?"

"He intended to give me rare exploration access to a new planet that was discovered two months ago. It was found by accident during research to establish a new hyper corridor. No one has been there yet to conduct a survey. It would have been a rare opportunity for me." She paused. "Don't think that you must make the journey there for me. It's up to you where you take this ship. You're the captain."

He smiled as he realized the best medicine for the hurting woman would be for her to go back to work. "Does this new planet have a name, and how do we get there?"

"It was given the temporary name of Io 4. The hyper corridor transition location is forty minutes away, and the hyper corridor length is three light years. I hoped to find sites to study, but we never received any indication of what the planet was like. The discoverers did not even orbit the world, but logged its location. Perhaps it might be a suitable place for his team to call home."

Zina climbed into the navigator's chair and fastened her harness. She rotated into a lift position. "What coordinates do you want me to load, Captain?"

"Lay in the course for Io 4." He watched as her face brightened with a smile.

"Course laid in. All hatches are secure, and external ventilation has been terminated and sealed."

Cade thumbed the communicator. "Cygnus 3 control, Searcher is ready for lift."

"This is Cygnus 3 control. The Searcher is cleared to lift. No traffic is reported in our space lanes."

The Searcher leapt into space. Zina scanned her instruments. "Thirty minutes to Hyper Jump Corridor transition."

Cade looked over his instruments. "Planetary drive functioning at normal levels. Hyper drive instruments indicate the drive ready for ignition."

Zina studied her navigation screen. "I'll count down from five for Hyperdrive ignition." A few minutes later, she counted down, and Cade slid the drive control full forward as he terminated the planetary drive. The hyper star drive produced a quiet hum, announcing its operation. Zina reported, "Three hours and two minutes until emergence." She unfastened her harness and left her chair. "I'm going to check on the team."

Chapter 2

Cade engaged the planetary drive as the Searcher dropped out of hyperspace. "Zina, how far are we from Io 4?"

She scanned her instruments. "We are thirty thousand miles and closing rapidly. I'm transferring the planet's image to the main screen."

Cade looked at the screen. "Reducing power twenty percent. Give me coordinates to establish orbit."

"Course laid in. Orbital entry in five minutes."

Cade eyed the computer and adjusted to the displayed flight path. "Orbital altitude achieved. Cutting planetary drive, he slowed the Searcher to indicated orbital velocity."

Zina released her harness and left her navigator's seat. She moved to the auxiliary console. "Scientific scans in progress." She examined the readouts on the console's monitor. "It is a small planet, with a diameter of twenty-five hundred miles." She made another adjustment. "Distance from its star is eighty-five million miles."

Cade's gaze settled on the instrument, displaying the distance from the surface. "I've never seen this before. Recheck optimum orbital altitude."

She adjusted several controls on the console. "Preliminary Orbital altitudes are calculated according to a planet's diameter. I may have to make minor adjustments due to the planet's actual mass. I show that our orbit should be close, according to the planet's diameter."

"We need to make more than a minor adjustment. We're gaining a hundred miles of altitude every orbit."

Zina adjusted another instrument's control. "Power up the planetary drive and take us into orbit one hundred miles closer than our initial orbit."

Cade navigated to the new altitude. He watched his altitude readout. "We have gained ten miles in one complete orbit. I'm going to move us ten miles closer." He powered the drive and moved to the new altitude. "Firing nose thrusters to reduce our orbital velocity by ten percent." He gazed at the read-out for another complete orbit. "Our distance remains constant for this orbital altitude and velocity."

"I've run some numbers." Zina pushed a control, producing a hologram image of the planet. Equations appeared on the image. "The mass of this ship, our velocity, and the altitude we are maintaining has produced an interesting outcome. The planet is not solid. It must have a void of at least thirty percent of its volume." She paused. "I can send a probe to the surface and measure the gravitational pull and velocity, to determine a more accurate estimate of the planet's mass."

"I have a better idea. Let's examine the planet's surface features before we do anything else." He looked at his instruments. "Our orbit has stabilized. We'll record this altitude, and velocity, in our log for future explorers to this planet."

"I've initiated the infrared spectrometer, and I'm seeing some unusual images." Zina made an adjustment. "I'm sending the scan to the main screen.'

Io 4s appearance on the screen changed as surface temperatures registered in red, yellow and blue. Ninety percent of the planet's image reflected a uniform surface temperature, but a huge rectangular area was blue. As they circled the planet, several other blue forms appeared. All of the cooler areas were geometrical in shape. Cade pointed to the largest rectangle. "What are the dimensions of this area? It can't be a natural formation."

"Calibrating instruments to planet's circumference." She was silent for a moment. "The rectangular area is three miles by one mile."

"What kind of elevations are we reading on the surface?"

"Surface elevations are nearly negligible, within one foot of variation." She looked at Cade. "I can only arrive at one fantastic conclusion. We are not orbiting a planet. Planets are not perfect spheres. Cade, I'm not the kind of person who scares easily, but I don't like this. I believe the object is artificial. For a monolithic construct to be the size of a planet, it could only be a creation of the forerunners." She frowned, and her ear frills raised slightly. "I've seen the records concerning forerunner structures, but there is nothing on record of this magnitude. It could be extremely dangerous to land on the surface of this enigma."

"I'm setting sensors to alert us if our orbit changes." He left the pilot's chair. "Let's get some caff and consider what our course of action should be."

When they were seated in the galley, with caff in hand, Cade tapped his fingers on the table. "My father told me about the forerunner structures found on Arzor. One of the facilities was benign, as it held plants and trees from around the galaxy. The other structure contained high-tech machines that were beyond the ability of scientists to comprehend. It almost proved to be the end of Arzor."

Zina took a sip of caff, and set her cup on the table. "The problem is, we have no idea which function is designed into the monolith below. Is it something safe, or something deadly?" She picked up the cup and swallowed another sip, before easing the cup to the table. She rotated the cup in her hands. "I suggest we should launch a warning device and station it in a high orbit. We set it to transmit the raw information concerning the possible danger of setting down on the planet. We then leave this area and report what we have found to the nearest Space Patrol post."

"I agree. Prepare a probe and set it up as a warning to transmit the message you suggested."

"I'll go down to engineering and put it together." She stood and hurried out of the galley.

Cade left the galley and returned to the bridge. He looked at the screen and watched the relic of the forerunners slowly pass beneath the orbiting Searcher. The display was still showing the artificial planet in infrared mode. The ship was passing over the large rectangular cool spot when he noticed a beam of light flash from the area and strike the ship. An aural alarm sounded, and the ship's security computer announced, "Intruder alert. Cargo bay three."

"What in Gorgon's name is happening?" He switched to the security video, and observed a man carrying the unconscious body of Zina. Maska charged the intruder and left her feet as she pounced, only to find empty air. The big cat raised her head and roared a challenge, daring the man to face her. Cade switched to the view of the planet in time to see the beam of light disappear. He moved to the pilot's console and lifted a safety cover to activate the ship's force field. He split the view on screen so the security video was displayed on one side, and the planet on the other. He drew his blaster as he saw the light beam reappear. This time, it was aimed at the bridge. For a brief instant, he saw the face of a man where the beam struck the force field. The face dissolved as it appeared to scream. The beam of light turned from white to yellow-green, before it disappeared.

Cade changed the live security feed to view the security record. He went to the time just before the first beam of light was shown on the monitor. He switched to the cargo bay record and ran the scene in slow motion. A man suddenly appeared, from a flash of light, in the cargo bay. He held a weapon in his hand and fired it at Zina. She collapsed to the floor, and the man picked her up. Maska appeared and sprang through the air for the intruder, just as the man disappeared in another flash of light.

He reversed the video and paused it with the man in full view. Magnifying the image, the man was humanoid and had very human features, but his skin was pale green in color. The alien's eyes had purple irises, and was wearing a dull black tunic with a coating that appeared as a dusting of light gray, luminous particles.

Cade moved to the auxiliary console in the center of the bridge area and pulled up a history file. He selected a file and opened it. He sighed as he looked at an alien that could be the twin of the one who invaded the Searcher. "Xiks!" He scanned a list of Xik weapons with images of each and a description of the damage produced with their use. The weapons inflicted nightmarish brutality in most instances. He considered the purpose of the light beam, and could only arrive at one unbelievable conclusion. "They have a teleportation device." He scanned all the information in the file but didn't find any reference to the Xiks having such a capability. "The Xiks must have mastered the use of equipment left behind by the ancients when they abandoned the planet."

Going to the captain's cabin, he went to another secret compartment and pressed a spot on the wall. A door opened to reveal a different wrist communicator. "It's still here." After removing the one he wore, he fastened the new one to his wrist. He pushed a depression, and a personal force field encased his body. The device was the product of research and development, but it proved to be unreliable at times, so it was seldom put to the test during the war.

Cade figured he had nothing to lose by wearing it, and he could control the ship's force field with the device. Closing the hidden compartment and leaving the berth, he went to the cargo bay and took up position behind a crate, as he attempted to mind-touch Maska and Aeolus, with the command, *"Hold position."*

Depressing the control to take down the ship's protective screen, he pulled the blaster and set it to stun, before leveling it toward the spot where the Xik had materialized earlier. He was gambling that those on the planet would believe the bridge to be protected, but the cargo bay would still be vulnerable. He didn't have to wait long as the light flashed, and two Xiks appeared. Stunning them before they could react, he immediately reactivated the ship's force field.

Cade rushed to the two and relieved them of their weapons, wrist devices and weapon belts. He searched the unconscious aliens and decided to remove their outer clothing as he found several small devices still tucked in various pockets on their uniforms. He left them naked except for their underwear. He went to another locker, and opened it to find tangler restraints. He put their clothes in the locker before returning to the two aliens. He secured them and managed to suspend them eight feet apart from cargo tiedown hooks on the bulkhead.

Maska growled and approached the two inert bodies. She reached out a paw and poked at the feet of one of the aliens. Their feet were about six inches from the deck plating. She looked at Cade, and he saw a twisted view of her thoughts. Wanting to rip out their throats, she flicked her tongue against her upper lip in anticipation.

Cade tried to form a picture of interrogating the aliens. Maska laid down, licked at her paw and began grooming herself. Using an antigravity cargo handler, he moved two crates, stacked one on the other, against the wall between the two aliens.

Finding an electrical extension in a locker, he inserted metal pins in one end and suspended the probe-like end from a cargo hook, located on the bulkhead near one of the captives. Making sure the metal pins were not grounded, he connected the other end to a power outlet. After placing a piece of raw meat on a small crate, he moved a chair to a spot directly in line with the crates, but far enough back so he could see both captives. They would see him, but not each other. He sat and waited for them to awaken.

The Xik to his left side began to move his head. He opened his eyes and glared at his captor. Cade didn't speak but stared back at the alien. The second alien began to stir and groaned as he opened his eyes. At first, he looked around in confusion, and then settled his attention on the seated human. Cade rose from his seat and withdrew the knife and a honing stone from his belt. He began to sharpen the cutting edge. He glanced at the two aliens. The one on the left continued to glare in defiance, but fear was etched on the face of the one to his right. The alien's body was shaking as he looked at the knife.

Cade put the hone back in its place on his belt. "I'm going to ask each of you a few questions. Answer me truthfully, and you will live. If my eagle detects a lie, or you refuse to answer, I will cut out your heart and feed it to the cat." He moved to the alien on the left.

He could feel an oily thickness, a miasma of evil, emanating from the alien.

The Xik spat at him and said, "You're of filthy Terran stock. I won't tell you anything."

Cade reached to the wire hanging near the alien, where he had placed it during his preparations. He pressed it against the alien's skin, producing a scream as the voltage hit him. Cade pulled his blaster and stunned him into silence. Reaching down, he picked up a piece of raw meat and tossed it toward the chair where he had been sitting, and Maska pounced on it. She put on a show by tearing the meat viciously as she ate. Cade wiped his hands on a rag and moved to stand near the chair as Maska carried the last bit of meat to her cage.

He looked at the second alien as he used the rag to wipe the blade of his knife. The Xik was shaking with fear. He did not detect the same evil rising from the second alien. He sighed as he slid the knife into its yoris hide sheathe. "Your friend wasn't very cooperative, but on the positive side, he will furnish several meals for Maska. "I just have a few painless questions, and I expect truthful answers. Do you want me to spare your life?"

The alien nodded his head. "I am not a warrior. I'm a scientist, and I didn't want anything to do with taking your female."

"What is your name?"

"I am Karoo, a scientist of the fifth level."

"Karoo, all I want to do is to bring her back so we can leave. How many more of your people are down there?"

"There are two. The captain and her navigator. We had a crew of six when we landed here two years ago. One of the crew died our first year when he was electrocuted trying to work on one of the ancient machines. Another died when he tried to teleport to the bridge of your ship. Our ship expended its planetary drive fuel, so we have been stranded here."

"What kind of weapons do they have at their disposal?"

"The only weapons on our scout ship were blasters, such as the ones we carried with us when we boarded your ship, and concussion grenades."

Cade cleared his throat. "This artificial planet, or whatever it is, seems to be a product of the forerunners. Did your crew find any weapons after you were stranded?"

"No, we didn't, but there is the most wonderful world down there. It's a jungle and zoological paradise, with so many creatures that I haven't catalogued even a portion of the life forms." Sadness replaced his fear as he sighed. "Now I won't be able to finish my work because of these fanatics."

"My friend who was taken from this ship, is a Zacathian. She is an archaeologist, and you sound a lot like her. She lives for the discovery of new things." He paused. "If you help me get her back, I will consider allowing you to continue your work here, or I might give you the option of coming with us."

"You would trust me? I don't know how much help I can be, but I'll do what I can."

"I did not kill your crew member. I faked it by stunning him, to help free your tongue. Do you still want to help me?"

"I have no choice, because he will want to kill me when he wakens."

"I'm Cade Storm. I won't allow him the opportunity to kill you. The choice is yours to make. You will not be harmed if you decide not to help me."

Karoo didn't hesitate. "I would rather be in the company of sane people than where I have been. You can count on me to help."

"When I removed your clothes, I found small devices that appeared to be some kind of weapons."

"Those are concussion grenades. They have the effect of rendering a person in a disoriented state, making it easy to take him captive. It is preferred when you need to question someone without waiting for the effects of a stunner to wear off.

Cade went to the locker and retrieved the bundle of clothing he had taken from Karoo. He carefully removed three grenades from the tunic. He placed them in the locker. He couldn't find any other devices, so he carried the clothes to Karoo and released him from the tangler. When the alien was dressed, Cade said, "Let's go to the galley and discuss our next move over a cup of caff."

When they were settled at the table, Karoo sat with a cup of caff at hand and drew a rough sketch on paper. "Here is the access opening that appears to be a rectangular cool area on your scanners. Our disabled ship is sitting inside, near one end of the opening. The control panel that was used to pilot the artificial world is here." He drew a small square. "The controls for the teleportation equipment are located here on the panel." He placed a small x at one end of the control panel, then indicated a circle several feet from the x marked on the sketch. "This is the location of the teleportation pad." He drew a square box across the large room from the control panel, and placed another x near the square. "This is the cage where they put your friend, and the small x is the keypad pedestal. I believe the cage was meant for examining a troublesome creature, but it can hold people just as well."

"Do the two remaining crew members stay in any particular spot for long periods of time?"

"Since the only chairs located in the entry chamber are the seats along the console, they usually stay there. A fresher is located not far from the console. He drew a square to signify its location."

"Are the wrist devices you wore, the controls for the teleportation machine?"

"Yes. Press the red button, and you will materialize on the pad, but it will take a moment for you to move when you arrive."

Cade drew in a deep breath. His plan would require him to place his life in the hands of Karoo. He took a drink of caff and said, "My friend, here's my plan."

While Cade went over his plan, Zina looked through the bars of her cage at her two captors. The captain was a female Xik, and the Zacathian noticed a difference in behavior between her and the lone crewman.

"Captain Karolin, they should have returned by now. I say we torture the captive and find out how many people are aboard that ship."

"We will wait. The captain of the orbiting ship may have been killed, and our men may not have found the control to shut down the force field for their return."

Zina watched as the crewman began to work himself into a frenzy.

"Captain, we know you are one of the unaffected, but you need to act on behalf of your crew."

Zina wondered. *What does it mean to be unaffected?*

Captain Karolin drew her stunner and dropped her crewman. She removed his weapon and walked to the pedestal that held the keypad for Zina's cage. She fingered the keys, and the door opened. The Zacathian stepped out of the cage, and the captain handed her the two weapons. "For what it is worth, I surrender to you." She started to walk toward the open cage.

Zina called to her. "Help me put the other guy in the cage."

Karolin helped Zina drag the unconscious Xik into the cage. The captain searched the body of her crewman but did not find any other weapons. She stayed in the cage as Zina walked out.

Zina turned and said, "Come out of there. I realized you were protecting me from brutal torture. You are not my enemy."

Karolin walked out of the cage and pushed the door shut. "Thank you. I have endured the company of the affected for too long. I'm glad it's over. I'm ready to be taken to your prison authorities."

"What does it mean to be unaffected?"

Before the Xik captain could answer, a whirring sound brought both women around to face the teleportation pad.

Karoo appeared and was holding Cade's body. He said, "I'm losing my grip; he's going to fall."

As Cade fell, he rolled and pointed his stunner at the two women, with Karoo standing next to him, holding his stunner trained on the women as well.

Zina laughed, and asked, "What are you doing?"

Cade stood and holstered his blaster as he realized there was no danger. "We came to save you."

"I appreciate your attempt, but you're too late. Captain Karolin already released me. She stunned her maniacal crewman."

Cade exchanged glances with Karoo. The alien shrugged and returned his blaster to its holster.

"We had a great plan. Karoo would fake dropping me, so I would have time to get the drop on the enemy before they realized I wasn't stunned."

Zina smiled. "It was quite convincing, and I am sure it would have worked. Thank you for coming for me."

Cade cleared his throat. "I couldn't very well leave my navigator. How would I be able to find my way home?" He laughed. "I'm thankful you're okay. Karoo, how do I return to the ship?" Karoo showed him the combination to select. Cade stepped onto the pad and soon materialized in the cargo bay. Maska voiced her disapproval of his sudden appearance. He noticed the prisoner was awakening, so he stunned him again. "He's going to have one serious headache."

Cade went up to the bridge and guided the ship to a landing next to the disabled Xik scout ship. Using an antigravity sled, he moved the captive from the bulkhead and settled him onto the sled. He retrieved the alien's clothes and removed the grenades before tossing the bundle on top of the unconscious form. Moving the alien to the cage in the alien world, Cade placed him inside with his crewmate.

Captain Karolin was standing near the forcefield that served as containment for the jungle and its creatures. Karoo and Zina had entered through a large door that was set in a narrow strip of bulkhead that abutted the forcefield fence. They were walking at the edge of the woods and were discussing various animals and trees that stood around them. Cade looked upward expecting to see the ceiling of the cavern, but saw a blue sky, or perhaps an illusion. The jungle was in daylight, but he couldn't see the source of the light. He turned his attention to again watch Zina and Karoo. They were too engrossed to notice that Cade and the Xik captain were watching them. Maska settled next to Cade. The cat could sense the forcefield.

Cade went to the access door and opened it for Maska to enter, and Aeolus swooped down and flew through the open door. They both disappeared into the jungle.

Karolin moved to stand near Cade. She looked at him and smiled. "Those two may be from different worlds, but they are both moved by discovery." She paused. "You're from Terra?"

"I am from Terran stock. My grandparents settled on Arzor after…" His voice trailing off.

"After my kind burned off Terra. It was a brutal and unnecessary waste of life. I realize you must hate me. Many of my ancestral people are possessed with the demons of hatred for Terrans."

"I don't hate you. Why don't we go aboard the Searcher and drink caff while we talk?" They made their way to the ship and settled in the galley.

Cade sipped caff and looked at the Xik captain. "Have you been on Xikthar, or were you raised someplace else?"

"No. I grew up on Altamira, a world the Xiktharians had colonized long before Xikthar had been affected by the forerunner sickness. I'm actually an Altamiran, but my people are identified with our Xik ancestors. Living in an unaffected world did not prevent refugees from Xikthar from settling there as they fled from the Confederated Planetary forces. Unfortunately, the sickness is passed to some children of affected parents. The affected are aggressive toward people like myself and dominate the actions of their unaffected fellow Xiks, or in my case, the native Altamirans.

The unaffected people are of higher intelligence and are needed for the more technical-based occupations."

Cade said, "Like the occupation of ship's captain or that of a scientist such as Karoo." He paused. "Your crewmembers are the first Xiks I've seen. I was always told that you were humanoid but far from human. The two we have in the cage have purple irises, which somehow makes them look less human. But you have very human blue eyes and lighter-colored hair, and the same is true of Karoo. In fact, you are a very attractive woman by human standards, even with your unique skin color."

"Karoo and I, and other unaffected of Altamira, are not physically marked with the darkness of the affected." She paused. "Fortunately, the numbers of the affected are steadily declining. When Xikthar fell to the Confederation, the forerunner facilities were blown up and sealed by their forces. Many of the affected people died no matter where they were on the planet. It was as if they were tied to whatever power had been unleashed when the ancient structures were unearthed." She paused as she took another drink of caff. "When will I be turned over to the authorities?"

"I don't intend to turn you over. If I am allowed, by law, to take you aboard as crew, I need a couple more people to crew the Searcher. After that, I will take you home if that is your wish. If you choose to remain on the ship, the pay will be based on any discovery we may make that is profitable. In other words, the only pay I can guarantee is a ship beneath your feet and possible discovery. That is if you're interested." He paused as he took another drink.

"If you and Zina will accept me as a shipmate, I would be happy to sail the space lanes aboard the Searcher."

"I don't think there will be any problem with you being accepted. Zina wanted to come here to explore, but I think we can wait until after we transport the two affected Xiks to the nearest Patrol station. We can always return here in the future.

Chapter 3

Cade sat at one end of the table in the galley. Zina, Karoo and Karolin sat at the table with him. They had only been in the artificial world for two days, and Zina was ready to leave.

Cade looked around the table. "Beltane 2 is the nearest planet with a Space Patrol port. It's only two light years away. I'll feel better with the captives off our ship, so I suggest we go there and hand over our two prisoners."

Zina nodded her head. "I agree with the plan. Will we ask about these two staying aboard as crew members?"

"I intend to ask about the law concerning any restrictions that may be in force." He turned to the two Altamirans. "Go to your berths and strap in for a lift."

They left the artificial world behind and set a course for Beltane 2. Four hours later, they approached the planet, and Cade used the communicator to contact the patrol spaceport. "This is research ship Searcher. Requesting permission to land at your port."

A firm voice answered. Cade detected suspicion in the voice. "State your business, Searcher."

"I'm Captain Cade Storm, Beast Master, and I have two prisoners to turn over to you."

"You are cleared to land on pad 7. I'm transmitting a landing guidance beam for you to follow to the pad."

"I copy your instructions and will comply." He lined the Searcher up with the landing marker and settled the ship on the pad.

He switched off the antigravity flux generator and secured all flight processes. "Patrol tower, I have secured the ship, and we are ready for inspection."

He used his wrist communicator. "Karoo and Karolin, go to the galley and wait for me to contact you." They acknowledged the communicated order as Cade made his way to Cargo Bay 3. He opened the hatch and lowered the boarding ramp. Four armed patrolmen came up the ramp. Maska moved beside Cade and sat, lazily observing the boarding party.

A patrolman wearing lieutenant's bars approached and halted in front of Cade. He looked at the big cat and then at the Eagle as she flapped her wings for attention. "I'm Lieutenant Jace. It's clear you are what you claimed to be, a Beast Master. We don't see many people in your specialty anymore."

Cade stuck out his hand to greet the lieutenant. They shook hands. He handed the lieutenant a record spool. This is a record we made of a mysterious planet, Io 4. The planet is artificial and was a creation of the forerunners. You'll find a large amount of information on that cassette. There were Xiks stranded there. One of them died while trying to board my ship. I took two others prisoner, and they are affected." He led the patrolmen to the cage he had installed to hold the two prisoners.

Jace motioned the three patrol troopers to shackle the prisoners. When they had the two secured, the lieutenant ordered his men to escort them to the brig on base.

When they were gone, Cade said, "Lieutenant, we have two more aboard who are unaffected. They are from Altamira. They are descended from Xiks, but they are true Altamirans. Their actions on our behalf served to save the lives of my crewmate and myself. I would like them to remain aboard as crew members, if it is legal to do so. They have expressed the desire to stay with the Searcher."

The lieutenant raised a brow. "You're Terran, aren't you? I mean, you are not the descendent of non-Terran humans."

"I currently live on Arzor, but my grandparents and my parents are pure Terran stock."

"I'd like to meet these Altamirans who are okay with making peace with a Terran."

Cade said, "Follow me to the galley."

When they entered the galley, Karolin stood and introduced herself to the patrolman. "I'm Karolin, and my career was that of starship captain and pilot." She reached out her hand and the lieutenant shook hands with her.

Karoo stood and said, "I'm Karoo, a fifth-level scientist." He shook hands with the patrolman as well.

The lieutenant scratched his ear. He smiled. "I'm Lieutenant Jace. It's a pleasure to meet you both. How do you feel about remaining aboard the Searcher?"

Karolin smiled. "It is a pleasure to serve aboard this ship. I and my friend Karoo are unaffected people and we would be happy to serve in a crew with Cade and Zina."

The lieutenant rubbed his jaw. "There is no law against Altamirans serving aboard any confederation ship." He turned to Cade. "You will need to come to my office, and we will record them as active crew members. That way, if you are inspected by a patrol ship, they will have access to know they are aboard with your approval."

The two Altamirans could barely contain their excitement as Cade said, "Let's go do it right now. My archaeologist is eager to research a new planet." He walked beside the lieutenant as they made their way to his office to register the crew.

Jace settled into the chair behind his desk. "Have a seat, Storm."

Cade sat in the chair across the desk from Jace. The lieutenant's manner changed to one that was deadly serious. "I have a huge problem in my sector. My patrol squadrons are spread across a zone fifty light-years across, with one thousand inhabited planets. Many of these planets are lawless, and patrol authority is limited." He paused. "We have been struggling against slavers for several months. Recently, an important person was taken by these vermin."

Cade leaned forward in the chair and frowned as he nearly spat the words. "Slavers! I had no idea that evil still existed."

Jace stood and began to pace. "It exists, and I believe there will always be those who profit from the flesh of innocent people. The taking of an important person has focused more attention on the problem. We have no hope of recovering anyone who has been taken, but we want to take down the ones responsible. There's a planet, Thane, located half a light year outside of patrol jurisdiction. We have confirmed it to be the base from which the slavers operate. We sent in an agent who was able to send information concerning the location of the base. We have considered plasma bombing to eradicate the rats, but civilians live in close proximity to the facility, and there may be people held there that were taken by the slavers."

Cade watched Jace retake his seat. "Lieutenant, why are you telling me this?"

"Right now, our only recourse is to indiscriminately destroy their facility with ships sitting a safe distance from Thane. The slavers have a network of planetary defense weapons that have proven lethal to two of our patrol cruisers, even with their shields raised. We were successful in getting a small scout ship to the surface undetected. That was the agent I mentioned. I believe you and your team may be the answer to bringing these slavers to justice."

"Lieutenant, I have a confession to make. I stretched the truth about being a beast master, because I knew you would be more cooperative in allowing us to land. I didn't come here to cause any problems, but I'm not the man you think me to be."

"But I saw your team."

Cade exhaled a deep breath. "The team belonged to a dying Beast Master. He asked me to find a planet where they could be released in peace. I am descended from a Beast Master and learned within the past few weeks that I inherited his ability to communicate with a team." He sighed. "But I haven't tried to actually use it to lead the team." He paused. "Maska and Aeolus only heed my requests because their master instructed them to trust me."

Jace leaned back in his chair. "I'm sorry for trying to lay my problems on your shoulders." He opened a drawer and pulled out a pad. He pulled out three forms. "Fill out one for each of your crew."

Cade filled out the forms and handed them to Jace.

Jace laid the forms on his desk. "I'll load the information in our data file. The paper originals will stay with the patrol for filing. Thank you for your time." He stood and shook hands with Cade.

Cade began toward the door, but stopped and turned to face Jace. "What about the agent you sent to Thane?"

"The last report ended abruptly. The agent was either killed, or captured."

When Cade returned to the ship, he retracted the boarding ramp and closed the hatch. His mind was focused on the people who had been taken into slavery. He knew he would have a hard time forgetting their plight. He clenched his jaw as he came to a decision. He would make an attempt to destroy the base. Because of the danger, he decided to release the team from their responsibility to follow him. He went to Maska's cage and looked at the big cat. She stared back at him. He formed a picture of Maska and Aeolus with Zina. He then pictured himself as being alone. Along with the last image, he tried to send the thought, *"Danger"*. He watched Maska as she looked toward Aeolus, where she was perched. He felt a slight dizziness as he saw in his mind the image of Maska by his side and Aeolus perched on his left shoulder. He looked at the team, and they were both staring at him. The cat made a slight nod, as if verifying their intention to go with him. He smiled and tried to send a mental message of comfort and peace between them. He turned to make his way to the galley.

When he entered the galley, he found the crew celebrating. There was a chocolate cake sitting in the middle of the table. "Where did you find a cake?"

Zina smiled. "I programmed the recipe for Ben. It was his favorite dessert."

He drew a cup of caff. "Let's have some cake." While they were eating, Cade said, "I won't be going with you. The patrol has asked me to help them with a problem. I tried to get the team to stay with Zina, but they chose to go with me."

Zina's neck frill stood out, and some of the iridescence darkened. "You're not telling us everything. Is this a dangerous mission?"

"Yes, it is, but I've decided to volunteer my help." He looked at Karolin. "Since you were the captain of your ship, are you trained to navigate?

"Yes. I am capable of navigating this ship."

"Zina, since you're familiar with the Searcher, I want you to function as captain until I catch up with you." He paused. "I'll have

Jace record my instructions, making you the owner of the Searcher if things don't go well."

Zina's frill fanned wide. "Why can't I go with you in the Searcher?"

"I'll be going to the planet in a smaller ship, one that can evade planetary sensors. A heavy cruiser would be suspected of belonging to the patrol." He paused. "I was not only one of the pilots of this ship when it served as a heavy cruiser. I was trained to conduct commando tactics and usually was the first to hit dirt ahead of the troops."

Zina sighed. "I guess there's no way to talk you out of this. Do you want us to wait here for you to return?"

"That's up to you. I don't know how long this will take. If you want to go to another planet where you can conduct research, go ahead and do that. If Karolin and Karoo want to be taken to their home, find a way to make that happen."

Karoo cleared his throat. "I've been an official crewmember for less than an hour, but I would rather wait here for your return, if that's possible."

Karolin nodded her head. "I'm with Karoo. You have proven to be a man of honor, and you have treated us as equals. I would rather go with you on this mission."

"I won't put anyone else in danger." Rising from his seat. "I need to return to Jace's office. I'll ask if you can remain parked here." He turned to Zina. "The ship is yours." Turning, he left the galley and made his way to cargo bay 3. Maska and Aeolus were waiting near the hatch. As he pressed the release mechanism to open the hatch, Zina entered the bay.

"This is something you will need." She handed him a padded yoris hide shoulder harness. "Strap this on so the pad covers your left shoulder. Aeolus will perch there until she has a need to fly."

He took the harness and settled it over his shoulder. The front of the harness had clasps for two straps that wrapped around his back to the front, securing the harness in place. An engraved face of a cat, and the form of an eagle, adorned the front leather. Aeolus flew up and settled on the shoulder pad.

Zina smiled. "Now you look like a Beast Master. Be careful, and don't hesitate to rely on your team."

Storm opened the hatch and walked down the ramp with Maska prowling alongside.

As Storm approached the field gate, the guard opened the gate and moved back, as he watched the big cat walk through the opening at Cade's side.

Jace approached them. "Have you decided to help?"

"My team and I have decided to do what we can. Brief me concerning your plan to get me there undetected."

Chapter 4

Cade settled the small scout, a ship formerly owned by a criminal apprehended by the patrol, in a wooded area. The scout had optional horizontal landing skids, so he eased the ship between trees using antigravity flux generators to help avoid detection. He secured the ship and sent Aeolus out to recon the area for watchers. Maska slinked away from the scout and disappeared into the undergrowth.

Cade moved away from the ship in case the enemy had been able to track its arrival. He wore a commando camo, and his face was darkened with streaks of face paint. He carried a small rack that held four small, but powerful explosive devices. The rack was fitted to his back and slung from his shoulders. A holstered blaster and a long knife were fastened in their places on the belt. A bow was grasped in his right hand, and a quiver of arrows was slung over the pad on his left shoulder. The primitive weapon was used to great effect by the first-in commandos in the last war.

He suddenly looked through the eyes of the eagle. He saw an alien perched on a platform attached to a tree. He began a slow journey toward the alien's position. The man appeared to be asleep, giving Cade hope the scout ship's arrival was not observed. He moved to within thirty feet of the sentry. He readied an arrow nock to string, and drew back on the bowstring. He released the arrow, and the alien fell from his perch. Cade moved silently to the fallen man and confirmed he was dead. He pulled away the arrow and dragged the body into the dense undergrowth.

He spied another watcher through the eyes of Aeolus. He was about a quarter mile ahead. There was a ridge of hills just past the watcher's position, and a path led through a narrow rift that cut across the ridge. He pulled out the detect Jace had furnished. It showed him to be a mile from the structure believed to house the control room for the planetary defenses. He had hoped to bypass the next sentry, but the alien was directly in his path. He approached the man warily, but stopped behind a tree as the detect vibrated, signaling an alert. He took out the detect, while using the tree to shield the device's illuminated screen. The display showed the position of a land mine. It was located in front of the tree where the watcher was positioned. Cade attempted what he called mind talk, seeking an alternate path over the ridge. *"Danger. Need new way."* The communication worked, as he viewed another passage through the tall ridge. A narrow, shallow rift was revealed through Aeolus' eyes. Maska slinked near and Cade glimpsed a vision showing him the cat would take the lead. He stayed with Maska as she carefully negotiated obstacles without making a sound. She first led him away from the sentry position, and then angled toward the ridge. He could just make out the narrow rift. Aeolus found no sentries stationed along the new path. He checked his detect, but there were no warning alerts. He moved through the narrow gap and soon found himself looking down into a small valley. It was dark, but a bright blue moon made it possible for him to make out a heavy freighter sitting on four fins, with a tall, slender ship sitting about twenty yards from the freighter. He checked his detect, and it directed his attention to a structure that stood close to the end of the valley. There were no area lights in the valley. He figured they didn't have the area illuminated to help conceal the ships from overhead observers.

He summoned Aeolus, and the eagle settled on his shoulder pad. Cade pulled a bomb from its rack. The device had a loop fastener that the eagle could grasp in its talon. He turned the timer to eight minutes. He formed a picture of placing the bomb against the smaller ship's tail fin on the side facing the larger ship.

He took a second bomb and set it for 10 minutes. He communicated to Maska, instructing the cat to take the bomb to the top of the building, where he would drop it next to the main entry door. He pushed the buttons to start the timers and sent the animals to plant their bombs. Cade followed behind the cat. He watched through the eyes of Aeolus as she set the bomb next to the spaceship and then soared away. Maska came around the side of the building after laying the bomb at the door.

A loud explosion caused instantaneous chaos. The smaller ship toppled into the freighter, rocking the larger ship. Cade could see a wide gash in the side of the freighter. He was satisfied that neither ship would be able to lift. The second bomb went off, and Cade rushed around the building and entered the large hole where a door had been. The men who were stationed in the building were unconscious. Cade drew his blaster and laid waste to the control panels and computers. He set a bomb for two minutes and placed it under the control console before rushing out of the building. Maska ran ahead, and he followed at the fastest pace he could muster. A loud explosion announced the destruction of the planetary defense control room.

They made it to the gap and traveled to the other end of the rift. He set the timer to three minutes on his last bomb and laid it at the end of the rift as he continued to run. They weren't heading toward the ship as much as they were going deeper into the forest. The last bomb detonated as he pressed a button on his wrist communicator, sending a message to the communications probe he had dropped off on his way to the planet. Within minutes, he saw two heavy cruisers swoop in and land out of his line of sight in the valley. He heard a smattering of blaster fire before the whine of a mass stunner blanketed the hidden valley. Everything grew quiet as he continued to follow Maska.

Storm felt a dizziness and was again looking downward through the eyes of Aeolus. Through the moonlit twilight, he saw a person perched in a tree with a large predator slamming at the trunk with clawed front feet. He formed the question, *"Where?"* He moved rapidly in the direction indicated by Aeolus. He could soon see the great eagle circling. He felt a momentary dizziness and saw the scene through the eyes of another. Maska was at the scene and was carefully stalking the huge creature. The scene was brighter due to the cat's night vision. Storm tried another mind send. *"Hold."* His vision revealed the cat had halted its advance

He was soon in sight of the beast and the person in the tree. He pulled the blaster from its holster and made sure it was set for stun. He moved toward the beast and fired the stun charge at close range.

The creature was nearly seven feet tall, standing on its hind legs. It didn't seem to be phased by the stunner as it swung quickly to face him. It tried unsuccessfully to swat him with a massive clawed paw. Cade stepped back and changed the setting to kill as the creature turned its full attention to him. He hated the idea of killing the beast, but he had no choice as the tree holding the refugee was cut nearly a third of the way through, where the beast had been using its claws to rip. Quickly leveling the blaster, he pulled the trigger. The beast tottered and collapsed lifelessly to the ground.

A woman's voice cut through the deepening darkness. "Why did you kill it? I was safe up here."

Storm looked at the woman clinging to the tree. "The beast would have cut the tree down in another few minutes. You would have been a meal for the creature."

"Go away. I don't need any help."

Storm moved near the dead beast and looked up but could not see her clearly in the darkening sky. Through Maska's eyes, he could see the woman's hair was matted, and her face was so filthy that he wouldn't have known it was a woman except for her voice.

"Look, if you want a safe place to spend the night, and food for your belly, come with me." The woman did not make a move and seemed determined to remain in the tree. Maska came out of hiding and went to the dead beast and poked at it with her paw. She turned her nose up and snarled in disgust at the rancid odor rising from the dead creature. The cat then looked up at the woman, before turning her attention to Storm.

"Is that big cat your pet?"

"No. She's a friend. She won't hurt you."

The woman climbed down and slowly moved toward Maska. She put out her hand, and the cat bumped the top of her head into the palm of the offered hand. The woman scratched behind Maska's ears. "What a beautiful cat. What's her name?"

"Maska, and the eagle up there is Aeolus." He pointed at the soaring raptor, barely visible in the night sky. The eagle swooped down and lit on his shoulder perch. "My name is Cade Storm."

She seemed reluctant to say anything else as she wiped at the dirt on her face. "My name is Melody."

"We're going back to the ship. If you want to come along, follow us, but remain silent. There may be others around."

When they reached the scout, Cade used his wrist device to open the hatch. Aeolus flew in through the open hatch and Maska followed behind Cade and the woman as they entered the hatch. When they were inside, he secured the hatch and showed her to the small fresher. You can clean up in there. He went to a locker and pulled out a jumpsuit. I think this will be more comfortable after you shower. I don't believe there is a clothes processor on this ship. She went into the fresher, and Cade set the ship's perimeter sensors to detect any who might approach. Maska and Aeolus settled into their resting area in the small vessel. He tried another mind send. *"Good work, team."* Aeolus issued a low answering trill, and Maska stretched, voicing a contented purring sound.

Cade thought about the massive change in his life resulting from his short stay on the muddy planet of Cygnus 3. He shook his head as it all seemed like a dream. He went to the caff dispenser and drew a cup. He carried it to the table and took a seat. A sound at the door of the small galley drew his attention. A striking woman stood in the doorway. She had dark eyes and was toweling her hair dry, revealing a raven sheen that seemed to shift from black to blue with every movement. He remained silent as he stared at her for a moment.

Melody frowned. "You have a silly look on your face. Why are you looking at me like that?"

He cleared his throat. "You look like one of my people. I mean, you look to be of Navajo descent."

"You can stop gawking at me. I'm not a Navajo or whatever you just said."

He quickly changed the subject. "Is this planet your home?"

"No, I was brought here from my world. We didn't have ships that sailed among the stars. I was taken as a slave and brought here. I was purchased by a man in the town, but I managed to escape and fled to this jungle." She paused. "Is there something to eat? I'm really hungry." She sat at the small table across from Cade.

He stood and reached over to the dispenser, and selected a hot meal. He handed her the plate. "Do you want caff, or a cold drink?"

"I think something cold would be good." She glanced at Cade. "Stop staring at me. I don't like it."

He drew his plate from the dispenser. He focused on his plate and ate in silence. When he was through, he placed his plate and utensils in the receptacle, and left the galley. He went through the doorway in the bulkhead to enter the bridge. He climbed into the pilot's chair and activated the com unit. "Patrol one, this is Storm. What's our status?"

Jace's voice came back. "We've secured the Slaver operations center. The freighter you grounded, without blowing it up, held twenty people who had been taken as slaves. They are all alive and undergoing medical evaluations. We found another fifteen locked-in cells within a building north of the valley. One of them was the agent I told you about. You've done a great service, Cade."

"The credit goes to my team. By the way, I found a woman who escaped from the slavers. She isn't a native of this world. I'll leave her with you when I get back to Beltane 2 to rejoin my ship."

Cade left his seat and returned to the small galley. He drew a fresh cup of caff and settled across from the woman. She had finished her meal and was sitting silently, staring at the empty drink container. Sadness darkened her face. He looked over the rim of his cup as he took a drink. So much of his life since leaving Arzor had been a continuous journey through conflict, beginning with his service during the war. The woman sitting across from him seemed to be an oasis, a respite from his life of facing ugly realities. Her beauty held his mind captive as he couldn't look away from her. He shook his head and set his empty cup on the table. "It's time for us to leave. You can strap in at the navigator's position up front with me, or you can strap in on one of the bunks."

"I'll sit up front. I didn't get to see outer space while in the hold of the slave ship. Where are we going from here?"

"I'm taking you to Beltane 2. My research ship is waiting for my return, and I'm going to turn you over to the patrol so you can be repatriated to your world."

"I don't want to be turned over to the patrol. Leave me on this planet. I was doing just fine before you interfered."

"Interfered?" Cade rubbed his jaw with his left hand as he considered her words. The woman's beauty was becoming an afterthought due to her unreasonable opinions. "Melody, you would be dead right now if I hadn't intervened. That beast wasn't trying to make your acquaintance; you were going to be its supper."

She crossed her arms and glared at him. "Men are all alike. You have to thump your chest and act like you did something spectacular."

"What have I done to earn your hatred?" He felt sorry for the woman, but he couldn't figure out why. He gently said, "Look, if you don't want to be turned over to the authorities so they can return you to your family, where else would you want to go? You can't stay here. This is a big planet, and there are bound to be people left who will hunt you down and enslave you again."

She gazed at him with dark eyes piercing his heart. He knew she was going to vent again if he didn't look away. As he broke free of her gaze, he noticed her lips pursed and twisted to one side as she seemed to be considering his words. "I prefer going with your ship for the time being, as long as you're not the only other person aboard."

Cade looked away from her and wondered what the woman's problem could be. He was beginning to think that leaving her on Thane might not be a bad idea. They were still seated at the table, and Cade thought about the time he was wasting on a person who didn't want his help and seemed to hate him for some reason. He leaned forward and rested his left elbow on the table, resting his chin on his cupped palm. After cooling his jets for a few minutes, he set his personal dislike for the unreasonable woman aside. He leaned back and settled his hands on the table. "I'm willing to take you aboard the Searcher until you make up your mind about a permanent destination."

She had an angry look on her face. "Fine."

Cade shook his head and stood. "Let's go strap in, so we can begin our journey to Beltane." Going to the pilot's chair, he strapped in, and watched the woman hook her restraints, making sure she did it correctly. Powering the antigravity flux generator, he carefully maneuvered the scout through the trees until he was in the open. Piloting the ship up and out of the atmosphere, he laid in the course to the hyper corridor transition that would take them to Beltane. Within three hours, he was guiding the scout along the landing beacon for a vertical landing at the patrol spaceport. When the ship was secured, he went to the aft section of the scout, where Aeolus flew to her shoulder perch, and Maska rose from grooming herself, to stand next to him. He scratched behind her ears before he opened the hatch and made his way to the Searcher's gangway. Melody trailed a few steps behind. He turned slightly to look over his shoulder, to see if she was following him. His quick glance was met by a glaring stare from the woman.

Zina appeared at the hatch. "I'm glad you made it back safely." Maska gracefully ascended the ramp, and Aeolus flew through the hatch to find her resting spot. "I see you've brought company."

Cade walked up the ramp and looked back to see Melody had halted at the foot of the ramp. A glance at the girl's face revealed she was staring at Zina. "Melody, this is Zina. She's the first officer and navigator for the Searcher." He realized the possibility she had never seen a nonhuman alien. The aliens on Thane were humanoid and very similar in appearance to humans. "You've never met a Zacathian before, have you?"

The girl shook her head, but quickly recovered. "Zina, forgive my manners. I come from a world that has not journeyed among the stars. In fact, we are quite primitive compared to the wonders I have seen since I was forced into slavery."

Zina held out her hand. "I do not take offense. My anger is for those who buy and sell flesh for the purpose of slavery. I'm pleased to meet you, Melody."

Melody reached out and held Zina's hand. "You are very kind, Zina."

Zina looked at Cade. "We have a lot to talk about. Let's go up to the galley and enjoy a meal."

Cade looked around the cargo bay. "Where are the new members of our crew?"

"That's one of the things I need to update you about."

Cade watched as Melody moved to walk beside Zina. The two women carried on a conversation all the way to the galley. Zina punched a code on the food dispenser and soon set three plates of hot food on the table. She set out the utensils and three plastic cups holding cold beverages. When they were all seated, they began to eat, and Cade found the food to be excellent.

"I didn't realize the replicator could make food that tastes this delicious."

"This is a recipe I programmed for Ben." Sadness colored her face and voice. "It was his favorite meal."

He reached over and gently patted her hand. "He was fortunate to have you for a life mate." He noticed Melody looking at him with curiosity in her eyes.

Zina cleared her throat. "We lost our new crewmembers. A ship set down at the civilian port, and it was manned by unaffected Xiks. Jace told Karolin about the ship and its crew. She went for a visit and discovered they were from a colony near the frontier. The entire population of the colony is made up of unaffected people. She and Karoo asked to be released from the Searcher crew."

"I'm happy for them. Now we are down to just the two of us again."

Melody said, "Don't forget you said I can sail with you on this ship."

"I didn't forget. I was talking about the flight crew. We could use one more person to serve as engineer of this ship."

"I'm willing to try. Can Zina teach me how to be an engineer?"

"Space-traveling worlds have set down directives concerning interference with sub-interstellar cultures." Cade paused as he saw an angry look cross her face. "These directives are for the protection of developing worlds from people like the slavers."

"Well, your directives didn't do much good, did they?"

She seemed to be extremely agitated as Cade stared in disbelief at her during the outburst. "I had nothing to do with the directives. They're not mine, but I can be prosecuted for violating them. The slavers on Thane are either dead, or in prison now. Some may have escaped capture, but we try to do what is right. They are paying the price for not only interfering with your world, but also because they took people to sell as slaves. We aren't the bad guys."

Zina cleared her throat. "It seems like you two have some kind of personal aversion for each other. We need to tone things down and find common ground if we are to be cooped up on this ship together." Zina looked at the girl. "What is the name of your home world?"

"I'd rather not say. Where I am from is of no importance."

Zina looked at Cade and raised an eye ridge at the girl's deliberately uncooperative attitude.

Cade raised a finger to the side of his head and moved his finger in a circular motion while rolling his eyes.

Zina sighed, her neck frills darkening with her frustration. "Let's move on." She turned to Cade. "Your father sent a message for you through the patrol, since he didn't know how to contact you. He has asked that you return to Arzor as soon as possible."

Cade left his seat, went to the caff dispenser and drew a cup. He returned to his seat and took a sip of the hot liquid. "I don't believe I'll be going back any time soon."

Melody asked, "Why would you not go home to see your family?"

He glared at the girl. "Perhaps it's the same reason you don't want to return home. It's interesting that you are quick to ask me this when you seem to be angry with Zina for asking where you're from."

"That's different. I have a personal reason, so it's none of your business."

"Personal reason! Hasn't it occurred to you that my reasons are personal as well?"

Zina said, "You two are like acid and water. You don't mix without exploding."

Melody stood. "I would like to rest. Can you show me to my room?"

Zina left the table and said, "Follow me. I'll show you to your billet and the fresher you will be using." They left the galley and Cade remained seated as he stared into his cup of caff. After a few minutes, Zina returned and drew a cup of caff before sitting across from Cade.

She sipped caff and set the cup aside. "When I first met you in the bar on Cygnus, you said I sounded like your father lecturing you. It's not difficult to see that you and your family are experiencing some kind of rift." She took another drink and held the cup for a moment, before returning it to the table. "I don't know what the problem is, but I can tell you this much. I would give anything to be able to see Ben sitting here, sharing time with me. When our family leaves this life, there is no way to see them again in this world. No way to resolve differences. No way to hold them in your arms one last time." Her tears began to flow as she couldn't say more.

Cade smiled and reached across the table to hold her hand. "Message received." He hesitated as he pulled his hand back. "I left for what is probably a very dumb reason. My future is, or was to be, the inheritor of my family's ranch. I would be very happy to continue my life there. The problem is that the population of settlers on Arzor is limited by the amount of land the natives have allowed for off world settlements. Recently, areas to the north and south of the original settlement allotments have been opened, and the climates are a little friendlier to humans, which is good news. My personal problem is that my parents want me to marry an available woman that I don't love. They kept pushing her toward me because she is descended from the Amerind people of Terra." He paused and took another drink of caff. "It will seem idealistic to you, but I really want to spend my life with someone I love, and not someone who is conveniently available."

Zina softly said, "I take it your father insisted that you cooperate for the good of the family."

"Yes, he was very insistent. I rebelled and enlisted in the military to get off the world. I was seventeen at the time. I spent four years in the war, and three more tramping around from planet to planet."

"It seems to me that your last captain was nearly correct. When I inquired about you, he said you were running from home." She smiled. "Your motivation was to seek a place where you would find a woman you could love."

He sighed. "I never really thought about it that way. I have this emptiness, and I guess you're right. I was hoping to find that one special person. When I saw Melody, after she cleaned up aboard the scout, I thought she could possibly be the one." He lifted the cup and took a drink before lowering it back to the table. "Her reaction to my misplaced interest in her…" He turned his gaze to stare at the bottom of his cup. "She doesn't know me, and I have only known her for a few hours." He paused with a sigh. "Did I really think a jaunt through the universe would help me to find happiness? Her actions make me realize how naïve my reasons were for leaving Arzor."

Melody was standing out of sight in the hall, listening. She silently turned and went back to her berth, tears flowing down her cheeks. She entered and closed the door behind her before laying upon the bunk as she thought about Cade. *I am attracted to this warrior I've known for only a moment of my life. But I can never let him into my heart. He's a decent man and he would detest me if he knew what I've had to do for survival, what I had to do at the hands of others to live. I had everything a girl could want in my father's estate, until warriors sworn to a rival chieftain took me prisoner. I was a slave in my world before slavers from space took me for their sport. To return, there would be a return to shame and ridicule. My brief respite with freedom was on Thane, when I escaped from my master. Even such a short breath of freedom is preferable to my former torment as a slave. Now, I wish I had taken my life.* She decided she would leave the ship when they reached another habitable world. She went to sleep with regret filling her soul.

Back in the galley, Cade frowned. "The illusion that she could be the one was destroyed by her strong dislike for me. And that's putting it mildly."

Zina finished her caff. "You and I can't begin to understand what she has endured at the hands of men. Any trust she may have held for others, is surely weakened by what she has been through."

Cade frowned. "You know, I really haven't considered the evil she has probably suffered. I'll try to be more understanding of her moody behavior."

Zina cleared her throat. "I said earlier that the two of you seemed to be opposites. I know well that opposites can be attracted to each other. If by some chance you find that you like her, and she likes you, ask yourself this question; 'Will you be able to love her if you learn of things she has been forced to do for survival'?" She paused. "If your answer is 'no', then you need to remain aloof to her presence. She doesn't need her soul battered any worse than it has been to this point."

"Zina, I see why Ben loved you. You are a very smart, compassionate person. I appreciate your council. You have given me something to think about." He rose from his seat. "I need to go visit Lieutenant Jace for a debrief. I'll ask if it's okay for Melody to stay with us for a while."

Chapter 5

Cade sat across the desk in front of the lieutenant. "Lieutenant, the woman I told you about during our raid is aboard my ship. She insists on staying with the Searcher, and she will not tell me her home planet. She appears to have a problem trusting anyone. Her name is Melody." He paused a moment. "I told her she could stay aboard until she decides where she wants to be left."

Jace picked up a piece of paper and handed it to Cade. "She is free to choose her destination. I will send a patrolman to your ship with a form to be signed by her, showing that she is a willing passenger."

"That will be fine." Cade looked at the paper Jace had handed him. "This is the title to a scout ship."

The Fleet Admiral Trent at Central Planetary Patrol wanted to reward you. Unfortunately, credits are stretched thin, but I recommended giving you the scout you piloted during the mission. I believe it will fit in one of your cargo bays." He paused. "It would come in handy if you continue to explore planets, or you can sell it for quite a hefty sum."

Smiling, Cade said, "There is a small two-seat skiff in a launch tube on my ship, but the Scout would make a better craft for research. I appreciate you giving me the ship, but it's not necessary."

"I'm not accepting no for an answer. The ship is yours. Now go fit it into your cargo bay."

"I'd like to register a name for it, Seeker."

Jace grinned. "I'll register that name now. It's fitting for a research vessel."

Cade was able to bring the Seeker in through the large cargo hatch located across from the personnel hatch in cargo bay 3. The scout was thirty feet long and the cargo bay measured thirty-three feet across, and was the only cargo bay of the three that was that wide. There was still plenty of room for the animals and space enough for people to move around the craft. Zina helped, but it took some time as several crates had to be repositioned to make clearance for the stubby wings and tri-fin tail structure of the craft. After closing the large cargo hatch and dogging it shut, they went up to the galley. Zina drew two cups of caff, and they settled at the table.

Melody came in after they were seated and drew a cup of caff. She sat across from Cade. She looked at Zina and then at the cup sitting on the table in front of her. "I'm sorry for being so rude earlier." She sighed as she turned the cup slowly, revolving it round and round. "There's no excuse for my behavior."

Zina smiled. "We understand. You have been through a lot, and you don't need to apologize."

Cade watched the girl turn her face toward him. Her eyes met his, and she said, "Cade, I don't have a family to return to. There is nothing for me where I came from. Please let me stay on the Searcher for now. I'll leave when we land on a planet where I feel comfortable."

Realizing the traumatic path her life had traveled, he felt the urge to go to the girl and wrap her in his arms to comfort her. He knew that would only draw her ire. "You can stay with us as long as you want. Zina can show you around the engineering bay. If you are still interested in trying your hand at maintaining the machines, Zina will hook you up with a learning session in her laboratory."

Melody grinned. "Thank you. I would like that very much. It will be good to feel needed and useful."

He turned to Zina. "Before you give her the tour, we are going to set coarse for Arzor. You will have time for engineering studies while in HyperSpace."

Zina nodded and turned to the young woman. "Melody, come with me and help secure the ship for lift." The two women left for cargo bay 3. Cade sat quietly as he thought about Melody. He finished the caff and placed his cup in the receptacle before making his way to the bridge.

Cade was alone with his thoughts; *I know dad will try to push someone else on me when I see him again. Perhaps I should do as he asks. Maybe the love that I hoped to find really doesn't exist.* He leaned back in his seat as he considered the possibility that he might have to settle for something less than love. He sighed and said, "I need to adjust my expectations to match reality. Happiness with my life may not be in the cards."

Zina returned to the bridge and went to the computer on the auxiliary console. "Cade, I just remembered a planet that is located near our first emergence point. It's called Faeroe. The planet has recently been opened to off-world visitors, and they have something there you may be interested in."

Cade left his pilot seat and moved to stand next to her. "What do they have that would interest us?"

"I'm pulling up a file to show you." She paused as she viewed images on a computer screen. "There it is. Take a look."

Cade looked at the screen to see a herd of horses. "Are they of Terran stock?"

"According to the first in contacts, this world is just beginning travels in their near space neighborhood. They claim the animals are native to their world. According to the locals, the horses are accustomed to a variety of climates."

"I'm definitely interested. Go ahead and lay in the coordinates to Faeroe. We'll take a closer look at their stock."

Melody entered the flight deck. "I finished straightening up cargo bay 2." She took the seat she occupied earlier. "How long will it take to reach Arzor?"

Zina said, "We're not going directly to Arzor. We're going to make a short detour to sit down on a planet called Faeroe."

"No! I don't want to go there." She nearly collapsed as she dropped into one of the chairs. She leaned on the armrest and looked at Cade. "Please, don't take me there."

Cade was puzzled. "Why are you so upset? We're going to check out horses that are native to that planet." He could see the girl was shaking, fear shown on her face like a dark shadow.

"I was a slave in that world. I was brought there by pirates who bought me as a slave in my own world. The pirate ship landed on Faeroe. I was given by the pirates to a monster living there. He seemed to be connected to them somehow." Horror invaded her numbing mind as she feared what Cade would think if he knew the whole truth. *I can't tell them how I was stripped of clothing and dignity and physically abused within sight of my father's fortress. A political rival of my father, backed by an off-worlder, sold me to the slavers after my defilement. I'm nothing more than useless filth to my people now. I will never go back. Even my own family will find me to be damaged and a liability. The slavers took me to Faroe, where my treatment was just as evil.* With that thought, she stood and turned her back to Cade. She opened the top of the jumpsuit and lowered it from her shoulders to reveal the whelps on her back. "The price for my resistance. I can't go back there. Even this ship will not be safe in that world."

Cade felt the heat of anger rise to the surface as he looked at her scarred back. He heard Zina ask, "What kind of person could do such a thing? I would relish cutting the throat of such a monster."

Melody pulled the blouse back in place and sealed the seam. "Those scars are easy to see. It's the scars inside that are difficult to bear. I will never let someone hurt me like that again. I'll kill myself first." She returned to the chair and slumped into it.

"What is the name of the person who did this?" Cade waited for her to regain composure.

"His name is Zande Dern. He is not a native of Faeroe. He arrived before the planet was opened to off-world trade. He was dissatisfied with my determined resistance to him, so he returned me to the pirates. They brought me to Thane."

"That means he went there illegally. I guess the natives accepted him since he's settled there."

"The people did not accept him with open arms. They feared him and had no choice. Law officers tried to take him into custody but were killed for their effort to keep the law intact." She paused to wipe tears from her face as she struggled to find composure. "The people fear contacting the patrol because of threats to their families."

Cade sighed. "That is exactly why interstellar planets are supposed to respect rising planets, by not interfering with advanced technology. This Zande character probably has blasters or plasma rifles. He can bully the populace without having to respect their lower-tech weapons."

"It isn't hand weapons that the people fear." She paused as she rose from her chair. "He has a machine he called a battle droid. It does his bidding."

Cade went to his pilot chair and sat down, deep in thought. A frown furrowed his brow. Cade leaned back and stared at the overhead steel plating. He activated the ship's transmitter. "Space

Patrol port controller, Searcher requests delay for departure. Inform Lieutenant Jace that I need to meet with him again after I get some rest."

"Searcher, you are cleared to remain berthed. The lieutenant says to catch some sack time."

He left his seat. "Zina, reinitiate the ship's systems for surface operations."

"Aye, Captain." The Zacathian gazed at his face as she asked, "How long will we be parked?"

"I'm going to the galley to think. We may be here for a while." He made his way toward the galley, deep in thought.

Melody, still standing beside her chair, watched him leave the bridge. "What's going on? What does he have to think about?"

Zina finished her task at the computer. "Ship secured and external ventilators are functioning." She turned her attention to Melody. "I believe he is considering another dangerous path. A path that will take him to Faeroe."

The girl began to shiver in fear. "Going there to obtain horses is insane. You must talk him out of it."

Zina hesitated a moment. "It is not for that reason. I believe he cares for you and is now determined to bring this Zande to face justice."

Melody settled into her chair. No longer shaking with fear, she nearly whispered, "He can't have feelings for me; I don't care about him. I'll tell him so he won't go off and get himself killed. If he knew everything, he would know how worthless I am."

Zina smiled, her neck frills flaring slightly with iridescent blue and green color. "I have known Cade for only a short time. He has proven to be an honorable man, loyal to a fault. He is the kind of man who finds worth in every person he meets. Whether he decides to go or stay will not be determined by your words to dissuade him."

Tears streaked the young woman's face. "I don't want him to be hurt or killed because of me. I should have remained silent about my fears. It would be better for him if I die."

Zina continued to smile. "Melody, I am not human, but I have observed human faces for many years. Your words may attempt to deny your feelings toward Cade, but your heart paints a very different message within your eyes and upon your lips. No matter how much you may protest, his feelings for you will not be dependent upon your past but on who you are today."

Looking downward at the deck, Melody sighed. "My heart does not matter. I can't allow him to see what I really am on the inside. I'm a shell. An empty vessel that doesn't deserve a second look from any decent man." She paused as she lifted her face to look at Zina. "He will be wasting his time on a wretched castoff like me. I won't allow him to go into danger on my behalf." She stood shakily. "Tell him to drop me off on Faroe before I can bring trouble to him. It's better to leave me there." Her emotions caused her to feel faint. "I'm completely drained. Please help me to my berth." She took a faltering step but sagged as she began to wilt due to stress.

Zina moved alongside her and put her left arm around the girl for support, to assist her. She helped the girl to her berth and stayed with her for a few minutes.

Cade settled at the table in the galley, slowly turning a cup on the table, holding it between his hands as he thought about his one encounter with a battle droid during the systems war. The machine could endure several blaster hits and still deliver death to great numbers of warriors. The one he had witnessed in action had a variety of built-in weapons. Fortunately, there was a limited number of the machines, and they were supposed to have been destroyed after the war.

Zina entered the galley and drew a cup before taking a seat. "Melody is resting in her berth. What's your plan?"

Cade raised his left hand to scratch his jaw. "I haven't settled on a plan yet. I want to talk with Jace before sticking my nose into another situation that doesn't concern me."

She lifted the cup to her lips and drank as she peered at him over the rim. "You have surprised me."

Cade settled his hands on the table. "In what way?"

"I'm not ashamed to say that I had a very low opinion of the man I met in the bar on Cygnus 3. You didn't seem like the kind of person to get involved with the problems of others. When you went to the mortuary, I didn't expect you to return for me and the team." She paused. "You have put yourself into dangerous situations because of your concern for others."

He exhaled a deep breath. "When you met me, I had just looked at a crumpled piece of paper for the last of… I don't know how many times. It was a message from my father, asking me to come home. I've spent so much time avoiding my responsibilities to the family that I lost sight of who I was. I rediscovered who I am during my brief stay on Cygnus. Captain Sartre and you, were the catalyst that helped open my eyes. You were willing to trust me when I didn't trust myself." He paused. "I believe it will now be possible for me to deal with the expectations of my family. My future may not be what I hoped, but the welfare of my family is more important than my happiness."

"Earlier you implied that Zande and his war machine are none of your business. I think your feelings for Melody has made it your concern."

"What feelings are you talking about? She's made it clear that I'm not on her radar scanners." He paused. "But I don't like what he did to her or what he's doing to the people of Faeroe."

Zina's ear frills fluttered slightly as they took on a pink and purple color. She raised her right brow ridge and smiled. "This is a good thing. I mean, you not having feelings for her. As you mentioned, she probably doesn't have you on her radar." She finished her caff and left her seat to place her cup in the receptacle.

"I'm returning to the bridge to check our ground operations instruments. Perhaps you should check in on your team."

"Good idea. They're probably getting restless, waiting for us to find a suitable planet to settle them on." Cade made his way along the ship's central corridor to cargo bay 3. He was surprised to find Melody sitting next to Maska on a mat of hay. Aeolus was settled on the hay on her other side. She didn't notice Cade as she softly spoke to the big cat while stroking the fur on its chest. Maska was lying on her back, purring like a kitten. He listened as she said, "It's amazing that we understand each other."

He cleared his throat so as not to startle the girl. "I thought you were resting in your billet." He paused. "You've made quite an impression on my friends." He was happy the girl could find peace in the company of Aeolus and Maska.

Momentarily startled, she turned her face toward him and smiled. "I hope you don't mind me visiting your animals."

"They aren't mine. They choose their own friends, and it looks like you are now in that company." He moved closer to the three and sat on the hay a couple feet away from Melody.

She gently touched Aeolus' breast feathers and softly stroked them. The big eagle closed her eyes and seemed content to allow the girl's touch. After a few minutes, Melody continued to focus on the beasts as she asked, "Why are we remaining here at the patrol station?"

He stared at her profile as she continued to look at the animals. "I will inform Jace about the possibility of Faeroe being used as a slaver base of operations." A frown furrowed her brow as she continued to avoid turning her face toward him. "I will also inform him about the possibility that this Zande is in possession of a battle droid."

Melody turned her face to him and stared into his eyes. "You're just going to tell him, right? You aren't planning on going there, are you?"

"If the patrol needs my help…"

Melody didn't let him finish as she reached out and lay her hand atop his. "Let the patrol handle him. He's dangerous… as dangerous as his war machine."

The gentle touch of her hand sent electricity through him as he thought, *I want to lift my hand and hold hers in mine, but that'll probably anger her. She doesn't care about me but fears I will take her back to Faeroe.* She lifted her hand and he noticed a blush on her cheeks. She turned away from him as he said, "I haven't planned anything yet. The space patrol is more than capable of investigating the activities on Faeroe." He paused a moment. "You will need to tell Jace about Zande and his war machine, along with what you witnessed concerning slavery."

She didn't turn to face him but looked downward. "That will be very difficult for me, but I'll do it. Others were held there as slaves, and this is how I can help them." She rose to her feet and brushed straw from her jumpsuit. "I'm tired. I'll return to my room."

"Try to get some sleep. We'll go talk with Jace in the morning." Cade rose and stood watching her as she entered the corridor and walked toward the crew deck. He sighed as he realized how much he cared for her.

Melody entered her berth and sat on the bed. Tears flowed as she thought about the few minutes she had spent with Cade. *How could I let my guard down? Touching his hand and expressing my concern for his safety. I've got to leave this ship as soon as possible. I nearly let my feelings for him overcome my grip on reality.* Her thoughts turned to Cade's beast team. She smiled as she wiped away her tears. *They accept me without reservation.* As she settled on her bunk, she considered how much better her life would be if her past could be erased. She eased into sleep and dreamed about the unconditional friendship she had with her only friends, Maska and Aeolus.

Cade stood by his bunk. He had slept, but it wasn't a restful sleep. He went to the fresher and washed his face before going to the galley. He entered to find Zina and Melody eating breakfast. He went to the dispenser and punched the code for a meal. He glanced at Melody and noticed she seemed to be deep in thought. He carried his plate to the table and sat across from her. "Were you able to sleep?" She looked up from her plate and gazed at him. Her face held an expression of defeat and sadness.

"I slept well." She paused a moment as she continued to gaze into his eyes. "Are we going to see Jace?"

He nodded and stared deep into her dark eyes. He wondered for a moment why she didn't yell at him for looking at her. "Yes. I believe it is necessary. How do you feel about it?" He remained focused on her eyes, but he could see her lips tremble."

"I intend to be brutally honest with the lieutenant and you." She sighed as she gathered her strength. "When the meeting is over, you will understand why I am someone to be avoided. You will know that my life is not worth your time, and you will realize why I hate all men because I detest myself."

Cade thought about the problems he had considered to be insurmountable in his own life as he realized the woman sitting in front of him was barely holding herself together after the things she had endured. "Let me be clear. No matter what I hear today, I will never condemn or hate you. I will always be your friend." He noticed a tear streak on her cheek as she turned her attention to the plate in front of her.

"I told you not to look at me. It makes me uncomfortable."

Cade looked away and focused on Zina. The Zacathian wore a smile and nodded at him. He cleared his throat. "As soon as we finish breakfast, we will go visit the lieutenant."

Chapter 6

Cade and Melody were seated next to each other, across the desk from the lieutenant. She had described how she was chained to other slaves in the hold of the pirate ship.

She glanced at Cade and continued her story. "Two other young women and myself were delivered to Zande Dern." She hesitated a moment and stole another glance at Cade. He was watching her intently, which made her nervous.

Jace asked, "How were you treated by this man, Zande?"

"He wasn't a man. He's a monster." She looked at Cade again before taking a deep breath. "He demanded my cooperation in an intimate relationship. My refusal led to lashes across my back." She looked at Cade. "He took me by force." She suddenly stood. "I need to go." She took a step and saw Cade standing before her through the flood of her tears.

Cade wrapped his arms around her and felt her bury her face against his chest as she cried uncontrollably. He said softly, "Pretend I'm not here and cry all you want. I won't let you go."

She tried to speak but couldn't control the shaking of her voice. She wrapped her arms around him and held tightly to him. She didn't know how long they stood locked in each other's embrace. She finally was able to stop crying. She didn't want Cade to release her, but she knew these brief moments couldn't lead to anything else. She released her embrace and moved her hands to push him away. "I'm okay. Let me go."

Cade lowered his arms to his side, and she stepped back. His heart was aching for the woman as she backed away from him. Cade turned to Jace. "I'll take her back to the ship and return afterward."

Jace nodded. "I'll see you later."

Cade walked alongside and reached for her hand, but she pulled away from his grasp. He looked at her, but she kept her face turned away from him. "Melody. You don't have to suffer by yourself. Let me be a part of your life. Let me help ease you of your sorrow and pain."

Melody lashed out angrily. "You deceive yourself in the moment, thinking you have feelings for me." She stopped walking and turned to face him. "You're a good guy, and I know you feel sorry for me, but that isn't the basis for a relationship. If you fool yourself into thinking you can accept me, you will regret it. I'm damaged and can't even find it within me to like myself."

Cade stood looking at her dark eyes for a moment. "I know you're wrong. I will never turn away from you, if you will give us a chance. No one gets through life without being hurt or damaged in some way. You're not alone. Give me a chance to comfort you."

"No! I'm not interested in you, and I don't want you to know me any better. What I revealed today is not the worst that has happened, and I will never tell you about the greater humility I have suffered. I hate you, so forget about me."

"Why do you hate me? I haven't done anything to you."

"When the beast was trying to get me back on Thane, I was afraid of the creature. Even with my fear, I hoped it would kill me. That was the only way for me to escape my broken life. You prevented my release from this pain when you killed the beast."

Melody's words sobered his heart. He realized the woman no longer had a heart for life, much less for love. Exhaling a deep breath, he said, "Let's return to the Searcher. I'll respect your right to hate me and will strive to interact with you only when it comes to our crew requirements." They returned to the ship without further conversation.

Zina met them in the cargo bay. "How did it go, Cade?" She noticed a grim expression on his face.

"Melody gave us the facts, and I'm going to return to the patrol office now that she is safely aboard. I'll be gone for a while." He glanced at Melody and turned to make his way back to Jace's office.

Zina noticed that Melody had remained stationary where she had stopped. The Zacathian woman moved to stand in front of the motionless girl. Melody's face was blank, and her eyes were fixed as if she was staring through the fabric of time. Zina took her hand and gently asked, "Are you okay, Melody?"

Melody shifted her gaze to look at Zina. She shook her head and whispered, "No."

Zina continued to hold her hand. "Let's go up to the galley and have some girl talk."

Melody nodded and allowed Zina to lead her to the galley. When they entered, Melody settled into a chair while Zina drew two cups of caff.

Zina placed a cup on the table in front of Melody and then sat in the chair next to the girl. Zina sipped some caff and set her cup on the table. "I see it was very hard for you to tell someone about your ordeal."

Melody picked up her cup and absently sipped a little before returning the cup to the table. "I lost control of my emotions, and the next thing I knew… Cade and I held each other in an embrace while I cried."

"It seems like you should be happy that he tried to comfort you, but you seem upset."

"Zina, I can't let him develop feelings for me. I would be a weight too big for him to bear. I need to flee his presence."

"I know you have been through a lot, Melody. You have experienced things that a person should never have to face in a lifetime." Zina hesitated before continuing. "Open your heart to Cade. I know you have feelings for him, and he may just be the best person to help you overcome your bad experiences."

"No. I've made up my mind. I will leave this ship before he returns to Arzor. I will even stay on Faroe if it is the next place we visit. I will accept whatever I face, and it will be without Cade."

"It seems to me that you're trying to protect Cade, and it's because you love him. You are even willing to stay in the world that caused you to quake in fear with the prospect of going there. Sounds like love to me."

"No, I hate him, and I told him so. I just don't want him to die because of me."

Zina sighed. "You're the only one who can change your mind, but I see it's not going to happen." She paused. "Melody, Cade sees your life as being valuable. He knows you have worth, regardless of the monsters you have been forced to deal with." Zina rose from her seat. "I'm going to wait for Cade in the cargo bay with the team." She left the galley and made her way to the cargo bay.

Cade sat across from Jace. "What does your file have concerning the battle droid?"

Jace frowned. "I have quite a bit of technical data. For the machine to be humanoid in shape, it can pack a lot of weapon hardware." Jace looked intently at his screen. "The vulnerable spot on the droid is the rear base of its skull, where a human spinal cord would connect to the brain. It is a difficult weakness to take advantage of because the machine has sensors to locate any attacker."

"If I can't flank it, what would be powerful enough to attack it from the front?"

"A sixty-gage crawler mounted disrupter, fired from a quarter mile away. Any closer would put you in the kill range of its defensive weapons."

Cade grinned. "Any chance you have such a weapon stored away?"

Jace shook his head. "I've inquired over the patrol interstellar communications net. No one even knows if any still exist after they were outlawed." He selected another screen. "When the war ended, engineers completed tests with long-bore plasma rifles. They modified the rifle with a small magnetic field generator coupled to a magnetic field condenser."

"I don't understand. What effect did this modification produce?"

"The rifle could be used to fuse any known metal. The idea was to weld movable segments of the droid to hamstring its mobility. The only problem is that you have to be within one hundred yards, and the rifle charge will last only long enough to fuse one joint."

"If it really works, it gives me an idea. Do you have access to any plasma rifles and the devices needed to modify them?"

"I will send out a query over the patrol's interstellar net."

Cade shifted to another subject. "Tell me about Faroe."

Jace changed to a different screen. "That world is not ready for interstellar travel and should not have been opened yet. However, a heavy interstellar freighter was damaged by pirates. It escaped capture but had to land on the nearest planet due to extensive damage. It was one of those quirks that can happen. The crew was mostly non-human, so Faroe was introduced to creatures from beyond their star system. Thus, we have a prematurely opened planet. There are many restrictions and laws regulating interstellar trade, but that does not keep criminal-minded people from going around the law." He leaned back in his chair. "The patrol is not allowed to maintain a permanent base, so we make periodic visits to check for interstellar rats."

Cade exhaled a deep breath. "This is an example of the right thing being wrong. If the patrol had a permanent base there, perhaps the citizens would have been more forthcoming about Zande and his war machine."

"You have a point, but doing things the other way around may not have worked out either. The powers that be, try to do the best they can. It's up to the patrol to put things right." Jace sighed. "Unfortunately, the patrol can't make a move against Zande if the citizens do not file a formal complaint. Melody's testimony isn't any help because she isn't a native of Faroe."

"Judging from what Melody told us, the citizens are silent out of fear." Cade paused. "Has Faroe been mapped by the patrol?"

"Yes. We have the topography and the major towns. Do we know where this Zande character has settled?"

Cade scratched his chin with his right hand. "She didn't say anything about the location of Zande's operation. I will send her back to you when I return to the ship. She may be able to get us in the general area. Perhaps she knows something near to where she was held."

Jace placed his left arm on the desk and leaned toward Cade. "It seems you plan to pay Zande a visit. I admire your courage, but this may turn out very bad for you." Jace stood and paced back and forth in the space between his desk and the wall. "Do you have a plan?"

"Not yet. I will need to consider any new information Melody might provide, and I will need a copy of Faroe's maps. I also have a list of things I may need." He reached into his pocket and handed a folded paper to Jace. "If it looks like success is possible, I will move Seeker from Searcher's hold and park it so the equipment can be loaded. I'm returning to the ship. Expect Melody shortly."

Melody sat alone in her quarters. She spoke aloud as if affirming her identity. "Cade, finding worth in my life has reminded me who I am. I am not the sniveling creature men have driven me to be. I am Chief Natahay's daughter. Even though he no longer holds me worthy to share his campfire, I am still his warrior daughter. My short time aboard the Searcher has reawakened my true nature. I will not stand aside and let good people die for me." She stood and moved to look into a mirror. "I see you, Eagle Feather. Your arrow will again fly true, and your sword will be wielded for the good of the tribe." Eagle Feather could feel conviction and confidence welling up inside her. "I will not yet reveal my true name, but I will act according to my truth." She glanced down at her jumpsuit. "This needs to go, but not now."

Cade entered the ship and went to the galley but found it unoccupied. He continued up to the bridge and found Zina.

"Cade, you're back. How did the meeting with Jace go?"

"We are still gathering what information we can find." He paused. "Where's Melody? Is she still upset?"

Zina sighed. "I believe she may be on the verge of a nervous breakdown. She's in her berth."

Cade reached with his left hand to rub his forehead. "I hate to put her through more questions, but I need her to talk with Jace again. It will probably be easier for Melody if I don't accompany her." He hesitated a moment. "Would you please ask her to return to Jace's office?"

"I'll let her know. If she's still upset, I'll go with her." Zina turned and made her way to Melody's berth. She knocked lightly on the door. "Melody, it's Zina. Can I enter?"

"Come in, Zina."

Zina almost gasped when she saw the girl. "Melody, you look different."

Melody smiled. "Perhaps it's because I braided my hair."

The Zacathian raised her right hand to her mouth for a moment, then eased it downward. "Your hair makes you seem more mature, but your bearing is more...?" She wasn't sure how to express what her eyes beheld.

"It really isn't anything other than I have decided to look at things in a more realistic way."

"If you say so, Melody. Cade asked that you visit Lieutenant Jace again. They are trying to collect more information."

"I'll be glad to pay him another visit. I'll go right now." Melody moved past Zina and walked with a determined step as she made her way to Jace's office.

Melody knocked on the door frame as the door was open.

Jace looked away from his paperwork and up at her. He said, "Come in, Melody. Have a seat." He watched her settle into the seat, and he found himself staring at her.

"It's rude for a person to stare like that."

Jace cleared his throat and looked at his desk. "Sorry. I didn't intend to be disrespectful, but you don't look like the same Melody I saw earlier."

"You would be surprised to know how often I hear that. I guess my appearance changes when I'm not being emotional."

Jace raised a brow and nodded. "Cade and I were wondering if you overheard any references to nearby landmarks or towns while you were a prisoner?"

"Give me paper and a pen, Lieutenant."

Jace handed her the requested items. He watched her draw for ten minutes before she handed the paper back to him. He raised his brow. "This has a lot of detail. A river, with its name. Two towns and the temporary patrol spaceport. You have Zande's property marked and even distances recorded." Jace shifted his left arm so his elbow rested on the desk and his hand cupped his chin. "This is amazing. Are you sure it's accurate?"

She icily responded to his question. "Do you doubt my powers of observation?"

"Well, no."

"Now that you have my information, give yours."

Jace asked, "What do you mean?"

Melody rose quickly and slammed her right hand against the desk. She almost smiled when Jace nearly fell out of his chair. "What does Cade plan to do with this information?"

Jace looked upward at the woman's face. "You are very different than earlier."

"In what way, Lieutenant?"

He cleared his throat. "You're scary."

"Now, about those plans."

"Cade doesn't yet have a plan because he's waiting for the map of Faroe and the information you just provided." He hesitated a moment. "He did give me a list of materials he thought would be of use. I'm to load the materials in the scout ship."

"Show me his list."

Jace opened a folder on his desk and handed the list to her.

She looked over the list and nodded her head. "Hand me another piece of paper. I'll list what I want added."

"I don't think Cade intends to take you along. It will be dangerous."

Still standing, Melody slammed the desk with her fist and Jace involuntarily fidgeted again. "I will go, and you are not to mention my list or my participation to anyone. Understood?"

Jace sighed. "I think you might be more dangerous than Zande. I'll be glad to see you away from my base. I just hope you won't get Cade killed."

"My intention is to do whatever it takes to prevent that. I will give my life if that's what it takes." She turned and left the office.

Chapter 7

"Space Patrol port controller, this is Seeker requesting departure."

"Seeker, no traffic within twenty; you are cleared for lift."

Cade engaged planetary propulsion and directed the scout ship toward the hyper corridor. After the ship was established in hyperdrive, He checked the Astro navigation computer. "Emergence in four hours." He settled back and began to focus on the task ahead when a voice invaded his solitude. He was startled because the voice reminded him of Melody, but it didn't sound quite the same.

"Would you care for a cup of caff?"

He left the pilot's seat and swung around to face aft in the small ship as he moved his right hand to the butt of the blaster at his side. His body froze in position as he gazed at the woman standing by the caff dispenser. She was clad in what appeared to be leather breeches that reached to her ankles. Moccasins with high ankle coverage were laced to her feet. She wore a sleeveless leather jerkin, with the dark brown cloth sleeves of an undershirt reaching near to the elbow. A leather band snugly circled her head, positioned above her brow. He moved his hand away from the blaster and continued to stare at the woman. He was pure Amerind stock, but his people on Arzor wore clothing that was in keeping with the extreme weather swings. They wore broad-brim hats and lightweight modern clothing that could both protect and help cool the body. This woman was straight off the pages of a history book. "Who are you, and how did you board this craft?"

She shook her head as she laughed. It took a minute for her to regain composure. "Do I look so different that you can't recognize me?"

Cade rediscovered his ability to move and took a couple of steps toward her. "It doesn't seem possible, but you're Melody?" Even with his confession of recognition, his mind still rebelled at the idea.

She picked up a cup of caff and, handed it to him, and took a second cup for herself. "Let's sit and talk." She settled in a seat at the small galley table, and he sat next to her. "She smiled, and her countenance softened. "This reminds me of our last time aboard this ship, on Thane. You were staring at me like you are right now."

"I remember you getting angry. I told you that you looked like one of my people, the Navajo tribes." He continued to look at her in awe. "Are you Navajo?"

"In my world, my people dress like this for hunting or war." She paused as she looked earnestly into his eyes. "The Navajo and my people are enemies." She hesitated and looked closely at Cade for his reaction. "I'm a member of the Sioux nation."

"Melody, I will never be your enemy." He sighed. "Our written history records the ancient times when we were on Terra. The various nations fought with each other, and when they weren't warring, they would be in strong disputes with one another. When Europeans began to settle and displace tribes, there was no early unity against the invasion. When it was too late, some nations joined together against the tide that was unstoppable." He paused. "It seems like we haven't changed much over the centuries."

She cleared her throat and sighed. "Eagle Feather. This is my real name. Melody was a name of convenience, chosen by the slavers."

"Your name is important, and I'm humbled that you have revealed your true name to me. No matter your name, I still have strong feelings for you. Do you still hate me, Eagle Feather?"

"Continuing to look into his eyes, she said, "I can't hate you, but it is not possible for me to love you. I am the daughter of a chief. Though female, I am, or was, next in line to succeed him. Even though I have been publicly humiliated and disgraced, I intend to return to my world if I survive this planned encounter with Zande. If I can't redeem myself in my father's eyes, I will join the ranks of my nation's warriors and live out my life without a mate." She paused. "If I am restored to my former position, I will be required to take a husband from our nation."

"I see." Still gazing into her eyes. "I will do everything in my power to return you to your people." He paused a moment. "Perhaps I will find a willing partner among the Navajo people of your planet." He noticed an odd expression cross her face. She seemed taken aback for a moment.

She lowered her gaze to stare at the cup before her. "Yes. I suppose that is possible." She continued to stare into her cup. "Have you developed a plan for dealing with Zande?"

"I have some weaponry that Jace procured, but it will only serve to place some restrictions on the robot's mobility and hamper the accurate targeting of his weapons. I will need to come up with some kind of trap that will be sufficient to destroy the machine." He sighed. "There is a lot to figure out before we can engage in battle."

She smiled. "You said, 'we'. I'm happy that you have included me in this effort."

"Let's look at the maps Jace had loaded in our auxiliary computer."

Eagle Feather sighed. "There is one more thing I need to tell you." She paused. "I discovered that I can communicate with Maska and Aeolus."

"That's amazing. I didn't know that a beast team could communicate outside of its team."

Smiling, she said, "I guess that makes me part of the team."

Cade looked past the girl and noticed Maska and Aeolus were both watching the humans. He reached out to them and pictured the four of them walking together. He felt a tingling warmth in his mind as Maska uttered a low growl with a slight nod of her head.

Eagle Feather smiled. "I saw the image of us that you formed." A blush reddened her cheek as she said, "I guess the three of you approve my membership."

He was stunned by her last revelation. "You can connect with my communication with the team?"

She frowned. "I didn't know until now. Is it a problem?"

"No. It may prove to be an important part in our arsenal." He tried to think about the things his grandfather had told him about beast master abilities. *My grandfather never said anything about two people communicating mentally.* He suddenly remembered the day he met Captain Sartre on Cygnus 3. *He looked into my mind. I need to ask Zina about these things. She was with a Beastmaster for years.* He realized it would be necessary to accept mind-to-mind communication as a natural part of a Beastmaster's life for the time being.

The woman interrupted his thoughts. "Are you okay? You seemed lost in thought for a while."

He smiled and said, "Let's look at those maps."

After a couple of hours, Eagle Feather exhaled a deep breath. "I believe the landing site you selected will be the perfect place for our base of operations. The cliff drops off almost two thousand feet and should serve the purpose, but I don't like your idea of being the bait."

"The plan will be effective if I can maintain a quarter-mile lead on the machine. I will need to be much closer to using the plasma welder. If I can fuse his blaster-equipped arm at the shoulder and one leg at his hip joint, the machine will move at a slower pace. I'll carry the three rifles Jace provided, so if I get the chance, I will try to fuse the blaster arm at the elbow as well. If I do it correctly, the blaster will not be of use."

She sighed. "There are a lot of ifs involved. Give me one of the rifles, and I'll flank the machine. We'll have a better chance of immobilizing the arm if I follow your shot."

"Your plan makes sense, but remember, the robot is capable of tracking multiple targets." He stopped for a moment in thought. "If we can procure a couple of horses, we will have a better chance."

"Cade, we have done about all we can until we land and are able to finalize our plan by actually seeing the lay of the land. We should have a meal before reaching our emergence point." She went to the dispenser and programmed the meals.

When they were seated with their meals, Cade asked, "Where did you hide on a small ship like this?"

She grinned. "The fresher is a tight fit when you're trying to brace yourself for launch."

They ate in silence, but Cade's mind was in a tailspin every time he glanced at the woman across from him. He thought about his feelings for her. *Eagle Feather is a different person than Melody. She's confident and reminds me more of a warrior who has my back than the woman I fell for. Here I am, holding someone in my heart. A woman who said she hated me and now tells me she won't be mine, even if she wants me. I have to let go.* He finished the meal without tasting it. "I need to take my seat. We are close to emergence."

She stood and asked, "How long will it take to reach Faroe after we leave hyperspace?"

"About two and a half hours." He moved forward and settled into his seat. Eagle Feather sat in the navigator's seat.

Three hours later, Cade was carefully guiding the scout into a small clearing. He set the ship down and killed power to the magnetic flux generators. He had entered the atmosphere at the north pole of the planet and skimmed at a low altitude as he approached his targeted landing site. He hoped the approach tactic had kept his ship from being detected. He opened a storage compartment located to the left of his seat and brought out two wrist com units. He put one on his left wrist and left his seat. He moved beside the woman and handed her the other unit. "This device has three functions. The most important is communication. You can transmit to my unit by pressing this button." He demonstrated by pointing out the corresponding button on his device. "Or, it will activate when you say, 'transmit'." He then pointed to another control. "This button activates the ship's hatch to either close or open. On the bottom of the wrist controller is a third button." He turned his wrist to show her the location. "Depress this button to activate or deactivate the ship's force field. When we exit the ship, we'll test the system." He started toward the aft section. "Let's get our gear. I need to change clothes." He opened one of the storage lockers and pulled out camo clothing. He also pulled out two universal translator badges. He handed one to the woman. "Pin this to your tunic. Jace said it includes the language spoken in this world." She pinned the translator on and opened another locker as Cade entered the fresher to change out of his spacer jumpsuit. When he exited the fresher, he found the woman standing with a quiver of arrows slung at her back and a bow nestled against the quiver with straps. A leather bag hung at her right side, suspended there by a long strap that crossed over her left shoulder. A canteen hung from the knife belt on her left side, just behind her sheathed long knife. "What's in the bag?"

"Jerked meat and protein bars." She hesitated. "I think the best way I can serve the plan is for me to strike out and scout for things that may prove to be a problem in the near future. After we identify the location for the trap, I will go while you build."

Cade struggled with his desire to protect her, but he realized this was not the weak Melody he had known but a very determined warrior. "Your plan makes sense."

Smiling, she said, "I value your trust in me. I won't let you down." Her mind was focused on something else. *What is happening to me. I can feel his emotions. He was weighing my plan against his desire to protect me. How is this even possible?* Her thoughts were interrupted by Cade.

"I need to explain something important. Follow me." He led her back to the bridge. "I have the ship's communicator set for the patrol's frequency. There is a light patrol cruiser in high orbit above Faroe. When we complete the mission, press this key..." He indicated by pointing it out. "And transmit the information. The cruiser will be here in a matter of minutes. If you are unable to reach the ship, press the transmit button on your wrist and say, 'Transmit ship,' and you will communicate with the patrol through the ship's transmitter. This is very important. Don't forget."

"I understand." As soon as she spoke, she could feel a darkness in his emotions. She was feeling frustrated with this new ability.

Cade exhaled a deep breath. "If something goes wrong, and I'm not able to return to the ship, be very cautious about returning here."

Her ability to sense his emotions caused her to feel the warning was his last effort to protect her. "Let me make something very clear to you, Cade. If something happens to you, I will not leave this planet because I will die trying to protect or avenge my teammate." She paused. "If you want to protect me, do not die. We will leave together, or not at all."

He grinned. "Let's lighten up a little. I fully intend to survive. You do the same so you can return to your world after this is over." He walked past her and opened the hatch. "Let's get started." Maska and Aeolus exited the ship quickly. Maska disappeared into the forest, and Aeolus soared high above. Cade and Eagle Feather moved cautiously after they sealed the ship and engaged the force field. They walked through a heavy stand of trees, but the undergrowth was thin and easy to push through. Cade and Eagle Feather each carried a detect that held the maps Jace had loaded. The devices would help them find their way in unfamiliar territory. After twenty minutes of traveling through the trees, they found themselves in a wide, open area.

They were standing about a hundred feet from a sharply defined rim of the mountain they were on. Mountains shrouded in haze populated the vista. Trees, with leaves that varied from green to blue and yellow, grew on the sides of the mountains, with snow capping the peaks.

Eagle Feather looked out over the expanse in awe. "What a beautiful vista. This reminds me of my world."

"It is an amazing view." He had stopped to stand next to her. In his mind, he could sense an emotion of peace, and he was startled to realize it was her emotion. He interrupted the moment. "I want to take a closer look over the cliff." He moved carefully as he inspected the ground for possible loose soil. The entire area was solid, exposed rock. Moving within a foot of the edge, he looked down. A sheer drop that looked to be a mile deep, but he realized was only eighteen hundred feet according to the topography survey. The drop ended on a rocky surface. "This is just as I hoped. Now, it is time for good old physical effort." He moved back to stand in front of the woman. "Time for you to go." An old saying that was recited between Norbies and Humans back on Arzor came to mind. "Warrior, may your strength be one with your bow and knife to give victory over your enemies."

She smiled. "May your bow arm be strong and your knife hand true in your quest." She turned and left the clearing.

Cade watched until she was out of sight. He could still feel her emotions, even though he couldn't see her. He said to himself, "I really need to ask Zina about these things. It's like she's inside my head." He paused. "How can an ordinary person live a normal life with another person's emotions in his head?" He sighed before he made his way to the ship to retrieve materials needed for the task ahead.

Chapter 8

Eagle Feather knelt behind a tree as she used her eyesight, and Aeolus' eyes to investigate the overgrown clearing. It was her second day of reconnoitering with the aid of Aeolus. The nearest inhabitants were located in a small town nearly three miles away at the foot of the high hill country where now stood. She had observed myriads of animal life that ranged from a mouse-sized creature, to a big tawny cat that was nearly the size of Maska. Her most important finds, a herd of wild horses and this abandoned homestead in the overgrown clearing. *Though it looks abandoned, the log house appears to be in good condition.* She watched Aeolus swoop down from the sky and settle on the ground near the cabin. The Eagle had found a small creature in the weeds and clutched it tightly in her talons as she tore at it with relish.

The woman left the tree line and maintained caution as she went to the door of the cabin. A short length of concrete walkway, littered with debris, lead to the front door, indicating the cabin had been more than a temporary hunting lodge. She opened the door and found a tidy, if dusty, dwelling place. Wooden furniture with cushions occupied one side of the large room, and a dining area with homemade tables and chairs was on the other end of the room. A stove, sink and cabinets completed the dining area. The floors were wood and solid. A fireplace was located between the two defined living areas.

She noticed pictures hanging on the wall on the living room side of the great room, so she moved closer to look at them. There were four pictures there. "These are all pictures of the same couple. This one shows a young man and woman standing in front of a partially built home." She focused on the structure. "It's this cabin." Each of the other pictures showed the same couple, but years had passed between each of the photos. The last picture showed a smiling elderly couple holding hands. A tear trickled along her nose as she looked at the happy couple. She said softly, "I wonder what became of them?"

There were two more rooms. One was a bedroom, and the other was a fresher. "There's no sign of power sources in this cabin. There are oil lamps in the rooms, so how can there be running water?" She turned one of the taps on the fresher sink, and clear water flowed. She turned off the tap and made her way back to the entry door. She went outside and closed the door behind her. She walked around the house and found a large stainless tank perched on a five-foot-high pedestal. Piping led into the house, and on the opposite side of the tank, piping went down into the ground.

Hearing running water gurgling, she moved through the tangle of overgrown weeds. She found a narrow stream and followed it to find the source. A large pond, or lake, was the source. A small structure stood near the edge of the water, and she realized it was a pumping station for the cabin. The energy was apparently provided by the sun, with a battery system to power the pump on demand.

She noticed a pathway leading from the pond, so she followed it for a short distance before finding the corral she had seen through Aeolus' eyes earlier. The fence was in fair shape, with a few sections needing repair. A large, three-sided shed, with a third of the front walled, served as a stable. "This will do perfectly. I need to return to Cade and tell him my idea." She began walking toward the cabin when she found the grave. Her emotions almost got the best of her. "So, this is what happened to the couple who lived here." She stood by a grave with a wooden marker inscribed in a language she could not read. A translation device only worked by processing vocalized language. A skeleton and torn clothing lay scattered on and near the grave. The clothing identified the remains as those of a man. She sighed, and tears ran down her cheeks. "He buried his wife and, at some point, realized he was near the end. A life of love and dedication." She sighed. "Will I ever experience that? Growing old with the one you love." She wiped away her tears and went to a nearby shed. She found a shovel. "It's time he's laid to rest beside her." When she finished her task, she began the journey back to the site where she left Cade.

Cade was exhausted as he inspected his handy work. He felt Eagle Feather's approach before he saw her. He turned his attention to the tree line where he knew she would emerge. Happiness filled him with warmth as he watched her confidently stride from the cover of the trees. Maska voiced a rumble as she lifted her head to lazily look at Eagle Feather, but the cat remained in her comfortable place in the sun. She stretched and lowered her head to continue her rest.

Eagle Feather walked to where he was waiting and halted in front of him. "I see you've been busy while I was gone."

He wanted to tell her how happy he was to see her, but her lack of greeting held him back. "I have the trap ready. Let me show you how it will work."

She looked at the contented Maska, basking in the sun. "Have you considered that the animals may welcome this as their new home?"

He turned his head to look at Maska. "I've thought about it a lot." He sighed and turned to gaze into the woman's eyes. "I didn't realize how attached I've become to these animals. They seem like family."

She continued to stare into his eyes. "When I return to my planet, I will miss the team as well." She forced herself to look away from him. "Tell me about the trap."

He turned and pointed toward two tree trunks protruding from the ground at about a twenty-degree angle. The exposed trunks were about five feet in length above ground, twenty feet apart, and the bark had been removed. Both logs' elevated ends pointed toward the cliff. "I've positioned a small diameter titanium cable in a shallow trench, covering it for concealment." He led her near the cliff. "I moved two large boulders and placed them close to the edge, twenty-five feet apart. Each end of the cable is securely fastened to one of the two boulders."

He went down on a knee and put a finger on a round metallic object that was partially buried under the edge of the boulder opposite the cliff. He stood and pulled a small remote from his pocket. "Each boulder has a strong explosive device positioned to force the rock over the cliff. The explosives for both boulders will be set off with this remote device I'll be carrying." He returned the remote to his pocket. "I'll lure the machine between the two tree trunks. When the machine passes the elevated ends, I will detonate the explosives. The boulders will drag the cable up the logs and catch the machine near its midsection. The impetus of the explosive force, and the weight of the boulders will carry the machine over the edge."

Eagle Feather looked over the setup. "I don't like it. The trap is too tight, and the machine will be virtually on top of you at this point. What if you lose consciousness in the attack? How will you set off the explosives?"

"It is a tight area, but it needed to be close enough to the cliff to assure the droid won't fall short of going over the edge. I've programmed the remote as a dead man switch. When I relieve pressure, the explosives will detonate."

"Dead man switch?" She suddenly felt like Melody again. "This is too dangerous. There has to be a safer way."

"The only weapon we have at our disposal capable of destroying the robot is a two-thousand -foot cliff and gravity. Even at that, it may not kill the machine, but it will separate Zande from its protection." He sighed. "If something goes wrong, it will be left to you to kill the man as quickly as possible. If the machine survives the fall, it will be neutralized with the loss of direction from its master."

"As much as I want to kill Zande, I would rather we leave this world. Take me to my planet and leave me there. The scales will not be balanced if I… if you die too." *I almost said, 'if I lose you. He is not mine to lose, but he is my friend.*

"Everything will be all right. It is a simple plan, but success will depend on our working together. We need to rest a few days to prepare for the ordeal ahead. The trap is finished, so we just need to get ourselves ready."

"I have found a necessary diversion for us. Aeolus and I have discovered a herd of wild horses and an abandoned corral that needs a little work. It would be an ideal situation for breaking two mounts."

"Great news. Our ability to stay ahead of the robot as we lead it to the trap will be greatly improved. How far away is this place?"

"It's about three miles."

Cade said, "Let's go have a look." He retrieved his quiver and bow from a nearby tree where he had suspended them from a low branch. He settled them in place on his shoulders as Maska got up from her comfortable place in the sun and moved alongside Eagle Feather. As they walked, Maska bumped her furred head gently against the woman's leg. Eagle Feather reached out and scratched behind the big cat's ears, eliciting a deep rumble of satisfaction with the attention. Cade smiled as he watched the gentle caress. He looked at Eagle Feather's face as he heard her laugh. A broad smile deepened the dimples that were always an asset for her beautiful face, but now revealed a happiness that Cade had not seen her display in the time he had known her. He smiled as he thought about how happy she looked at this moment. *This is the first time I have seen her like this. Her beautiful face has transformed from a woman who has been hardened by evil men to the visage of a young girl, unaware, innocent, and untouched by even the briefest knowledge of such evil. If only she could hold her present happiness for the rest of her life.* He sighed. *But life isn't like that. All we can do is treasure the happy moments so we can walk through the difficult ones.* He suddenly realized she was looking at him. Her face was still glowing with a smile.

Eagle Feather's heart was light with contentment. She felt a joy she had not known in a long time. In fact, she thought, she could not remember ever being this happy. She turned her attention from Maska and looked at Cade. He was smiling as he watched her scratch behind Maska's ears. He looked up and gazed into her eyes. She felt her heart skip a beat, and her thoughts centered on Cade. *This is more than a feeling of another's emotion or a fleeting vision shared by a beast master's communication. I heard his voice in my head. He said, or thought, 'Melody's beautiful'.* She was happy with his thoughts of her, for a moment, until it occurred to her that he might know her personal thoughts as well. *I can't let that happen. I need to block him from my mind somehow. I need to be Melody. I must hate him in my thought's, if not my heart.* She cleared her throat, and the smile faded from her face. "Why are you staring at me? It makes me uncomfortable." She watched the smile leave his face.

Cade was confused. He didn't know what to say. *We've made eye contact many times since she regained her confidence. I assumed she had feelings for me or at least was not threatened by my unsolicited interest in her. The reality is she sees me as an ally. Her feelings are clear, as the happiness she had a moment ago is completely gone.* He realized it was time to refocus on the problems at hand. "Forgive me, Melody. It won't happen again." He nearly groaned aloud as he realized he used the name he first knew her by.

"See that you don't." She paused before saying, "It's appropriate that you continue to call me Melody. You have become too familiar with me, and it's not right for you to get the wrong idea." Her heart ached because of the words she spoke, but she knew it would be for the best. The name would remind her to remain aloof in her dealings with Cade.

He shrugged his shoulders and continued to scan the path ahead while they walked. He changed the subject. "Tell me more about the corral and the place we are going."

She told him every detail about the homestead. When she told him about the grave, she sensed sadness in his emotions. She tried to detach herself from this unwanted connection to Cade, but she couldn't think of a way to shut him out.

Cade felt deep remorse for the unnamed couple who had lived such a solitary life. He thought about his own lacking and how it would affect his future. *Am I destined to die without someone to mourn my passing? If I go tomorrow, there will be no grieving widow or children who will miss me.* It suddenly dawned on him that his parents were urging him to marry, not for their sake, but his. *I'll set things right when I get back to Arzor. Either I will take a wife there, or perhaps I will find one among the Nation on Melody's planet.* He glanced at Melody and saw she was looking at him, so he quickly averted his eyes. He realized she had asked him something while he was lost in his thoughts. "I'm sorry. What did you ask?"

"I was asking what you thought about my idea concerning the abandoned homestead."

"I believe you're right. It'll be an ideal place to train a couple of mounts, as well as provide us a place to rest and restore our strength."

When they finally stepped into the clearing, Cade looked at the cabin and smiled. He could picture a young couple working to build a house in which they could grow. He wondered why they didn't have children. Was it by choice, or were they unable to produce offspring? He said, "I'd like to visit the grave first."

Melody led him around the house and along the worn path that led to the grave site. When they stood at the foot of the graves, she watched Cade go to his knees. She knelt beside him.

Picturing an elderly man digging the grave to bury his wife, and at a later day, using his last strength to cover her grave with his body, stabbed his heart with compassion for the couple that held such a great love. Cade looked up at the sky and then closed his eyes with his face still tilted skyward. "Great spirit, I pray for the peace of these two spirits. My friend and I will borrow their home, which was built with love, for a short time. We will respect their lives and the property they have left behind." He bent and touched his forehead to the earth and then stood. He looked at the lone headstone and wondered, in silence, what story the alien writing held.

Melody stood beside him and said in a near whisper, "Your words were good. May their peace be as enduring as their love."

Nodding his head, he replied, "Time to inspect the corral and see what it will take to make it usable." He followed her through the undergrowth until they stood by the rail fence. He walked around the perimeter, testing the strength of the post and the rails. There were three posts that would need replacing, along with six rails.

Melody accompanied him on the circuit around the fence as she said, "The small shed near the grave site held a shovel and some woodworking tools."

"I'll check it later and see if I need to return to the ship for anything that might be lacking in the shed. Let's check out the cabin."

"First, let me show you the lake and the pump that supplies water to the cabin." She led him along the path until they stood on the shore of the lake.

Cade looked out over the lake. In the distance stood a tall mountain with its peak hidden by misty fog. "I see what the homesteaders saw in this property. It would be a great place to settle."

Melody knelt and dipped her finger in the lake. "The water is inviting. I'm going to take a swim later."

Cade said, "I'll join you. The water looks tempting, but it might be cold."

"I don't think so. I haven't got a swimsuit, and you probably don't either."

Cade felt his face warm with a blush. "Uh, that's right. Guess I'll swim after you are through."

"There're clothes in the cabin. I'll look through them for swimsuits. I'm sure they swam in this lake."

Cade grinned. "Well, they were married, so they may not have needed swimming clothes."

"I'll look anyway. It's late in the day, so I vote that we do some of that resting you mentioned earlier. We can repair the corral tomorrow."

Cade recognized the happy little girl's face he had seen earlier. He realized it had been a long time since she was able to enjoy herself. "Okay. I agree. We need a little downtime. It may be hard to come by over the next few days." He followed her to the cabin and got his first look inside. He was surprised at how it appeared to have been sitting unoccupied for so long, and yet the only hint was dust. He looked at the pictures Melody had told him about, and he was touched by the lifetime of love recorded through so few photos. He then went to the kitchen part of the great room and inspected the stove. It was a wood burner, but there wasn't any wood stored on the rack. The fireplace was clear of ashes, and there was no wood stacked near it either. He went outside and walked around the cabin. At the rear, he found a small storage shed attached to the house. He opened it and found an axe. "I'll look for some fallen dried limbs tomorrow." He returned to the front of the cabin and went inside. Melody was wearing a piece of clothing that had a blouse with short sleeves, which left her back uncovered to the waist, and was attached to shorts, creating a one-piece suit.

She held up a pair of shorts. "I believe these will fit you."

He took the shorts and went into the fresher to change. When he came out, she was already gone. He made his way to the lake and found her frolicking in the water like a child. He waded into the lake and found it to be cold. As he drew near, she began splashing water in his face. They were enjoying the water and each other's company for quite a while when she turned her back to him as she wiped water from her eyes. She suddenly straightened and turned to face him. Cade saw her smile had been replaced with a frown.

"Cade." She sighed. "I found this suit and winced when I realized my back would be bare. I almost changed my mind about going for a swim." She hesitated. "Only three people have seen my scarred back. The monster who wielded the whip, Zina, and you." Tears began to flow as she tried to gather herself. "Knowing you can see them now makes me feel so ugly. I was able to forget them for a while, but now I'm resisting the urge to run for the cabin to cover my back."

Cade waded nearer and wrapped her in his arms, pulling her gently to him. He said in a near whisper as if fearing the universe would hear his words. "I know you don't like me and probably prefer not to hear what my heart has to say, but I will tell you the truth. "You are a beautiful woman, and I don't find your back to be ugly." He continued to hold her. "I know you don't want me to comfort you like this, and I realize you will be unable and unwilling to see me as anything more than an ally. But for me, no matter what I do in the future, and no matter whom I may marry, you will always hold a part of my heart."

Melody made a weak attempt to push him away. "You know I've already rejected you."

"I have one last thing to say, and I will never speak to you again about my feelings. If I live to carry the weight of many years, I will remember every moment spent with you. I will cherish everything about you; even your scarred back is precious to me." Tears began to trickle down his cheeks as he released his hold on her. He turned his face away, trying to hide his tears. "I'm through swimming." He turned and waded out of the water and walked toward the cabin.

Emotions wracked her body as she continued to stand in waist-deep water. She nearly choked on the words she was forcing between sobs. Words she wanted to say to him but couldn't. "It's not my back that's ugly; it's the darkness inside me. I love you, but if I let you into my life, you'll wind up hating me. Your family will turn against you for loving a woman like me." She sighed as she gained control of her flaming emotions. "Your words of love were so sincere… so beautiful. I will always remember, and forever regret, turning you away." She slowly waded to the shore and walked back to the cabin. She entered the cabin and went to the fresher. She found his bathing suit draped on the side of the tub. She looked in the bedroom and discovered he was gone. She went outside and looked around. She called his name several times. It was getting dusk, and Maska came padding up to her. She formed a picture of Cade and mentally asked, "*Where*"?

Maska answered with the image of the scout ship.

Melody sighed and returned to the front door. She opened it wide, allowing Maska to enter. Aeolus swooped down from the sky and entered to land on a wooden chair back. She smiled at the animals and tried to send a feeling of peace to the team. Maska stretched out on the floor, and the eagle tucked its beak under a wing. She closed the door and swung the lock bar into place. Going into the fresher, she peeled off her suit. It was no longer sopping wet but damp. She hung it over the shower rod and placed the shorts Cade had worn there as well. She pulled a towel from the fresher's closet. She shook the towel to remove any dust and wrapped it around her.

She went into the bedroom at sat at the small dressing table that had obviously belonged to the woman in the pictures. She undid her braid and brushed her hair as she gazed into the mirror. She closed her eyes and thought about the moment of happiness felt while she was in the lake with Cade. She suddenly felt a wave of dizziness. She could see a hand holding a picture of her. Melody realized she had made a connection to Cade's mind, just as she was able to do with the animals. She examined the scene in her mind. It was as if she was lying on the bunk aboard the scout. *How can he have a picture of me?* She shook her head and sought to clear her mind. She remembered a brief moment in Lieutenant Jace's patrol office. He took a picture of her. He had said it was normal procedure to record displaced people, to aid with possible future identification and repatriation.

She murmured to herself. "I told him I would never go back to my home world. Now, I know it's necessary for me to return. I'm shamed no matter where I go, and my shame holds me prisoner. I need to go home and learn to embrace my fate." She went to the kitchen, picked up her supply bag from the place she had left it on the counter, and withdrew a protein bar for her meal. She washed it down with water before returning to the bedroom. The temperature in the room was getting cooler, so she went to the dresser and found warm sleepwear. She removed the towel and pulled on the heavy clothing. She lay on the bed and pulled a heavy blanket over her. Sleep was hard to find, as she thought about the two times Cade had protectively embraced her.

Chapter 9

A noise wakened her. She pushed the blanket away and stretched. Light showing through the curtained window affirmed the fact that she was well into a new day. She rose from the bed and went to the fresher before going to the front door. She opened it, allowing Maska and Aeolus to quickly leave. She, again, heard the sound that had awakened her. She realized it was the sound of wood being chopped. She left the door open and returned to the bedroom. She went through the dresser and found a pair of denim pants and a plaid, long-sleeved, wool-lined shirt. On a shelf in the closet, she found a pair of lace-up boots that were either new or hardly worn. She tried them on and found them to be the right size for her feet. When she was dressed, she banded her hair into a ponytail before going to the kitchen to retrieve a piece of jerky from her bag. She ate while making her way to the corral.

Cade was setting a fence post into place when he looked up to see Melody approaching. "I wasn't sure it was you. You look a lot different this morning."

"You should have knocked on the door to wake me. It must be near to midmorning."

He cleared his throat as he tamped the soil tight around the post. He avoided making eye contact. "I figured you could use the extra sleep. Besides, this fence repair is nearly finished. There was no need to wake you."

She looked across the enclosure and noticed he was working on the last damaged section. "How long have you been working?"

He continued to focus on his task. "I didn't sleep well last night. My mind was busy planning what needed to be done concerning this repair."

"So, you started… when?"

"It was just a while ago." He risked a glance at her. She was standing with clenched hands against her hips and a frown on her face. "I was here before dawn. What does it matter?"

"We are a team in this effort. Just because I unintentionally gave you the wrong idea yesterday, it doesn't change the fact that we need to work together."

Cade picked up a fence rail and began placing one end in its tenon. Melody moved quickly to lift the other end and force it into its slot. Cade said, "I don't remember any ideas being tossed around yesterday. In fact, I can't remember anything notable that occurred, so forget yesterday. It's in the past and meant nothing." He picked up another rail, and she helped him set it in place.

She took a deep breath to help harden her resolve. "You're right. Nothing memorable happened." She picked up another rail, and the two of them set it in place. She timidly asked, "We're still a team, right? We need to function as friends who have each other's back, don't we?"

He could tell she regretted being so brutal with his feelings, even though she saw him as nothing more than a temporary friend.

"You're right. We need to depend on each other to finish what brought us here." He stepped back and surveyed their handiwork. "The corral is ready. Let's look inside the stable." They went through the open part of the stable and found the closed end held two stalls and a tack room. Cade went to a rack holding two lightweight saddles. He tested the chest straps and cinches. "They look good, but they could use some oil."

Melody opened a crude cabinet and found three one-gallon-sized cans. She opened one and sniffed. "I can't read the script, but it smells like leather oil." Folded rags lay on one shelf. She selected one and poured a small amount on the rag. She went to the saddle rack and tested the oil. "It looks and feels right. I'll rub down the saddles."

Cade went to a nearby wall rack where there were several bridles hanging. He picked out the two he thought were the best and carried them to a table near the saddle rack. He got a rag from the cabinet and joined Melody in oiling the leather bridles and saddles. They also found several pairs of well-worn leather gloves on a shelf below the top of the table. They each selected a pair to clean and oil. When they were through, Melody checked coils of rope hanging from pegs on the wall. "The fibers feel brittle. I don't think they will hold against a struggling horse."

"That's okay. I brought synthetic rope from the scout this morning. We'll divide it into two lariats after we have lunch."

"Okay. I have jerky in my supply bag. Would you like one?"

Cade smiled as he walked with her toward the cabin. He pointed to a thermal transport container sitting near the door of the cabin. There was also a stack of firewood on the opposite side of the door. "I used the scout's dispenser to prepare two meals that will need to be heated. Bring in the container, and I'll get the fire going in the stove."

He went to the stove and carefully placed thinner slices of dried wood he had collected in the combustion area. He took a flamer from his pocket and started the fire. The tinder was burning strong so he placed two pieces of wood in the stove and closed the door. When the stove was hot, he opened the thermal container and removed the meals. He transferred the combined food from the two plates and placed it in two frying pans, separating the meat from the tubers and beans. He didn't need to cook the food but only had to warm it. He found two plates in a cabinet and washed them to remove any dust. He soon had the food hot enough, so he divided it between the two plates and set them on the table, along with utensils and two glasses of water.

Melody sat at one side of the table, and Cade settled across from her. "Cade, this food smells good. I've only eaten jerky and protein bars for the last three days." She took a bite of meat. "It tastes as good as it smells. Thanks for doing this."

"I'm happy to do it. I need to eat too." They ate in silence for a while until Cade said, "I don't know anything about the seasons on this world, but I've noticed a definite drop in temperature over the last two nights." He paused as he took his last bite of food. "If it snows, we will have to delay our schedule. Hopefully, we only experience cooler weather for the next four to five days."

Melody lifted her glass of water and took a drink. "I guess you want to put the plan into action within a week."

He sighed. "It would be better to have a few more days, but the weather may not cooperate." He took a drink of water before saying more. If we have snow, it will be tough to stay ahead of the machine, even with horses. Not only that, but I checked the data being recorded by the scout's auxiliary computer. With the approach of winter, the length of daylight hours is decreasing, indicating the nearness of winter. Shorter spans of daylight will make it necessary to plan accordingly. We can't chance luring the machine into the trap in the dark." He paused. "I may be concerned about nothing."

"You are doing what a successful leader would do. You're looking at the variables and calculating the probability of success."

He stood. "I better get some wood for the fireplace if we expect to sleep comfortably tonight."

"You're going to stay with us tonight?"

"If it's okay with you and the animals. I think the floor will be a good place to curl in front of the fireplace."

Melody smiled. "Maska told me it'll be fine for you to stay. Is there anything I can do?"

"Well, since I prepared the banquet, you could wash the dishes."

"It's the least I can do to show my appreciation for your fine cooking."

Cade left the cabin and went to a stack of wood he had split earlier. He gathered an armload and carried it into the cabin. Using some tinder he had shaved, using the axe, he soon had a blaze dancing in the fireplace. He made three more trips to bring in the rest of the wood. He saw the dishes were done, but Melody was not in the great room. He figured she was in the fresher, so he went back outside and split more firewood. He worked for about an hour. It was beginning to get dark, so he leaned the axe against a tree and gathered another armload of wood. He carried it into the cabin and added it to the supply in the rack.

Melody was in the bedroom. She put on the warm night clothes she had worn before and went to the great room. Cade was putting more wood on the fire. "You need to shower soon if you're going to. The water is cold, and it will probably get colder with the sunset." She sat in a chair near the fireplace. "I placed some clothes in the fresher. I didn't find any nightwear for you, but I picked out some warm clothes."

He rose from where he had knelt to stoke the fire. "I better take a shower. You and the team may not be able to stay in the cabin as bad as I smell." He went to the fresher.

Melody looked over the available seating in the living area. There was a long wooden couch that was very heavy. She dragged it so it was near the fireplace, on the bedroom side of the room. Melody then positioned a chair to sit near the opposite side of the fireplace, facing the couch. Sighing, she thought; *That's the proper amount of separation.* Returning to the bedroom, she brought out two quilts from the linen closet. Folding one in half lengthwise, she lay it so that the wooden couch would have a more sleep-friendly surface. She left the other for Cade to use for a cover. Going to the door, she opened it for the animals to enter as she sensed Maska waiting outside. The cat curled up near the fire, between the couch and chair, while the eagle roosted on one of the chairs at the table. She settled into the chair and basked in the warmth of the fire.

Cade came out of the fresher. He was wearing pants that reminded him of corduroy and a lined, long-sleeved blue shirt. A glance told him the seating arrangement, so he went to the couch and took a seat. "This is kind of pleasant. It reminds me of home."

She stretched lazily. "It reminds me of some good things on my world. Mainly the security and comfort I found in my father's lodge." She sighed as she gazed into the crackling fire for a moment.

He got up and put another log on the fire. He settled back onto the couch. "Tell me about your world."

"Where to start?" She leaned forward and held her hands toward the fire. "Almost three hundred years ago, two colony ships left Earth for a newly discovered planet. By coincidence, one of the ships carried four hundred men and women who were of the Sioux Nation. The other ship transported four hundred men and women of the Navajo people."

Cade said, "That was several years before Terra was burned off by the Xik."

"I guess so; we didn't know. The ships were traveling through hyperspace when an anomaly occurred. It was determined by the flight crew that a supernova had impacted the hyper corridor. The ships made a normal emergence, but they were in an uncharted star field. Fortunately, there was a habitable planet only three months travel under planetary drive. When the ships established orbit around the planet, they found three continents. One was occupied by a small population of very primitive humanoids. Scanners showed the other continents to be home to lower life forms only. One continent was covered in snow and ice. The other was very much like Terra. The ships had expended their hyperdrive fuel, and there were no other habitable planets within light-year distance. The green continent was the largest of the three, and it had a major river that divided the land nearly in half. The Sioux Nation settled on the western half, and the Navajo settled on the eastern side. The crews of the two ships, not of the tribes, ten people from each, decided among themselves where they would settle. Over the years, they intermarried and became one with the people.

Cade asked, "What level of technology has been attained by your people? You said one time that your world did not travel in space."

"The whole point for the two tribes to leave Terra was to live their lives more in line with the ancestors. We have technology that is somewhat primitive compared to your planet, Arzor. We have landline telephones, electricity, automobiles and civilian aircraft. We have our Articles of Nations that provide for certain rights and justice. We do not build machines for war. We ride horses when tribes war against each other, and our weapons are somewhat basic. Arrows, spears, knives and single-shot rifles."

"Incredible. I've never heard of a civilization binding itself to such restrictions."

Melody sighed. "Unfortunately, it creates a huge disadvantage when off-world thugs with high-tech weapons move in."

"With your world being planet bound, Central Control will not interfere with the business of your world. However, Central Control would come down on any interstellar parties that interfere with the more primitive planets."

She sighed. "Unfortunately, we never knew about Central Control and its space patrol. We had a rude awakening when Lim Jardin found a large deposit of precious metals on Navajo land. No one can overcome their alien technology." She paused. "They are slowly devouring my world."

"Is he…?"

Melody exhaled a deep breath. "The one who shamed me? Yes."

Cade felt as if his blood would boil. Even if they had desecrated a woman he did not know, he would still want to cut out the man's heart. Knowing Melody made his anger flame ever higher. He was seething inside. He looked at the woman sitting across from him. She was staring back at him, a strange look on her face. Cade took a deep breath and brought his anger under control. "What's wrong?"

She stood and walked over to the couch and sat beside him. "I've never seen you so angry." She rested her left hand on his shoulder. "You made a terrible sound, like the growl of a beast."

He leaned forward and rested his right elbow on his right knee, propping his forehead on his clenched fist. "I'm sorry. I've never felt so much anger toward a human being. I can't even think of this Jardin as anything but a deranged beast that needs to be put down."

She squeezed his shoulder. "Look at me."

He straightened up and leaned back. He turned his head to look at her face. He wanted to take the pain from her, to somehow make her forget what was done to her.

She sighed. "I wish I had never told you and Zina about my troubles. I am not worth the pain I have caused you. Here we are, facing danger, perhaps death, because of what was done to me by a heartless man. You shouldn't be here. I shouldn't be here. Killing Zande will not change the past." She paused. As far as Jardin, I hate him, and when I return to my world, I will do my best to kill him and his crew. Not because of what he did to me, but because of what he is doing to my people and my world."

Cade turned his face away from her. "One reason I'm here is to prevent the jerk from harming other innocents and to free any slave still in his possession."

She frowned. "Things you wouldn't have known about if I hadn't revealed them in a moment of fear and weakness."

"I know what you're driving at, and you are partially right. My greatest reason is you. I promised not to mention my feelings, but I think this needs to be said. I don't want to kill him because I think I will somehow be able to win your love. That's not it. From my view point, the greatest damage Zande did, was to make it impossible for you to trust your love to anyone. He ruined two lives. Yours, and mine." Melody turned her face away from him and sat in silence. He got up and put another piece of wood on the fire. He then moved to sit in the chair she had vacated. He looked down at Maska. She had lifted her head to watch him stoke the fire and then settled back. "Tell me about the process to redeem yourself. It was something you said several days ago."

Frowning, she said, "It's something that would best be left out of my history lesson."

"It won't hurt to tell me. It's just the four of us here, and neither Maska nor Aeolus seem interested in history."

She exhaled a deep breath. "Though my people are not living lives that are comparable to the ancients. I mean, after all, we do have automobiles and live in brick-and-mortar houses. In the case of honor and integrity, the bar is still set as high as the ancestors placed it." She paused. "Like truth, honor and pride are difficult to regain once it is lost. My situation is extremely difficult when it comes to our laws and traditions. The honorable thing would have been to kill myself, but the means and opportunity presented itself too late when I began to feel that living was important. I guess, deep down, I'm a coward."

Cade frowned. "Please don't say that about yourself. I believe your world was a better place because of you, and you will return to set it right again."

She continued after exhaling her breath. "The matter of redemption is a tough one. There are three options that are possible. First, a warrior can stand before the gate of the chief's citadel and challenge the tribe's best warrior to a fight, usually to the death. If the warrior wins, the shamed person he fought for will be restored. Second, the shamed person kneels before the gate and calls out for the chief to witness his or her sacrifice by suicide."

Cade was stunned. "It's hard to believe your people still adhere to such barbaric traditions. They should have developed into a more civilized society."

"Do you mean, be more like the slavers and rapists that seem to be imbedded like ticks in even the most advanced worlds?"

Cade sighed. "You have me there. What about the last method of redemption?"

"It is a choice of servitude. All stigma is removed except for the fact you spend your life locked into dirty jobs that no one wants to do. There are several levels of opportunity if you call it that. In my mind, the best is a lifetime warrior. The rest of the options are similar to cleaning stables, working with sewer infrastructure, farm labor and many others. You get the idea. You live in a barracks environment and can never marry or have a relationship. You live to serve the public."

"Do you really want to go back? Stay on the Searcher as a member of my crew. If we visit a world you like, you could stay there."

"It's tempting to do just that, but I still want to help my people. Even if I'm shoveling human waste out of a septic tank, I will still be looking for an opportunity to destroy the aliens."

"What's the name of your planet?"

"When the colony ships landed, the people saw the planet was very much like Terra, so they named it New Terra. You won't find it on a star map. Only the slavers that stumbled upon our world and Jardin know the coordinates." She sighed. "I may never find my way home, but I will search for the rest of my life trying to find it, if necessary." She looked at the fire and then turned her gaze on Cade. "If I find a way home, I will never tell you how to get there. You have already challenged too much danger on my account."

He rose from the chair. "I'm ready to turn in. Can I have my comfortable couch back?"

She stood. "I was hoping you'd tell me about Arzor."

"Maybe tomorrow. We need to rise early in the morning if we want to bring home a couple of horses."

"Melody smiled. "This cabin does have the feel of home. I'm going to miss it." She went to the bedroom and left the door open when she entered. She nestled in the bed and slipped into a restful sleep as she thought about how talking about her shame seemed to relieve some of the burden from her heart. She was happy that she had decided to talk with Cade about her past and her possible future.

Chapter 10

The next morning found Cade and Melody one mile into an expected three-mile hike to the canyon, where she had found a herd of horses during her reconnoiter three days earlier. Cade had instructed Maska to remain behind to avoid spooking the herd. Aeolus soared high above, scanning the area for the herd's location. "Melody, I've been thinking about a memory of a conversation with grandfather when I was young. I was amazed that he could communicate with animals. I loved horses, so I asked him if he communicated with his horse like he did with his team. He told me that the brain of a horse did not process in the same way, but he could convey a sense of peace and calm to his horse when it was agitated."

She asked, "Do you think we can influence the horses enough to help us rope them?"

"I don't know if it's possible. My grandfather was talking about his horse, which was very familiar with him. I can't claim to have even one percent of his ability, so that would be another variable to consider."

She said, "Still, I think we should give it a try. It wouldn't hurt to make the attempt."

"You're right as usual, Melody." Cade heard a familiar sound as he saw two horses through the eyes of Aeolus."

She said, "I heard the whinny and shared Aeolus' image as well. They are nearby. How close do we need to be for our attempt?"

Cade removed his backpack and laid it beside a tree. He removed his leather gloves from his belt and pulled them on. Freeing the lasso from its belt hook, he uncoiled it enough to grasp it for a toss. He looked at Melody, and saw she was prepared as well. She nodded at him to signal her readiness. He saw through the eyes of the eagle that the two horses were grazing while moving slowly toward them. He tested the wind and was satisfied they were downwind from the animals. Aeolus' vision revealed there was a lightly beaten trail the two were following. He and Melody were standing on that path. He tried sending a picture to her of him standing behind a tree on the far side of the path and her on the other. He saw her silently comply by moving behind a tree.

He took his place and stood ready to act. They held an advantage by watching the two horses' approach through the eagle's vantage point high above. Cade concentrated on the animals, sending what he hoped would be calming assurance. The horses suddenly bolted and were running toward them. Cade moved his arm to prepare for his throw. Using Aeolus' eyes, he tossed the loop at just the right time. He yelled, "I've got it." As he got the words out, he was suddenly jerked from his feet and was being dragged down the path. The horse suddenly came to a halt as Cade saw through the eagle's eyes that it had swooped down, flapping its wings to hover in front of the horse. Cade jumped up and heard Melody laughing as he regained his footing and secured the rope to a tree.

Melody called out, "I've never seen anything that funny in my life. I believe the horse caught you instead." She laughed so hard it caused her to cough.

The stallion was mostly black, with white areas standing out on its neck, right flank, and left hip. While concentrating on his captive, he said, "I may find your effort as funny when you catch your horse."

"I have already captured her."

Cade turned to see Melody standing beside a gray mare, with her hand resting on the neck of the beast. The lasso was still coiled in her hand.

"How did you do that? Is that horse domesticated?"

"No, silly. I did what you told me to do. I used my mind to calm her spirit. Why didn't you do the same?"

Cade felt a little miffed at the woman. "I tried to calm the beast, but I think my effort is what caused them to bolt." He felt disappointed in himself. He never considered himself to be a beastmaster, but he had convinced himself that he was like his grandfather. He sat by a tree and reclined with his back against it.

Melody stood in front of him and felt cloudy emotions in his mind. She was concerned and angry with herself that she had laughed at him. "Are you okay? Did you get hurt?" He didn't answer, but she could sense sadness. She again felt regret because of her ability to feel his emotions. "I'm sorry that I laughed at you. I thought you would find humor in the moment."

He sighed. "You did nothing wrong. It's on me. I realize that I'm not a beast master. I believe the animals are able to make possible my communication with them. With you, it's different."

Melody sat beside him. "Different, in what way?"

"You're a natural at this, a true beast master. I'm a fake."

"Oh no! I will not sit here and listen to you wallow in self-pity. I wasn't with the team when you destroyed the Slaver base on Thane. That was you and your team. Don't you see, I can communicate with them because of you." She hesitated. "Can you see into my mind at times? Answer truthfully."

"Yes, I can feel your emotions and sometimes your thoughts. I intend to ask Zina about this when I see her again. She was a partner to a beast master for years, so she should be able to shed some light on this ability."

"I have experienced the same ability. It is annoying to feel someone else's emotions and thoughts, but there it is. We are emotionally interconnected."

Cade considered her words and thought about the implication of such an intimate connection. *Shouldn't this be the best reason for us to stay together? To live out our lives together? I should bring it up for her to consider.* He almost gave in to the need to discuss it with her. *No, I can't do it. Every time I try to open my heart, she rejects me. Perhaps this connection is common with beast masters.* Her words did serve to lift the doubt from his mind. He may not be the perfect beast master, but he did have a team, if only for a while. He smiled and said, "Perhaps you can calm my horse a bit, as well."

"Welcome back, teammate. I will be glad to give it a try." She paused. "You at least have to see the humor in our efforts today."

They both rose to their feet. Cade laughed. "Yes. Anyone watching would have found it to be quite funny." He had received some bruises and scratches from his wild ride at the end of a rope. "It was a little painful, though."

They led the horses back to where they had left their packs. After retrieving them, they began the short journey back to the homestead.

They led the horses into the corral and closed the gate. Cade sensed the horses were becoming agitated, and he realized Maska was approaching. "Before we remove the ropes, we should begin acclimating them to the presence of Maska."

Melody nodded. "Good point. We can't afford having a horse panic at a crucial time because of her presence. I'll try to impress them with trust while you make it clear to Maska that the horses are part of our team." Two hours later, the night was closing in. Maska was stretched out in the corral, lying between the two horses as they grazed on the tall grass in the corral without fear. "Melody stretched, flexing her back. "I'm ready for a rest. Using your mind to impress thoughts on an animal is a lot of work."

Cade sighed. "I'm with you." He looked at Maska for a moment and then said to Melody. "The weather is warmer tonight. I think it would be best for Maska to stay out here, near the horses. Spending the night together should really help cement their trust." Cade formed a scene in his mind, showing the cat sleeping near the horses. Cade focused on Maska and sensed her agreement with staying in the corral. "We'll start training with the bridles early in the morning." When they entered the cabin, Aeolus flew in and settled on her favorite chair while the door was open. Cade placed some tinder in the fireplace. "I'm going to get a fire going. Even though the weather is a bit warmer, there's a chill in here."

She nodded. "While you do that, I'm going to take a cold shower. The fire will be welcoming when I'm through."

With the fire going, he sat on the couch and focused on tomorrow's plan. *We need to train the horses to accept the bridle and the saddle tomorrow. I hope we can begin breaking them for riders tomorrow as well. At least, we need to start training. The longer it takes for us to initiate the plan, the greater the possibility that someone will stumble upon us.* His thoughts were interrupted when Melody came out of the fresher.

"Your turn. I didn't want to mention it, but you don't smell too good."

Cade rose from his seat. "That is mean. I didn't tell you that you smelled awful."

She grinned. "You just did, and I already realized how smelly I was after tramping beside horses on a dusty, hot day."

Cade shivered while enduring the cold shower. When he finished, he put on a clean change of clothes that Melody had placed in the room for him. He went into the living area and put another piece of wood on the fire. He returned to the couch and sat.

Melody came out of the bedroom and went to her supply bag in the kitchen area. She walked to the couch and sat down next to him. She held out a strip of jerky and a protein bar. "I prepared a meal for us to share."

His insides felt like jelly. There was a gap between them, and they weren't physically touching, but he was affected by her nearness. He took the offered food and felt electricity as his hand touched hers. "Thanks for the food."

Melody caught her breath with that brief touch as she thought; *I couldn't help myself. I wanted to be near him. Our time together is growing shorter, but my feelings for him are getting too strong. How can an insignificant touch cause such a fire in my heart. We must finish this business with Zande soon. I don't want to doom him to the misery my life would bring to him.* She wanted to slide further away from him on the couch, but she couldn't. "You promised to tell me something about Arzor tonight."

He involuntarily cleared his throat as his heart raced faster than he wanted. He took a bite from the jerky and chewed for a moment. "There's not much to tell. The planet is nowhere near Terra-like. There are two different native races. One of them, the Norbies, have two horns on their heads and average seven feet in height. Their vocal cords are incapable of producing translatable language, so they communicate through sign language. They are friendly, for the most part. The Nitra are a different story. They are war-like and are said to be cannibalistic." They talked until midnight. When he finished, she hadn't asked any questions for several minutes. He turned his head to look at her and realized she was fast asleep. He reached his right hand to lightly grasp her left shoulder. He gave her a gentle shake. "Wake up. It's time for you to go to bed." His effort caused her to lean against his shoulder. He sighed. Her scent was intoxicating. He had noticed a pleasant natural scent beginning with the first time he met her. It wasn't perfume. He had long considered it to be the aroma of her personality and spirit. Whatever it was, he would always remember it. He gently pushed her away and stood. He carefully picked her up and took her to the bedroom. He lay her on the bed and pulled the blanket over her. He paused for a moment, looking down at her face before returning to the living area, leaving the door open as she had done the previous night. He put more wood on the fire and laid down on the couch, thinking about how difficult it would be to forget her."

Melody opened her eyes after Cade left the room. She sighed as she thought about him. *Why is he so kind to me? I've never known anyone like him. He only knew me for a few hours when I overheard him tell Zina that he thought I could be the one. Tragically, my heart belonged to him from the moment I first sat with him aboard the scout ship on Thane. He is suffering under a delusion of love because of the pressure placed on him by his world. I was too willing to accept the illusion that I could be loved by him and that he could love me unconditionally.* She sighed. *My past can't fit into his world.*

How could I be so cruel to him? I feigned sleep so I could get closer to him without my feelings being exposed. I feel an emptiness inside, a longing for his gentle touch, to simply have him hold my hand in his. How can such an innocent desire have such a hold on me? He treated me so respectfully tonight despite my efforts to reject the feelings he believes he holds for me. I can't do that to him again. I dare not give in to my love, either. My willpower is too weak for me to stay aboard the Searcher after this mission is over. I'll ask Jace to help me find my way home. Perhaps the patrol has a place for displaced people like me to stay. The turmoil in her mind finally gave way to a restless sleep.

She awoke to a room filled with sunshine. She sat up quickly with the realization she had overslept. She entered the great room on her way to the fresher and saw Cade in the kitchen area. She didn't say anything but hurried into the fresher. When she came out, she walked over to the table and sat. She looked at the stove and saw a pot with a small trickle of steam emitting from its spout. The pleasant smell of caff permeated the room. Cade turned from the counter and noticed she was seated at the table. He picked up the pot and poured caff into two cups sitting on the counter. She watched as he stirred lightener into the cup. "Why did you let me sleep so late?"

He carried the cup of caff to the table and set it before her. "I realized this morning that we needed to eat a good breakfast if we expect to have the strength we need for the task ahead."

She protested. "I could have helped you with this. There is no reason for you to do this for me."

"Don't get angry. I did this because we need to eat something substantial. I went to the ship and dispensed four meals. Two for our breakfast, two for lunch, and a thermos full of caff. I think I've been suffering from caff withdrawal."

She picked up her cup and took a sip. "This is really good."

He came to the table and set a steaming plate in front of her. He went back to the counter and returned with his plate, cup of caff, and utensils for both. He sat and glanced at her. He quickly looked down at his plate when he realized she was looking at him. He didn't want to raise her ire.

She shifted her attention to her plate and took a bite of food. She savored the taste and realized having a meal was a real treat. "This seems tastier than when we have it aboard ship. Thank you for preparing it."

"Well, it's nothing. At home, I prepared meals a lot of times. It was real food, not dispensed, though we do have dispenser processors in the house."

Melody ate several more bites and took another sip of caff. "I don't remember going to my room last night." She thought, *Why did I say that? Am I forcing him to say something that I can berate him for?*

"Oh, yeah. You fell asleep. When I woke you, I guess you were still mostly asleep as you went to your room. I thought about checking on you to see if you got into bed okay, but I figured I would have heard you fall if you didn't." He cleared his throat. "If you were wider awake due to moving to the room, you would have been angry for my intrusion, so I just left you alone."

"Thank you for respecting my privacy." She felt bad for causing him to lie, but she knew it was because of her own attitude.

Cade looked at her briefly as he said, "We need to finish our meal. We have a long day ahead." He felt like he was walking on eggshells because she was quick to reveal her dislike for him.

Cade watched Melody train the horses for almost three hours. He was amazed at the empathy she seemed to share with the animals. She not only accomplished the task of saddle and bridal training, but she was well into training the horses to accept a rider. He watched with more than a little trepidation as she fitted her left foot in a stirrup and swung up, and seated herself on the gray horse's back. The horse didn't rear but seemed unconcerned about the whole thing.

She held the reins without putting pressure on the bit. "Okay, Shadow. Let's go for a slow walk." She gently bumped her heels against the horse's flanks, and they began a slow trot alongside the fence in a clockwise direction. Melody gently tugged pressure on the right side of the bit, directing the animal to maintain its distance from the fence. After several circuits, she urged the horse to a faster gait. They went around several times before she reined in while saying, "Whoa."

She dismounted and then swung up into the saddle again. The horse remained calm, so Melody dismounted.

"Melody. If you find your way home and have to take servitude, ask to be the horse whisper of the tribe. You are really good at this."

"You know, I could live with that. I love horses. And with my newfound ability, the chief would probably agree to that request."

Cade tilted his head toward the mare. "I noticed you named your horse."

Melody smiled. "Yes, her light gray color reminds me of a shadow."

"I suppose you named the other horse as well."

"I do have some ideas. But he is your horse, so you should name him."

"I don't think it's a good idea to name them. That would feel like a commitment to keep them after we leave this world."

"When Zina told you about the horses here on Faroe, you wanted to come here to purchase some for your ranch, so why not take these?"

"I guess you're right. There's not enough room in the scout, so I'd have to bring the Searcher here to take them. What about Shadow? Wouldn't you want to keep her?"

"When we leave here, I intend on going with the patrol to search for a way home. I won't have a way to keep a horse. I hope you'll be okay with taking Shadow with you."

Cade felt the tendrils of darkness churn within. He knew to expect her departure from him, but her words added a finality to her intentions. He had never experienced an emotional roller coaster like the one he now rode. He took a deep breath. "It's fine. I'll take them with me." He turned away as he shed a tear. "I'll go set out our lunch." When he entered the cabin, he washed his hands before pouring himself a cup of caff. He took a drink before removing the plates from the thermal container. He set them on the stove to warm them after adding wood to the stove. He settled into a chair at the table and was soon lost in thought and memories.

Melody entered and stood for a moment, looking at him with the realization he was hurting. She was hurting, too, because she knew where his mind was taking him, and she was the cause. She didn't say anything but went to the fresher to wash her hands and face before going to the table. She silently settled into her chair, and Cade didn't show any sign that he was aware of her presence. She thought *This is for the best. We need to begin severing our bond so that it will be easier later.*

Cade pulled loose from his thoughts and realized Melody was seated at the table. He got up and went to the stove to gather up the two plates. He set them on the table and poured a cup of caff, which he set in front of her, on the table. He started to sit but realized he couldn't endure sitting across from her. He picked up his plate and cup of caff, before going outside. He sat on a crude bench sitting near the house and set his cup next to him. He took a bite of food and found it difficult to chew or swallow. He forced himself to eat, knowing it was necessary.

Melody remained seated at the table against her will. She struggled to remain aloof, to keep herself from going to him. She wanted to find a way to comfort him, to make him understand that he didn't really feel love for her. He would forget her once she was gone. She forced herself to eat, but it wasn't easy. She continually wiped tears from her face and struggled to keep from sobbing aloud. She finally swallowed the last knot of food. She went to the fresher and washed her face. The cold water helped her to regain her composure. She went outside and saw the empty plate sitting on the bench. She went around the house, heading for the corral. She saw Cade leaning against the fence. He had his arms folded on the top rail and was resting his chin on them as he seemed to gaze at the horses. She moved to stand near him, resting her hands on top of the rail. "Cade, remember how we agree to be friends. We are still friends, right?"

He didn't answer right away. After a minute, he said, "I can't be your friend. We are two warriors with a mission that has bound us together as a temporary team. If we can get the other horse trained for a rider today, we'll take them out for a run before dark. Tonight or in the morning, we will talk about everything you can remember about your time here. We will come up with the best tactic to succeed." He paused. "If all goes well, we will be on our separate ways two days from now. I'll take the scout back to Beltane, and you can catch a ride with the patrol cruiser orbiting this planet."

Her heart felt like it was exploding, but she had to play her part with resolve. "Sounds like a good plan."

Cade pushed away from the fence. "Let's get busy. We're wasting daylight.

By late evening, Melody had worked her magic with Cloud. She said the white patches made her think of clouds against a stormy sky. Cade swung up into the saddle, and the horse proved to be as tolerant of him as it was to Melody. He rode around the inside of the corral fence several times before dismounting. "We'll take them out for a run tomorrow." He paused. "I'm going to stay in the scout tonight. I'll bring breakfast tomorrow when I return."

She answered. "I'm going, too. I want a hot meal tonight after a warm shower."

"Whatever." He turned to Maska, who had just returned from a successful hunt. He asked her to protect the horses during the night. The big cat agreed to stay. Cade felt the panther was happier staying outside. He didn't say anything else but went to the cabin to retrieve the thermal container and the thermos. Melody followed him in silence. As they walked toward the ship, Aeolus followed along in the sky. When he opened the hatch, the Eagle flew in and settled on her perch.

Melody went directly to the fresher. When inside, she stripped off her clothes and put them in the processor before she showered.

Cade waited to initiate the food dispenser until she came out of the fresher. She was wearing her freshly cleaned clothes and had her head wrapped in a towel, helping to dry her hair. He initiated the dispenser and soon had two plates on the table. He dispensed two cold fruit drinks and set them by the food. He sat in a chair, and she sat down opposite of him. He remained silent as he began to eat.

She took a sip of her cold drink. "It seems like two warriors on a team should not isolate themselves one from another in silence."

"I'm not trying to isolate you with silence. I'm focusing on a plan."

"Since I'm taking part in the foray, it's best if we discuss things together. We need to be on the same page."

He opened a swing-down door on the bulkhead, separating the small bridge from the cramped living quarters of the scout. The door formed a desk, and a storage area was revealed with the desk opened. He withdrew a piece of paper and a pencil. "Tell me everything you can remember about Zande's homestead. I want to know if he has hired guards. Does he keep the battle droid in a specific place to stand guard? Even the smallest detail may be helpful." He pulled out a folded map that he got from Jace. "See if there is anything on this map that helps you to approximate the location of Zande's place." They discussed the layout until it was nearly eleven o'clock. Cade gathered the papers and placed them in the desk's storage area. He swung the desk up and closed it. He got up from his seat and moved to fold down two of the bunks. There was enough aisle space that a person could walk between them if one needed to go to the fresher or forward to the bridge. He pointed to the port side bunk. "That's your bunk tonight." He laid down on the starboard side bunk. He didn't have any trouble falling asleep. Two days of training with two short nights of sleep had caught up with him.

Melody opened her eyes. She was lying on her right side, and she could see Cade in the soft night lighting of the ship. He was lying on his left side, so she could see his face. She wondered if he was really asleep. She focused her mind on looking into his emotions. He was in a deep sleep and was not yet dreaming. His right hand was at the edge of his bunk. She reached across the narrow aisle and gently touched his hand. She felt the quickening of her heartbeat as she carefully took his hand in hers. *I will never experience this again. No one will be able to quicken my heart with a touch of a hand to mine. She moved his hand to her lips and softly kissed it.* She said in a whisper, "I will always love you." She eased his hand to its original position and released her grasp before falling into a restful sleep with the thought of her clandestine kiss. In her dreams, his hand was replaced with his lips against hers.

Chapter 11

Cade sat on Cloud and looked down the slope through binoculars. The tree cover to the east of the mountain slope was thick enough for Melody to be hidden from the battle droid. He heard her voice on the communicator. "I'm in position and will have a clear shot." He said, "Understood." He had one of the modified plasma rifles hanging from a saddle loop. The other was laying across his legs at his thigh level.

The two most dangerous parts of the plan were this first move, and being the bait in the trap. He urged Cloud ahead at a slow pace. He didn't want to alert the machine too early. He communicated with Melody. "I'm moving toward the target." She acknowledged receiving the message. He got to within a hundred yards of the target and raised the rifle, focusing through the scope on the machine's left arm. He aimed at the hinged area of the left elbow and fired as the droid turned its attention to him. He saw the beam from Melody focused on the shoulder almost simultaneously with his shot. The rifle reached the end of its discharge, and he threw it down to take the second rifle. He focused on the right hip and pulled the trigger as the machine swung that leg forward to begin pursuit.

Cade knew Melody should be riding toward her next position near the trap. The machine was slowed, as it lumbered with a noticeable limp toward Cade. He turned Cloud and urged the mount to run full speed up the slope, toward the top of the mountain. He looked back and saw the machine was moving more quickly than expected, but it was not closing the gap. Further down the slope, he saw a man running out of Zande's homestead. Cade hoped Cloud would have the stamina to continue at top speed toward the top as the slope increased a little. He caught a glimpse through the trees of Melody racing ahead of him. She cut out of the tree line and outdistanced him in her dash to make it to the top ahead of him. He saw Zande through the eyes of Aeolus. The man mounted his horse and followed the droid, but his horse was not as fast as the machine. Finally, Cade could see his goal. He heard Melody over the com unit. "I'm in position. Be careful; that machine will get to you in a hurry." He tersely answered, "Copy."

Cade reined in Cloud and leaped from his back. He slapped the Stallion and yelled, "Go!" The stallion departed as Cade moved past the jaws of his trap. He saw the droid approaching too fast and realized the trap should have been deeper. He had underestimated the machine's speed. "I won't be able to avoid his attack." He backed up, so that he stood between the jaws of the trap and cliff. The machine did not slow down. It passed between the logs in an instant, and Cade fell backwards, releasing the trigger as the machine's sword slashed through his right side. His head hit the rocky ground as he heard the explosions. He was losing consciousness as he saw the machine pass above him, catapulted in the direction of the cliff.

Darkness was closing in, and he heard a man's voice say, "You destroyed my machine; now it's your turn." He could no longer see, and the threat seemed detached, and distant. He heard a woman shout just before darkness overcame him.

Melody had watched helplessly as the droid inflicted damage on Cade, causing him to fall backward onto the ground. The trap sprung, and the droid went over the cliff just as Zande rode up and dismounted, unaware of Cade's accomplice. He approached the fallen Cade and pulled a blaster from its holster. Melody had an arrow nocked to string as she shouted at the man. She released the arrow as the man swung around to face her. Her timing was on the money. The arrow embedded itself in Zande's groin before he could aim the blaster. He screamed, dropping the blaster; he reached for the arrow in an attempt to pull it from his groin. Melody set another arrow and called out, "Remember me?"

Zande looked at her as he groaned. "You! You'll pay for this."

The next arrow hit him in the chest. "I don't think so, rapist. You are the one with payment due." She set another arrow and released it. He lost his throat and ability to scream as he went over the cliff. Melody threw down her bow and rushed to Cade. Kneeling beside him, she cried out, "Don't die. Stay here with me." She pressed her com transmit button and said, "Transmit, ship." She nearly yelled into the device. "Cade is seriously injured. Bring medical help. Hurry."

A voice answered, "Patrol six copies. Arrival in three minutes."

Melody unlaced her jerkin and discarded her quiver. She took off her undershirt and pulled the jerkin over her bare torso. Quickly securing the laces, she used the shirt in an attempt to slow the bleeding of his gashed side. Blood was flowing from his head. She held her blouse over the gash with some pressure, but she didn't know if it would stop the bleeding. She looked into his mind and saw darkness. She began pushing herself into his mind' forming a picture of the two of them holding hands and standing in a green field. She felt light coming into his mind as a hand touched her shoulder. She looked upward, through her tears, to see a patrolman. We'll take him to the ship. She backed away as three men placed him on a stretcher and carried him in through the cruiser's hatch. Melody followed with Maska and Aeolus right behind her.

They were in a large entry room. A clear wall of glass, or some similar material, separated the room from the medical suite while allowing observation of the medical section. A decontamination entry area with an entry hatch was attached to the glass wall. Two orderlies were cutting away Cade's clothing. Another orderly hurried over to her.

"Melody, the animals will have to stay on this side of the glass. If you want to go into the medical facility, you will need to go into that fresher," he indicated a door to her left, "Discard your clothing and shower with the soap furnished in the unit. There are suitable clothes for you to wear in the unit."

She hurried into the fresher and stripped off her clothing. She remembered her hasty lacing of her jerkin when she saw in the mirror that she had minimal coverage of her torso. She showered and scrubbed with the soap that was there. Stepping into the drying chamber, she was dry in a minute. The clothing was a white medical jumpsuit with short sleeves, and a pair of disposable shoes. She stepped out of the fresher and looked for Cade. Seeing him through the glass wall, Melody went to the door of the chamber and entered. She felt some pressure on her body, and then the hatch on the medical side opened, allowing her into the medico. An orderly instructed her where to stand while preparations were being completed for Cade's procedure. He was covered with a sheet, but she could see his lifeless face. She wanted to go to him, but the medical team needed their space to do what was necessary.

The cargo bay was set up like a hospital. There were two tissue infuser knitter tables. The men lifted Cade to the surface of one of the tables. A doctor was examining the wound to his head, as two of the men swung the infuser trolly over the unconscious warrior. The doctor said, "Set the infuser so travel begins six inches below his breast and retraces two inches below the groin. She stood there for thirty minutes, but she was still in his mind. She was holding firm to the peaceful scene with them holding hands. She was sharing other memories with her mind, but she couldn't know if her efforts were helping. She felt a hand on her shoulder.

"I presume you are Melody."

"Yes, doctor. How is he?"

"It will be a while before we can make a viable prognosis. For the moment, we have cleaned his body and used surgical glue to hold him together. The tissue infuser will promote rapid knitting of damaged tissue. We had to drill a small hole in his skull to insert a tube that will administer proteins that will repair physical damage to his brain." He sighed. "These procedures will take four to five days, but his vitals are weak. If he holds to life for forty-eight hours, his chances will be good."

"Is there anything I can do?"

"He needs blood, and soon."

"Take my blood. Take all of it if necessary. My life isn't important."

The doctor smiled. "You shouldn't think that. I have a feeling my patient would say that you are important."

"Please give him my blood." Tears ran down her face.

The doctor motioned for a technician. "Let's set her up for transfusion. Let me know when she's ready."

The technician retrieved a wheeled stretcher sitting by one of the walls, and rolled it to her. He helped her to lay on the surface, with her arms positioned on two arm supports that swung out to give access to her arms. As the tech placed the access ports, Melody heard a female voice.

"His vitals are beginning to slip."

Melody cleared her mind and remembered the lake, how her heart raced with Cade holding her in his arms. She was hoping he would experience the scene with her. She remembered one moment after another, pushing her memories toward his mind. She felt Maska and Aeolus join her in her attempt to help. Tears streamed from her closed eyes as she heard the nurse again.

"I don't understand what is happening. His vitals are climbing. His heartbeat is strong." Another voice, a man's voice, invaded her mental field of battle. "Brain wave activity is rebounding. He is dreaming." She heard someone else, the doctor's voice. She realized he was speaking softly near her right ear. "Looks like your blood has turned the tide. No need for tears." She felt a tissue brush against her cheeks, but she continued to funnel her memories of their time together through the mental conduit, the connection she and Cade shared. She knew the truth. It wasn't the blood alone. It was their love. She fell asleep and continued to share her connection and her dreams. She was dreaming about sharing a kiss with Cade, when someone gently touched her shoulder and woke her. She looked at her arms and realized the IVs were gone. She was still lying next to Cade. She suddenly realized that she shared moments that did not happen during their time together. The kiss never happened.

She turned her face and looked up to see the doctor.

He smiled and said, "You were sleeping so peacefully that I let you sleep. The two of you have been through a tough ordeal."

"How long have I slept? Have we made the journey to a base with a hospital?" She felt something stuck to her forehead. She reached up and felt a small box with wires running from it to her head.

"Please don't touch that device. You have been sleeping for twelve hours. Cade is not entirely out of the woods yet, but he has made phenomenal progress." He paused. "Progress that can't be logically explained." He cleared his throat. "We are still on Faroe. Your team has not left the ship, and they refuse to eat."

She sat up on the stretcher and looked toward the glass wall. Maska and Aeolus were staring back at her. She sent a mental picture of Cade and said in her mind, *"He is well. Go and hunt. Protect Cloud and Shadow."* The two left their station and went out of the hatch. The doctor's voice drew her attention.

He was holding a notebook-sized electronic device in his hand. "Just as I thought. You're a beast master."

"No, I'm not. You must think so because the animals left when I sat up. They probably left because they saw that I was okay."

"Melody, medical science refutes your words." He held the screen of the device in his hands for her to view. "Notice the screen is split down the middle. On the left, we see your brain wave activity. On the right is Cade's."

She stared at the screen for a moment and then looked away. "You recorded my brain waves without my permission."

"I apologize for doing so without your permission, but I did it for my patient's benefit. Your brain waves match exactly. Even now, as you communicate with me, your brain waves are connected in some way. The only variations are when you communicate outside of the connection." He continued to hold the device for her to view. When you looked at the animals, there was a noticeable change in your pattern. The same thing happens when you are talking to me, but the underlying pattern remains identical to Cade's."

She sighed. "Does your culture require that you not expose patient information? Will my words be held in confidence?" She turned to look him in the eye.

"I am bound by oath to keep medical information confidential. But consider the possibility that what has been done here, could be beneficial for others with serious injuries."

"I will tell you what little I know, but you must not tell Cade."

"I don't understand, Melody. I believe the love the two of you share is the main reason he even has brain waves. Why would you not reveal this to your lover?

She angrily reacted with a lie. "I do not love him. We worked together as a team, and he had misplaced feelings for me. He knew I would be leaving when we completed our mission to free Faroe from the clutches of a monster."

The doctor sighed as he bracketed her last statement, recorded on his device, with markers. He looked her in the eye. "You say you intend to leave soon."

"Yes! I need to search for a way to get home, and I don't want to remain in his presence, building false hopes in him. He's delusional about caring for me."

"I see. This connection you have with another beast master is new to me. But I believe Cade will suffer catastrophic regression if you leave before he has recovered."

Melody's face went from one of determined confidence, to a countenance reflecting pained concern. "Regression? Will his life again be in danger?"

"I don't know. What I can see and measure is the fact that your brain waves seem to be sustaining his mind and body. Without a mind, the body will die."

Melody leaned forward on the stretcher and rested her elbows on her legs, so she could cradle her forehead in her hands. "I will remain with him until he recovers, or Jace discovers the way home for me." She paused. "Why are we still on Faroe?"

"We are still parked where we landed. I told the captain that it would be best for Cade to stay planet-bound until he recovers. We are still in the first forty-eight hours of his recovery, but this ship has been ordered to another assignment. It will depart on the fourth day."

"But that means you will leave him behind. He will still need medical help."

"Captain Brown, the captain of this patrol cruiser, went to the town with our patrol marines and arrested four aliens who were lackies for Zande. They also liberated six slaves. A patrol heavy cruiser is on its way here to take the prisoners and freed slaves to Beltane. The townspeople are very happy that you and Cade rid them of Zande and his battle droid. They have given the thirty acres where the cabin and corral are located to Cade, and they have requested that the patrol establish a permanent base on property that adjoins the homestead." He paused. "The heavy cruiser is also bringing a prefab facility that will adjoin the cabin, and will be equipped with everything that will provide care and comfort for the two heroes of Faroe."

"I'm not a hero, but Cade is the one who put his life on the line for others.

"In life, it is the humble who turn out to be heroes. The cruiser will be here tomorrow, so the homestead should be ready for Cade by the end of his fourth day of recovery." He looked at the device in his hands again. "I don't know how you are sustaining this connection, but you should probably continue for the time being. By the way, if you haven't done so, try to help him with memories of other people you both know."

She pursed her lips. "I haven't thought about it, but there are only two people I am aware of that we both know. Zina, the first mate on his ship, and Lieutenant Jace."

"Try to reinforce some memories of those two, as well as memories you have of the Searcher and his team. As of now, the only memories I can be sure of in his mind, are yours."

"I'll do whatever it takes to get him back on his feet."

"That's what I want to hear. I will write a medical paper on what you have accomplished, but I won't release it to the profession until after you have left. Only doctors will see such a report, so there is very little possibility of Cade seeing it."

She smiled. "Thank you for your promise. It is in Cade's best interest."

"Melody, I know you must be starved. Go up to the galley and eat something."

"I'm not leaving him."

The doctor chuckled. "I can see how much you don't like him. I'll have something sent down for you to eat." He handed the brain wave monitor to her and left the room.

She stared at the matching set of brain waves. *I don't know how the connection still exists. I'm not making any effort to hold him.* She suddenly realized that she may not be able to end the apparent symbiosis of their two minds.

Chapter 12

It was the fourth day of Cade's treatment. The heavy cruiser had arrived, and the prefab was being erected. Melody had not left Cade's side except for visits to the fresher. The tubes in his skull were removed on the second day, and the tissue knitter was reprogrammed to cover from the top of his head to just above his groin on that same day.

She spent sleeping hours on the stretcher next to him, and most of her waking hours were spent seated in a chair, holding his hand, which was extended beyond the range of the tissue knitter's travel. The doctor entered the room. He had told her on the second day to call him Doctor Bill.

Bill said, "I have some interesting things to update you about. We will be transporting Cade to the prefab in about two hours. The scans show his wounds to be healed, but we won't take him off the knitter in the prefab until morning, to be on the safe side. One of our nurse physicians, and an orderly, will remain with you for about two weeks. The necessary medical monitoring and observation should be completed by then. She will begin backing down the drug that has kept him asleep early tomorrow. He should be awake by late afternoon." He paused. "The Searcher is on its way, and will be here late tomorrow. Captain Jace is assisting the second officer in bringing Cade's ship to Faroe. He is to finalize the agreement to maintain a base here."

"That's good news. It'll be good to see my friend, Zina, again. I have some questions she may be able to answer."

"This cruiser will leave today, after we have Cade established in the prefab. After we leave, his health will be in the hands of the nurse-physician, and you."

"I understand, Doctor."

"The heavy cruiser, Hermes, that brought the prefab has been ordered to remain in support of Lieutenant Jace." He paused. "I'm leaving the brain wave monitor with you for additional data. You can remove your device when he regains consciousness. I guess that's all I have for now." He left the room.

She realized Cade's hand was still resting in hers. Melody gently raised his hand, bringing it close to her lips, softly kissing his hand. She leaned forward in the chair and rested her head near the edge of the bed, but away from the path of the knitter. She fell asleep, but was awakened by activity in the room.

She sat up and realized they were moving Cade to a stretcher. Two men carried him through the decontamination room and out the cargo hatch. Melody followed them. She saw the prefab for the first time. It was nearly the size of the cabin, and was positioned parallel to the west side of the house, with about ten feet separating them. The front had a small covered porch that protected the entry door. They carried Cade inside, with Melody following closely behind.

They entered a great room that had a sitting area on one side, and a galley on the other. She noticed all modern conveniences, including a meal dispenser in the galley. There was a doorway in the middle of the wall opposite the entrance, and it opened to a wide hallway. The orderlies carried the stretcher through the hall entrance and then turned to enter a room through a doorway on the right side of the hall. Following them in, she saw the tissue knitter located near the wall opposite the hall door.

The men, with the help of two others, slid Cade onto the surface of the knitter. They swung the overhead trolly into place and programmed the machine before turning it on. The emitter began the process of sweeping back and forth in its journey to heal. A woman nearby in the room approached Melody.

"I'm Sarah, the nurse-physician Bill told you about. You and I will be working together to get Cade back on his feet."

"I'm Melody. I don't know how much help I will be, but I'll do my best."

Sarah said, "Let's go take a look at our patient." They went to the knitter and stood side by side. "Bill told me about you two because of medical necessity. I am bound by oath to protect your rights, and Cade's. I know about your extraordinary mental connection to him." She held out the monitor. "Bill and I are both apprehensive about the ability you will have to disconnect when it's time. Have you given it much thought?"

"I intend to talk with Zina when she gets here. She was bonded to a beast master for years. I hope she has some experience or knowledge about this empathy, or whatever it is."

"Okay. Don't worry too much until we find a reason to. For now, I want you to consider remaining near him. There is a bed in this room, and another in a room across the hall. There is a fresher located near the end of the hallway."

"I've been maintaining physical contact with him by holding his hand, even when I sleep. Do you think that contact is necessary?"

"It depends on the range of your shared esper talent. We will do a little medical analysis tonight. I will keep a check on vitals and brain waves while you sleep across the room. If there is a problem, we will move a stretcher next to the knitter." She pointed to a small table with two chairs sitting on one side of the bed. "I will see that your meals are brought in so you can continue to stay near him, like you've been doing. There is an easy chair on the other side of the bed for you to rest during the day. If all goes well, I'll turn off the knitter early in the morning, and begin the process of bringing him out of the induced sleep at the same time." She looked at her watch. "It's time for supper. The orderly will bring it to you. Afterward, you'll be given some time alone with Cade until bedtime, when I'll begin regular monitoring of the instruments." She left the room.

Later that evening, Melody lay upon the bed across the room from Cade. She had spent the last three nights by his side, holding his hand while they slept. She was afraid of going to sleep, fearing dreams that would prove her love to Cade. She didn't want that to happen, knowing the time would come for her to leave, severing her connection to him. She tried to put him out of her thoughts by focusing on Zina, Bill, Jace and Sarah. She finally fell into a restless sleep.

She awoke and realized Sarah was standing beside Cade. Melody asked, "Anything odd happened last night?"

Sarah turned away from Cade and walked over to stand by Melody's bed. "We had an uneventful night. In fact, neither you nor Cade dreamed much, according to the brainwave monitor. His vitals are normal and steady. I've shut down the knitter and swung the trolley away from the table. He's received his second dose of the drug that will wake him." She paused for a moment. "I'll send in your breakfast. Let me know if you notice any change."

"How long before the medicine takes effect?"

"It will take at least two more doses. Possibly, he'll wake in four hours. Hopefully, you'll see activity on the brain wave monitor that will be different than your readings." She turned and left the room.

Melody got out of bed and walked over to stand by Cade. She picked up the brain monitor from a table sitting next to her. She looked at the monitor and saw their waves still matched. She heard a knock at the door, and turned to see the orderly bring her food to the small table. He set the tray down, and left. She didn't have any appetite, but she knew she would need strength to see the day through. After finishing breakfast, she returned to her bed. She laid down and made up her mind to avoid going near Cade. She soon fell asleep.

She heard a voice in the distance. "Wake up, Melody." She opened her eyes to see Sarah.

"He's awake."

She sat up quickly and swung her legs over the side of the bed. She hurried to stand beside Cade. Looking at his face, she found he was staring at her.

He turned his head toward Sarah, and then turned his attention back to Melody. He tried to speak, but his voice was raspy.

Sarah handed a glass of water to Melody, and elevated the head of the bed. "Help him to drink slowly through the straw."

Melody held the glass near him, and maneuvered the straw between his lips. He sipped slowly until the glass was empty. She handed the glass to Sarah. "Cade, do you know me?"

A slight smile crossed his lips. "Yes, you're Melody, the woman I love."

She felt her heart skip a beat. *I'm so stupid. I've made things worse.* Her mind was awhirl with random thoughts.

He turned his attention toward the nurse. "Hello, Sarah."

Sarah looked at Melody and then back to Cade. "You know me?"

"Of course, Sarah. You and Doctor Bill have worked with Melody to heal me."

Sarah looked at Melody with amazement written on her face. She knew that the only way Cade could know her and Bill, was through the connection Melody shared with him." Sarah was busy writing a note concerning their conversation.

He reached out and grasped Melody's hand as he gazed into her eyes. "I'm a little hazy on why I'm here." He paused and looked around. "In fact, where exactly am I?"

Sarah looked at Melody. "I'll leave you two alone for a while. Bring him up to date on the where and why." She left the room and went to the one-way observation window, located in the hallway.

Cade gazed up into her eyes. "Can I have more water?"

She went around the bed and poured another glass full from the carafe. She held it close so he could drink. He finished the glass, and she returned it to the cart. "Seriously, Melody, I have been trying to remember, but I can't remember how I got here."

"Do you remember Maska and Aeolus?"

He looked around. "I do remember. Where are they?"

"They are out hunting. Do you remember Zina and Lieutenant Jace?"

"Yes, I do. Zina is my navigator on the Searcher." He looked proud as he remembered. "Jace is a patrol officer."

"Do you remember what planet we are on, and why we are here?"

"No, I don't remember. Isn't that strange? Most of my memories seem to be about you. I remember a special kiss we shared."

Melody raised her right hand to her forehead. "Do you remember that you are a beast master?"

"Yes, I can communicate with Maska and Aeolus."

"Anyone else that you can remember communicating with, in the same way you do with the animals?"

"I think we had a connection, Melody, and you are a beast master too."

She looked at the brain wave monitor and saw his wave varying from hers. "I am going to add to your memories by telling you why we're here. We are on the planet Faeroe. You and I came here to destroy a battle droid. Do you remember what that is?"

"Some kind of robot?"

"Yes, it's a machine that is banned. A man brought the machine to this planet for the purpose of taking power and control over the people. You and your team destroyed the machine and the evil man, Zande. Is any of this coming back to you?" She could tell that he was struggling to remember.

"I don't remember."

Melody took a deep breath. "Remember that we have a connection. What I am going to tell you will make more sense if you believe in the existence of that connection. You were severely injured by a battle droid. You had a deep gash on your right side, and you received brain trauma when you were thrown to the ground by the machine's attack. I looked into your mind and knew you were close to death. I know you think we are in love, but we're not. You believed you were in love with me, but I rejected you." She saw Cade's face fall, and anguish was written in his eyes.

"But the kiss, and our embrace."

She hated herself, but it was for his own good. "Cade, I funneled images of you and me to help strengthen you. I wanted to save your life at all costs. Many of the memories of our interactions were true, but the kiss and embrace were manufactured by me."

Sarah entered the room in a hurry. "How can you be so heartless? You may cause him to relapse."

Cade said, "It's alright, Sarah. I believe she is telling the truth." He looked at Melody. "I must be pretty stupid to think a beautiful woman like you could have any feelings for me." He turned his face toward the wall.

Sarah sighed. "Melody, go outside. I need to remove his cath. He'll be able to walk with assistance." Sarah noticed her tears and handed her several tissues. "Go on. You've done enough damage here."

Melody felt like she was going to faint. She left the prefab and made her way toward the corral without conscious thought. She saw several people who were obviously locals, working around the stable and clearing debris from around the outside of the fence. She went to the fence and looked in at Cloud and Shadow. One of the men approached her.

"Are you Melody?"

"Yes, I am. Who are you?"

He was wearing a broad-brimmed hat, which he removed and said, "Miss Melody, I'm Harold, the mayor of the town of Lawrence.

The town where that demon machine was kept." He paused. "The town wanted to do something to help. With winter coming on, we knew you would need feed and hay for your horses. The men are making the stable tighter to keep the horses safe."

Melody smiled. "You really didn't have to do all this work."

"You and your man didn't have to free us from evil, but you did. We are grateful and hope the two of you will consider living here one day. We'll even remodel the house so that it will be more comfortable."

"Let everyone in Lawrence know how much we appreciate what you have done."

Harold grinned from ear to ear as he returned his hat to its perch on his head. "We heard Cade was still recovering from injuries. We hope he will get well soon. The town plans to have a celebration when the two of you are able." He turned and made his way back to the stable.

Going to the cabin, she entered and went to the couch where Cade had slept during their few nights together. Settling on the end near the fireplace, where he always sat while they talked, she closed her eyes and felt sadness, like a knife, stabbing at her mind. *The happiest days of my life are those I've spent with Cade. I will never experience that again.* She sat for a long time, before returning to the prefab. When she entered the great room, Sarah was just entering from the hallway.

"You're needed in Cade's room."

"Did something happen? Is Cade okay?"

"Gee. Funny how much concern you have, since you don't love him."

Melody ignored the remark and hurried into the room. She stopped abruptly when she saw Zina, Jace and two people she didn't know. "Zina, I'm happy to see you."

Zina went to her and gave her a hug. "I'm relieved you are safe." She paused. "I want to introduce you to someone." The unknown woman approached Melody as Zina said, "This is Anna, Cade's mother."

Melody felt her knees start to buckle. She regained composure. "I'm pleased to meet you, Mrs. Storm." She reached out and grasped Anna's hand.

"Please, Melody, call me Anna."

Melody saw the man approach her. He reached out and grasped her free hand. "I'm Curt, Cade's father."

"I'm pleased to meet you." Melody felt unworthy to meet his parents as if she were somehow equal to them. *They would cringe if they knew my shame.*

Cade was sitting on his bed, with his legs over the edge. "Melody, how is it I have memories of you, Zina and others, but not my parents?"

Sarah said, "I think we all need some enlightenment concerning this question. Let's all go to the prefab's galley and listen to Melody's explanation over a cup of caff."

Melody went to Cade. "Is it okay if I assist you?"

He smiled. "I'd appreciate your help." He slid off the table, and Melody placed her right arm behind his waist to steady him. She looked up and saw Anna smiling at her. They were soon gathered at the table with caff sitting in front of each.

She exhaled a deep breath as she looked at the faces around the table. She was seated at the end of the table, with Cade in the first seat to her left, and Anna sitting opposite him, and to Melody's right. "Well, no pressure here. I will begin by telling you I am not a good person. If there is anything good within me, it is only because my friends, Cade and Zina, have made me a better person. Enough about me." She looked at Anna, and then Curt. "I know Cade found out he is a beast master since the last time you saw him."

Curt said, "Zina told us. We were shocked that he inherited his grandfather's ability."

Cade said, "Since I recently discovered it, I was probably shocked too, but I don't remember."

"There's no need to go into how I arrived on the scene." Melody was reluctant to reveal her past to his parents.

Anna smiled. "We want to know, Melody. Don't be afraid of the truth."

Melody's eyes watered as she tried to hold back tears. "I was a slave on the planet Thane. I escaped and had to climb a tree to avoid being eaten by a giant creature. Cade and his team saved me." She felt a tear roll down her cheek.

Anna handed her a tissue. "Don't cry. None of us here condemn you for being a slave. That is an evil that was forced on you."

Melody steeled herself, and continued. "Being around Maska and Aeolus, I discovered that I had the ability to communicate with them."

Curt exclaimed, "Astounding. For two people to meet in one little small corner of the universe, both with such a rare ability, can only be termed as fate."

Anna noticed that Melody was not pleased with his words. "Curt, don't be so melodramatic."

He started to protest, "But, Anna."

She cut him off with a look. "Go ahead, Melody."

Melody glanced at Curt. "What I have to say next is even harder to believe. Cade and I can communicate with each other, just as we do with Maska and Aeolus."

Zina was incredulous. "I've never heard of such a thing. I was bonded with a beast master for more than twenty-five years. I asked him if he could communicate with other sentient beings. He said that a beast master could look into the mind of another to get a sense of emotion and character, but nothing more."

Melody swallowed as she came to grips with the lie, she had to tell. "When Cade was lying injured, I looked into his mind and felt impending death. I was aware that he believed he loved me." She paused as she glanced at Cade. "Even though I rejected him, he continued to be delusional concerning his feelings. When I am gone, he will realize that he was not in love. I used the knowledge of his feelings to save his life. I fed memories to him of us. Many were true, showing our interactions as crew members and friends. But I also showed him a sweet embrace and a shared kiss. These were not real, but I gladly lied to him in an effort to save his life. He is an honorable and brave man. His mother and father should be proud of him, just as I am proud to have known him." She hesitated. "It is my hope that his memory will improve, with the help of the memories I returned to him." She hesitated. "I just hope my desperate action doesn't convince him that my feelings are the same as his."

Silence prevailed, and everyone at the table digested what Melody had said. Finally, Anna asked, "What do you plan to do now, Melody."

She looked toward Lieutenant Jace. "I will make an official request to Jace to have the patrol look for my home world. I intend to return there as soon as possible." She hesitated again. "Doctor Bill said it would be best if I continued to spend time with Cade. He thought the time we had spent together could help him recover his memory. I think it is a bad idea." She looked at Cade and saw tears flowing, as he looked at her and wiped at his tears with a napkin. She felt like the worst of traitors.

Anna smiled and reached out to take Melody's hand. "I believe the doctor has a point. Please promise a worried mother that you will at least try. I know you're concerned about encouraging affection that you do not welcome, but you have laid it in the open for me and

Curt to see. We respect your desire to return home, but please stay longer. Perhaps together, we can retrieve his memory."

"I will stay for a while."

Sarah said, "It's time for supper. Let's make use of the dispenser, and we can get to know each other over a meal."

After they dispensed the food, they all sat around the table. Friendly conversation and occasional laughs created the feeling of a celebration. Melody kept glancing at Cade. Not drawing much food from the dispenser, he ate very little. He quietly left the table and went out the front entrance. Melody was worried he might get lost. She picked at her food, and finally left the table. She went out the front door, unaware that Anna was trailing behind her. Melody saw smoke rising from the cabin's chimney. She went to the front door and entered. Cade had built a fire and was sitting at his usual spot on the end of the couch. Going to her chair, she sat down. "You remembered making fires here?" She nodded toward the fireplace.

He looked at her and smiled. "Not really. I just felt comfortable doing it." He closed his eyes for a minute and looked to his right. He reached to rest his hand gently on the couch. "Did you place a memory of you, falling asleep next to me, here?"

"You remember? I didn't place that memory. It really happened. I asked you how I got to bed. Do you remember what you said?"

He gazed into her eyes. "I told you that I woke you, and you walked into the room and laid down. I also said that I almost went in to make sure you didn't fall off the bed."

"That's right. I think your memory is coming back."

"Actually, I lied to you that morning. I carried you into the room and put you on the bed. I pulled the covers over you and came back in here."

His confession caught her by surprise. Melody knew he was recovering memories. "Why did you lie about it?"

He sighed. "I didn't want to upset you." He nearly choked, and his breathing came harder as he tried to suppress his tears. "I wish my memory wasn't coming back. I wouldn't have known to miss you. My heart wouldn't be broken." He took a deep breath. "I am able to remember that you don't love me. That is the toughest memory for me to endure."

"Cade, it's not you. I've told you before that I am not worthy of anyone's love, and..." Cade interrupted her.

"Look, Melody, stop telling me what's best for me. I reserve that evaluation for myself to make. Stop using me as an excuse for not loving me. It's alright. I will get over you." He looked away from her a moment and sighed. "All I ask is that you make the effort to know my parents, spend time with each one and use our empathy to put them in my memory. It will be the last thing I ask of you."

Melody nodded. "I will begin with your mother tomorrow, if she is willing."

Anna carefully closed the door of the cabin. She had heard enough to know Melody was in love with her son, but had some reason to resist her feelings. She walked back to the prefab, thinking how much she would love to have Melody as a daughter-in-law.

Chapter 13

Two weeks after he had been injured, Sarah was giving Cade his last checkup. He was seated on the edge of the knitter table. "You are in perfect health as far as your recovery goes. I suggest you get more exercise. You're gaining weight."

"Believe me, Doc, I know it well. I feel flabby and slow."

"How about your memory?"

"I'm not there completely, but I feel close. Melody did a great job of helping me remember my family." He paused. "Jace is going to take them back to Arzor aboard the Hermes. He's scheduled to arrive sometime this morning."

"Speaking of Jace, he requests that you meet with him aboard his cruiser the moment he lands. He said it was patrol business."

Cade scratched his chin as he considered what the future held. He had never been one to make long-range plans. "The patrol may have another problem they can't handle. I don't think I'm physically or mentally ready to get involved again, at least anytime soon."

Sarah said, "Not to make this meeting out to be mysterious, but he has requested that I accompany you to the meeting."

"That doesn't sound like a mystery. He probably wants your evaluation of my recovery." He paused. "I'm not going to burn up any brain cells trying to figure out his reason for the meeting. Let's just roll with the flow."

Sarah laughed. "Okay, let's just drift down the stream."

Cade slid off the table. "See you later, Doc. I'm going to visit with my team until summoned."

Cade left the prefab and walked toward the cabin. He focused on Maska. *"Where?"* He viewed the stable through her eyes. He found her stretched out in the sun, outside the fence. He felt guilty about not spending much time with the team during his recovery. He sat next to her and leaned against a fence post. He picked up a piece of straw and stuck it in his mouth. He looked around at the scenery. The distant mountains were glistening with snow. He felt a chill in the air and remembered one of the locals telling him winter was only days away. A scratchy sensation in his mind alerted him that Maska was looking through his eyes at the mountains. He heard the big cat's mind talk. *"Nice... Happy."* He smiled. The few times he had communicated with Maska during his recovery, he found that their communication had greatly improved. They could speak through what Cade thought of as 'mind talk'.

Aeolus' wings stirred the air with a whirring sound as she flew down and landed on the top fence rail, just to his left. *"Hunting good."* He glanced up at the eagle. She held a rodent in a talon as she tore at it with her razor-sharp beak. He wondered, once more, if Faroe would be the animals' choice for their new home. He felt a nudge at his back. He reached into a pocket and retrieved a sugar cube, one of the villagers' gifts to the homestead. Holding the cube on the open palm of his left hand, he raised the offering over his left shoulder. A gentle nuzzling removed the cube from his hand. He grinned, knowing he would receive another request. A nudge at his right shoulder was not as gentle. He knew, without looking, that Cloud wanted his prize. He pulled out another cube and offered it over his right shoulder. Cloud wasn't as gentle as he teased by bumping his teeth against Cade's palm while taking the cube.

Cade felt a familiar, faint vibration in the air. He glanced at Maska. She rolled to her feet and sat, looking every bit like one of the ancient statues of an Egyptian goddess. The cat was gazing upward at the ship descending from the heavens under magnetic flux drive. Cade stood and made his way back to the prefab.

Sarah met him at the door. "Jace was serious about us meeting him upon arrival. He sent for us moments before landing." She had a concerned look on her face. They walked to the ship together, where a marine guard guided them to Jace's office.

He motioned them to enter. "Have a seat. Sorry about not explaining the need for this meeting, but I have several things to cover." When they were seated, he asked, "Would you like some refreshment before I begin."

Sarah said, "Now you are causing me to worry. What's wrong?"

Jace sat back in his chair. "Nothing's wrong. I have some news, and a couple of proposals." He cleared his throat and then sighed as he looked at Cade. "I wanted to break some news to Cade before I tell…," He hesitated. "Before others hear."

Cade was beginning to feel concerned. He wondered if something happened to his sister back home on Arzor. "What is it, Jace?"

"I've found New Terra. I have the coordinates."

Cade slumped back into his chair as reality hit him. "I see."

Sarah asked, "New Terra? What does this mean?"

Jace looked at Cade. "I know how close the two of you have become."

Cade shook his head. "We're not close! She doesn't feel anything for me."

The light of understanding flipped on for Sarah. "Oh. That's the world Melody is from. So that means…" Her voice trailed off as she looked at Jace.

"Yes. I will be taking her home. I'll tell her after we finish our meeting here." He looked at Cade. "I'm sorry."

"There's no need. It's ironic. When she was first aboard the Searcher, she insisted that she didn't want to go home. In fact, the driving force for me to punish Zande, was the fact that her experience with him destroyed her will to face her people. I thought I loved her, but I can see now that I pitied her. I mistook my compassion for love." He hung his head. "These memories make it clear that my recovery is complete." He sighed. "I deserve pity as a man who wishes he had never recovered his memory." He tried to clear his mind. "Sorry for my rambling. You said there was more?"

"When we liberated the slaves held by Zande, two of the women declined to be repatriated. One of the girls was an engineer aboard a starship that was boarded by pirates. The other was taken from her home world. It seems her planet did not advance into the star lanes, and is an uncharted world. They have expressed the desire to return to service aboard a ship, if possible."

Cade sighed as he realized what was coming next, but he remained silent.

"I know you will probably reject my proposal, but I witnessed a positive turnaround for Melody while she was under the care of you and Zina." He paused a moment. "I know you need at least one crew member, and these two are qualified and need to get on with their lives. Even if the Searcher remains parked here for a year, I believe these two will rediscover themselves, without returning to space. Will you consider taking them aboard, if only for a short time?"

"Jace, I know you mean well, but I haven't the slightest idea what I will be doing tomorrow. I made a promise to Zina, to return her to her home world, and I still need to find a place for Maska and Aeolus. I may not even keep the Searcher." He looked down at his hands, resting on his knees. "I'm not sure how long I would be able to pay them if they came aboard."

Jace continued to press. "I know there's a lot of uncertainty. But I believe you can make a difference in their lives, just as you did with Melody."

He sighed. "Okay. Fine. I will interview them and make a determination." He started to rise from his chair.

Jace said, "There's more."

He settled back into his seat. "What more could there be?"

"Head quarter's brass has offered a proposal. You have accomplished more in the struggle against slavery and piracy than the Patrol has in the last fifty years. They seem to attribute this to the fact that you see things through a fresh perspective and a willingness to act." He opened a folder and took out a paper. "This is their proposal, and it is amazingly brief. It seems they are leaving a lot of room for interpretation and action. That is, your interpretation and action." He handed the paper to Cade. "I will give you an overview. They will commission you as a Lieutenant in the Patrol's marine organization. Your responsibility will be centered around the slave trade and piracy, with me serving as your liaison. You will not be brought in on every incident. Only the toughest missions, like the two you've already carried out, will be assigned to you. Your vessel can continue carrying out research or whatever civilian occupation you may choose for your ship and crew. In a sense, you can do as you please, but with the understanding, the call may come. You will not be required to put your ship or crew into dangerous confrontations, but you and your team will potentially be exposed to danger. As for your crew, they will be paid the same as cadet patrolmen."

Sarah asked, "Why did you ask me to be here?"

"Due to the hazards Cade and his team face, you will be assigned to the Searcher as its medical officer, just like any other Patrol ship. You will be given a raise commensurate with the responsibility. The medico sitting in the prefab will be transferred to the Searcher. A small part of cargo bay 2 will be closed in to create the medical office, if Cade agrees to the contract." He focused his attention on Sarah. "I know this is sudden. You can choose not to take the position, and we will find someone else."

Sarah smiled. "Are you kidding? Life is not as boring when Cade is around. I want the job, and you really don't have to give me the raise."

"I'll give you a few days to decide, Cade. In the meantime, I need to go visit Melody. The two candidates are in the galley, waiting for your visit." He left the office.

Cade looked at Sarah. "Since you might be my medical officer, I would appreciate it if you would sit in on this meeting."

"Aye, Captain. Happy to oblige."

He looked at her as he stood and shook his head. "This will be one messed up crew. Let's get this over with." They made their way to the galley.

He entered the galley to find the two women seated at the table. They both stood as he entered. Sarah entered after him. Cade said, "I'm having a cup of caff. Would you women care for something to drink?" He could see the two were on the ragged edge. They reminded him of the dirty-faced girl he found on Thane.

One of the girls, with nervous dark eyes, timidly said, "I'll have some caff." She pulled a cup from the dispenser and returned to the table, but continued to stand.

Cade gently said, "Go ahead and have a seat." She shakily settled into a chair. The other girl had dark red hair and brows, and her skin was red-toned. He asked, "Would you like caff, or a cold drink?" She didn't speak, but pointed to the caff dispenser. He drew her a cup. "Do you prefer a lightener?" He watched her nod. He stirred in the cream and handed the cup to her. He watched her silently return to her seat. He sat down opposite the two, and Sarah sat next to him with caff in hand.

He looked closely at the dark-haired girl. He suspected she was descended from an Amerind population. "What is your name?"

"Nizhoni."

"You're of the Navajo Nation?"

"I am not pure blood. My great-grandmother was not of the blood." She quietly asked, "Are you of the blood?"

He smiled. "Yes, I am." He saw her smile for the first time, and she seemed at ease.

He turned his attention to the young woman with the ruddy complexion. "What's your name?"

The girl hung her head and remained silent. Nizhoni asked, "May I speak?"

Cade looked at the Navaho girl. "You can talk to me anytime you wish. What do you want to say?"

"She hasn't spoken since our ordeal."

Reaching across the table, he gently laid his hand on hers, and said, "I will not let anyone hurt you again. If you stay on my ship, you will be part of a family. That's how I see my crew."

The girl raised her head and looked him in the eye for a long minute. "I believe you. My name is Riley."

"I am pleased to meet both of you. My name is Cade, and the woman sitting next to me is Sarah, the medical officer of my ship, the Searcher. Would you like to take a look at our ship?"

Cade and Sarah led the two girls to the cargo bay and down the ramp. They met Jace and Melody at the foot of the gangplank. Cade noticed Melody carrying her kit bag. Cade ignored Melody and said to Jace, "They're going to tour the Searcher. Is that okay?"

"That will be great. I guess the interview went okay."

Cade nodded. "They will be a great addition to the crew. We'll be on our way." Cade, Sarah, and the other two new crew members, resumed their walk to the Searcher.

Melody turned to watch as they walked away. Jace stood next to her, watching them as well. Melody asked, "Who are those two women?"

Jace turned his attention to focus on Melody's reaction. "They are going to be part of the Searcher's crew." He continued to watch her face. He could see a shadow of concern.

"One of them looks to be Amerind."

"She is Navajo. Her name is Nizhoni."

He saw jealousy darken her face. "Most Amerind names have special meaning. Do you have any idea what hers means?"

She angrily snapped, "Beautiful!" She reined in her emotions. "Her name means, Beautiful." After speaking, she thought; *His parents were hoping for a blood match. It looks like they'll get it.* She reluctantly turned away and walked toward her destiny. She had one last regret. *He didn't even say goodbye. I guess I succeeded in turning his heart away from me.*

Cade led his new crewmembers up the gangplank of the Searcher.

Zina was waiting in the cargo bay. "Jace informed me you were bringing two new crew members."

Cade said, "Girls, this is my first officer, Zina." He then turned to each girl and told Zina their names. They stepped forward to shake hands, but Zina dispensed hugs instead. At first, Cade feared they would not be familiar with the Zacathian people, but both girls seemed to accept her hugs without hesitation.

Zina said, "Follow me, girls, and I'll give you a tour of the Searcher."

The three went toward the lift, engaged in conversation. Cade noticed that Riley was just as talkative as the others. He grinned as he remembered Melody's similar meeting with Zina the first time. He turned to Sarah and said, "I'll give you the nickel tour on our way to the galley. He stopped the lift in cargo bay 2. "This is the area where your medical facility will be located."

She looked at him. "So, I guess you plan to accept his offer."

He sighed. "Meeting Nizhoni and Riley reminded me that I had a reason, other than Melody, for taking down Zande. Slavery and piracy destroy people's lives."

Sarah smiled. "I think you have a third reason for expanding your crew."

"Yes, Jace was right. I believe this may be the best medicine for them to overcome the pain and humility they've endured. Just a brief few minutes of knowing Zina seemed to take away a large chunk of their fear. My experience with you, Doctor, tells me that your character and personality will go a long way toward healing them."

"Careful. Your compassion is showing." Sarah paused. "I once heard you say that the love you felt for a certain woman was actually compassion. Has your compassion ignited even an ember of love for either girl? Their challenges have been equal to those of Melody."

"I guess you're my psychologist as well as my doctor. I lied when I said my love for Melody was only compassion for her because of the ordeal she went through. But it doesn't matter anymore, because she didn't even have compassion for me, much less love." He resorted to a lie. "Enough of that. I'm over that fiasco in my life." They reached the galley and entered.

Sarah marveled at the size of the galley. They each drew a cup of caff and sat across from each other at the table.

Cade laughed. "I didn't introduce you as a new crew member. I guess I didn't think of it because we are already familiar with you."

Zina entered the galley with her charges in tow. "Did I hear you say your doctor is joining our crew?"

"Yes, she is. Our crew went from two to five."

Zina said, sadly. "You mean from three to five. Melody was part of the family."

"Of course, I wasn't thinking. Let's all sit and get to know each other. The women did most of the talking, while Cade did most of the listening. His mind wandered, as he drank his cup of caff. He remembered Zina telling him that she didn't want to inherit the Searcher because no crew would want to ship under a female Zacathian captain. *Here we are, with a female crew. I bet they would all sail with Zina.* He sat and marveled at Zina's ability to put people at ease. She was like the favorite aunt at a family reunion. He suddenly remembered that he might soon lose her. He had promised to take her home. He really didn't want her to go.

He leaned forward in his chair. "While we are all assembled, I need to ask each of you about the events of today." The women fell silent. "Zina, I promised to return you to your home world, but I've seen how important you are to this ship. I hope you will consider staying aboard as my first mate."

"Cade, I will stay as long as you want me. We've had some adventures, and I believe there will be more in our future."

"Nizhoni, you haven't had much time to think about this, but Jace is leaving soon. "Do you want to stay, or go?"

"You are willing to sign me up? I'll stay with the Searcher."

"Riley…"

She didn't wait for his question. "I'll stay. I feel like part of a family."

He turned to Sarah. "I've already gotten Sarah's answer. She will be our medical officer."

"Zina, will you take Nizhoni and Riley to Jace's ship to retrieve their personal belongings?"

Zina answered, "I'll contact him and let him know we're on the way."

She started to exit, but Cade motioned her to stop. He took the neatly folded paper from his pocket and signed it. "Give this to Jace. Tell him he can make me a copy later." He watched her hurry away with the girls in tow.

Zina led the girls up the gangplank of the Hermes. A patrolman escorted them to the crew's living level. Nizhoni went to her former cabin and opened the door. Melody was just inside and about to leave the room.

Nizhoni said, "I didn't know someone else moved in. I came to pick up my belongings."

Melody smiled. "I noticed someone's things were here. Come in." She sat on the bed and watched as Nizhoni stuffed her clothes into a kit bag. She noticed the girl folding a leather Jerkin and pants. They were like the ones she owned. She also opened a storage locker and took out a quiver and bow. She laid them next to the bag. "I heard you are a new crew member aboard the Searcher."

Nizhoni looked over her shoulder at Melody. "Yes. It's a wonderful ship, and the captain is amazing. He even got Riley to speak."

"Riley is the other new member?"

"Yes. We were both held as slaves by Zande."

Melody felt a chill run down her spine. "You were a slave?"

"Yes. In fact, Cade was the one who led the team that freed us." Nizhoni suddenly turned around. "Wait, are you the warrior named Melody?"

"I guess so."

Nizhoni looked at Melody's kit bag next to her on the bunk. "Are you leaving? I heard that you and Cade were lovers."

Melody flew hot. "I never had feelings for that man. We only worked together." She noticed a stunned look on Nizhoni's face, and realized she had overplayed her reaction. Or was it jealousy?

"I don't understand. I see light in Cade's heart and eyes when he talks to me or Riley. Why do I see only darkness in your heart and eyes?" She paused a moment. "Please forgive my words. I realize a man like Cade would only see light in you, just as he does with me. If he is not taken, I would gladly be his woman."

Melody felt smaller than a worm. "I didn't think to tell him goodbye. Please tell him for me when you see him. Nizhoni's words cut her to the soul as she realized the truth in them. Cade would never see the dirt that she felt clinging to her soul. He would only see her as being a human-like himself. A human who he would love, only wanting her love in return. She sighed as she realized it was too late for her. She watched Nizhoni finish her packing. *Perhaps she will be the one to whom he gives his heart.*

Nizhoni said, "I'll tell him of your farewell."

Melody watched sadly, as Nizhoni left the berth.

Cade met up with his parents and walked with them to the Hermes. Anna hugged him when they got to the gangplank. As he hugged her, he said, "I'll try to come home soon for a visit. I own a fast ship, so it will be easier to make the trip."

Anna whispered in his ear. "I know you have your mind made up, but you are wrong about Melody. She loves you deeply, but is trying to protect you from something in her life. I've never seen you care so deeply for any woman, and I'm afraid you may never find love again. Don't give up on her."

"Mother, even if you were right, we will soon be light years apart. That is what she wanted. I tried to change her mind. I opened my heart and even cried for her to stay. One thing you are right about, I will never love anyone again."

Anna released her hold on him. "That is the worst thing I have ever heard. Mothers always hope for their sons to give them grandchildren."

"Don't worry, mother. I didn't say I wouldn't marry. I will settle down without any further looking for the right woman. I will marry for the family's sake, and I will treat my wife like a queen. I'll utter the word 'love', and give myself to her completely. You will have grandchildren, if I survive long enough."

Curt stepped close to his son and gave him a hug. "I heard every word, and I respect your decision. I'm proud of your desire to fight against slavery. Hosteen would have been very proud. Don't worry about the ranch. Your sister and her husband are going to take the reins."

"That makes me happy. Sis is very smart, and I'm sure she will do you proud." He hugged them both again. "I guess you need to settle in. Jace will take good care of you." He watched them until they moved out of sight in the cargo bay. He turned away and decided to visit the corral.

He sat down and leaned against a fence post. The team wasn't around, so he just sat in silence. Feeling the vibration in the air, he looked up to watch the cruiser climb toward space. "Goodbye, Melody. I hope you find peace and whatever else you may desire." Rising from the ground, he made his way to the Searcher. Entering the galley and selecting a cup of caff before sitting at the table, he thought it was probably time to eat.

Zina entered the galley. "The girls are organizing their rooms." She poured a cup of caff and sat across from him. "Cade, I'm thankful that you wanted me to stay on the Searcher."

"I'm glad you are willing to put up with me. I was just thinking. We will probably be spending a lot of time planet-bound here. What do you think about that?"

"I think it's great. I didn't stay because I wanted to continuously fly around in space. I am here because it feels like family." She paused for a moment. "I never told you about my family situation." She sighed. "My family disowned me, kicked me out. They were angry because I had the nerve to insist that I was a scientist. I was fortunate to meet Sartre when he visited the science foundation on my planet. I told him about my desire to travel to other worlds and explore. We were kindred spirits. I know it seems odd that two different species can actually fall in love, but we did. My parents expressed their hatred toward me and the human I bonded with. That was the last I saw them."

"You have a new family now. The Searcher is still a research ship. When we do lift, if it's not to carry out a patrol mission, I want you to have a site that you want to visit in mind."

"You mean it?"

"Yes, I do. What good is a research ship if we don't research something?" "In the meantime, I believe it's about time to eat. I want to make it a rule that we always dine together when we aren't on shifts. That's what families do."

Chapter 14

Jace stood on the bridge of the cruiser, Hermes. Melody stood next to him, wearing her native leather attire. "This is as close as we dare approach." He pointed to a display screen. "Our sensors show the location of the pirate's defensive detects. They have so many that this alone would be grounds for patrol intervention. This ship is making a record for patrol review." He hesitated, then continued. "There is a brand new surveillance vessel watching this planet from a higher orbit. Observing this planet is its first assignment." He handed her a small device with a pin attached. "Attach this pin to the inside of your clothing. We will have the ability to track you, and watch your progress." He didn't tell her the top-secret tech on the spy ship would enable observers to read a paper lying on the ground. He watched as she fastened the pin to the shirt under her jerkin.

Melody asked, "How do I get down there?"

"There are several options, but I think the southern pole is the best one. We come in at the center of the pole and follow a fifteen-degree course to this beach." Pointing out the area, he continued, "I will keep the skiff low and swing up next to the tree line. You'll leave the ship and travel due north until you bump into the citadel."

"I'm familiar with those woods."

"Keep in mind that your people, or the invaders, could be dug in where they weren't when you left. You will need to use extreme caution." He looked at her. "Are you sure you want to do this? From what you told me, your own people are not going to celebrate your arrival."

"I know the risks, but they are my people, and I want to help them."

"Okay. Let's make it happen." Jace led the way to the hanger bay, where the skiff was parked. The skiff was painted flat black. Jace opened the hatch and climbed in. Melody followed, carrying her bow and quiver full of arrows. Jace took the skiff in a wide arc to keep the distance between the skiff and the detects. At a good distance from the southern pole, Jace turned the ship toward the center of the grid on his heads-up display. When he drew within a quarter mile of the surface, he leveled off and followed the fifteen-degree radial showing on his panel. There were no lights on the craft, so it would be difficult to spot in the darkness. "Two minutes to the shoreline." Swinging the craft to starboard, he settled it within a foot of the trees so that the port side faced the trees. Opening the hatch, he watched Melody disappear into the darkness. Securing the hatch, he retraced his route via the South Pole. He soon stood on the bridge of the Hermes, looking at the distant planet.

His first officer stood next to him. "Do you think she's capable of surviving, sir?"

Jace continued to gaze at the world spinning in space. "Not as Melody. But the invaders on her planet will rue a meeting with Eagle Feather."

"I don't understand, Sir."

"It's nothing. I was just remembering my brief encounter with a scary woman in my office. I believe she will survive." He thought about the angry woman punching his desk with her fist. "Our task is completed. Set course for Faroe."

Eagle Feather knelt behind a tree. Her face was streaked with the face paint she requested from Jace. He obtained it at the same time he got her the native leathers. She thought about her endgame, returning to her tribe; *I will stand before the gate of Sioux fortress when I have only one arrow left.* She strapped a leather cover over her quiver to prevent the arrows from dispersing in the water.

Her plan was to cross the river and scout the Navajo lands. She wanted to find the strength of the invaders. Staying within the tree line, and moving north, allowed her to keep the river in sight. Locating two watch posts, revealed the sentries were negligent in their duty. Both posts had talkative warriors who were completely uninterested in watching the river. She finally found what she sought, a shallow wash that led down to the water. Scanning the nearby trees revealed the absence of sentries in the immediate area. She crawled on her belly along the wash until reaching the water's edge.

Easing her outstretched right hand into the water, Eagle Feather tested it. *The Great Spirit is with me. It is mid-summer, and the current is sluggish.* She knew, near the end of summer, the current would be stronger, but crossable with effort by a strong swimmer. Winter would bring raging current with deadly eddies. Crossing the river in winter, would be possible by using the only bridge spanning the gulf. Before easing her body into the river, she pulled out the only other piece of technology she had accepted from Jace.

She scanned the far shore for watchers with the detect. *There is a sentry two hundred yards upstream, and another at three hundred yards downstream.* She realized her crossing point couldn't be more perfect. If she drifted downstream, she should still have some distance between her and the southern sentry.

Eagle Feather repositioned the quiver and bow, strapping them against her chest and belly. She didn't want to chance the quiver drawing attention as she swam. Once her armament was secure, she slid into the warm water of the river. Her fortunes held as she found it easy to resist the current with measured strokes, allowing noiseless passage. Taking the current into account, she angled upriver, so her exit point would be well between the two sentry positions. She kept to a steady rhythm, fighting an urge to increase her speed, an urge brought on by the approaching dawn.

She finally reached the far shore and crawled across the open expanse of beach, until she reached the trees. Ignoring aching muscles and exhaustion, Eagle Feather moved deeper into the trees. She burrowed and pushed her way into a dense thicket. Pulling the detect out of a pouch, she set it to stealth mode. When Jace gave it to her, he revealed it contained new tech, the ability to render opposing detects useless. Removing her quiver and bow, she collapsed into a restless sleep as she thought about Cade and Nizhoni.

Meanwhile, the crew of the Searcher seemed to enjoy their extended stay on Faroe. Almost two weeks had passed since the departure of the Hermes, and Cade was continually amazed at the progress made by his new crew members. He couldn't understand how they made progress so much quicker than Melody. Cade stretched as he prepared for his usual afternoon run. Cloud stood impatiently next to him. "I'm almost ready, have patience, Cloud." He heard a woman's voice, and looked up from his preparations to see Nizhoni approaching. She was wearing lightweight running gear like his. The weather was getting colder, but a runner would be warm enough in the lighter material once the exercise began.

"Captain Storm, I used to run every day before…" She didn't finish the thought but moved on to make her request. "Mind if I run with you?"

"Look, just call me by my name. I want the crew to feel like family. You need to stretch to get your muscles ready." Nizhoni seemed to be making the best progress of the two, to the point she was somewhat bold during her interactions with him. He found it difficult to believe she was ever a slave.

She began her preparations. "Thank you, Cade. It's better to have a running mate than to go it alone."

He nodded, but didn't say anything. He kept stretching to keep his muscles warm, as he waited for her to finish. When she was done, they started with a slow jog as they went down the mountain. Cloud paced alongside Cade.

As they jogged, Nizhoni asked, "Why is your horse jogging with you?"

He turned his head toward her with a grin on his face. "You'll find out when we reach the bottom of this slope."

She was happy to be running with Cade, to be sharing some one-on-one time with him, even if they paced along in silence. She found the jog to be too easy because it was downhill, but it served the purpose of warming her muscles. They finally reached level ground and continued into the town. She noticed the villagers were greeting him as he passed.

Cade came to a halt in front of a small café. He said to Nizhoni, we will take a short break before heading back." Several villagers came out of the café to herd the two inside.

As she accompanied Cade, she heard one of the villagers say, "He brought Melody with him." She tried to clear up the mistake, but the crowd was laughing while each person greeted her. There was so much noise that she couldn't make out individual voices.

Cade took her arm and guided her to a seat at the table, which the owner always held for him. "Two coffees, please."

The noise began to subside as the people gave them room. Nizhoni felt like she was on stage as there were so many people standing and staring at her. She could only see a few feet of floor between the table and people standing at least four deep, shoulder to shoulder. She looked at Cade. "Does this happen every afternoon when you jog?"

He laughed, and softly answered in a near whisper, "It is annoying, but it seems to give them joy. Normally, the crowd would have thinned out by now, but I think they're waiting for you to sing."

"What? Did Melody sing to them?"

He grew serious. "No. But she will forever be their hero. This is the first time they've seen her in a while, so they're happy."

"But I should tell them who I am. It's not right to fool them like this."

"Nizhoni, I am happy to hear that you are a person who respects truth." The owner pushed his way through the crowd and set two cups of coffee on the table. Cade said, "Melody, this is Irving, the owner of the café."

Irving was nearly jumping from the floor with this personal introduction. "Miss Melody, it is a pleasure to meet you for the first time."

Nizhoni looked questioningly at Cade. He closed his eyes, gave a slight nod, and quickly moved his head to one side toward the excited owner. It was obvious to her that Cade wanted her to perpetuate the lie. "It is my pleasure to meet you as well, Irving."

The happy café owner turned toward the crowd. "Okay, everyone has seen the lovely couple. Now go, unless you want to order something." The majority of the crowd left, while many seated themselves at the tables and the bar.

Cade remarked, "It looks like we're good for business."

She looked into Cade's eyes. "I'm surprised that you are okay with them believing a lie."

"You're right. I wouldn't normally allow it." He gazed around the room. "Look at these people. They suffered nearly as much as you at the hands of Zande." He returned his gaze to look at her. "Look around. What do you see?"

She looked around the room. There wasn't a frown or tear to be found. She felt tears trickle from her eyes as she turned back to Cade.

Cade took a napkin and reached across to gently wipe away her tears. "I see you understand." He watched her nod without saying anything. They finished their coffee, and Cade said, "If it makes you feel any better, Melody is not the one who freed them. Melody was her made-up name. She didn't use her real name. So, in a sense, their praise is for a name, and idea. They will never see that Melody again, but they will see the name, when they see you." He stood, and Irving rushed over.

"I hope to see you and Miss Melody again tomorrow."

Nizhoni said, "Please call me Melody. There is no need for the honorific." She felt a little better. She didn't tell him Melody was her name; she merely told him to call her that. It didn't feel quite as much of a lie. She followed Cade into the street where Cloud was waiting. They had an audience while they did a few stretches, before beginning the uphill leg. Within a few minutes, she felt the difference in the amount of effort required. She maintained her pace alongside Cade. "I met Melody while aboard the Patrol cruiser packing my belongings."

Cade glanced at the woman running beside him. "I didn't know that."

"We actually talked for a little while."

Cade nearly stopped running, but resisted the urge and kept pace. "I'm glad you got to meet her." He didn't say more, but he began to count his steps to himself, as if the process would somehow blot out memory and conversation." His legs were feeling the effect of the steeper incline.

"I realize that you may not have had time to tell her goodbye."

He didn't like the direction her conversation was going, and once more wondered about her confident boldness, and outspokenness. "I said goodbye."

Nizhoni kept her attention on his face as they ran. "If that's so, why did she ask me to tell you goodbye?"

He came to a halt. He turned away from Nizhoni as he felt his emotions rise to the surface. "I didn't say goodbye in person." Cloud moved alongside, and Cade set his foot in the stirrup and swung up into the saddle. He wanted to urge Cloud to a full gallop up the grade.

"Hey. Don't leave me here. Let me ride with you."

He wiped away his tears without turning in the saddle to face the girl. "You should have brought a horse with you." He didn't ride away but settled into silence.

Nizhoni said, "I'm sorry if I hurt you, but you can't move on unless you are willing to talk about your pain." She paused a moment before quietly saying, "Believe me. I found out the hard way."

He reached down, swung her up, and placed her behind him. "You'll need to hold on. This saddle isn't built for two." He held the horse to a slow pace, and the cold was penetrating their clothes without the exercise to keep them warm. "I guess this is the last time wearing light jogging clothes. It's really getting cold."

She snuggled tightly against him and didn't say anything else. She realized her words had laid open emotional wounds, and she regretted telling him the truth.

Cade lowered Nizhoni from the horse at the foot of Searcher's gangplank. The crew had been staying aboard the Searcher most of the time. Cade rode Cloud to the stable and removed the saddle and bridal. The horse had not worked up a sweat, so Cade laid a blanket across his back and fastened the straps to hold it in place. Cloud moved alongside Shadow, joining her in a meal of oats. A small atomic-powered heater hung in one corner, to keep the stable pleasant. He went to the Searcher and secured the hatch after entering. Maska and Aeolus were settled in their usual spots. He went up to the captain's cabin and used the fresher for a hot shower. Changing into a spacer jumpsuit, he left his berth and headed for the galley. He entered to find everyone seated and ready for supper. Zina was hovering around, mothering everyone.

Cade made his selection from the dispenser and sat at the table. Nizhoni was in line to draw her plate. She sat next to him. He glanced at her. *She's as beautiful as Melody, and yet I feel nothing. There is no fire in my chest. If she can't stir me, how will any woman be able to reach my heart?* He ate his meal and occasionally added his opinion to random conversations around the table.

He smiled as he viewed the scene, knowing how much peace the meal gatherings seemed to bring. Watching Riley as she laughed and talked with the others in the ship's family made him realize there couldn't be so much happiness with any other crew. When they were through eating, he went to his berth and pulled on a warm coat.

Going down to the cargo bay, he left the ship with Maska and Aeolus going out ahead of him. It was still daylight when he reached the cabin and went inside. The animals entered with him and took their usual places as he lit a lamp, and then knelt at the fireplace. He got a fire going and continued to kneel, warming his hands for a few minutes. Rising from his task, he went into the bedroom. Remembering the night when he carried Melody into the room, and gently laid her on the bed, he noticed the robe she had worn, lying on the covers. Picking it up, he held it to his face and inhaled a deep breath. Her scent was still clinging to the fabric. He held it for a few minutes and then carefully folded it and placed it in an empty drawer. Returning to the great room, he found Nizhoni, wearing a heavy coat, standing by the fire, warming her hands.

"I didn't realize someone had come in. He looked at Maska, and wondered why the cat didn't alert him. Maska merely stretched a little more as she lay between the couch and Melody's chair. Nizhoni was standing next to the lazy cat.

"I will be honest; I followed you here." She looked around the room. "I like this cabin. I would be happy to live here."

"Why did you follow me?"

"Because I like to talk, and I want to talk with you."

He settled into his usual spot on the couch, and motioned her to take the chair. He felt a little uncomfortable with her seeming familiarity with him.

She sat down and looked at Maska reclining between them. "I guess Maska is the dividing line."

He chuckled and asked, "What dividing line would that be?"

Nizhoni changed the subject. "Is this where she would sit?"

He hesitated before allowing a slight nod.

"And you would sit there to talk with her?"

He managed to say, "Yes. Is this what you wanted to talk about?"

"It is." She looked toward the bedroom. "That was her room, and you stayed on the couch. Isn't that so?"

"Yes, that is the way we spent the nights."

"I admire Melody."

Cade felt surprised. "Why do you admire her? You hardly knew anything about her."

"She loved you without there being intimacy between you."

Cade felt ready to bolt from the room. The girl across from him seemed to know everything, and it made him uneasy. "You're invading personal memories. Can't you drop it?"

"We are alike, you and I. I was living a happy life in my world. I had a man who was bond-sworn to me. He was the love of my life, and the date for our bonding had been set. Everything changed the day I was taken prisoner. A blow to my head knocked me out." Tears flowed as she began gasping to hold back sobs that were near the surface. "I awoke, trussed up tightly in rope with a hood over my head. I could hear screams of fighting and death. I never got to experience the intimacy I longed for with my love. My people believed that act to be a part of bonding, which I still believe to be true." She began crying more desperately as Cade got up and carried tissues to her. He felt her pain. She finally calmed enough to finish. "I do not know if he's still alive, and will never know. My father died before my eyes, and I don't know if my mother…" She trailed off with a deep sigh. "You and I are in the same boat, but different circumstances led us to this point. We will never be able to embrace those that we love most in life." She fell silent.

He took her hands in his, and gently urged her to stand. He guided her to the couch and settled her next to him. He wrapped his right arm around her and held her close to his side in an effort to comfort her, and himself. They sat quietly for a long time. Her head rested against his shoulder. Cade thought she might be asleep, but she stirred a little.

"Cade, I haven't known you but a few days. I was dwelling in a dark place until I met you on the Hermes. I saw an honorable man, one who could be trusted. You have brought light to my darkness and helped me to find peace. I know you will never love another woman, and I'm sure that I will never love another, the way I loved Chayton." She hesitated a moment. "I want us to be close, to lean on each other."

"What do you mean?"

"Chayton is the one I love, and long for bonding with. That's not possible now, and may never be. I want us to have a closeness that borders on that, but more like a brother and sister. A closeness that doesn't require intimacy." She reached with her left hand and cradled his right hand in hers. We can trust each other enough to do this, and remain loyal to our true loves, should we ever reunite."

"I understand what you are proposing is a way for us to find it possible to continue our journey, but there are dangers in that type of relationship. You could fool yourself into thinking you love me, like I did with Melody. Believe me, that is a painful path to walk."

"She didn't say more, but leaned on his shoulder.

They remained there until Cade heard her breathing hold steady with sleep. He picked her up and carried her to the bedroom. The memory of carrying Melody drifted through his mind as he gently lowered Nizhoni onto the bed.

She grasped his hand in hers as he was turning to get the blanket to pull over her. "Stay with me. Lie next to me for comfort. That's all I need."

He helped her remove her coat, and pulled the blanket over her. "Please stay."

He lay next to her on the bed, fully clothed. He heard her breathing grow regular. He felt at peace as he fell asleep.

When he awoke, he was alone. He went to the fresher and washed his face. Maska and Aeolus were no longer in the cabin. He made his way to the Searcher and went to the galley. Zina was seated with a cup of caff in hand.

"You're the only one that didn't make it for breakfast."

"I made a fire in the cabin, and fell asleep."

Zina drew a plate for him, and herself. "I waited to have breakfast with you." She set the plates on the table, drew a cup of caff from the dispenser, and placed it in front of him. "You look well rested today. There seems to be a glow about you."

He laughed, "I slept the whole night through and felt refreshed." He saw Nizhoni come in and go to the caff dispenser.

She carried it to the table and sat across from him. "Are we going to run down the mountain this afternoon?"

Cade noticed Zina raise a brow, and her ear frills betrayed her interest in the conversation. "No, I'm going to work out, on the land the Patrol engineers have cleared for their spaceport. Patrol marines are going to be stationed there, so a huge field for physical training has been laid out." He paused for a bite of food. "I'm taking my bow and practice while I'm there."

"That's great. I need some target practice myself."

A quick glance at Zina revealed her neck frill changing color, as he asked, "You know how to use the bow?"

Nizhoni took a drink of caff. "I trained as a warrior on my planet. If you want to practice martial arts, I was tops in my class."

Cade looked at Zina and thought she was going to choke on her caff. "I don't think it would be a good idea. I'm a lot bigger than you."

Nizhoni retorted, "Don't worry, I won't injure you, unless you are more out of practice than I."

Zina spewed her caff into the cup and left the table laughing. "Cade, I think you're afraid of her."

Cade frowned. "Alright, you can come with me. But I won't go easy on you."

Zina said, "I'll put on a coat and go too. I'll referee."

Cade's face reddened. "It's not necessary."

She smiled. "It's no trouble; I'll get my coat."

Cade went to the cargo bay hatch and waited for the women. Zina arrived first and was bundled up to keep warm. Nizhoni left the lift and walked toward the hatch. She was wearing her native gear, with a long sleeve, skin tight shirt under her jerkin. Cade recognized it as being thermal wear. She was carrying her quiver and bow, with a long knife hanging from her belt. Cade asked, "Where did you get the gear?"

"It was with the belongings I brought from the Hermes."

They reached the practice field after thirty minutes of walking. Cade tested the ground. "It's not frozen, but it is hard and will hurt in a fall."

For the first time, he noticed her headwear. She reached up to remove the decorative jewelry from the headband above her brow. He looked closely at the thin band she handed to Zina. It looked to be silver, with three silver bangles at the back. A silvery feather hung from the middle one, and the bangles on either side held a small falcon. On the left side of the narrow metal band, were suspended two ivory disks on separate golden wires, with a chief's headdress etched on each. He stood looking at it in awe.

Nizhoni noticed his interest in her adornment. "This is only a reproduction. Mine was lost the day I was captured."

"That means, you are a princess, daughter of the chief."

"That's what it used to mean. My people are probably all gone by now. I wear it to remind me of them, and who I was."

"That's another reason why we shouldn't practice martial arts."

She began warming up. "I'll be ready in a minute."

Cade began to warm up as well.

They soon faced each other, and Cade tried to dissuade her one more time. "We should really wait until we get a mat to cushion your falls."

Nizhoni stood defiantly, facing him from six feet away. "Enough talk. You're the aggressor."

Cade sized her up. *I'll keep it simple. Feint to her right and grasp her left wrist when she tries to throw me, pinning it to her back. That should be safe. No harm, no injury.* He made his move, but the expected counter was not there. He suddenly saw the sky as he landed square on his back. He heard Zina laughing as he tried to get his breath back. He finally said, "I wasn't ready."

He could see deep concern in Nizhoni's eyes as she bent over to look at him. "Are you okay? Why did you come at me so recklessly?" She held out her hand and helped him to his feet.

He sheepishly answered, "I underestimated your ability. I wanted to save you from injury by making a quick move to pin your arm behind your back. I guess it was me that needed protection." He moved his arms and swiveled at his waist, trying to shake off the pain.

Nizhoni grasped his right hand. "I'm so sorry. Are you hurt?"

"Mostly, my ego is bruised."

Zina called out, "Not as much as your backside."

He glanced at her and saw she was holding up a piece of paper with his name and Nizhoni's written at the top. A big zero was drawn beneath his name, and a big number one under Nizhoni. "Really? You have to keep score."

"If I'd known it would be this much fun, I would have brought a device to record the whole thing. It was amazing."

Nizhoni said, "Don't take it to heart. She loves you."

"I used to think she did, but now I'm not too sure."

Nizhoni picked up her quiver and positioned it on her back. Picking up the bow, she said, "Pick a target for me."

He pointed to a tree about twenty-five yards away. A small branch grew about six feet from the ground, on the side facing them. He said, "It will be a difficult shot, with the branch facing head-on. Hit the branch at its base, cutting it from the tree."

He watched as she tested the tension on the bowstring. She wound a turn on the upper string notch.

Pulling an arrow from her quiver, she said, "This is like trying to split an arrow with a second shot. You would have to make it difficult. I'm out of practice, but I'll do my best." She set the arrow, and pulled the string toward her cheek as she sighted the target. She released the bowstring, and the arrow traveled true, imbedding itself in the tree as the branch fell to the ground.

Cade went to her and rested his right hand on her left shoulder. "I've never seen a more accurate shot. You are truly skilled." He saw her blush at his words.

She smiled. "I'm honored that you would think so. Thank you."

Zina said, "I think we need to head back to the ship. It's getting colder, and Cade looks to be in pain." She returned the chieftain tiara to Nizhoni.

Cade rubbed his lower back and said, "I believe I've had enough for one day."

Nizhoni gently settled the adornment so that it encircled her headband. The two chieftain medallions dangled over her left ear as she moved next to Cade. "I'll give you some support as we walk."

He started to protest, but realized his right hip was bruised enough that her aid helped ease the pain of walking.

They were near the cabin, and Cade said, "I think I'll stay here. You two go on to the ship."

Zina protested. "But it's near to lunchtime."

"I'll be alright. There's a food dispenser in the prefab. Go ahead, I'll rest easier in the cabin." He watched them as they walked away, and then entered the cabin. He went to the fireplace and stooped to make a fire and realized how stiff he was. "How can a small woman manage to toss a horse like me over her shoulder?" He got the fire going and found it hard to stand up; his hips were so sore. "I knew I was getting too flabby. I'll start working out in earnest, tomorrow." He eased down onto the blanket Melody had placed on his couch that first night. The door opened, and Nizhoni entered the cabin.

"You're still wearing your coat; take it off."

Cade grimaced. "I'm beginning to think your sole purpose is to torment me. Go away."

She went to the counter and set something down and returned to the couch. Unfastening his coat, she pulled it off one arm and then the other. With the coat removed, she released the seal on the blouse part of his jumpsuit.

Cade asked, "What are you doing?"

"Sarah gave me some ointment to rub on your back."

"Well, let Sarah do it, she's the doctor."

"Stop acting like a child. Help me pull down the top of your jumpsuit."

He reluctantly complied with her orders.

She looked around the room and then went to the dining area and picked up a chair. She set it near him. "Move to the chair and sit so you face toward the chair back."

He gingerly rose and moved to the chair. It was painful, but he straddled the chair seat and leaned against the chair back, as she went to the counter and returned with the ointment.

"Now tell me if I rub too hard."

He felt warmth penetrate his back as she rubbed in the ointment. "That feels good." She rubbed his back for a long time before stopping.

"You can stand up now."

He struggled to extricate his legs from the chair.

When he was clear of the chair, she said, "You need to rub ointment on the backs of your legs." She paused. "And anywhere else you hurt." She went into the bedroom and returned after a few minutes. I laid out some loose clothing. Go in there and remove that jumpsuit so you can massage your muscles with that ointment."

"You're definitely the daughter of a chief, and you're too bossy." He went into the room and closed the door. It took a while, but he rubbed the ointment into his backside, from his waist to his ankles. "That's the last time I'll spar with her."

Her voice called from the great room. "I heard that, and you're wrong. We need each other to improve our skills. I intend to join your team."

"That's not going to happen. You can't communicate with the animals."

"But I can communicate with you. That's what com-links are for."

"Gee! I want to say some things that I learned from the Pomeroy kids when I was young. But if my mom finds out, she'll wash my mouth with soap again." He laughed at the memory. "I agree to us working out together, but I'll have to think about you becoming a team member."

He walked out of the room and found he wasn't as sore. Nizhoni had two plates of food sitting on the table, along with two cold drinks. Going to the table, he took a seat, pulling one of the plates to him.

Nizhoni sat next to him. "Do you feel better now?"

"Yes, a lot better." He suddenly had an image of Maska standing by the door. "Would you go let the animals in?"

Nizhoni got up and said, "It feels like I'm a member of the team." She opened the door, and the animals came in quickly. "It's snowing." She closed the door and returned to the table. "Cade, this is what I was talking about last night. We can be comfortable with each other, and help one another like I did for you just now.”

“Since you are the one who threw me for a loop, I guess you should have been willing to help me.”

“I really like you, Cade, and I believe you like me, even though I might be a little annoying.”

He shook his head. “A lot annoying and too bossy. I just don’t believe your idea to be a moral one.”

When they were through, Cade moved to the couch and sat in his usual place.

Nizhoni hurried over and sat next to him. She leaned against his shoulder.

Cade turned his head toward her. “We probably shouldn’t get in the habit of being this close.”

“Why not? Aren’t we good for each other? And we have vowed that we will never find love again, which means we won’t fall in love.”

“Yes, but others may get the wrong idea.”

“I don’t care what others think. The way I see it, we can’t experience intimate love now, but there are other kinds of love. If we are good for each other, and we have peace, isn’t that a type of love?”

“You have a way of confusing me. I agree there are different kinds of love, but we can’t stay here together.”

"I want to stay every night I can, just like we did last night. It gives me comfort. Don't worry, I already told Zina about it."

Cade was exasperated. "That's just great. She'll think I'm taking advantage of you."

"No, she said someone besides her needed to keep an eye on you."

He tilted his head to look up at the ceiling as he thought, *I'm about ready to take the scout and return to Arzor to marry one of the women my folks suggested.*

Chapter 15

Melody marked eleven silver lines in a row, right next to the image of a skull on her arrow. She had already buried ten arrows in the bodies of ten aliens. She carried a bag with ten trophies, the blasters she took from their dead hands. The alien invaders were at a disadvantage because her detect made her invisible to their sensors.

She had worked her way to a vantage point where she could see the mine, and the starship sitting a short distance from the entrance to the mine. She couldn't believe how the number of aliens had increased while she was gone. As she surveyed the scene, she saw some motion near the top part of the vertically parked ship. A hatch opened, and a metal balcony extruded from the ship's surface. An alien wearing a scarlet cloak stepped out onto the platform and was casually looking at the activity of a hundred or more aliens on the ground below. She said under her breath, "This is too good to pass up." She pulled one of two special arrows from her quiver; she set the nock to string. This arrow had a lightweight but potent bomb on its tip. There was no wind. She pulled the bowstring to her cheek and added some elevation before releasing it.

Eagle Feather watched as her present blew past the startled alien and exploded inside the ship. The caped alien was thrown to his death, and the ship began to topple. It hit the ground, and a mighty explosion ripped the air as Eagle Feather held tight to a tree, resisting the instant hurricane that tried to tear her away. She hoped there weren't any slaves in the mine. The entrance was not facing the ship, and she had not expected such a catastrophic result. Alien bodies were strewn on the ground below, and the ship continued to shrink in on itself, as if an intense fire was burning on the inside. Using caution, she backed slowly away from the scene and moved deeper into the forest. She burrowed into another thicket and ate a piece of jerky. Her hands were still shaking, and her ears were ringing.

Several miles away, a messenger entered the Navajo fortress. He hurried to Lim Jardin and made his report. He handed a bloody arrow with a skull on its shaft, and eight silver slivers painted in a row next to the skull. "Lim asked, what's this?"

"It is one of ten arrows like this one, except for the number of stripes. Those arrows were pulled from the bodies of ten men, and their blasters were taken."

"Damned. How many men do we have?"

"Counting the ten that stay in the Citadel to guard the people left here, we have another twelve serving as sentinels, and another hundred at the ship."

Looks like we'll have to quit mining for a while and use everyone to put down this rebellion." He paused. "Any idea how many renegades we are facing?"

The messenger nervously cleared his throat. "At this point, we can only be sure of one."

"What? How did you arrive at that number?"

"The arrows. The bodies were found in sequence with the numbers on the arrows. Whoever it is, moved without a trace and left a path of ten dead men, with a numbered arrow buried in each."

A flitter settled in the courtyard, and a man exited before the rotors stopped turning. He ran to face Lim. "The ship has been destroyed, and all of our men, over a hundred in number, are dead."

The first messenger holding the arrow said, "The last arrow we found, number ten, was within two miles of the mine. It was probably the same person. That leaves us with less than twenty-five people."

Lim looked around and found a place to sit. He was nearly in shock. "One person? How can one of these savages do so much damage?"

The first messenger cleared his throat. "I don't believe it's one of them."

Lim gazed at him. "An off-world mercenary?"

"I can't be sure. The explosion seems to point in that direction, but the cargo is very unstable. It could be a crazy local who has no fear of blasters."

"Go use the communications unit set up in my office. Contact our pirate friend, Dirk. Tell him we need reinforcements."

The messenger hurried to carry out his task, as Eagle Feather was sizing up another target. A flitter had flown by at a low altitude. She decided to travel in the direction it had flown. She came across two more sentries and made them proud owners of arrows eleven and twelve. She traveled for hours, using thirteen through twenty, before coming in sight of the Navajo citadel. She was on a high bluff, overlooking the impressive structure. She could see the machine's rotors, but it was on the far side of the courtyard and out of range. As she scanned the scene, she spotted an antenna mast sticking up from the roof of one of the buildings. It was out of range as well. She faded back into the undergrowth. She had ten arrows left, not counting the one she was going to save for her chief, and the remaining explosive-tipped arrow. *By destroying the ship with all of the aliens around it, I've done enough. I need to take the blasters I've captured and make my way to the Sioux fortress.* She decided to take the easy way and cross by bridge. She reached the bridge to find two of the aliens standing guard on her side, and two native guards were on the opposite side. She quickly killed the two aliens without bothering to number the arrows. Walking calmly toward the bridge, she saw the warriors on the other side watching her. She threw the two bodies into the river and crossed the bridge. When she reached the two guards, they signaled a third to come out of hiding.

The third man appeared to be their officer. He asked, "Who are you?"

"I am Eagle Feather."

The man looked at her more intently. "By the spirits, it is you. How did you get here, and what were you doing over there?"

"I killed a hundred and twenty of the invaders, and destroyed their starship."

The man laughed in her face. "Who would believe a disgraced female could do that?"

Before the man could take another breath, she dropped the bag of blasters, and in the same motion, she held her knife firmly against his neck. "I am not in the mood for small talk. However, I can cut out your heart if you need further evidence of my mood." She released him, and the other two backed away a step. She picked up the bag of blasters and handed it to the officer. "You carry the blasters and escort me to the fortress gate."

When they stood before the gate, Eagle Feather shouted, "I, Eagle Feather, have come to redeem myself. But first, I seek audience with the Chief." She knew a messenger was on his way to announce her presence. She removed her quiver, and laid it and her bow on the ground, along with her long knife. She had earlier turned off the detect, and it remained in her belt bag.

The chief called to her from the wall above the gate. "You have come to claim redemption. Which do you claim?"

"Before I do that, I have weighted words to speak before you and the council." She knelt down on both knees and put her forehead on the ground. She remained like that for a minute.

The chief said, "Weighted talk will be allowed."

She stood as the door swung open, and entered to face her fate.

Meanwhile, in the Navajo citadel, Lim got more bad news. Dirk told the messenger that he couldn't return for a couple of months. He also received a report concerning ten more numbered arrows."

Motgrey, Lim's lieutenant, stood nearby. "Sir, I've received word that our guards at the bridge are missing. It would seem our mercenary has crossed over into Sioux territory. Do you want me to gather some men and go wreak havoc?"

"You idiot! Haven't you been paying attention? We have thirteen men at most, and we won't have reinforcements for at least two months. We will hold our position in this citadel for now."

Eagle Feather entered the great hall and was escorted to the chief's audience chamber. She entered to see the chief, her father, seated at the far end of the table. Four elders sat along each side of the table, leaving her a seat at the end opposite the chief. She went to one knee and waited for his command.

"You may be seated, Eagle Feather."

She took her seat and waited for him to speak.

"We are curious about the journey that has returned you here. Each elder will have the opportunity to ask a question of you, before you speak your weighted words. Do you agree?"

"Yes, my Chief."

The elder seated at the chief's left spoke first. "When we last saw you, you were shamed by the invaders. What happened after that?"

"I was taken from this world to another, light years from here. Chained, I was shamed again by an alien named Zande."

The elders began to murmur with one another, and Eagle Feather could see disgust on their faces.

"Because I resisted even after beatings, I was taken to another world where I escaped. I was chased by a wild predator and climbed a tree, but I considered giving my life up to the beast. A mighty Navajo warrior who was the master of a panther and an eagle, rescued me. Wishing to avenge me, he went with me to the place of Zande, where I put an arrow in Zande's groin, and two more in his evil body."

Another elder asked, "Are you saying a mighty warrior thought you to be worth his effort? Did you not tell him the nature of your shame?"

"I did, and he swore his love for me. I lied and told him I did not love him. My real reason was that I knew he deserved better than a shamed woman."

An elder on the other side of the table spoke. "It is difficult to believe you. Who would want you?"

"Cade Storm is his name." She paused. "He destroys the rat nests where he finds slavers and pirates like the ones infecting our world. He works with a Galactic Patrol to protect planets like this from those who have greater technology. Cade Storm was severely injured during the battle he and I fought against slavers."

A fourth elder asked, "If this man is your champion, why is he not here, by your side?"

"If I were to go against my troubled heart, and call him to me, he will come. I don't want to hurt him because of my shame; I have told him to stay away, that I hated him." Tears began to flow down her cheeks. She saw her father lean forward with a look of understanding on his face.

The chief said, "I believe Eagle Feather did leave a champion behind. Now for her words."

"I have raided the invaders across the river. I killed over one hundred and twenty of their warriors, a hundred of those with a starship I destroyed."

An elder said, "Not possible! Do you expect us to believe that?"

"I am willing to face your mightiest warrior, knife to knife." She paused as she scanned the group around the table. "His death by my blade will prove the truth."

The chief exhaled a deep breath. "If you are telling the truth, you have stirred up a hornet's nest against us. We have avoided confrontation with them. What do you say in your defense?"

Eagle Feather felt anger building beyond her ability of restraint. "My defense? Aliens are destroying the Navajo, and we will be next. They aim to colonize this planet. Don't you understand? We can strike now. They can't have many men left after my rampage; that's why they haven't crossed the river yet."

The chief said, "You are the one who does not understand. Your words do not carry weight with us. State your redemption choice."

She sighed. "I choose servitude because I'm willing to die with the rest of you, when the aliens have enough numbers to walk over the Sioux. I choose to die with the rest of my people."

The chief looked around the table, and each elder nodded. "You will be assigned to the stables, with the added remedy of ankle shackles. You will toil there the rest of your days."

She stood and stepped to one side of her chair. She went to one knee and bent her head in acceptance of the sentence.

Chapter 16

Zina contacted Cade on his wrist communicator. He and Nizhoni were in the prefab, working out. Cade had requested a mat be sent, and Jace sent it on the next ship.

"Cade, Jace just contacted me and said he will arrive in about thirty minutes. He said he had information concerning your next assignment."

"Thanks, Zina. Tell Jace I will be there the minute he lands."

Nizhoni was standing next to him, wiping sweat from her brow with a towel. "We should take quick showers before we meet him."

"There is no we. It is only me. I haven't decided to put you on the team."

"I'm going to get a shower before we go." She turned and left the building."

Cade shook his head in frustration. "How does she expect to be a team member if she can't accept no for an answer?" He left the prefab and headed for the Searcher. When he had showered, he put on a fresh jumpsuit and made his way to the cargo bay.

Nizhoni was waiting for him. "I can't wait to see some action. I'm getting tired of beating you at martial arts."

Cade only grinned. He was coming out on top three out of five times, but he held great respect for her skills. They left the Searcher as Hermes settled on its fins.

When they entered Jace's office, the lieutenant looked at Nizhoni. "Is it okay for her to attend the briefing?"

"Jace, she hasn't paid attention anytime I've told her to do something. She may as well stay."

"We'll go over things in the conference room. Follow me."

Jace led them to a room that would seat about fifteen people. When they were seated, the lights went low, and Jace stood near a section of wall that began to glow with a blue light. "This briefing will cover some of the newest technology we have for fighting slavers and pirates. There are things that you cannot reveal to anyone. Is that clear, Nizhoni?"

"I will not reveal confidential information to anyone."

"Cade, as you know, I recently returned Melody to her planet, New Terra."

Nizhoni stood suddenly. "New Terra? Melody is from New Terra?"

Cade turned his head to look at his friend. "What's wrong, Nizhoni?"

She sat down. "I am the daughter of the Navajo chief on New Terra."

Cade asked, "Why didn't you say something before this?"

"I don't know. I guess it never came up."

Cade shook his head. "You have talked my ears off for what, three weeks? And there was something that you actually didn't think to talk about?"

Jace said, "It seems the princess has a vested interest in this planet. We have a top-secret surveillance ship in a very high orbit above the planet. Melody wore a micro tracker, and you are about to see what happened after she reached the surface of New Terra." Jace began the video.

Cade gasped as he watched Melody inch her way through a shallow ditch. "This was recorded from space?"

"Yes. I told her we would track her, but I didn't reveal how well we would see her. She actually did not move according to plan. She was supposed to stay on the Sioux side of the river, but she apparently never intended to do that."

Cade and Nizhoni watched as the brave Melody crawled out of the water and scurried for the trees.

Jace stopped the video. "She carried thirty-one arrows and two special arrows with explosive tips. She had us put a small skull on each arrow, and she numbered each arrow with a succession of stripes showing the number of each. She successfully killed ten invaders with her first ten arrows, and then this happened." The video rolled again.

Cade wanted to reach out and pull her out of the forest, to protect her as he watched her survey a camp with a starship parked there. A hatch was clearly seen, and an alien stepped out on a balcony-like structure. Melody was so close, he could see the bow string almost touch her cheek as she sent an arrow through the hatch. Cade gasped as the ship violently exploded, killing every invader at the site.

Jace stopped the video again. "She goes on to kill at least twelve more of them; the last two guarded the lone bridge that crosses the river. She recovered at least ten blasters, which she seemed intent on giving to her people to use against the enemy. We believe she tried to get the chief to attack the few remaining aliens and it appears there are less than a dozen left alive. Cade, your woman decimated her foes, but the worst enemy was her people. I will reluctantly show you one last clip."

Nizhoni said in awe, "She is truly a great warrior. I wish that I could have been by her side."

The video continued, and Cade felt like he was standing next to Melody as she went down to her knees, touching her face to the earth. She stood, and he watched her enter the fortress. They couldn't see her, but a small red x continued to mark her location, invisible to them because she was in a building. The x remained stationary for quite some time, and finally moved along the roof until she emerged from a side exit, with two guards escorting her. She was forced to sit, while a blacksmith hammered home rivets, fastening shackles to her ankles. Anger rose to a boiling point as he leaped to his feet. "Those animals! She left safe-haven and returned to help her people and where did it get her? They don't deserve her." He looked at Jace with blood in his eyes. "When do I go? I'm ready now. I'll kill anyone in that filthy world that stands against my freeing her."

Nizhoni stood next to him. "You must control your anger, Cade. You will be so blinded that you will be of no use. I will go with you for the sake of my people and Melody. We will save her, but we need to be disciplined and have a plan."

Cade knew she was right. He had never been this angry in his life. He looked at the brave Nizhoni and smiled. "You're right, little sister." He looked at Jace. "I'm sorry about my outburst and language."

Jace sighed. "I understand. I don't know how I would react if it were me and someone I cared about. The good news is that this technology will be of major importance when we take the bastards down. You will both carry one of these."

He handed Cade a detect. "This unit will nullify the enemies detects. You will be electronically invisible. Melody used hers to great success." He handed a small disc with an attached pin mechanism to Cade. "You will wear one of these, somewhere under your outer garments. This is what allowed us to track, and watch Melody." He held out two arrows. "This arrow is the same as others, but the skull adds an element of superstition every time the enemy sees one. This other arrow has the explosive tip, and is like the one Melody used on the starship." He paused and looked Cade in the eye. "I want you to hear me out before going nuclear about the plan."

Cade looked at Nizhoni, and she looked at him with the same puzzled look. "What is there about the plan that would make me angry?"

"We intercepted an encrypted transmission sent from the Navajo citadel on the day Melody destroyed the starship. It was easy for the surveillance vessel to decode. Lim sent a request for pirates to reinforce his depleted army. Dirk, a homicidal maniac on the Patrol's most wanted list, replied that he couldn't comply immediately, but he would be there in two months." He paused again. "This is a big deal. We have intercepted a couple of other messages between Dirk and Lim. Two ships, carrying three hundred slavers and pirates, will arrive in five weeks from today."

Cade sighed. "So, the part that would make me angry is that we need to strike when the ships arrive, and not now."

Nizhoni took his hand in hers. "I am as fired up as you to start killing vermin. But this makes sense. The bottom line, our job is to clear the space lanes of these thugs. This is the best way to do it."

Jace raised a brow. "Cade, I like her. Is she your Sage, or are you two a couple?"

Cade lightened up and chuckled. "I would say, she is almost both, but an annoying little sister that I never wanted would be a better description. She just can't seem to stop bossing me around." He paused as he made a show of pulling his hand away from her. "It makes sense that we need to wait and bag all the rats at one time. What's the plan?"

"You and your Sage will arrive in your scout, a week before the two ships arrive. It's my belief that the two of you should find a way to enter the citadel and neutralize the bad guys. The Patrol will neutralize those at the ship, and try to take as many prisoners as possible. Hopefully, they will provide valuable intel concerning other pirate bases." He hesitated. "You probably already know this, because of the way Lim treated Melody. I correctly identified Dirk as a maniac, but Lim thinks of himself as some kind of deity. He will kill off the Navajo people within the citadel if he thinks he's going down. You will need to take him before he realizes his end is near." He handed Cade a memory cube. "This contains the entire video surveillance of Melody's raid. You and Nizhoni need to watch it together and put it to good use. It's encrypted, so you will need this." He handed a small leather sheathe to Nizhoni. "You can down load this on the scout's auxiliary computer for study."

Nizhoni said, "We'll get on it right away."

Jace cleared his throat. "I actually have a pressing problem that the two of you will need to take care of first."

Cade asked, "What kind of problem?"

"It isn't what you signed up for, but you and your team are the best options I have available, and time is of the essence. A Carnelian prince has been taken hostage by a terrorist organization." Jace pulled up the image of a planet on the screen. "This is the planet, Edda." He pointed to a large island, and the image zoomed in, showing a thick jungle, or forest. "They are holding him somewhere on this island, or small continent, and have announced they will execute him in forty-eight of their hours, which is about thirty-eight hours from now."

Cade looked at the dense forest. "What are their demands."

"They have no demands. Their goal is for their religious cult to overthrow the monarchy, and thus the civil government of Edda. Even if I could reassign our spy ship from New Terra, its technology would be hampered by the growth covering the sector." He sighed. "It is a monumental task, and it will be difficult to succeed."

Nizhoni asked, "Any idea where the terrorists would have entered the jungle?"

Jace pointed to a spot on the east side of the wooded area. "They were pursued by the local gendarmes, but they lost them a mile in."

Nizhoni scanned the view as if trying to penetrate the tree cover. "How wide is the forest?"

"Roughly an average of sixteen miles."

She looked at Cade. "I have an idea, but it could backfire."

Cade nodded. "We go in from the west." He looked to Jace. We need some infrared scopes that can be accessed wirelessly. They need to be compact enough for one to be strapped to Aeolus. Nizhoni and I will each carry one, with monitors to view the Eagle's scope."

Jace said, "The marine contingent on this ship has the equipment you need." He raised his wrist com toward his face. "Lieutenant, I need you in the conference room ten minutes ago."

Cade said, "Jace, we can't take time to play patty cake with these guys. They won't be leaving the forest after we are gone, even if we don't get to the prince in time."

Jace replied, "I've already made that known to the authorities there. If you can manage to bring one out, I'm sure the locals can coax some info out of him."

One hour after their meeting, Cade engaged the Seeker's hyperdrive. He checked his instruments and left the bridge to assist Nizhoni. "I see Aeolus is cooperating nicely."

Nizhoni held up a finger with some blood showing. "For the most part. It would be better if I could talk to them like you."

Cade laughed. "She just told me she's sorry. It was a reflex, and she won't try to take off your finger again."

"I need something to wrap my finger with, so I don't get blood on any of the lenses."

Cade opened a cabinet and took out an adhesive dressing and an antiseptic wipe. He knelt by Nizhoni and cleaned her finger before applying the dressing. He gently kissed her finger when finished. "All better now?"

She didn't answer as she tested the camera harness. "It seems to work fine. The chest camera gimbals in the direction Aeolus turns her head." She stood from where she had been kneeling while putting the gimbal harness on the eagle. "I've already tested the display goggles." She handed one of the assemblies to Cade.

Cade was familiar with the technology from his days in the military. He clipped the wireless receiver to his belt, and adjusted the goggles to his head. The goggles held infrared detector lenses and also functioned as binoculars. Warm-blooded beings would be seen clearly in the lenses, and any target picked up by Aeolus would appear on a wrist monitor worn by both warriors.

Cade returned to the bridge. "We will reach our emergence point in fifteen minutes.

Nizhoni entered the bridge and strapped into the navigator's seat. She looked out her starboard port. "I still find traveling through Hyper Corridors disquieting. The white, featureless tunnel causes a feeling of isolation from reality." She turned her attention to the instrument panel to avoid looking at the white void outside. The hum of the hyperdrive quieted, and she could feel the planetary propulsion system engage.

Cade announced, "We'll land in twenty minutes." A short time later, Cade carefully guided the ship through total darkness. Using his instruments, he set the scout down in its horizontal configuration, just inside the tree line. Going aft, he found Nizhoni securing her quiver over her shoulder. Lifting his quiver, he fastened it in place. They slung their bows and exited the scout. Securing the hatch and engaging the ship's force field, he signaled Maska to reconnoiter, and Aeolus took to the air.

Cade looked at his wrist monitor. "My sight through Aeolus' eyes, and the monitor coincide." He looked at Nizhoni. "You will see what she sees." Scanning ahead through the darkness, his glasses revealed two watchers in trees to his right, some distance away. "I have two targets; they're twenty feet above the ground, in trees. Set your detect device, to counter-surveillance mode." He heard

Nizhoni in his ear. "Copy. I'm going to move ahead." He clicked his tongue once, signaling through the com that he agreed. He moved with stealth until he was in the range of the two watchers. They were in trees ten yards apart. He set an arrow to string, and hit the first target in the throat. He did the same to the second before the first hit the ground.

He scanned for more targets. To his far left, he saw another watcher. He used the zoom lens to get a closer look just as an arrow took the watcher out. Nizhoni was on the hunt. He moved forward, and used his detect to look for booby traps. He avoided two, and decided to remind Nizhoni. "Be sure to use your detect device. I've found two mines. These sentries should lead us right to our goal." He heard her tongue click four times, signifying she had found that many.

Nizhoni held her wrist communicator near her ear. It annunciated the time to be fourteen hundred, local. She spotted two more watchers, and put an arrow in each. She looked in the direction she knew Cade would be, and spotted two targets falling from their perches in the trees. She eased forward and spotted a man on the ground, using a tree for concealment. She started to set an arrow, but hesitated. *Could it be the prince? He could have escaped.* She slung her bow and moved silently toward the figure. She stopped when she heard Cade in her ear.

"Aeolus has found our target. Three men are standing over one who is trussed up and blindfolded."

Drifting silently behind a tree, she raised her bow and nocked an arrow to the string. Holding the arrow against the bow with her left hand, she bent to pick up a small piece of a rotten limb. She tossed it so that it hit in front of the watcher's position. He made the fatal decision to reposition himself on the side of the tree, away from the sound. He fell with an arrow through his neck. She resumed moving, not knowing where she was in relation to the three men Aeolus had seen. She finally saw three standing heat signatures and one lying on the ground. She moved closer until she had a clear view of the men. She heard Cade again.

"Aeolus can only detect the three with the prisoner. All the others are dead. Do you have eyes on the target?"

She clicked once into her mic.

"I'm not sure which is the leader. I'll take out the one with the sword. You pick one of the others. I will stun the one that's left. Follow my shot.

She clicked once as she pulled the string to her cheek. The guy with the sword fell as her arrow hit the second terrorist. A slight flash indicated the firing of a stunner. She could tell the weapon was aimed high to hit the target in the head. He fell limply to the ground, just missing the squirming captive who had been spared the effects of being stunned, because of Cade's well-placed shot.

Cade moved slowly into the clearing, checking his detect as he went. He knew his partner was keeping him covered in case something unforeseen should occur. He found no other targets, and

Maska slinked into the clearing. The cat had taken out a watcher hiding behind a tree, possibly saving Cade's life. She stretched out on the ground and seemed to lose interest in terrorists. Cade moved to the captive and waved Nizhoni in, as he knelt to remove the hood covering the man's face. The prince looked around in confusion at the bodies as Cade cut the rope holding him.

Nizhoni went to the stunned terrorist and secured the unconscious man's hands behind his back with handcuffs, before placing cuffs on his ankles to prevent him from trying to run.

The prince got to his feet and was still confused. "What happened? They told me I was going to die soon. They told me so many times."

Nizhoni said, "They were mistaken. It was they who died instead."

"Who are you people? You will receive a huge reward for saving my life."

Cade grinned. "No reward is necessary, Prince Redstone. I'm Cade, and my partner is Nizhoni." He pointed at the two bodies pierced with arrows. "This is what we do. We don't care for terrorists, pirates, or slavers."

The prince looked at Nizhoni. "Did she kill one of these?"

She said, "Yes, and if memory serves, I left twelve arrows out there in the woods, with bodies attached."

The prince said, "Not only are you a strong woman, but beautiful too. Are you married?"

Cade looked at her and chuckled. "She's already taken. You wouldn't want her anyway. She's too bossy and talks too much."

"I am not bossy. I'm just organized."

"How are two descriptions like that even put in the same conversation? You are bossy, but you are organized. One has nothing to do with the other."

Redstone said, "I see. It sounds like you two are married."

Cade slung the unconscious terrorist over his shoulder. "Like that's ever going to happen. Let's get you home." Nizhoni led the way, monitoring her detect for explosives. Dawn was lighting the sky when they entered the Seeker.

Cade contacted Jace before lifting. "We have the package, where do we deliver?"

"I'll send coordinates for Edda's spaceport. How did it go?"

Cade said, "We saved the package, left twenty-two packages as fertilizer, we have one lucky captive that isn't wearing an arrow or sporting Maska's teeth prints, and Nizhoni received a marriage proposal."

Jace replied, "I'll await your return for a clarification. A marriage proposal?"

Nizhoni punched him in the arm as she took her seat. "That wasn't a proposal."

Cade said, "I distinctly heard a proposal. A prince marries a princess. It makes sense."

Nizhoni punched him again. "You don't make sense."

Cade set the scout down, at the spaceport. When he opened the hatch, two gendarmes stood waiting for the prisoner. A large crowd had gathered, and a large chorus of voices greeted the prince as he left the ship and was directed to a microphone, a few yards distance from the ship. He motioned for Cade and Nizhoni to join him.

A person approached and carried a tray with a towel over it. He asked the prince, "If I may, your highness. I will clean your face and straighten your hair."

"You may proceed, but do it quickly."

The man, obviously a servant of the royals, spent less than a minute and had the prince presentable before stepping away.

"I was rescued from a terrifying ordeal by these two warriors. My death was imminent when they struck the blow to free me. This man, Cade, and his woman, Nizhoni, are to be commended for their selfless heroism." The crowd roared its appreciation for the two.

Cade noticed a portly man and an attractive woman approaching and the crowd was parting to allow them passage. People bowed as the couple passed by.

Nizhoni remarked, "His woman?"

Cade said softly. "I think he's trying to smooth over your rejection of his proposal." She punched him harder this time.

The king approached the Microphone. "Fellow citizens of Edda. The actions of these two deserve recognition. I am conferring the Medal of Freedom on each at a reception in the Palace tonight. The event will be televised so that all may witness the honor being bestowed on these two." The crowd cheered.

The king turned to Cade. You and your wife must come with us to the Palace. We will have an early, private celebration."

Cade received a call on his wrist communicator. "I'm watching a live feed. Please accept the king's hospitality. Failure to do so will cause a political incident." Jace chuckled. "Don't forget to take your wife."

Cade looked at Nizhoni, who was listening. "Looks like we're going to a party."

Nizhoni muttered, "Live feed? I hope none of my friends see this."

Cade smiled. "You have no friends."

She punched him again.

Chapter 17

Cade set the scout down in its usual spot, not far from the Searcher. He climbed out of his seat and quietly moved next to the fold-out bunk where Nizhoni was strapped in. He disconnected the restraining strap, gently grasped her shoulder, and shook her. "Wake up, Nizhoni, we're back on Faroe."

She moaned, "Leave me alone. Let me die in peace."

He moved further aft and opened the hatch, allowing Maska and Aeolus to exit the scout.

Going back to her bunk, he picked her up and carried her out of the ship. He was almost to the prefab when he met Sarah.

Sarah stopped him. "Is she okay? Was she injured during the mission?"

"Yes. Her stomach was hit with at least a gallon of alcohol."

Sarah hurried ahead and opened the door to the prefab. She followed Cade inside. "She's been drinking?"

"King Redstone insisted that we attend a banquet in celebration of his son's rescue." Cade gently lowered Nizhoni to the bed in the room that housed the knitter. "The king also invited us to a pre-banquet celebration."

Nizhoni moaned and mumbled, "I shouldn't, but just one more."

Cade looked at her and said, "You've had at least twenty more than you needed."

"Doc, do you think she'll live? I kept telling her not to drink so much."

"I'll mix something up that should clear her cobwebs." She left the room and was gone for about fifteen minutes. She returned with a glass of greenish liquid, which she set on a bedside tray. She went to another cabinet and returned with a plastic bucket. "I think we're ready. Cade, lift her so she's in a seated position on the bed."

Cade lifted her and watched Sarah set the bucket on Nizhoni's lap.

Sarah picked up the glass. "I'm going to try coaxing her into drinking this liquid. I want you to hold the bucket with your free hand. Be ready to hold the bucket near her mouth." Sarah got most of the liquid into the girl and stepped back. Nizhoni started into heaves, and Sarah exclaimed, "Now!"

Cade lifted the bucket just in time. "Ugh! That is disgusting." It seemed to Cade that she was going to fill the bucket with vomit."

Sarah brought a cold, damp rag and cleaned the girl's face. "What did you do to make her drink so much?"

Cade shrugged his shoulders. "I have no idea." He glanced at the contents of the bucket. "I doubt she will ever drink like that again."

"I'll look after her, Cade. You look beat. Go and get some rest."

Making his way to the cabin, he went inside where he laid down on the couch and fell asleep. He awoke and realized it was dark. Sitting up, there was enough light that he saw Nizhoni sitting across from him in Melody's chair. He got up and went to the table and fumbled for a moment, lighting a lamp. The cold air bit at him, with his breath frostily floating from his face. Nizhoni was so still, he feared she might be dead. Noticing Maska lying in her usual spot, he checked Nizhoni and found her to be breathing okay. He went to the fireplace and built a fire, then turned his attention toward Aeolus' favorite chair, and saw the eagle perched there.

Nizhoni pierced the silence that seemed to muffle the room. "Cade, I'm so ashamed. I've never drank more than one glass and only to be sociable."

Cade shrugged. "I was worried about you. I tried many times to get you away from the alcohol, but you pushed me away." He went silent as he looked at her, huddled on the chair. "There must have been a reason. Was it because you killed terrorists?"

She sighed. "No, it wasn't that." She stood up and moved to the couch. She sat, but didn't lean on him. "It's because of New Terra. Reality has set in with the knowledge that I will soon be back home." She paused a moment. "I'm not sure where to begin, but I will try to tell you what I feel. The first time we met, on the Hermes, I was a physical and mental lump of hopelessness, and fear. I wasn't sure I wanted to trust anyone. Your gentle, understanding words to Riley, and your kindness to both of us helped me to begin righting my ship. It's difficult to explain, but I needed to be loved, and I felt love from you, Sarah, and Zina. It was a feeling of family. I needed the two weeks that you lay next to me at night. The security that someone cared about me. You even put your trust in me to be part of the team. You were there when I needed someone the most. If not for you putting up with my bossy behavior, and giving in to me almost every time, I wouldn't be where I am right now. Our mission on Edda proved I'm back. I am the warrior princess, and I will return to New Terra because of you."

Cade shrugged his shoulders. "I didn't do that much. You had the strength within you. After all, you did throw me for a painful loop."

"I may have had the strength within, but you brought it out." She paused. "I will no longer need you to sleep next to me. I'm able now, to look forward to the future. It's a future that you helped restore."

Cade grinned. "I guess this means you will no longer boss me around, or ignore my orders."

Nizhoni smiled. "Don't count on it. I hope to remain your annoying little sister."

Cade grew serious. "To tell you the truth, I leaned upon you, too. Your persistence helped turn me around when I was feeling abandoned and alone. I will miss lying next to you and hearing your steady breathing in the night."

She poked his shoulder playfully. "I have to admit that you have changed since I've known you. You were so serious and seemed to be on a roller coaster, rising to light and then going down into the dark." She hesitated. "Was it because of Melody leaving?"

He tilted his head to stare at the ceiling, without seeing it. He was reluctant to open his wounded heart to Nizhoni. He sighed, and relaxed enough to lower his gaze to the floor. "I don't know. Having you around has helped to change my perspective, but my time with Melody impacted me like a spear." He hesitated again as he considered what to say. "I've never experienced love, or at least felt love for a woman. That is until I met Melody. There is no logical reason, no single thing that I can point to and say, 'That is why I feel this way.' Is it her face, or bearing, or her distinctive scent that makes my heart jump with her mere presence? Can it be her spirit, or character, or innocence, or a lack of innocence? Is it because I try to explain my feelings to her, when I can't understand them myself? I was so affected by the dangerous elixir of the heart that I confessed my love to her several times, and she rejected me." He fell silent for a minute. "I was on a roller coaster, but that ended when she left. My highs and lows are now flatlined. I know I'll never find all the things I loved about her with another woman."

Nizhoni wiped at her tears. "If any man ever tells me what you just said, and names me as the subject of his affection, I would never let him go. You need to go to her. Tell her how much you love her."

"I've already made that attempt. It only brought me grief." He realized how at peace he was, even with thoughts of Melody. "The time you and I have spent together, has helped me to move on. At least, I'll be able to move on once I've completed my effort to restore her, to the position she held before the invaders arrived. I love her too much to let her cruel father crush her into the ground."

Nizhoni stood. "Tonight, I will sleep in my berth on the Searcher. I hope you have a peaceful night, Cade." She went to the door and left the cabin. When outside, she reached into her pocket and turned off the recording. *I hope he will forgive me for this, but I intend to have Melody hear his words if I see her again.*

He awoke the next morning and threw off the blanket. He suddenly felt a bone-chilling cold. He was still dressed, just as he was when he slept by Nizhoni. He got up and decided to go to the Searcher to find warmth.

He entered the galley and found Zina seated in her usual spot. She looked up from her caff, but didn't say anything as he went to the dispenser for a cup.

Zina looked up from her caff when he sat across from her. "I notice Nizhoni stayed aboard the ship last night."

"I know she did." He took a drink of the warming caff.

"I hope you didn't break her heart; that would damage my image of you."

Cade leaned back in his chair. "I told her you would have the wrong idea about us."

Zina icily said, "Nizhoni informed me she would be staying with you at night. What is there to misunderstand?"

"I thought you knew me, Zina. We slept side by side in the same bed, fully clothed."

The Zacathian grinned; her neck frills glowed in iridescent colors. "I must admit, that wouldn't surprise me."

"The truth is, she found comfort with someone by her side. I didn't understand that until last night, when she told me she was able to resume living her life. I was surprised to discover that her time with me, has helped me in the same way."

Zina took another drink of caff. "It seems like you both found healing in the times you've shared together." Another pause to take a drink. "I was concerned about you when Melody left, but it appears your heart has healed."

"It's a false appearance, a mirage. The raw wound will always be here." He patted his left chest. "I'm going to have breakfast before changing into suitable clothing, to take a walk with my team. I've been neglecting them."

As Cade prepared for the cold, Melody faced a new day on New Terra as she suffered a cruel reality. She woke to another day and felt the cooler air of late summer. She left her burrow in the matted hay. When she took a step, her shackles chafed at her ankles, but she was getting used to it. She talked to herself, something she did to maintain her sanity, if indeed she still possessed such. "I didn't know redeemed people were treated like this. How can such inhumanity be heaped on people?" She took measured steps to reduce the amount of pain she would suffer, when putting too much pressure on the shackles. She hobbled to the horse trough and scooped up water in her cupped hand to take a drink. She splashed the cold water on her face in an attempt to clear away the dirt. She noticed manure in her hair. A result of sleeping in the hay that was too fouled for the horses to eat. She was the only redeemed person in the stable; at least, she was the only one treated as such. Her body trembled at the sound of her tormentor, Brack, approaching.

"I've brought your breakfast, wench." He dropped the garbage lid to the ground, spilling some of the contents. "I'll be back in twenty minutes."

Melody hobbled to the lid and sat beside it on the ground. She wasn't permitted to sit on any of the few chairs and benches around the stable. Her breakfast was edible leavings from the previous day, along with other trash that had nothing to do with food. She picked out a bone that still held meat, along with evident teeth indentations in the meat that was left. She gnawed at the resistant meat and thought about how a person would do anything to cling to life. Finished with the bone, she returned it to the lid and picked out a piece of bread and an apple with a bite out of it. She finished her meal as Brack returned.

He picked up the lid and kicked her right hip. "The stalls are waiting; get to work. She painfully gained her feet, determined that she would not give them the satisfaction of finding her dead. She went to the barrow and pushed it to the first stall. She shoveled manure mixed with hay, but her mind took her to a more pleasant place as she mechanically did her work.

Memories were all that sustained her, and helped her to survive in a corner of her mind. She tried to imagine what his kiss would be like. *The water of the lake feels warm, and I see Cade entering from the shade. He's so loving and kind. She felt his embrace as he kissed her.* Tears flowed from her cheek as she was jolted into reality by a hand striking her left cheek, knocking her to the ground.

Brack stood over her, glaring at her. "A piece of manure missed the barrow." He pointed to fresh manure on the floor. "Pick it up with your hands."

Knowing he would knock her down again, she crawled to the spot. She knew it had not fallen from her shovel, but there was nothing she could do. She bracketed the mound with her hands and slid them together. She held most of it as she reached up and over the edge of the barrow, dropping what didn't cling to her into it. Brack walked away, so she crawled to some hay and wiped her hands as well as she could. *He motivates me to live until the invaders come for my people. I hope they kill him before me. I will laugh at his death.* She had another thought. *Perhaps I will kill him myself, before I die.* Her thoughts helped her to get through the day.

Brack made his way to the door that gave entrance to the fortress. The door opened, and the messenger said, "The chief asks if she still lives."

"She has a strong will, and clings stubbornly to life." He scratched his beard. "She will die if we stop giving her the scraps from the garbage."

The messenger shook his head. "The chief has ordered that she be given a meager amount to sustain life. It must be her choice to give up and die."

"I can beat her with a strap several times a day. That should weaken her will."

"Do not do that either. In fact, the chief is feeling generous and has ordered that you no longer touch her, but let her give up because of her circumstances."

Brack shook his head. "The chief is underestimating his daughter. She will not surrender to the specter of death. Of that, I am certain."

The messenger said, "Nevertheless, you have your orders. Obey them, or you will join her in shackles."

Brack turned and went to a nearby bench. He sat down, deep in thought. *I never liked the chief's orders concerning the princess, but I've had no choice. She is a warrior, one of the best. I'm glad for the order not to strike her. I made the suggestion of lashes to maintain the illusion that I agree with the chief. How can he do this to his daughter?* He stood and went back to the stable. He didn't approach her, but watched as she stubbornly did her work. He couldn't help but admire the woman's tenacity.

Late that evening, Melody made her way to the corner of the stable where her straw bed waited. When she reached it, she found the old straw was gone and had been replaced with fresh hay. A blanket hung from the rail that separated her stall from the others. She looked around and caught a glimpse of Brack, quickly ducking behind a corner of the feed building. *Why would he do this? I bet my father doesn't know.* She fell asleep and slept well that night, snuggled in the blanket.

The next morning, she awoke to find Brack standing silently, watching her, holding the trash can lid.

"Princess, I want you to know that I don't agree with the chief. I have been doing as he ordered, because I had no choice. I'm here because of my own redemption. I'll try to make your life easier, but it will be bad if I'm found out. So please, continue in your determination to live. Living is the only way for you to defeat your father's purpose for putting you here, whatever it was." He nodded toward a bench sitting in her stall along a wall. "I put that there for you to sit on while you eat." He turned to go, but her voice stopped him.

She said, "Thank you, Brack. I will not forget your kindness this day."

He turned back to her and said, "I hope the day will come when your father will open his heart and embrace you." He walked away.

She picked up the lid and found a ham sandwich separated from the trash with a piece of heavy paper, and a thermos holding coffee. She set the lid of the garbage to one side and ate the sandwich slowly while sipping coffee between bites. She thought about how her world had coffee, and Cade drank caff. They were one and the same. When she finished her meal, she left the thermos sitting by the lid and went to work. She barely noticed the shackles as her spirits were lifted by the kindness shown to her by the man who had been her tormentor. When she finished her work for the day, she took a few minutes to wash her face and hair in a bucket of water taken from the trough. She was surprised to find a plate with a cooked potato and a piece of roast. The plate was resting on her bench. A glass of juice sat next to the plate. She enjoyed the best meal she had eaten since she left the Hermes.

Melody's mental state improved with her physical strength over the days to come. She lost track of time, but the stable master's kindness gave her hope that better days were ahead. One day, her routine was interrupted when three warriors entered the stable compound with a black stallion, rearing and bucking wildly. It was trying to throw off the three ropes being desperately held by the warriors. A fourth warrior threw a lasso over the head of the struggling beast and added his weight to the others. She heard one of them shout, "The chief is mad if he believes this horse can be mastered."

There were two massive posts buried in the middle of the corral, about six feet apart. Large iron rings attached to plates, were bolted to the posts at about four feet from the ground. The men, two on each side, managed to put their ends of the rope through the rings, and then they pulled the ropes until the horse didn't have any slack. Melody feared they would strangle the beautiful animal.

"Brack came to her and said, go to your stall for now. The chief is coming to look at his prize. Stay out of sight."

She hurried to her stall and was able to watch the stallion from her vantage point. She saw her father approach the horse, but the creature kept kicking his hind legs, and his back half continued jumping and straining against the ropes. The chief backed away, and she could hear him say, "This animal is beyond training."

One of the warriors asked, "Do you want us to release him?"

The chief said, "I think it would be a kindness to put it down. I'll decide in the morning."

The warriors departed, and the chief returned to the fortress. She watched the horse continue to struggle as Brack approached.

"You can continue what you were doing, Princess."

"I can train that horse."

Brack looked at her. "That animal is a killer."

She tried something she hadn't done since she was with Cade. She reached out and touched the brain of the horse. The stallion ceased struggling against the ropes. She was soothing his mind with peace and calm. "If my shackles are removed so that I can ride, I will train him."

Brack asked, "Why do you believe you can do it?"

"I trained wild horses before returning to New Terra. An off-world alien called me a horse whisperer. Let the chief know I have made the offer."

"But you might be killed."

"That's why my father will agree to allow it. He would see it as an honorable way to let me die. Trust me. Let him know about my offer."

Brack left her, went to the door, and knocked. After a few minutes, the messenger opened the door.

"Is she still alive?"

"Yes, she is. But I think we have a new opportunity. She insists that she is able to break the devil stallion the warriors brought in today. Since she has asked for the opportunity, I thought it would be an honorable way to be rid of her."

The messenger rubbed his chin. "Yes! I will ask the chief. He will probably want to do it right away." The messenger closed the door.

Brack shook his head as he murmured, "I hope I haven't sealed her death." He returned to the stall where Melody was cleaning. "I sent the message."

She looked up and saw another man approach her, so she went back to her work. She heard the man tell Brack, "Remove her shackles, but they will be put back if she survives. The chief will witness her attempt."

Brack nodded and said, "Yes, sir."

She stopped shoveling as Brack said, "Follow me." He led her to the blacksmith's shop. She sat on the ground, and the smithy rested the left shackle over an anvil designed for the purpose. The anvil was fastened to a stubby pedestal.

"Don't move, miss, unless you want a smashed ankle."

As the smithy drew back a large hammer, she closed her eyes and held her breath. She heard the clang, and felt the shackle loosen.

"Okay, put that foot aside and move over to this end." He indicated the end with a jerk of his head.

She moved around to the opposite end, so the rivet and her foot would be in the right position. She closed her eyes again as the hammer crashed down. She was free of the shackles. She stood and almost laughed, but restrained herself.

Brack said, I see the chief is in position. Good luck."

She approached the stallion slowly, sending peaceful thoughts to him. She formed a picture of her scratching behind his ear. He remained calm, with his hooves still defiantly planted spread out, as if anticipating someone would tip him over. She inched closer as she heard her father ask, "What's she doing? Why isn't the horse struggling like before?"

She gently lay her right hand against the stallion's left jaw, and stroked as she whispered, "You are so beautiful, and strong." She formed images of her placing a bridle on his head, and then walking beside him with reins in her hand. Looking into his left eye, she no longer saw fear and resistance, but calm and acceptance of her attention. She reached to the near pole, and pulled the release point of the knot, allowing the rope to go slack. The horse did not go into a frenzy but remained calm as she crossed in front of him to loosen the other ropes. When they were free, she asked him to lower his head. The horse obeyed and lowered his head so she could take the lassos off his neck. The horse was free of restraint. She glanced at her father and saw him standing with a look of shock on his face.

She walked toward the tack room, and the horse followed her, nudging at her shoulder until she lifted her hand to stroke the right side of his jaw. Lifting a bridle, she slowly and carefully put it on his head. When she had it secure, she pictured herself riding on his back. The horse knelt, and she swung her right leg over and slid onto his back. She urged him to trot around the enclosure. After a few times around, she gently tugged the reins and said, whoa." She slid off his back as Brack cautiously approached with an apple. She removed the bridle from the horse.

Brack softly asked, "Do you want to give him an apple?"

She grinned. "He'll accept it from you." She pictured Brack offering him the apple.

Brack grinned as the horse gently accepted his offering. "I've never seen anything as amazing as what you just did with this horse."

The messenger came over and moved carefully to stay away from the stallion. "The chief wants to see you." He escorted her to the chief as Brack treated the stallion to a light brushing.

She went to her knees and bowed her head in respect. She waited for the chief to speak.

"That was the most impressive display of horse whispering I have ever observed. When did you discover the talent?"

She looked up. "When I was on Faroe with the warrior called Cade Storm. He taught me how to spirit train." She stretched the truth with her explanation, but she knew it was an explanation he could embrace.

"Is the horse trained well enough for me to ride?"

"Not yet, My Chief. He is growing used to the bridle, and I will move to saddle training later today, or tomorrow."

"If I leave your shackles off, will you voluntarily stay here?"

"I have already made that promise, My Chief. I will stay here and willingly die with my people when the invaders come for us."

He turned to the messenger. "Instruct Brack to leave the shackles off." As the messenger returned to tell Brack, the chief said, "Eagle Feather, if you succeed, you will be given housing as a reward."

She bowed her head again. "Thank you, My Chief."

"You may go."

She stood and looked toward the top of the fortress wall and saw her mother looking down at her. Her mother smiled and waved her hand. Melody smiled and waved back. Watching as her mother left the wall, she turned away and returned to work with the stallion. Happy with the brief glimpse of her mother. She felt life glow inside her chest, with her brief return to the land of the living. After settling a saddle on the stallion's back and pulling tight the cinches, she walked the stallion around the corral several times. Speaking softly the whole time, even though she didn't think the horse would understand, she talked about the time she had been with Cade. Peace filled her soul as she walked along the fence. Later in the evening, she led him into the stable and removed the saddle and bridle. She put him in the stall next to hers and put oats into his feed bucket. When she went to her stall, she found her evening meal sitting on a small table in front of her bench. Hurrying to the trough to wash her hands, she returned to find Brack standing outside her stall.

She looked down and realized she had a full dinner on her plate, and a glass of wine sat next to it. "Brack, you brought too much. Someone may notice."

"The Queen Mother asked me to bring it to you. She prepared it herself."

Melody began crying. She couldn't help herself as she thought about her mother's love for her.

Brack held out a napkin for her to wipe her face. "Don't cry, Princess."

Taking a deep breath, she dried her tears and smiled while thinking about her mother. She sat and enjoyed the meal so much more, knowing it was sent to her with love.

After sleeping peacefully that night, she awoke refreshed the next morning. Sitting up, she glimpsed from the corner of her eye, someone sitting at her table. She turned her head and saw her mother. Leaping out of bed, she went to her knees in front of the queen. Tears streamed as she tried to hold her voice steady. "My Queen."

"Save the honorific for others. I'm here as your mother."

"Mother, I'm honored by your presence, but I'm no longer worthy."

She watched as her mother stood and walked around the small table. She bent over and reached out to Melody.

"Take my hand and stand."

Melody stood, and her mother embraced her, hugging her tightly. "Mother, I'm filthy. I have dirt and manure on me." She realized her mother was crying.

"I've missed you, my baby. I didn't know I would see you again." She continued to hold tight to Melody. "I don't want to lose you again."

"Mother, father will be angry if he finds out you came here."

"He knows I'm here. I am tired of his unbending belief in the old ways. He actually said you would be better off dead. I'm ready to break our bond. I don't care if he puts me in the stables with you."

"Please don't turn from him. He's still my father, and I love him."

"Even after everything he has done to you?" She stepped back and looked at her daughter. "You are a better daughter than I ever was. I would hate my father if he threw me into the manure and wanted me to die."

"When I was taken, I wanted to kill myself. I thought our code was right." She sighed. "I met a man, a good man, who helped me see my own worth. He stood by me, even knowing how I had been shamed. He even vowed his love for me. He is Navajo, and was born in another world, light years away from here. He said his people learned to adapt to the changes in the universe. Changes that we should have adopted as well. The Great Spirit loves his people, but I believe he doesn't want us to cling to ancient traditions and codes." She sighed. "I understood how father felt, because I was raised in his world. I didn't have to come back here. I could have stayed with the man I love, but I chose family. I chose my people, and I wanted to help save them, but I have failed. All I can do now, is wait for the death that will come to us all. The invaders want what we have, and they have the power to take it."

Her mother hugged her again. "Let us set aside our fears, for we will either whither before the wind, or we will bend and flourish." She paused. "Eat the breakfast I made for you before it gets too cold."

Melody sat and ate, while her mother watched her with a smile on her face. When she was finished, her mother kissed her and carried the plate as she returned to the fortress.

Melody began work early as she rode around the corral several times. The horse adjusted quickly and was comfortable with the saddle. She saw her father watching, and her mother was looking on from the top of the fortress wall. She urged the horse to a faster gait. She wheeled the horse away from the fence and gently kicked his ribs as she urged him to go faster yet. They sped toward the far fence, and the stallion jumped with plenty of room to spare. They soared over the fence and were soon out of sight.

The Chief roared. "I didn't think she could be trusted."

A warrior asked, "Do you want me to give chase?"

"Nothing we have, can catch her on that horse."

Brack stood leaning on the far fence. He shouted, "She's coming back."

She was closing on the corral with blazing speed, and the horse cleared the fence again before wheeling to a stop, next to the fence nearest the Chief. She leaped off the horse and gave a whoop. "I've never ridden that fast before. War Eagle is the best."

The Chief walked over to the fence. He cleared his throat. "Will you walk beside me as I ride around the corral?"

She smiled. "Yes, My Chief."

She watched her father swing up into the saddle. He took the reins and urged the horse forward. Melody walked alongside. "I named him War Eagle, but he doesn't have to keep that name."

The Chief smiled, "I think the name suits him. The first few times I ride him, I want you alongside until he gets used to me."

"I will be honored, My Chief." She walked alongside her father, talking about horses and the old days. She enjoyed every minute of her time with him. After the chief returned to the fortress, Melody removed the saddle and bridle. She gave War Eagle an apple from the supply Brack had left. As she curried the horse, Brack approached.

"I've been instructed by the Chief to show you to your new bunkhouse." She followed him through the gate and stepped into the outside world. He continued to walk until they entered the trees, and approached a log cabin.

He opened the front door. "This is it."

She went in and immediately recognized her old bed. The quilt her mother had made for her years ago was lying on the neatly made bed. Her old chair was there as well. It was one large room, but she thought it was beautiful. A small kitchen and sitting room took up the front half of the cabin, with her bedroom area, her old desk, and a small enclosed fresher populating the back half. A fireplace was set into the middle of the wall that spanned from the kitchen to her bedroom. She felt like a little girl again, and the cabin was as grand as a palace. "I love it." She turned to Brack. "Isn't he concerned I'll sneak away?"

"When you returned with the horse, you removed any mistrust he may have had." He cleared his throat. "I've been told to remind you that you are still required to do your stable work, and you cannot have a relationship." He lowered his voice and said, "But I will remain your friend."

"I will do as he has instructed. Thank you for being my friend, Brack."

"I need to go, Princess." He stopped at the door. "By the way, you have been given one day a week to rest. Let me know which day you want when you have decided." He went out the door and closed it behind him.

She walked around the room and touched everything, as if assuring herself she was not dreaming. She heard a knock at the door, and her mother came in with a picnic basket.

"I brought a meal for us to share on your first day in the cabin," she said, as she carried the basket to the counter. "If you want to shower before we eat, I laid out some things for you in the fresher."

Melody exhaled a quick breath. "A shower. I haven't been able to take one for ages." Turning to make her way to the fresher, she stopped short. Turning to her mother, she asked, "How is my little brother? Did he witness my shaming that day?"

Aiukli looked up from her task of setting the table. "No, he was kept in our private quarters. When it was over, your father sent him to stay with my sister in her village. Natahay has not yet ordered his return."

"I'm glad he didn't see it." She went to the fresher and enjoyed a long shower.

Chapter 18

Cade focused on the ground ahead, mindful of slushy divots or ice. There was a snowfall, but most of it didn't stick as the ground was still too warm. Nizhoni jogged alongside, and they were both wearing heavy sweat suits.

Cade watched his breath as each exhale produced white vapor that drifted up and dissipated almost immediately. He was breathing in through his nose and exhaling through his mouth to keep from bringing the cold directly into his lungs. He came to a halt and Nizhoni stopped too. "We'll turn back now. The conditions are too bad for running." They began jogging toward the ships. "We'll put in some heavy exercise in the prefab to keep in shape."

Nizhoni didn't answer but kept pace. When they got to the prefab, they went to the caff dispenser and drew two cups. They sat at the table to warm up. Nizhoni took a sip and set the cup on the table. "I remember some things about the entrance to the secret tunnel, I told you about. I was so young when my father showed it to me."

Cade took another drink of caff. "That is good news. Do you know if anyone besides you and the chief know about the tunnel?"

"All I can remember is what he told me. He said only the chief knew about the tunnel, and it was to be used only in a dire emergency."

"Well, I believe we have reached that minimum requirement. How about the inner structures of the citadel? Can you recall which room the tunnel terminates within?"

"I hate to say it Cade, but all the rooms look alike to a little kid."

Cade stood, "Let's get rid of these heavy coats and go to our sparring room." Cade noticed a com alert glow on his wrist communicator. He opened the connection to hear Zina's voice.

"Jace just contacted the ship, and needs to talk to you. He said it's urgent."

Cade glanced at Nizhoni and they both headed for the door. Maska and Aeolus fell in beside them as they made their way to the Searcher. They entered and Cade went up to the Bridge with Nizhoni following close beside him.

Cade pressed transmit. "Searcher calling Hermes."

Jace's voice came back immediately. "We have new data and I have more hardware to show you. Bring the Searcher to Beltane for a meeting."

Cade wanted to ask why the Searcher needed to go, but he said, "Searcher copies, and will lift immediately." He looked at Zina. "Is all the crew aboard?"

She looked at the locator on her wrist communicator. "They are present."

Cade used the inner ship communicator. "Prepare for lift in ten minutes. All departments report readiness to first officer Zina." He switched to the designated frequency for Faroe Patrol Base. He didn't know if any ships were at the base, but it was best to broadcast his intention to lift. Searcher to any ship on this frequency, Searcher is lifting from Faroe in eight minutes."

A Patrol cruiser answered, "Searcher, this is Patrol heavy cruiser Pisces. We have been tasked to provide traffic control while a permanent station is built. You are clear to five thousand miles. Clear for lift."

"Searcher copies." He strapped down and looked to Zina in the navigator's seat.

"Captain, all stations report secured for lift. External ventilation has been terminated, and all hatches are secure."

"Cade hit the communicator. "We lift in five." In minutes they were well on their way.

Zina said, "Course for Beltane laid in. Hyper corridor transition in two hours. Time in Hyper Space will be four hours.

"You have the bridge, Zina. I'm going to meet with the crew in the galley." He transmitted the information over his wrist com as he made his way to the galley. He went in and drew a cup of caff before sitting. Riley was the last one to enter. Engineering was farthest from the galley.

Riley sat down and was obviously very happy. "This is our first trip as a crew."

Cade said, "I didn't think about that. I guess we have become a bunch of land lubbers."

Sarah said, "I don't mind being planet side one bit."

Cade took a drink of caff. "I don't really know much, but I wanted to let everyone know that we were summoned to Beltane. He instructed me to bring the Searcher. I have no idea why, but we will know in a little over seven hours. Since this is a short jaunt, we won't need to set up shifts. That's all I have for now. If your stations are secure, you can relax until we get there."

Cade went back to the Bridge. He strapped in and turned to Zina. "If you want to take a break, go ahead. I'll watch the store."

Zina remained in her seat. "I've been thinking. He can't be giving a new assignment. We are too near your deployment schedule."

"I was thinking the same as you. He said he had new intel video, so I believe it has everything to do with New Terra."

"Cade, how do you think our Melody is doing?"

"I don't mind telling you that I pray for her every day. I keep seeing her in leg chains and it eats at my stomach. Time seems to be crawling while I chomp at the bit, wanting to go to her." They talked until Cade heard the marker chime sound.

Zina announced, "Transition in five." She counted down five seconds and felt the planetary drive shut down as the hum of the hyper drive engines sounded their steady song. "Four hours to emergence." She looked across at Cade as she released her seat straps. "I'll take that break now."

Cade nodded, "I've got the stick. Take your time."

Nizhoni entered the bridge and settled in Zina's seat. "Cade, I've been thinking. When we have successfully completed our mission to New Terra, I've realized that I may never see you again."

"Are you kidding? When you and Chayton are bonded, I intend to lay between the two of you for two weeks."

She tried to punch his arm, but he was just out of reach. "Don't you dare tell him about that. He might not understand."

She fell silent and Cade turned his head to look at her. "Why the long face?"

"I can't help but wonder if he's still alive. When we watch the spy video, there aren't many of my people in view."

"You need to hold on to the belief that we will find him. We have to, if you two are going to name your first son after me. And as for that, you will see me when you invite me to his naming ceremony. Don't think for a minute I won't do my best to pay you back for all the times you've bossed me around."

She brightened. "You're right. We'll find him." She paused. "I'm serious about that sleeping together thing. Don't bring it up."

Zina settled in one of the jump seats. "I want to talk to Chayton myself. I'm going to tell him how you two have been thick as thieves."

Cade and Nizhoni both answered, "We are not!"

They all three talked until Zina said, "Time to reclaim my seat. Swap places with me." Nizhoni moved to the jump seat and Zina strapped in. Zina said, "Five minutes to emergence." She scanned the instruments. Two minutes, and sensors show no traffic. "One minute and I will count from five." They soon left Hyper space and planetary drive engines were now carrying the load.

Cade broadcast over the ship's com unit. "All departments, we land in twenty minutes." A few minutes later, Cade requested landing clearance. When they were settled on the concrete pad, Cade called Jace. "Do you want me to bring any of the crew?"

Jace replied, "Bring your Sage for now."

Zina looked at him. "Sage?"

He laughed. "It's a code name for knucklehead." She still looked confused. "Nizhoni!"

Nizhoni left her jump seat and punched his arm. "I heard the whole conversation. Didn't you remember I was sitting here."

He laughed. "I didn't forget, Sage."

They left the ship and went to Jace's office.

When they were seated, Jace said, "First, I want to show you recent events on New Terra." Video appeared on a screen on the wall to Cade's right. Jace said, "There's a lot of other scenes, some of which would be tough for Cade to watch, but conditions for Melody seem to be improving on the most recent surveillance."

They watched the entire event unfolding around a magnificent stallion. When Melody approached the horse, without her ankles shackled, he wanted to jump up and cheer her on. She gentled the stallion as easily as she did the horses on Faroe. When she jumped the fence and raced away, Cade thought she was gaining her freedom, but she returned and jumped the fence again. An older man entered the video and swung up into the stallion's saddle.

Jace stopped the video again. "This is the same man she pleaded with when she stood before the gate. It has to be her father. We also isolated the woman who appears to be her mother." He started the film going, and they were watching Melody walk with a man toward the tree line. As they moved beneath the trees, the foliage wasn't concealing much. They saw the man lead Melody into a cabin. The man left shortly, and a few minutes later, a woman entered the cabin. Jace stopped the video. "The woman is her mother. She is carrying what is obviously a picnic basket. The implication is that her successful training of the stallion has resulted in her being given comfortable quarters. She leaves every morning and works at the stable. She returns every evening."

Nizhoni said, "I'm so happy for her."

Cade breathed a sigh of relief. "This takes a load off my mind. Thanks for showing this."

"I'm giving you a copy of this for your research." He picked up a storage cube and handed it to Nizhoni.

Cade asked, "Will that be all?"

"Nizhoni can return to the ship. I need to talk to you about something not related to the mission."

Nizhoni left her seat. "I'll see you back at the Searcher."

When she was gone, Jace leaned back in his chair. "I have another crew member candidate for the searcher."

"I don't know if we can take on another person with problems right now."

"This person doesn't have emotional damage. It will only take a minute. He's waiting just down the hall."

Cade nodded his head.

Jace reached for his mic. "Send Zangari in for the interview."

Cade was surprised to see a male Zacathian enter the office. He stood and offered his hand in greeting. "It's good to meet you, Zangari. How can I be of assistance."

Zangari shook hands with Cade during the greeting. They both took a seat. "Captain Storm, I am an archeological student looking for an interesting subject for my final thesis. I'm currently traveling aboard a ship with inadequate equipment available. During a chance encounter with Lieutenant Jace, he told me about your research vessel. I can pay you for a short-term use of you and the ship. I'm also a certified star ship pilot, if you should need my service."

Cade leaned back in his seat. "Mr. Zangari, I will need to have my first officer interview you." He turned to Jace and saw a hint of a smile. "May I have my first officer come over to interview him."

"Of course. Have her report here and I will show them to the conference room."

Cade called her on his wrist communicator. "I have another crew candidate in Jace's office. Can you come over for the interview?"

"Be right there, Captain."

"He said, "Mr. Zangari, I run a loose ship. Everyone aboard feels like family, and treated like family. How do you think you'll fit in?"

Zangari's ear flaps darkened a little. "Well, to be truthful, I'm not a very social person. Humans would say I'm a loner. And most humans are not comfortable interacting with a Zacathian."

Cade smiled. "For what my opinion is worth, I think you'll fit right in. We will wait for my first officer's opinion after your interview."

Zina came to the door and asked, "May I enter?" She saw Zangari as soon as the words were out of her mouth.

Zangari turned and saw her. He jumped up and nearly fell over his chair. "You have a female Zacathian for a first officer?"

"Actually, I am captain in name only. She is extremely bossy and runs the ship, and she is the science officer and navigator as well."

Zangari reached out his hand and shook hands with her. "I am impressed and extraordinarily pleased to meet you, First Officer Zina."

"She smiled and said, "The pleasure is mine." She looked at his hand still holding hers. "You can release my hand now."

He let go and said, "I hope to join your crew. You have questions for me?"

She looked at Cade. "It will be best if I take him aboard for the interview. Is that okay?"

"Go ahead. I'm okay with whatever decision you make. The call is yours."

She nodded, and led Zangari down the hall.

Cade looked at Jace. "What a look on their faces. I thought I was going to fall over."

Jace grinned. "I almost burst out laughing. I thought his jaw was going to hit the floor."

"I see why you asked me to bring the Searcher. Seeing the reactions of those two made it worthwhile"

"Actually, I needed you to bring the Searcher for another reason. I have some new tech to show you, and it will be used on New Terra." Jace left his chair. "Follow me".

Jace led him down the hallway, in the opposite direction from which Cade entered the Patrol facility. They stopped in front of an elevator and he waved his wrist identification disc across a sensor on the control panel. Two floors were listed on the panel. The door opened and they stepped into the elevator. The door slid shut.

Cade stood quietly for what seemed like a couple of minutes. He finally looked at Jace. "Why aren't we moving?"

Jace laughed. "We are in transit."

"I don't understand. I thought this was a conventional elevator, but I don't feel any movement, and we only had two floors to travel."

"This is an anti-gray lift. It is enclosed, and appears to be a run of the mill elevator, for several reasons. The best reason, is for safety. We are traveling horizontally, so a person would suffer severe and tragic vertigo if their senses weren't isolated from unstable surroundings." The door suddenly opened without warning.

Cade stepped out of the transport unit, and into a very large hanger. He looked around and saw at least two large ships, but his attention was drawn to a scout sized ship sitting a short distance from the elevator entrance. "Where are we?"

"We're fifteen miles from the Searcher's parking space. This facility was built at the start of the ten systems war. The Patrol space port and this hanger, were all part of a military research and development base. By the way, the Patrol had to conduct a background investigation on you. You were approved for top secret access to this facility. You can't reveal its existence to anyone."

Cade was drawn to the smaller ship, and walked toward it. "I've never seen anything like this before." The ship looked almost like a shadow. Its lines were blurred, but he could just make out a profile that resembled his scout. He stopped next to the ship, and reached out his hand to touch it. "It's really sitting here. I thought it was an illusion of some kind. It almost makes my head spin trying to focus on it."

Jace said, "Let's back away a few feet, and I'll demonstrate the purpose of its appearance." They stepped away several feet and Jace touched a depression on his wrist communicator.

Cade watched the ship shimmer and appear to turn into glass. "It's almost invisible."

"This is radical stealth technology. In simple language, the surface of the ship replicates what is behind it, from the viewer's perspective, and basically transfers a visual double to the part of the craft facing the viewer. You've never seen one like it because it is a one-off ship, the only one that exists." Jace touched his wrist, and the ship returned to its dark mode. "The indistinct outline is created by the same emitters that produced the invisibility effect. In most conditions, dark mode makes the ship nearly invisible to the eye."

Cade walked around the craft, and realized it wasn't shaped like his scout. Instead of a slender cylindrical fuselage, like most conventional ships, this one had a weird looking wide body. In fact, the ship was nearly as wide as it was long, and the sides were not rounded, but presented a flat surface. It was in effect, oval shaped with a flat perpendicular surface around the perimeter. Cade ran his hand along the side. "It definitely lacks sleek lines."

"The squared off construction enhances the cloak technology you witnessed."

"Cloak?"

"The team that designed the technology decided against blanket or cape. Not to mention a lot of other ideas. They decided it was like throwing a cloak over someone's head, concealing their identity."

Cade looked at Jace. "You told me at one time, that the Patrol didn't have the budget for new ships, but this thing must have broken the bank."

"Actually, you helped the Patrol obtain this ship. One of the people held with the slaves on Thane, was Frank Harland. He was actually the important individual that needed to be recovered. He owns the largest space craft builder in the known galaxy. He was extremely thankful for being rescued, but he also saw the need to improve the Patrol's ability to hamstring piracy and the slave trade. He was the right man for the effort because he also owns a company experienced in the building of war machines. His people designed and built the Searcher and her sister ships."

Jace used another control on his wrist device, and the ship lost its fuzzy appearance and looked like a normal, if not ugly, space ship.

Cade commented, "It looks like something from the distant past. It doesn't look fast."

"Hyper corridor speed is pretty much a constant for every ship, and this one is no different. But its planetary propulsion system will blow the Searcher out of the water when it comes to speed." He pressed another depression on the wrist control, causing a hatch on the port side to open, and a short ramp with steps deployed. The flat-bottomed hull was only two feet off the ground. "This ship doesn't have the configuration to make a vertical tail fin landing. It will only land horizontally, which simplifies the interior design." He motioned Cade to enter the vessel. "After you."

Cade climbed the two steps and entered the ship. "I can't believe the room in here." There was a hatch located in the bulkhead to his right. It was in the corner, formed by the bulkhead intersection with the port hull bulkhead. A military styled placard over the hatch read, "Engineering Access." To his left, was a bulkhead with a hatchway, its hatch standing open, located directly opposite the engineering access. The room was six feet wide, front to rear, but was nearly twelve feet, port to starboard in width.

Jace stood next to Cade. "Here's the quick overview. This is called a cargo bay, but it serves as an airlock if needed. A bulkhead can be installed just past the central access, to form a large storage locker. It can also remain open to accommodate Maska and Aeolus." He led him into the next chamber. "This area is fourteen feet port to starboard, and eighteen feet fore and aft. It has a larger galley than your scout, and it's on the starboard front corner. Four, fold out bunks are on the starboard side, two upper and two lower. Two more bunks are located on the common bulkhead separating the cargo area from the crew section. The bridge sits two and occupies the front six feet of cabin space. You will notice that the port to starboard dimensions narrow going forward, until the bridge is only eight feet wide. The ship presents a rounded wedge shape when viewed from above, overall length is forty feet. This ship is also equipped with the counter detect system used in the personal hand held detect used by Melody."

"My scout is thirty foot long and it just fits in the thirty-three feet wide cargo bay, so I can't transport it that way."

"That is why I had you bring the Searcher. Harland will send engineers to modify that section of your ship, free of charge."

Cade looked at Jace, and then looked toward the bridge. "I need to tell you something I've been thinking about. Let's go back to your office."

They entered the elevator, and both remained silent until they once again sat in Jace's office. Jace maintained silence as he saw Cade was struggling with what he had to say.

Cade was seated for a minute before he spoke. "I'm going to settle down. I have this crazy idea about staying on Faroe and running my own horse farm. I will need to buy more land adjoining the cabin, but my biggest need will be an interstellar freighter. I will probably have to sell the Searcher to purchase a transport capable of carrying a large number of horses. I want to partner with the people of Lawrence, sharing any profit with them. I've grown to know and love the people there." He hesitated a moment. "I plan to put my plan in action after I finish our mission on New Terra."

Jace leaned back in his chair. "I think it's a great idea, but it would be possible for you to continue helping the Patrol. You have already seen that your service doesn't require you to give up your personal business."

"I realize that, and want to continue taking down bad guys. The problem is, I'll need to take out some huge loans, and may be too busy to address other issues."

"Cade, I already have a couple of ideas to make it all possible. You can probably even keep the Searcher and own a freighter too. The Patrol has several storage yards with confiscated ships, and I know the Brass at Central would make you a gift of one of them." He paused. "I value your ability to attack the thugs head on." He grinned. "I also know you to be an honest and trustworthy man. Don't make a move too quickly. Let me be involved in helping you."

"Okay. I will give it some time after New Terra. Who knows what might happen?"

Jace leaned forward, both elbows on the desk. "In the meantime, we'll leave the Searcher as she is. Take her back to Faroe, and I'll deliver the shadow ship in a day or two. It's almost time for you and Nizhoni to travel."

"I'll return to the ship." He stood and started for the door.

Jace glanced at his wrist communicator. "By the way. I just saw the message that Zangari has removed his personal belongings from the ship on which he was a passenger."

Cade grinned. "Looks like we have a new crew member. That ought to liven things up." He left and made his way to the ship. On the way, he contacted Zina and told her to prepare the Searcher to lift.

"Will do, Captain. By the way, I took Zangari on as a temporary crew member."

"Thank you for handling the interview. I thought he could be a good addition to our gang. I'll be aboard in five minutes."

Chapter 19

Cade buckled into his seat and powered his instruments. "Fuel good for both propulsion systems."

Zina fastened her restraints. "All personnel are aboard, and departments all report secure for lift." She reached to the control panel and made adjustments. "External ventilation terminated and hatches are secured. What is our destination, Captain?"

"Set course for Faroe."

"Course laid in. One hour to Hyper Corridor transition point."

Cade contacted base control and requested clearance. After receiving clearance to lift, they began the trip home. Cade leaned back and was thinking about his conversation with Jace. He and Zina were both silent for a long length of time.

Zina interrupted his thoughts. "During my interview with Zangari, I was shocked by something he told me." She fell silent.

"What? Aren't you going to tell me what he said? He seemed like a nice guy."

"He knows my parents, and just talked to them last week."

"I didn't expect you to say that." He looked across at her. "What's the matter? Did something happen to one of your parents?"

"He said my mother teaches mathematics at university."

Cade stopped to think for a minute. "Didn't you tell me females were pretty much restricted from occupations like that?"

"Yes. I did say that. That's the way it was, twenty-five years ago, but I haven't been home since then." She grew quiet again.

Cade realized she was deep in thought. He had never seen her in such a pensive mood. He finally hazarded a comment. "I guess you are probably pondering a long overdue trip home."

She stirred and looked at Cade. "I left on such bad terms. I've been thinking about how hatefully I reacted to them. I can't believe they would welcome me, but…" She couldn't finish her sentence because of her crying.

Cade had heard somewhere, when he was young, that Zacathians could not produce tears. His long-forgotten source had been wrong. He had seen Zina shed tears over the loss of her bond mate, and now she was crying again. He released his restraints and move to stand by her seat. He stooped to give her a hug and said, "Zina, I have a feeling your parents would find joy in seeing you again. I can definitely see that you love them, so why wouldn't they love you."

She regained her control. "That's why I'm being so emotional. Zangari said my dad told him how they missed me." She dabbed at her tears. "They missed me, and I miss them."

"Zina, when we get back to Faroe, I'm sending you on another mission. Take the Searcher and go spend some time with your parents. Take as much time as you need. Riley will go with you, and I understand our newest member is starship pilot qualified."

"What about your assignment?"

"I won't need the Searcher, and I'll have the scout. I'm serious about this. I was on the outs with my parents, but seeing them again helped me realize that our disagreements were minor, compared to family love."

"We are nearing the transition. You need to strap in."

Cade went to his seat and secured his restraints.

"Transition in two minutes, Captain.

They were soon gliding at hyper speed. Cade said, "May as well have a late lunch. Do you want to go first?"

"I'm not really hungry. You go ahead."

"You have the bridge." He went to the galley and found the rest of the crew already enjoying their meal. He made a selection and took a seat at the table. He was curious about the new crew member, so he watched their interactions as he ate. Zangari was talking and laughing as much as the others. Cade thought, *So much for being a loner. He seems to be enjoying the company.* He continued eating slowly, and enjoying the caff he had drawn. He always felt at peace, when sitting with the crew.

Zangari turned his attention to Cade. "Where is Zina?"

"She's on the bridge. She'll probably come down when I return."

"Would it be okay for me to join her? Don't worry, I'm familiar with the bridge on one of these cruisers. I piloted one during the ten systems war."

Cade raised a brow. "Now you've surprised me. I thought Zacathians were never involved in war."

"That is true, but not an absolute. After talking with Zina, I discovered we have a lot in common. I, too, went against the grain. My parents disowned me for joining the military. They said it was dangerous. I asked them if they knew how many Zacathians have been killed during endeavors to expand knowledge."

Cade said, "You may want to go to the bridge and talk with her about home. She would love to hear the news from you."

The Zacathian nodded and left in a hurry.

Cade decided the bridge could do without his presence for a while. He motioned for Riley to move to the seat next to him.

Riley put her dishes in the processor and joined him. "You wanted to talk to me?"

"Yes, Chief Engineer. Zina has told me the great job you are doing in engineering. Are you still happy being in the crew?"

"Yes sir. There's no ship I'd rather serve aboard."

"I'm glad to hear it. When we get to Faroe, Zina will be taking the Searcher to her home world, for a visit. Our newest crew member happens to be a qualified and experience cruiser pilot. He will be piloting the ship, and Zina will assume the captain's chair. Are you interested in making the journey with them?"

"That would be great. I've never been to that world."

"Well, now's your chance. This is official ship business, so you will be paid as usual."

With so many things on his mind, it seemed to Cade that very little time had passed when they were once more parked on Faroe.

He went to his berth and changed into the heavy winter gear he wore when he boarded. As he left his berth, he saw Zina talking with Zangari. "I'm headed for the cabin. Let me know when you're ready to leave for home. I need to think about things." He left the ship with Nizhoni walking beside him. Maska and Aeolus went before them.

As they walked, he said, "Zina is taking the Searcher to her planet for a visit with her parents. She may not return before our deployment, so you may want to collect your belongings and put them in the scout, or the prefab."

Nizhoni stopped walking. "That news has slapped me with a dose of reality. You and Zina have been a family, actually a home for me. She brought warmth and stability to my damaged life." She fell silent for a moment. "I won't see her again, once I've cleared my berth."

Cade turned to face her. "That is the really hard part of life, little sister. There is always another goodbye to be said, and someone you love, to be lost."

She smiled, but a tear betrayed her fear. "You will remember your promise not to forget me, won't you? And your visits. You promised."

"It's impossible for me to forget you, and you'll probably grow tired of my visits to New Terra." He smiled and turned to continue walking toward the cabin, as Nizhoni returned to the Searcher. When he reached the cabin, he entered and looked around, and said to the walls, "This place brings me comfort. Each time I enter, it feels like home." He went to the fireplace and built a fire, and continued to kneel for a few minutes, as he warmed his hands. Satisfied the fire would continue burning, he got to his feet and went out to the stable.

He didn't see Maska or Aeolus, and knew they were out enjoying a hunt. He didn't stop at the stable, but continue to the lake. He settled on a wooden bench and looked out over the ice encrusted water. The trees stood strong with a burden of snow and glitters of ice. He looked again at the lake and didn't see ice. He saw crystal water with Melody standing waist deep a short way from shore. He sighed, and rose from the bench and walked slowly to the cabin. He felt Maska's approach, and smiled as she greeted him with a bump of his hand with her broad head. He scratched behind her ears as he entered the cabin. Aeolus winged in through the door before he closed it. Going to the couch, he settled into his usual spot and stared at the empty chair sitting across from him. He heard Melody ask, "We are still a team, aren't we?" He finally dozed off.

"Wake up, Cade. We have to do something."

He opened his eyes to see Nizhoni. "What happened? Is everything okay?"

"Yes, nothing's wrong. We came to see you."

He looked beyond her and saw Sarah standing behind Nizhoni. He wasn't quite fully awake.

Sarah said, "Zina is leaving tomorrow, but will wait for you to see her off. I'm not needed there, so I put my kit in the prefab bedroom."

Cade shook his head to clear the cob webs. "That's good. But you could have told me this in the morning."

Nizhoni said, "No. We have something to do right now."

Sarah wore a slight frown. "I'm sorry about barging in, but she insisted."

Cade felt like he was missing something. "Insisted what?"

Nizhoni held up her long knife. "I want to do the blood brother ritual with you."

Sarah held up a scalpel. "I told her we would do a blood-sibling ritual with a sterile field."

Cade was fully awake now. "It isn't really necessary to do that."

Nizhoni put on her pouty puppy look. "Please do this. We will be real siblings, and you won't be able to forget me."

Cade stood and said, "Oh for…!" He looked at her puppy dog eyes. "How do you do that? Okay, stab me and get it over with."

Sarah put the disposable scalpel in her shirt pocket. "We'll do this in the prefab. I happen to have some celebratory anesthesia in my kit."

Cade asked, "Celebratory anesthesia?"

When they entered the prefab, Sarah led them to the kitchen area. "This ritual would have been done around a camp fire. Picture the knife being swung across the flame, and promises made. An owl hooting in the night.”

Cade said, “Sarah, just jab our fingers. What’s with the story?”

“We have to set the scene, and I’m just getting to the exchange of spirits.” She handed them each a glass of liquid, and kept one for her. “Let’s sit at the table.”

Cade smelled the liquid in his glass. “Is this rubbing alcohol?”

“No. It’s whisky from the world of Ironious. Ironisians are famous for their liquor making skills.”

Cade looked at the glass. “What do we do next?”

“We drink for unity.” She turned up her glass and drank it down.

Cade took a drink and said, “This stuff is awful.”

Sarah was filling her glass again as she said, “You have to drink it down.”

Cade reluctantly finished the glass, watching Nizhoni down hers at the same time. “I’m glad that’s over. What’s next?”

Sarah refilled their glasses. “We drink one for brother hood.”

Cade and Nizhoni lifted their glasses as Cade said, “At least I won’t have to worry about infection. This will probably kill everything except my liver.” He downed the glass as Sarah and Nizhoni drank theirs. “I’m hesitant to ask, but what’s next?” He saw her refill the glasses. “How much of that do you have?”

She said, “Next we slice the fingers.” She took out two alcohol preps and wiped Cade’s right index finger.

He said, if you're doing that to prevent infection, you're wasting your time. I have enough inside me to handle that."

He watched her wipe Nizhoni's finger.

Sarah pulled the cover off the scalpel, "She took hold of Cade's hand and asked in a slurred voice, "Give me your hand."

"Can't you see? You're holding it."

"Oh! I am, aren't I?" She was giggling and her hand was shaking. She looked at Nizhoni and winked. She quickly sliced his finger and turned to Nizhoni and sliced hers. "Now put them together." When they had their fingers pressed tightly together, Sarah wrapped surgical tape around them. She straightened up and said, "Take two aspirins and call me in the morning if your cold isn't better."

"Cade asked, "What cold? Are you drunk?"

Sarah said, "Glad you mentioned it. We all have to drink another glass for thankfulness." She turned up her glass and emptied it.

Cade picked up his and asked, "Why thankfulness?"

"I didn't hit an artery, did I?"

Nizhoni drank hers down. "You know, this stuff tastes pretty good after two glasses."

Cade drank his and said, "It's because our taste buds have been cauterized."

Sarah took her scalpel and carefully cut the bandage from their fingers. "You are now one in the blood, brother and sister." She stood and said, "I'm going to bed." She left the kitchen and went down the hallway.

Cade looked at Nizhoni. "You look happy. You must be drunk."

"I'm very happy. I have a real brother." She sobered. "You may be the only blood kin I have left."

"He hugged her and said, "Good night, little sister. I'm going to return to my couch." He was still wearing his winter gear, so he went to the door and realized Nizhoni was following him. "Aren't you staying here?"

"No. I want to be near you until we complete our mission."

They went to the cabin and entered to find Maska still stretched out in her familiar spot, between the couch and Melody's chair. He went to the fireplace and added fire wood.

Nizhoni removed her coat and hung it on a kitchen chair. "Will you be okay on the couch tonight?"

"Yeah. It's pretty comfortable, and I can keep the fire stoked during the night."

"I'm going to sleep in Melody's bed tonight."

Cade sighed, "It's not Melody's. It's the cabin's bed."

"I didn't know her for more than a few minutes, but I can feel her when I'm here. It's a comforting feeling, because your love for her is so strong. I keep hoping that she will be my sister one day."

He stretched out on the couch. "Good night, sis."

He slept soundly that night, and awoke to find the fire reduced to small flickering flames. He got up and added tinder before putting in more wood. "I'll need to clear out the ashes when this burns down." He heard Nizhoni as she went into the fresher. He went to the door and let the animals leave, and then returned to his couch.

Nizhoni came in and sat next to him. They were both still dressed except for their coats. She moaned, "I have a headache."

"Let's get our coats on and go next door. Maybe Sarah will mix up that green stuff she gave you last time."

"I don't need it. That stuff was nasty." She put on her coat and followed him out the door.

When they went to the kitchen in the prefab, Sarah was at the table drinking one of the green tonics. She looked up and said, "No more blood rituals for me."

Cade sat beside her. "Nizhoni is eager to drink one of those."

Sarah pointed to the counter. There's a bottle of it over there. Shake it up and pour some in a glass."

Nizhoni was soon drinking a glass of the green concoction.

Cade said, as he left his seat. "I'm going to go to the Searcher and see if Zina will have breakfast with me."

Sarah said, "Wait for me. I need to get a coat." She went to the bedroom and returned as she pulled the coat on.

Cade walked with them to the searcher. They went to the galley and found Zina sitting with the others.

Cade said, "We came to dine with you, and then see you off on your adventure."

Zangari said, "I am honored that you allow me to pilot your ship."

Cade settled at the table with his breakfast and a cup of caff. "Just be sure to take care of my sister."

Zina smiled and her ear frills were pink with a blush. "I'm so happy that you feel that way."

The usual talk and laughter crossed back and forth across the table. Cade watched with a bit of trepidation. He knew things would not be the same if Zina should decide to remain with her family. When everyone was through eating, Cade held up his cup and said, "Here's to a joyful family reunion for my navigator, Zina." They all took a sip of caff, toasting to a successful trip. Cade stood and went to stand next to Zina. She stood and he hugged her tight. He said softly in her ear. "I want you to return, but if you decide to stay, it's okay with me."

Zina squeezed him in return, and said," Thank you for being a good friend."

They parted and Cade said, "I'll listen on my com for your launch clearance. He left the ship and walked slowly back to the cabin."

Chapter 20

Cade stood soaked in sweat. He looked at the mat and saw it was as wet. He laughed when he looked at Nizhoni. "You look like a drowned rat."

Rolf, one of the citizens of Lawrence, had been showing up every day to go everywhere Cade went. Rolf said, "I'll clean the mat and drape it over a rail."

Cade nodded. "That will be great, Rolf." The man had become something of a manager, doing whatever he could to help out. Cade had protested at first, but the man seemed despondent because his help wasn't wanted. Cade had given in, and the guy never intruded on their workouts or target practice. Cade realized Rolf would probably run along with him when the weather allowed for that exercise.

Nizhoni was wiping at her face with a towel. "I'm going to get a shower." She went to the small dresser by her bed sitting in the corner of the room and pulled out clothes before heading to the fresher.

Cade helped Rolf put the mat over the rack that was made for the purpose, and left as the man began sanitizing it. He went to the cabin and took a cold shower. When he was dressed, He heard a tone, signaling a request for communication. Cade pressed a depression on his wrist device. He said, "Transmit, ship."

Jace's voice came through. "I'm on the way with the ship. I'll be there in ten minutes. Meet me where you first landed the scout. Only you and Nizhoni are authorized to see the package."

Cade went to the prefab and found Nizhoni dressed. "Get your coat. We have someplace to be."

He exited the prefab and led Nizhoni to the landing site. He looked to make sure Rolf wasn't aware of them leaving. When they got to the site, the shadow ship was on the ground and in normal mode.

Nizhoni commented, "What an ugly craft. Did it crash here?"

Cade laughed. "No. That's our ride." Jace stood near the ramp and waited for them to approach.

Nizhoni asked, "Where did you get that antique?"

Cade shrugged as Jace looked his way. "I didn't tell her about this ship. I figured it would be best to wait until our departure."

Nizhoni punched him in the ribs.

Jace said, "Come aboard." He went up the steps and the two followed him. When they were inside, Jace closed the door. "I didn't give you any instructions concerning the actual operation of this craft, because its controls are exactly the same as the Searcher. The few differences are in its defensive capabilities." He led them to the bridge where he opened a small compartment and withdrew two wrist com units. They looked like Amerind wrist bracelets and were disguised by being almost long enough to reach the elbow. He handed the larger one to Cade, and the smaller one went to Nizhoni.

They clamped on like a regular bracelet, but Cade couldn't see any release mechanism. Jace instructed Cade to sit in the pilot's seat. He pointed out controls on the console, and indicated the corresponding control on their wrist devices. Cade and Nizhoni were instructed how to change the shadow ships camouflage, as well as how to fire the ships disrupters, and blaster arrays. He showed them how to fire small guided missiles equipped with warheads.

Cade picked things up quickly. Except for the camouflage, the weapons were the same as Searchers combat configuration had been. "I've got it, Jace." I'll go over it with Nizhoni several times before our deployment."

"Your deployment date is now. We have received intel indicating a few days plus or minus for the pirate ships arrival. In addition, after examining your reports concerning the citadel, it will be best if the two of you have more recon time to scope out the tunnel and terrain." He paused. "Patrol marines have been pre-positioned with two, all terrain wheeled assault vehicles, equipped with mass stunners. The plan is to wait for the ships to land and open their hatches before springing the trap."

Cade said, "It sounds like a good plan. We'll need to hurry and pick up our kits."

"No need. Everything you need is on the ship. There is one thing I need to show you." He led them back to the airlock chamber and opened the locker that was installed after Cade had seen the ship on Beltane. He opened the door and they walked into what was basically a storage closet. Native clothing hung on a rack, along with two quivers filled with red arrows. Several bows, knives and blasters were strapped to shelves. Jace picked up two head coverings with built in masks. He handed one to Cade.

Cade pulled on the mask. It covered from the top of his ears at the sides and back of his head. In the front there were two eye openings with silver lenses and the mask covered the bridge of his nose, leaving the lower part of his face exposed from nose to chin. "Does this have the capability I asked you to research?"

"Both masks will keep Melody from entering your brains."

Nizhoni wore a puzzled expression. "What do you mean?"

Cade looked at her. "I didn't tell you, but Melody and I can read each other's thoughts. We have a connection that just happens when we are near each other. The masks will also add a fearsome aspect to our appearance."

"I knew you two were meant for each other. No one else has that kind of connection."

"It's not like that, little sister." He paused. I need her to believe I am Red Arrow, so she will not accidently give me away, not to mention she would be angry that I came." He removed the mask and returned it to the shelf.

Jace said, "You'll have plenty of time to familiarize yourselves with the equipment. It's an eight-hour trip through the Hyper corridor. I've loaded all of the surveillance video onto the shadow ships auxiliary computer. Your call sign for this ship is Shadow

Hawk, and there are only two frequencies loaded on the communications control. One is the standard Patrol frequency, and the other is the dedicated mission frequency. When you need to contact me, the name of the ship is Nautilus. Call sign for the site Marine commander is Thor. There is an operator's manual loaded on the computer in case I forgot something, which I probably have. Next time we meet, we'll be on New Terra. The route is laid in and ready for lift. Good luck." He left the ship. Cade sent a message to his team, and waited for them to arrive. Maska bounded through the hatch without touching the ladder, an Aeolus followed. He secured the hatch and told Nizhoni it was time to strap in. He led the animals into the large living area. There was a roost fastened to the bulkhead for Aeolus, and some hay in the starboard rear corner of the room that serve as a bed for Maska. Jace had thought of everything. He and Nizhoni went to the front of the ship and Cade climbed into the pilot's seat. He strapped in and watched to make sure Nizhoni was fastened correctly.

Cade made sure the frequency was set for normal Patrol communications. "Faroe departure control, scout requests clearance to lift." He didn't use the call name, but used Seeker, the name of his scout.

"This is Patrol Cruiser Pisces, there is no traffic and you are clear to lift."

Cade lifted the ship and initiated the route data once he was a thousand miles from Faroe. He looked at the navigation computer.

"Fifty minutes to transition, and we'll have eight hours in Hyperspace when we transition."

Nizhoni looked at Cade. "This ship has a lot of room inside. A lot more than the scout, and it isn't a piece of junk." She unstrapped her restraints. "I'm going to give myself a tour. Apparently, you got one and didn't trust your sister enough to tell her."

"In my defense, you weren't officially my sister yet. Not only that, Jace said it was top secret and to not tell any blabber mouth about it."

"Blabber mouth? I might demote you from favored brother status." She left her seat and Cade didn't hear anything from her for a long time. Finally, he used the ships internal communicator. "Nizhoni, you need to strap in. We will transition in two minutes."

He didn't look away from the instruments when he heard her return. Not having a navigator added a little more pressure on him. "Make sure you're strapped in. Transition in ten seconds. He counted down to himself and disengaged the planetary propulsion and simultaneously engaged the Hyper Star Drive. For a moment, he thought the drive failed, but a quick glance out the window revealed the solid white mist of the corridor. "That's the quietest engine I've ever heard." He could not actually hear any hum at all.

He looked over at Nizhoni and saw she was dressed in one of the native costumes, from moccasins to the mask on her head. The mask gave the impression of a hawk's head, and her eyes couldn't be seen through bulging lenses.

"You look mean, except for your grin. How is your visibility?"

"The lenses seem to make everything much sharper. I see no problem with sighting an arrow with this mask in place, but we may need to practice a few times before the real deal."

"That unit is supposed to be infrared equipped. We'll have to check them out for that. We may as well have a meal, I'm hungry." He unstrapped and went to the galley, which was six feet from his seat. He went through the hatch and turned left. In two steps he was standing in front of the food synthesizer. He pulled a tray and a cold drink. He took two steps and sat at the table. The layout was the same as the scout, but a little larger.

Nizhoni sat next to him with her food. "I thought I'd be nervous, but my nerves are calm."

"It's because we didn't have to wait several days after the Shadow Hawk arrived. We didn't have time to worry." He looked at her. "You do know that you're eating while wearing the mask."

"I'm already used to it. It's surprising how light weight it is. Maybe Jace will let me keep it." She held out her left arm and admired the wrist controller. "I want to keep this too. They went to a lot of trouble decorating these. There is an engraving of Maska and Aeolus, along with an attractive warrior."

Cade asked, "They engraved my likeness?" He looked at his device. "That's a woman." He looked a little closer. "Well, I'll be. I'll have to read the riot act to Jace when I see him again."

Nizhoni smiled. "Are you upset they used a picture of the toughest warrior? I think it's great that Melody has her picture there."

"I hope she doesn't notice it." Cade suddenly thought about the team. He got up and went to the bulkhead that divided the living section from the airlock hatch area. He had noticed two wide, deep dishes that were secured to the wall with an attached frame. Two, almost invisible doors were positioned above the bowls. He didn't see any mechanism to open the doors, so he went through the rear hatch and opened the locker door. He entered the equipment closet and approached the starboard bulkhead. There was a machine, a smaller version of the one on the Searcher. He depressed and released the food side, and then did the same with water. He left the locker and returned to the room to see Maska and Aeolus sharing the replicated meat in the dish. He returned to the table and continued eating. Even though Cade knew Nizhoni feared what she might find at home, it was obvious she was excited to be going back. After they ate, Cade said, "It's time that I tell you my plan concerning Melody. Let's sit up front so I can scan the instruments."

When they were strapped in, he gave her an overview of his plan. "Melody must not know I'm Red Arrow. When we move against the citadel, I want to take Lim, alive. We will string him to a pole in front of the Sioux fortress, and Melody will announce that she seeks to redeem herself to her former status. She'll kill Lim while her father looks on."

"I don't know, Cade. Her father probably won't agree to that kind of full redemption."

He frowned. "I'm going to ask for a meeting with the chief and his council. In that meeting, I hope to find a father that really wants his princess returned. I believe I can convince him. While I'm meeting with him, Melody needs to be kept in her house."

"She'll probably be at the stables."

"If she is, I will request that Eagle Feather be sent out. I will have to do some mean talking, but I believe he will comply. When she is in her house, she needs to become the princess, in appearance. I have stuff in the back that we'll need to take to the cabin. I'll show you later."

Nodding her head in agreement. "Sounds plausible so far."

"When you see me exit the fortress gate, wait until I'm out of sight. Then you will accompany Melody to the place where she halts before the gate. You'll be carrying a quiver and bow."

"I know what you have in mind. She will make her plea for the redemption, and I'll hand her the bow and arrow."

"Right. She will have her best opportunity and Red Arrow will not be seen again. When Lim is dead, you can join me on our way to the bridge."

"I don't understand. You intend to leave her and go back to Faroe alone?"

"I can't change the fact that she isn't interested in Cade Storm, and I don't want her to sacrifice her heart by accepting me because she feels obligated. I'm trusting my sister to never tell her I was here. Do I have your promise? We may not be able to go over this again."

"I think you are wrong, but I promise not to tell her."

"This is only a rough plan, and we may have to play it by ear when the time comes." He paused. "Another reason to keep my presence secret is that she will probably need several months to convince others that a Patrol presence is in their best interest. You can do a lot to help her with that by getting the Navajo on board. The Sioux will fear the Patrol will make a pact with the Navajo, which will help them to be more eager to have a joint agreement."

"Cade, if the Patrol gets rid of the pirates, I'll make sure my people know. I'll do my best to persuade them."

"Nizhoni, get some sleep while we're in Hyper Drive. I'll sleep after we land and you can stand watch then."

Cade waited till she was on a bunk, and then dimmed the cabin lights. He went over the plan several times, but he would need to actually look everything over once they were on the ground. He sat back and went over the short history of the New Terra invaders. He was beginning to think the two anti-slavery missions he participated in, were pieces of a chain, part of a larger plan. *I'm missing an important piece of the puzzle.* He thought about the operation on Thane, where the pirates possessed an extensive planetary defense system. *That would be a massive endeavor, too big for a lone outfit. What is the material being mined on New Terra? What could be so important to cause scum like the pirates, band together in such numbers? Pirate ships are like lone wolves. Each is independent of the others, and are quick to attack each other because of greed. Amassing what amounts to a pirate army to strong arm a world is out of character.*

Cade released his restraints and went to the galley. He drew a cup of caff and sat at the table. He drank a few sips, as he pondered the first step he needed to take, when they reached New Terra. *We won't study the citadel first, as I had intended. I want to take a look at the mine site before anything else. I'll need to talk with the officer in charge of the marines that are already deployed with the mass stunners. They have oversight on the expected landing site, next to the mine.* He finished the caff, and drew another cup. He carried it to the bridge and settled into his seat. All he could do now, was wait.

Chapter 21

Cade awoke and looked up at Nizhoni.

"Six hours are up. I'm your wake-up call."

He swung his legs off the bunk as he sat up. "Thanks. Any alerts while I slept?"

"All sensors were quiet as a mouse."

He stood and went to give instructions to his team. *"Out, but do not be seen."* Maska and Aeolus acknowledged understanding. Going to the hatch, he opened it so the two could hunt. He then went to the fresher. When he came out, going into the galley, he settled at the table where he found a cup of caff and breakfast waiting. Nizhoni was already seated with a cup of caff in hand. He sat next to her.

He took a drink of caff and set the cup aside as he took a few bites of food. Still focusing on his breakfast plate, but thinking about what needed to be done, He said, "Sparrow Hawk."

"Were you talking to me, or mumbling to yourself?"

He smiled at her. "Until I board my ride home, at the end of this mission, your name is Sparrow Hawk. To prevent rumors that may ruin the mission, no one can know our real names, and that includes any of your people we may run into." He took another drink of caff. "I'm Red Arrow, and we will use these aliases beginning now, even when we are alone."

"I understand, Red Arrow. What's our first move?"

He told her about his thoughts concerning possible connections that might be emboldening the pirates, and his plans to check the mine before going to the citadel. "As soon as I'm finished eating, we will suit up as Sparrow Hawk and Red Arrow. Then I will let our superiors know that we need to meet with the Patrol marines on site."

Nizhoni left her seat and demurely said, "I'm going to get started. It takes a lady longer to apply war paint, and it's not proper for a gentleman to watch." She turned and went aft.

When he finished breakfast, he went aft and met Nizhoni as she stepped through the hatch, connecting to the airlock area. She was ready to go. Cade stood for a moment, looking at her face. The war paint, black stripes with white borders, was applied in a way that had the effect of making her look like a hawk. "Great job. I hope I can duplicate the effect."

"Get dressed, brother. Sister will apply your war paint so we match. You know, birds of a feather."

When they were ready, they stepped out through the hatch, carrying bows and quivers full of red arrows. They each carried a blaster, hidden in a pocket at the base of each quiver.

Cade used his wrist communicator. "Thor, Red Arrow seeks council."

A terse reply announced, "Route sent."

Cade opened his wrist device tracking screen. He said, "Follow me, Sparrow Hawk." After forty minutes, they were challenged by a sentry. Cade held up his right hand, palm facing the patrolman. "Red Arrow."

The sentry escorted them to Major Conner. "How can I help you, Storm?"

"I'd like to take a look at the pirate ship that was blown up."

Conner said, "There's not much to see, but follow me." They walked past one of the two military vehicles equipped with a mass stunner. "There's a bluff overlooking the site just past these trees. The Major came to a halt, and the three were looking out over a blasted valley. The crumpled hulk that was a starship lay in the center of destruction. Trees were laid flat for a hundred yards all the way around the ship, with their tops all pointing uphill. "I sent engineers down to examine the wreckage our second day here. They couldn't determine where the explosion originated.

Cade said, "The explosive arrow released by Eagle Feather, entered a hatch near, or on the ship's bridge. Major, were your men able to enter that part of the ship?"

"The bridge is completely gone. Is it important?"

"Major, it has been my experience that the computers on a starship are encased in hardened steel. I'm hoping that they survived, but it's obvious they were blown away from the ship. Do we have any tech available that can scan for wreckage outside of the blast zone?"

"Seems like you believe them to be important. The Nautilus has the capability of scanning the main wreckage to map a footprint based on the current condition of the materials that make up the wreck. They then scan with a discriminator, much like a handheld metal detector, but more complex."

Cade rubbed his chin. "I have a theory that might be proven if we can recover intact computers from the ship. I believe something far more sinister than slavery and piracy is taking place."

"I'll contact the Nautilus right now." He turned away from them and made his request via his wrist communicator. After a couple of minutes, he turned back to Cade. "They're scanning the ship now to establish its signature composition. Is there anything else, while we wait?"

"I'd like to examine the mine. Do you know what they were digging up?"

"Other than taking a quick visit to the ship, we've maintained our position to avoid detection."

"My partner and I will take a look."

"Since the two of you look like local citizens, it shouldn't be a problem for the mission if you're observed. Let me know what you find down there. If you need to contact me, hit your com unit."

Cade nodded and then looked to Nizhoni. He felt the momentary disorientation of seeing the area through the eyes of Aeolus. The eagle had identified the best path to descend to a point near the mine's entrance. Cade moved his head slightly, indicating the direction to Nizhoni, as he began making his way to the mine. They soon stood in front of the entrance.

Nizhoni surveyed the debris field created by the death of the starship. "The entrance does not face toward the ship. We can't even see the wreckage standing twenty feet from the entrance, and the force of the explosion was shielded from the mine entrance, by an outcropping of the mountain's south slope."

Cade looked upward and realized the mine was at the base of a mountain, or large hill, that projected up into the ridge that encircled the valley where the mine was being dug. He used his detect to scan the ground between them and the entrance, as they advanced toward the dark opening. They moved through the entrance and continued along the shaft. Light illuminating the shaft, was produced by still functioning systems.

Nizhoni asked, "What is that odor?"

Cade sniffed the air. "I've smelled this before, but I can't quite place where it was." He noticed the sides of the shaft were growing lighter in color. He went to the north wall and touched his finger to the surface material. A coarse powder covered his fingertip. He carefully lifted his hand toward his face and cautiously smelled the material. "The smell is definitely being produced by this white material." He suddenly realized what the invaders were mining. "Iteranium!"

Nizhoni asked, "What is Iteranium? I was thinking gold or something valuable."

"Iteranium is an extremely rare mineral. I am aware of two mines that produce this ore, and they are on planets light years apart.

This ore is used to make Hyper Fuel, and can also be used in weapons of mass destruction."

"Cade, this seems like a lot of time and credits spent needlessly when they could obtain the stuff to make fuel from a mine that's already functioning."

He sighed, "The mines are protected by strong military garrisons, and there are only two refineries that produce the fuel. Because the processed fuel is highly unstable, the refineries are located on separate, uninhabited moons." He paused. "They aren't mining for financial gain. The pirates are a part of something larger. War is the only possible answer I can come up with."

Cade's communicator signaled a connection request. He used his throat mic to verbally open the link. "Red Arrow here."

"This is Thor. We've located the computers, and a team has been dispatched to recover them."

"We're finished down here. Be there in a minute." They returned to the top of the ridge and found the Major waiting for them."

"Did you find what they were mining?"

"Iteranium." Cade saw by the expression on Conner's face, that he immediately understood the implication.

"That is the worst possible news you could have brought back." Conner paused a moment. "Thank God we didn't try to seal the entrance with explosives. In its raw form, it takes an explosion to set off a reaction. You can't even ignite the stuff with fire, and an electrical arc has to be massive to do the trick. The concussion combined with flash, caused by the detonation of a bomb in a confined space, produces catastrophic results."

Cade nodded his head in agreement. "The destruction of the starship was probably caused by a small sample of the ore, being kept near or on the bridge of the ship." He heard a flitter approach, its rotors producing a quiet hum as it settled to the ground near them."

Conner motioned to the craft. "The computers are in the flitter. Let's see what condition they're in." The three went to the flitter as the side cargo door opened. The flight engineer hopped to the ground as Conner stepped into the craft with Cade behind him. Nizhoni remained on the ground, peering in through the open door.

Cade looked at two, intact steel cabinets. They were scorched, and had wires dangling where the units were electrically connected to the ship."

The major ran his hand across one of the cabinets. "The steel casing has suffered only minor scratches and dents, along with the scorch marks. Nautilus should be able to access the information they contain."

"Have them taken to the Nautilus when it is safe to do so. The information they hold is more important now, with the threat of another war on the horizon." He looked at the sky. "How long before nightfall?"

The major looked at his wrist device. "Four hours to sunset."

"We're going to return to Shadow Hawk and finish preparing for our recon of the citadel."

Conner nodded. "I'll make a full report to Jace concerning your findings." He paused. "Contact me if you need anything else."

Cade nodded as he turned away from the major and began the return to the ship.

Nizhoni was silent until they were well past the outlying sentries. "Cade… I mean, Red Arrow, how much danger does Iteranium pose to this planet and my people?"

"Because the existence of the ore has been discovered, your chiefs will not be able to refuse a Patrol, or military base from being built on New Terra. The mine will probably be sealed, but it will have to be guarded against others who would come."

Nizhoni sighed. "I understand; after being off-world, we need a permanent Patrol presence here. But if the chiefs are told they have no voice, I know they will resist. It will be to the death, arrows against blasters."

Cade said, "I told you while we were traveling to this world, that we would probably have to modify our plans once we set foot here." He paused. "I still have the task of convincing them of the need for Patrol protection. Hopefully, I can frame it in a way that they will know it's in their best interest."

As they moved cautiously through the forest, Cade reached out to Maska. *"Return to the ship."* Maska answered, *"Yes, hunting good here."* He glimpsed, through the cat's eyes, the result of the hunt. Cade released his contact with the panther. As they neared the ship, Cade asked, "Where are the homes and civilian areas you told me about?"

"Civilization, as you would call it, is outside of a six-hundred-mile diameter boundary. Activities beyond the boundary are strictly peaceful, and county governments oversee each of the many counties. All conflicts between the Sioux and Navaho nations are settled within the confines of the boundary." She paused. "Now that I know how small the galaxy has become because of Hyper corridors, I'm painfully aware of how antiquated our way of life is."

He replied, "Some of the worlds I've visited, had demilitarized zones between bordering countries. Here, you have a militarized zone." He used his wrist device to open Shadow Hawk's airlock hatch. "If it weren't for off-world interference, it would be a better system than most." He paused. "The best system would be one of cooperation and peace. But that is the most difficult socio-economic system to maintain."

Maska and Aeolus entered the ship ahead of the humans. Cade set aside his quiver and bow after entering. "We'll take a meal before we hike to the citadel." He went to the galley and selected a meal and cold drink. He sat at the table as Nizhoni drew her meal. Cade took a drink and ate in silence as he thought about the task ahead. When they were finished eating, he said, "Make sure your provision pouch is full. We may not be back here before we have to make a move."

Nizhoni nodded. "I'm prepared."

He led the way to the storage locker, where he picked up two lengths of rope with grapples at the end of each. "We'll each carry a grappling line. We may discover the tunnel to be inaccessible, making it necessary to go over the top of the wall." With their preparations made, they both hitched their quivers across their shoulders and began their journey through the forest. Aeolus and Maska went ahead of them. After four hours of pushing through, and over, underbrush, they came in sight of the citadel. They were looking down at the citadel because they were on a high hill.

Cade clearly saw the sentries posted around the ramparts of the Navajo citadel. "I see twenty men, equally spaced around the perimeter. There is too much wall and too few guards. I believe the majority of their remaining men are those we now see."

Nizhoni tapped Cade on the shoulder and whispered, "I have several people showing on my detect. One is in a tree, with three others on the ground. She adjusted the far lens built into her mask. I can clearly see the one in the tree. He is looking out toward the citadel." She gasped and turned to Cade. "It's Chayton."

Cade rubbed his brow with his left hand. "I had hoped to complete this mission without revealing our identities, but it will be best if they see someone they know."

"Relax, brother. I can handle this." She put her fingers to her lips and whistled. "Chayton is climbing down from the tree. I'll continue to be Sparrow Hawk. I hope my mask's voice modulator works."

She paused as she focused her attention on the four now approaching their position. "Three have halted their advance and are waiting."

Chayton stepped into the open. "Who are you?"

Cade said, "I am Red Arrow, and my fellow warrior is Sparrow Hawk."

Chayton looked at them with suspicious eyes. "You are Navajo?"

Nizhoni said, "We are from a village outside of the boundary. We came here after speaking with a wounded warrior who escaped the area."

"I have never seen Navajo wear fearsome masks."

Cade improvised. "We have heard the men from the stars can read minds, but masks with metal thread can block those thoughts." He paused. "We were with a mighty Sioux warrior who killed hundreds of the invaders just a few days ago. Her name is Eagle Feather."

The Navajo warrior motioned his three cohorts to come forward, as he said, "We have heard about the death arrows. Her attacks provided enough chaos that I and my three friends were able to escape the citadel. We remained close to the citadel, looking for a way to help our people. We have been watching it for several days."

Nizhoni asked, "Do you have an idea about how many of the vermin are still breathing?"

"We have seen twenty-two different individuals. Most of the watchers on the wall have not left their posts during our surveillance. The leader, Lim, and his lieutenant, have not been on the wall."

Cade observed, "We have at least twenty-four to deal with, and I need Lim alive."

Chayton raised a brow. "It sounds like you're planning on paying a visit to those inside."

Nizhoni said, "That is our plan. Do you know where Lim is holed up?"

"He's in the throne room. He keeps Queen Aiyana there as insurance." He paused a moment. "Our Chief died battling the demons, and the princess was taken away. I will go with you into the citadel. It is better to die an honorable death than to sit here doing nothing."

Cade looked at Nizhoni. She turned away from them, and he knew she was crying. He went to her and put his hand on her shoulder. "Take off your mask and let your fiancé comfort you, and you will give them strength, as well."

She removed her mask and turned to face Chayton, tears streaming down her face.

"Nizhoni!" He moved quickly to take her in his arms. "Nizhoni, how are you here?" Tears ran down his cheeks as he held her tight."

She gently pushed him away. "We will wait until this war is over, before we dare to have a proper reunion. I have been taken from here and traveled among the stars. Red Arrow helped free me from the pirates and brought me here to destroy the invaders. He is of the blood, but comes here from among the stars to help us." She paused. "He is my blood brother."

Chayton bowed his head to Cade. "I am in your debt. Thank you for bringing Nizhoni home."

Cade smiled, "I really had no choice. She's very bossy."

She punched him in the ribs. "I'm not bossy."

Chayton shook his head. "You two are obviously siblings now. Save the fighting for later." He laughed. "If only for a moment, you have brought laughter and hope with you."

Maska entered the clearing, and the four warriors retreated a step before Nizhoni said, "She won't hurt you. She is a threat to the enemy, along with her winged friend, Aeolus." The eagle dropped from the sky to land on a sturdy branch."

Chayton said, "What beautiful animals. You say they are a threat to the enemy. How do they know what to do?"

"They can communicate with Red Arrow. They are a team." She reached down and scratched behind Maska's ear.

Cade looked at the sky. "The sun will set soon. Sparrow Hawk and I will reconnoiter under the cover of darkness. We'll share a meal of jerky before making our way closer to the citadel."

After eating, Cade led them in a wide arc, keeping well within the tree line for cover.

Chapter 22

Cade left the four warriors at a safe distance from the citadel. Nizhoni was wearing her mask to make use of the night vision screens. Cade followed her as she tried to remember the location of the tunnel entrance. She stopped several times and looked toward the citadel as she tried to get her bearings.

She looked at Cade and was obviously frustrated. "I remember it was within the tree line for concealment." Looking around the area where she had halted, she said, "It was disguised as a tree stump." She eyed the citadel for a moment. "There was something my father said about the central tower on the east wall. What was it? Day or night, site on the tower's right." She moved five steps and gazed at the tower. Moving her gaze from the tower, she scanned the area. "This spot aligns with the tower wall. The entrance must be further into the trees." She turned away from the tower and walked toward a tree she picked for reference. After twenty paces, she stopped in her tracks. "This is it." She stood next to a tree stump, or at least a good facsimile of one.

Cade knelt next to the trunk and gently tapped with a knuckle. "It looks like wood, but it's not." He carefully looked around the faux stump before grasping the top with both hands and swinging it on a pivot pin, revealing a dark vertical shaft. He reached down and felt the rung of a ladder. He motioned Nizhoni to lower herself into the darkness. She lowered her legs into the hole, and her feet found the rung. As she descended, Cade went over the edge and slid the top back into place. He didn't want someone to stumble upon the secret entrance. Their night vision goggles presented a clear view of their path as they carefully filed along, watching for anything that might make a noise if stumbled over.

They eventually came to the end of the narrow tunnel. It opened out into a room about twenty feet long and ten feet deep. The wall was made of blocks, with four door-sized wooden sections.

Cade noticed a light shining through several small holes in the wooden sections of the wall. He moved his right eye close to one of the peepholes and looked into a bare chamber.

Nizhoni was looking through another hole in the wall. She backed away and moved nearer to Cade. She motioned him to follow her into the tunnel. She whispered, "This is the basement level. One of these panels is a door, and if we enter, the dungeon would be to our left. To the right is a stairway that leads to a small room on the ground floor. It adjoins the great hall. The throne room, or room of meeting as we call it, would be to the left as we exit the small room, and the front entrance would be to the right."

"There may be some of your people in the dungeon, and that could mean a guard with a blaster, unless they can't spare a man for that duty." He thought for a moment. "When we get the word that the ships have been captured, you will enter the basement and quickly stun any possible guards. I'm hoping there won't be one. Go up the stairway and wait inside the room, until I lure Lim into coming toward the front of the great hall. The range of a stunner is thirty feet, while a blaster reaches forty feet. You will need to stun Lim before he is out of your range."

"I don't like the idea of you being bait. Something could go wrong."

"Don't worry, I'll stay out of his range. We'll need Chayton and his three warriors on the wall so they can eliminate all the sentries." He went back into the room and examined the four wooden panels. He found the latch mechanism on the panel second from the right side of the room, and he showed Nizhoni how to operate the latch. They then made their way to the tunnel entrance and climbed out. Cade swung the tunnel door shut, and they carefully made their way back to Chayton.

When they were all together, Cade pointed to the center tower on the east wall. "When the time comes, I will scale to the top of the tower. You four warriors will follow with your quivers and knives. You will need to kill all of the aliens on the wall. It will have to be quick, and quiet. I will make my way to the front courtyard and issue a challenge for Lim to face me." He paused. "There will be three of them, other than Lim, somewhere on the grounds. Do not hesitate to kill them on sight before they can use their blasters on you. Try to stay forty feet or more from your targets. The arrow is lethal at a greater distance than their hand blasters."

Chayton said, "If you use a grapple, it may make enough noise to attract attention."

"I will be in contact with a spaceship that can keep me informed if someone reacts to my presence." Cade paused. "It is a simple plan, but it should work. We probably have a couple of days to consider any possible improvements." Glancing up at the sky. "It will be dawn soon. Let's move further into the trees and get some sleep." When they found a place with a concealing brush, they settled down for rest. Cade communicated with his team and set them as sentinels. Falling asleep, he slept soundly for ten hours. Awakening, he found the others were already up. Sitting up, Nizhoni handed him a strip of jerky. He looked at his wrist com and saw it was four thirty in the afternoon. Feeling well rested, he looked forward to another night of reconnaissance.

He looked at Nizhoni and motioned her to move near to him. When she was settled, he smiled. "I've decided it would be best if you go to the Sioux Fortress with Chayton and his three men. Take Lim, if we manage to take him alive, and secure him to a tree. If Melody is in the fortress, announce that you have words to speak to the council, but you want Eagle Feather sent out to meet with you first. Tell her to wait until you return from the meeting with her father before requesting a full redemption. She must kill Lim in front of the fortress. You will need to campaign for her redemption, acceptance of the patrol, and unity between the tribes." He paused. "You will have to wing it, just like I would have done. And remember your promise. Do not tell her I was here. I'll leave as soon as we have freed the citadel."

"I'll do as you have asked, but you're making a mistake by leaving without her."

"We've already been over that. We'll sit tight until dark." He laid back on the ground and looked up at the sky. It was bright blue with a few fluffy white clouds drifting lazily in a westward direction. He dozed until he was shaken by a hand on his shoulder. He looked up to see Nizhoni.

"Your wrist com signaled a connection request."

He sat up and pressed the control to open the transmission. "This is Red Arrow."

Jace's voice responded. "Two heavy freighters are three hours out and inbound. Nautilus has decoded their flight plan and verified they will land at the mine, as we hoped. Conner will contact you when the ships are secure. Good luck."

Cade looked at the time. "They will arrive about two hours after dark. That will help us quite a bit. I will scale the tower at that time. The mass stunners will put on a light show that will serve as a distraction while I use the grapplers."

They all ate jerky and drank water from the canteen carried by Cade and Nizhoni. Thirty minutes before the landing, Cade guided Nizhoni into the tunnel entrance. She had her blaster in hand, set to stun. Cade led the warriors to the tree line closest to the tower. Inching his way slowly to the base of the wall, he uncoiled one of the grapple lines and prepared to propel it upward. Something in the sky caught his eye. *Good. They're putting on a show to throw fear into the population. The ships aren't using the flux generators for a quiet landing. They are using planetary propulsion rockets to broadcast their presence. Couldn't ask for a better distraction.* Stepping back from the wall, he began swinging the grapple in a tight, fast orbit of his right hand. Timing his release, he watched the grapple soar over the tower rampart. He tugged, and it held tight. Moving close to the wall, he began his climb to the top. When he reached the top, he felt a tug as one of the warriors was following him. Soon, all five men were on top of the tower.

They went to the steps leading down into the interior, and descended to the rampart where the watchers were stationed. He motioned two out the north-facing opening, and two to the south. He saw two watchers lose their throats before he descended to the ground level. He met an unfortunate invader and killed him just inside the ground-level entrance. *There should be two left besides Lim.* He saw another of the invaders walking toward the opening and used his knife again. A flash lit the sky for an instant and Cade thought he heard the mass stunner. He scanned the courtyard while remaining in the tower entrance. He got the signal from Conner. The ships were secure. He carefully eased out into the courtyard and felt an impact on his right side as he heard a simultaneous report of rifle fire. He went down as he glimpsed the gunman fall with an arrow in his throat. *That should be the last one.* Ignoring the pain in his side, he rose to his feet and went to the front of the main door. He yelled, "Lim, throw down your weapons and come out. You are under

Patrol arrest." He quickly transmitted to Nizhoni, "I'm out front; be alert."

Lim called out, "You won't take me alive, but I'll take you with me.'

"Cade held the stunner, but knew the target was too far. Lim came to a halt, holding Queen Aiyana in front of him for a shield. He saw the stunner raise as Lim aimed at him. He jumped to his left, but his injury slowed him. He felt a searing, icy feeling on his right leg as he hit the ground. He was still conscious and wondered why he felt so cold, as he watched Nizhoni fire her stunner at point-blank range. Lim crumpled, and Aiyana was cradled by Nizhoni enough to prevent injury. He dimly saw Nizhoni run toward him after gently lying her unconscious mother on the floor. He heard her yell something as she put her hand on his shoulder. He managed to say, "Remember your promise", as he lost consciousness.

Nizhoni frantically keyed her wrist communicator. "Cade is severely injured. I need medics in the courtyard now!" She knelt by Cade and glanced at his right leg. "Cade, stay with us. Help is on the way." His last words, though weak, rang in her ears as she said, "Even near death, he wants to honor her feelings."

A flitter settled outside the compound, and the gate was opened. Maska bounded in to stand by her wounded teammate. Four men came and moved Cade to a stretcher. They carried him to the flitter, with Maska following close behind.

Nizhoni turned to see Chayton. "Take care of my mother, and secure Lim until I return. We need him alive. I'm going with Red Arrow." She hurried to the flitter and climbed in beside Maska. The flitter landed near the two pirate freighters. Jace's ship, Hermes, was parked nearby. The medics took him from the flitter and carried him into the Hermes. Maska and Aeolus boarded the ship. Sarah met Nizhoni as Cade was being taken to the medical decontamination area.

"Nizhoni, we'll take good care of him. You return to your people and help them."

"Sarah, please let me know how he is."

"You have a wrist com. We'll contact you. I know you have some things left undone. Cade would want you to finish the mission."

Nizhoni nodded and returned to the flitter. Keying her wrist communicator, she said, "Jace, I need to borrow this flitter and its flight crew. I'm going to meet with the Sioux, and it will serve as a backdrop."

"I'll contact the pilot and tell him you're his boss until further notice. Be careful, Nizhoni."

One hour before dawn, the flitter settled just outside the tree line that sheltered Melody's cabin.

Nizhoni climbed out, followed by a female warrior carrying a package. Chayton and two male warriors exited behind them.

Nizhoni pointed to a spot and said, "Set it up right there."

The two women continued toward the cabin, as Chayton and his men unstrapped a wooden pole assembly that had been slung below the belly of the flitter. One of the Patrol crewmen assisted as they carried the seven foot tall, whipping post, with its heavy base formed by two logs attached to it in an X configuration. They set it up where Nizhoni had indicated. They then returned to the flitter and pulled out a squirming Lim Jardin. The prisoner tried to yell at his captors, but the gag tied around his head muffled his attempts. Freeing his arms from the tangler, Chayton secured a manacle to Lim's left wrist before threading the attached chain and second manacle through the large steel loop at the top of the post. They lifted the prisoner so his toes barely touched the ground as the second manacle was secured to the right wrist.

Chayton stepped back and said to the prisoner, "We wait for Eagle Feather to pay you a visit. You do remember her, don't you?" He said to the warriors, "Strip off his clothing, but leave the gag in place."

They cut his clothing away with their knives, snatching and ripping the clothes so violently that Lim was being slammed against the rough pole. Muffled screams made it past his gag. When they were finished, they returned to stand near the flitter.

While the warriors were carrying out their orders, Nizhoni knocked on Melody's front door. "Eagle Feather, it is I, Princess Nizhoni of the Navajo. I come seeking a parley with you."

Melody opened the door. "Nizhoni? How did you get here?" Melody suddenly stepped outside and looked around."

Nizhoni smiled. "He's not here. Cade said you told him not to follow you, so he honored your request."

"I wasn't looking for him. I just wondered what was going on. Please come in."

Nizhoni and her female guard entered and closed the door behind them.

Melody indicated her dining table and said, "Please sit, and tell me what you have to say."

Nizhoni sat, and her guard set the package on the table. Nizhoni pushed it toward Melody when she was seated. "Cade sent this to you."

Melody pulled the package closer and began opening it. "A warrior's clothing." She held up a doe-skin jerkin. A blue blaze of dyed leather in the shape of a pin feather, adorned each shoulder, and a large eagle was blazed in blue on the back. The head of a big cat, blue in color, was situated on the left breast of the jerkin. Leather fringe was attached below the shoulder on both sides of the vest. "I've never seen anything as beautiful as this." She ran her finger across the image of the cat. A tear rolled down her cheek. "It reminds me of…" She cleared her throat as she tried to control her emotions. "It reminds me of the team."

Nizhoni smiled. "There's something else."

Melody reached into the package and lifted a ten-inch, square box that was two inches in height. She removed the cover and carefully lifted a princess' tiara. Three silver feathers dangled from the back of the silver headpiece. On the left side, dangled two small, silver eagles. "Why did he send this to me?"

"He said that he never thanked you for being a part of the team, so he wanted you to dress as the warrior princess you are meant to be, on this your full redemption day."

"I've already been redeemed."

"Well, it seems that he believes you should be restored, and I happen to agree with him. Outside, I have a present that can't be included in that package. It is a loathsome piece of crap, disguised as a person. The piece of vomit is patiently waiting until I have a parley with your father. When I come out of the gate, it will be up to Eagle Feather to find the appropriate words as you announce your desire to reclaim your life with your act of vengeance."

"Is it Jardin?" Her countenance changed from the emotional Melody to reflecting Eagle Feather's smoldering hatred for the monster.

"Yes. It is the same creature that defiled us both." She paused a moment. "I know you would like to kill him immediately, but please wait until I return. I wanted to kill him myself, but you have suffered more than I because my father died in battle. I was never dethroned and treated the way your father treated you. Today, you show him who you are."

Eagle Feather's voice nearly matched the growl of Maska. "I will wait for your return."

Nizhoni stood. "While I parley, prepare yourself." She nodded toward the new clothing. Nizhoni left the cabin and walked toward the fortress gate. She saw Sioux warriors at the top of the wall, gazing down at her approach, while some pointed toward the naked man hanging by his wrists. She said to herself, "That woman can be scary. I wouldn't want to be her enemy."

She stopped twenty feet from the gate, and removed her quiver, bow, and long knife, laying them on the ground. She bowed, but remained standing as she looked up and said loudly, "I am Princess Nizhoni of the Navajo. I seek a parley with Chief Natahay."

The chief was already stationed on the wall. "Why do you come here with one of the enemy flying machines?"

"That machine is not one that belongs to the invaders. Guardians from the stars, came here to finish the task that was begun by Eagle Feather. A mighty warrior among them, Red Arrow, has rewarded Princess Eagle Feather's heroic, single-handed destruction of hundreds of the enemy by giving their leader into her hands."

"Why is Red Arrow not here to parley?"

"He was mortally wounded during his assault to free the citadel. His last order was for me to stand in his place." As Nizhoni said this, she looked over her shoulder and saw Melody standing at the tree line, listening. "The guardians came here to stop a plan that would have brought hundreds of invaders to replace the ones destroyed by

Eagle Feather. The guardians captured them and their star ships. We owe them much, and that is one of the things we need to discuss."

Natahay shouted, "Open the gate. We will parley."

Nizhoni was led to the council chamber. She looked around the table at the chief and the eight elders.

Natahay said, "Please be seated and speak what you have to say."

"The words I have, are living in my heart, and came to me while I was lost among the distant stars. I was taken from here by evil people. I was mistreated, and my lot was that of a lowly slave. Eagle Feather and I were held in a world called Faroe. Eagle Feather was taken away to another world, while I remained a prisoner. A mighty warrior, Cade Storm, freed Eagle Feather, and the two of them destroyed the monster that held me and others captive on Faroe. I discovered that there are more good people than evil ones, even among the stars. The guardians that came to our aid, are known as the Space Patrol. They guard the lesser advanced worlds from pirates and slavers." She paused. "The Patrol discovered the pirates were here to mine a very rare mineral used to power their star ships. If the pirates would have been left unchecked, our world would have been claimed by them." She paused again. "The Patrol has requested that they be allowed to establish a base and permanent presence on this world. They will only interact with our populations to the degree we allow, and they will not force us to advance our technology. We will still be in control of our lives to the extent we have already been."

Natahay said, "I am against their base. I don't trust anyone from the stars."

Nizhoni frowned. "My people have been severely affected by the invaders. Even now, medics of the Patrol are tending to the many Navajo who were injured by the invaders. Queen Aiyana and her council, have agreed to negotiations with the Patrol. It is my belief that the Sioux should join in those talks." She could see the elders were considering the consequences of being left out as they glanced across the table at the chief.

Natahay sighed, "There is merit in your words. We will discuss the possibility after you have departed. Do you have other words for us?"

"Yes, Chief Natahay. A mighty warrior, Red Arrow, seeks the restoration of the warrior princess, Eagle Feather. He found her bravery and dedication to honoring her people, to be extraordinary. He also praised her wisdom as she considered what was best for her people. She returned here from the stars, when she could have chosen to stay with the man, she held dear. She sacrificed happiness there for what she knew would be a hard life under a yoke of shame. Eagle Feather represents what is the best in each of us, and yet she still carries the flaws that we all share as well." She saw a tear run down the chief's cheek. "When I depart, Eagle Feather will be at the gate with her request. It will be the last chance for wisdom to triumph over an archaic view of the nature of a person's honor. If a person is humiliated by another, the humiliation can be overcome by the character and strength within the one who was victimized." She rose from her seat. "Thank you, Chief Natahay, for hearing my words." She turned and left the chamber to be escorted to the gate. She retrieved her weapons and saw Eagle Feather begin walking to meet her. They met halfway.

Melody said, "I heard you say a warrior from the stars, Red Arrow, was mortally wounded. Was he Cade?"

Nizhoni steeled herself to speak the lie. "No. Cade refused to come. He didn't want to anger you."

Melody closed her eyes. "I'm relieved that he stayed away, but I'm saddened by the death of Red Arrow."

Nizhoni began to resume walking, but Melody stopped her.

"I want you to stay here until this is over."

The Navajo princess nodded and remained standing on the spot where she was stopped. She turned to face the gate as Melody continued her approach.

Melody came to a halt, but did not remove her weapons. The silver tiara, shown brightly in the sunlight. Her long warrior's braid reaching to her waist. "I, Eagle Feather, stand before you and vow to avenge the cruelty I endured before this very gate. The garbage you see hanging from a post, is Lim Jardin, the leader of the invaders. He is the one who attempted to destroy my honor, and the honor of Princess Nizhoni." She drew the long knife from its sheathe and raised it skyward as she shouted, "My honor is still within my beating heart, and today I will send Jardin on the journey to the underworld. He will arrive there as less than a man. This is my action, to restore my life." She turned and began walking toward her enemy. "Remove the gag."

Chayton hurried to the captive and removed the gag.

Lim's body shook in fear as he saw anger etched into every inch of the woman's face. He looked at the knife she carried by her side, and he started yelling for forgiveness. His voice kept getting louder until he was nearly screaming.

"Today, you will enter the underworld as a half-man." She swung the knife and left ragged flesh where his groin had been."

He screamed continuously at the top of his lungs as she slowly walked back to join Nizhoni. She drew an arrow from her quiver and nodded to Nizhoni. "We will end his screams together."

"Nizhoni smiled and drew an arrow from her quiver. They both nocked their arrow to the string. "Quick, or slow?"

Melody said, "His screams are annoying me. Let's end it." Two arrows struck the heart of the writhing body, bringing his life to an end. Melody smiled and slung the bow over her shoulder. Both women turned to see Natahay rushing toward them.

The chief embraced his daughter. "I'm sorry, Eagle Feather. You didn't deserve to be discarded by your father. You are more of a chief than I, and you will one day take my place as chieftain of the Sioux."

As Melody hugged her father, she saw her mother hurrying toward them. The Queen hugged them both, with tears running freely. The warriors on the ramparts were whooping their approval with their princess.

Nizhoni walked back to the flitter and said, "Let's go, we've done all that can be done. The rest is up to them." They boarded the flitter and headed toward the Navajo citadel.

Chapter 23

Jace stood in the medico and stared at the massive damage to Cade's leg. He asked the surgeon, "What's his status?"

"I removed the primitive projectile from his side, and I have the knitter repairing the damaged tissue. The blaster damage requires tissue restoration, but some of the bone is gone. I have a fluid circulating in the wound to slow further loss from decay. To save his leg, we need the facilities at the trauma hospital on Osiris 3, but it is too far away from here. We don't have the luxury of time."

Jace stepped away from the surgical table and keyed the Patrol's interstellar net. "I need the current location of the hospital ship, Blue Star." He hurried toward the bridge of the ship, and he pressed a different button on his communicator. "Meet me on the bridge now." When he got to the bridge, the navigator was in his seat.

"What's going on, Captain?"

"Here are the coordinates for the Blue Star's location. Give me the coordinates that are nearest to halfway for our ships to meet."

The navigator did a quick calculation. "Here are the coordinates that will put us in the vicinity of the two hyper corridors we each have close access to. If we depart now, we can be there in three hours."

Jace transmitted the coordinates to the Blue Star. "Meet you there in three hours. Patrol priority red one." He didn't wait for the pilot, but strapped into the pilot's position. "Lay in that course." He keyed internal communication. "We make an emergency lift in five minutes. Secure all departments." He next contacted the Nautilus. "Hermes is making an emergency lift in three minutes. Clear our space to ten thousand miles."

"Hermes, you're cleared to ten thousand. We have contacted ground forces to pull back."

The navigator said, "External ventilation is secured, and all hatches are dogged. All departments have reported secure."

Jace initiated the flux generators and lifted the ship smoothly toward space. At ten miles, he powered the planetary drive and pushed the ship to top speed as the pilot entered the bridge.

Jace checked his instruments as the Navigator said, "Two minutes to hyper-transition." The pilot was strapped into a jump seat as the navigator counted down from five. The hum of the hyperstar drive replaced the muted roar of interplanetary drive units.

The navigator said, "Two hours and forty-five minutes to emergence."

Jace unstrapped and said to the pilot, "The stick is yours. I'm going to the medico."

Jace met the surgeon. "We will meet up with the Blue Star in less than three hours. That's the best I could do."

The surgeon exhaled a deep breath. "That's good news. This guy must be pretty important to you."

"He's important to all of us. He uncovered a plot that would have started another war between star systems."

Two weeks passed before the Hermes returned to New Terra. The ship settled near the mine, where two groups of dignitaries were waiting. Jace exited the Hermes and was greeted by a representative from each group. He reached out and shook hands with Eagle Feather and then Nizhoni. It's good to see both of you. I hear you two have succeeded in swaying both sides."

Eagle Feather smiled. "I believe Nizhoni deserves most of the credit. I don't know what she said to my father and the elders, but they have been very open to this meeting. The two women bracketed Jace as he approached Chief Natahay and Queen Aiukli, of the Sioux. Queen Aiyana of the Navajo, accompanied them.

Jace showed respect by bowing at the waist. "I'm Lieutenant Jace, representing the Space Patrol. It is an honor to meet the leaders of both nations."

Natahay said, "I hope we can reach an agreement that we all can embrace."

Aiyana nodded her head. "It is the wish of the Navajo as well. The councils for both of our nations are already assembled inside."

Jace pointed to the prefab that had been set up for the meeting. "Let's go inside and open negotiations over some refreshments."

Four hours later, they all exited the prefab wearing smiles. Jace said, "A flitter is assigned to carry all of you home."

Melody said, "I'd like to stay for a while. I want to talk with you."

Jace glanced at Nizhoni and saw her shake her head ever so slightly. He looked at Melody and said, "Wait for me in the prefab while I see the others off."

She smiled and returned to the meeting area.

Nizhoni moved to walk beside Jace. She whispered, "Don't tell her about Cade's condition. Tell her he's okay and building his ranch."

Jace said, "Don't worry. I'll keep lying, but sooner or later, she needs to know the truth."

She nodded. "I agree, but it should be Cade who tells her."

Jace frowned. "I truly hope he will be able to do that."

"Hasn't he improved? Sarah said he was doing better."

"His bones and flesh are being restored, but only time will tell if his nerves will regenerate enough for him to walk."

Nizhoni sighed. "When he is able to do physical therapy, I will go work with him. I can boss him around and push him to get better."

Jace laughed. "You might just be the medicine he needs for recovery." Watching her climb aboard the flitter with the rest of the delegation, he waited till they were in the air before returning to the prefab.

He entered to find Melody patiently waiting. "What can I do for you?"

"I have been wondering a lot about Cade, lately. Can you tell me how he's doing?" She hesitated. "I meant to say I've missed the crew of the Searcher and have been wondering about all of them."

Jace nodded his head. "I understand." He struggled with the lie he knew Cade would want him to tell. "Zina hasn't returned with the Searcher, and Cade is considering giving the ship to her."

She smiled. "That sounds like him. He has a tender heart when it comes to Zina. What else?" She leaned forward in her chair.

"Well, Riley has communicated almost every day. She is very happy aboard the Searcher." He paused. "She told Cade that she believed Zina may eventually bond with Zangari."

"I haven't met him, but he must be a great guy if Zina likes him that much. I'm happy for her. What else?"

Jace was beginning to get nervous. "There isn't much else to tell." As soon as those ill-chosen words left his mouth, he saw her face darken as she stood up and slammed her hand against the table.

"Cade! I want to know how he is doing. Is he healthy? What?"

Jace cleared his throat as he thought; *How is it even possible for Cade to be so lovesick over her? She scares me every time she puts on that Eagle Feather face.* He almost jumped when she slapped her hands hard against the table.

"I'm waiting to hear something."

"The Patrol gave Cade one of the pirate freighters as a reward. I haven't heard from him since he left with a hold full of horses." He fell silent as he felt the sting of another lie. He suddenly thought, *What will she do to me when she discovers the many lies I've told for Cade?* He rose from his chair. "When I hear from him, I'll tell him of your concern." He hesitated and then proceeded to say too much. "He probably won't contact you since you made him aware of your dislike for him."

She almost snarled as her lips pulled back to reveal her teeth. "I never said I didn't like him. I merely told him that I didn't love him."

Jace pressed his luck one more time. "For a man, they are one and the same. You rejected him, so now he's moved on."

Her face softened as she collapsed into the chair. She quietly asked, "Has he moved on, forgetting me?"

Jace felt sorry for her. How could two people be so in love and yet have hearts that are light-years apart? "Look, I can tell you are upset. Why don't you ask Nizhoni about Cade? She was close to him before returning to her planet."

She turned her face toward Jace. "How close?"

"She was part of his team. You know, Beast Master and all."

"She joined him on missions?"

"Yes. The two of them, along with the animals, took out a terrorist group and saved a prince from being executed."

Melody sighed. "Guess I'll call her and find out when we can meet." She stood. "Can I trouble you for a flitter ride home?"

"I have one waiting outside." He opened the door and walked with her to the flitter. He watched as the craft lifted and flew southwest, toward the Sioux fortress. He touched his wrist communicator and entered a communication request for Nizhoni.

"Hello, Jace. How did it go with Eagle Feather?"

"Not so good. She is seriously afflicted with problems of the heart. She kept grilling me for information about Cade. I told her that Cade was transporting horses in a freighter given him by the Patrol, and that I haven't heard from him lately. I'll tell you the truth, that woman scares me. When she finds out how I've lied to her, she may cut my throat."

Nizhoni laughed. "She's a sweet woman. She wouldn't do anything like that."

"I'm glad you think so. I told her you would know more about Cade because you were close to him, and part of his team."

"You didn't."

"I did, and she said she would arrange a visit with you so she can find out about Cade."

"Okay, you coward. I will handle it when the time comes. We will all be very busy over the next couple of weeks, so that gives me some breathing room. Thanks for the warning." She ended the connection.

Jace returned to the Hermes. Two Patrol marines, one to either side of the ramp, saluted him as he entered the ship. He went to the galley and drew a cup of caff. He took a sip and glanced at his wrist communicator. He received an alert for a communications request. He pressed the button to open the line. "Jace here."

"This is Sarah."

Jace leaned forward in the chair. "Has something happened to Cade?"

"No. He is still being kept in an induced coma. The reason I'm contacting you, is because the Blue Star is taking him back to Faroe. Scan's show his bone and flesh are properly restored and protocol calls for him to be awakened within the next twenty-four hours. He will still be under a knitter for a few extra days, but he will be experiencing pain. Even with the pain, he will need to rehab through the end of his recovery." She paused. "He and I will be left in the prefab, where I will work with him."

"I'll be there before you, and check out all the environmental equipment in advance."

"Thank you, Jace. I knew you'd want to be there."

Jace selected internal com and announced, "All departments, prepare for lift in ten minutes. He received acknowledgments from the pilot and navigator. He went up to the bridge and found them going through their checklists. He settled in a jump seat behind the pilot. "Lay in the course for Faroe." Jace thought about the animals. After transferring Cade to the Blue Star, he took the beast team back to Faroe and released them. The animals were familiar with Rolf, so he knew they would be okay. After the ship was in the hyper-space corridor, Jace released his restraints. "I'm going to turn in. It's been a long day." He went to his berth and flopped onto the bunk. He was asleep in minutes.

An alarm sounded and roused him awake. The overhead announced, "Touch down in two minutes." He relaxed and waited for the ship to land. He knew he had about twelve hours to wait for the Blue Star's arrival. He left his berth and headed for the cargo bay. He went down the ramp and found Maska sitting on her haunches, waiting at the end of it. "You know he's on the way, don't you?" He wondered if the big cat nodded its head coincidentally, or did it really understand him. "I need to check out the prefab and make sure it's ready for his arrival." He watched Maska suddenly gain her feet and run toward the direction of the prefab. "That's just weird. Animals don't understand human communications." When he reached the prefab, Maska was waiting. Jace laughed. "He won't be here for another twelve hours." The cat lay down and stretched by the prefab entry. Jace went inside and checked for any damage that may have happened while the facility was sitting empty. The townspeople had helped Rolf to build a cabin near the site where Cade had landed the Scout during his first visit to Faroe. Patrol engineers had assisted by installing advanced galley, environmental, and fresher equipment for Rolf and his family. Jace set the environmental units in the prefab, to appropriate settings. It was early spring, but the temperatures still dropped during the night hours.

Jace received the landing notification and went outside. The Blue Star landed on the pad near the prefab. The ship's cargo hatch opened, and Sarah came down the ramp. Maska ran to her and requested an ear scratch. Sarah grinned as she scratched behind one ear and then the other. Two orderlies came down the ramp with the gurney, carrying the sleeping Cade, rolling along between them. They left the ramp and followed Sarah to the prefab, with Maska keeping pace. Two more men came down the ramp, fighting to control the more awkward medical treatment table with attached knitter equipment. They transported it into the prefab and set it up, before all four of the orderlies gently lifted Cade and eased him onto the treatment table. Sarah set the adjustments on the knitter, and turned it on. Jace stood nearby, watching the procedure. Cade's legs began working up and down, bending at the knee and hip.

He asked Sarah, "Why are you flexing his legs?"

"We need to keep his limbs flexible and work his muscles and tendons. It helps improve his prognosis."

"When will he wake up?"

"I'm going to begin bringing him up in about an hour. He will experience tremendous pain with any movement, but he will have to move."

Maska stretched out near the door to the room and watched her unconscious human teammate. Aeolus flew into the room and lit on the floor next to Maska. Her perch was in the great room, near the front door.

Jace went to the dining area and picked up a chair. He took it in the treatment room and placed it near the eagle. She flew up and landed on the back of the chair. Jace went to the easy chair near the bed and sat as he waited for his wounded warrior to awaken.

About two hours later, Cade stirred and moaned loudly. He turned his face toward Sarah. His voice was raspy. "I can't stop moving my legs. I have excruciating pain."

"I will stop it for a while, so I can remove your catheter." She switched the leg exerciser off and turned her attention to removing his cath.

He moaned. "I need some water."

Jace went to the bedside table and poured a glass of water from a carafe. He put his right hand behind Cade's back and lifted him gently, holding the glass to Cade's mouth. He gulped down the entire glass full, and Jace lowered him to his original position.

"What happened after I blacked out?"

"Nizhoni stunned Lim and took him prisoner. Patrol medics treated a lot of injured Navajo people. It was very successful except for your injury."

"It feels like my right leg is on fire, and someone is trying to extinguish the flame with a chainsaw."

Sarah said, "I can help you get up and put some pressure on your legs."

He moved his legs a little and yelled. "I can't move. It hurts too much."

"It's okay. I will restart the flexibility exerciser." She flipped the switch, and Cade yelled again. "I can't take the pain. Turn it off."

Sarah switched it off. "Cade, it is absolutely necessary that we work that limb. If we don't, it will freeze up. Your muscle memory will be gone, and you will limp for the rest of your life."

"I really don't care. It would have been better if I had died on New Terra."

Maska rose to her feet and went to the table. She reared up and put her front paws on the surface of the bed. She looked him in the eye.

Cade saw an image of a squalling human baby. He sent a thought message, *"Hurts a lot."* Cade thought he saw a look of disgust on Maska's face. He watched the cat ease her feet off the bed and pad out through the doorway. Aeolus screeched and flew out behind her.

Jace said, "It looks like your team wants you to get well."

"I don't care. You can both leave the room; I'm tired."

Jace started to protest, but Sarah nodded toward the door. They went out into the great room.

Jace frowned. "I can't believe he's being so childish."

Sarah sighed. "I think there's more to it than physical pain."

"What more could there be? He's been seriously injured before, but he didn't act like this."

"No, he didn't, but he had a different caregiver involved with his recovery."

Jace settled into a chair at the table. "The scary woman stayed by his side the whole time."

Puzzled, Sarah asked Jace, "Why do you call her scary?"

He slumped in his chair. "Apparently, you've never been interrogated by her." He paused. "It will be necessary to break my promise to Cade. We have to convince Melody to come here and straighten him out. She's just scary enough to do it." He sighed. "I

have a call to make." He got up and made his way back to the
Hermes.

344

Chapter 24

"Nizhoni, this is Jace."

"What's up? Is Cade recovering from his injury?"

"As a matter of fact, he is apparently depressed and acts like a baby because of the pain. I believe he's given up."

"I assume you need me to do something to make him straighten up."

"Nizhoni, we are going to break our promise to Cade. Sarah believes Cade recovered so quickly the last time he was injured, because of Melody. We need to let her know what's happening and convince her to come here."

"Jace, are you so oblivious that your last interaction with Melody didn't give you a clue about her feelings?"

He shuddered. "She seemed on the verge of violence at times. Is that the feeling you're referring to?"

"Just leave it to me. I have an idea." She ended the connection. "Melody has a wrist communicator now that she serves as the Patrol's contact point for the Sioux." Holding her communicator near her face, she pressed a button and said, "Contact Eagle Feather."

Melody answered, "This is Eagle Feather."

"Melody, this is Nizhoni."

"No one's called me that in a long time. What do you want?"

"I actually need to have Melody come to my chambers in the citadel."

Eagle Feather frowned. "I'm quite busy right now. Is it important?"

"Yes, it is. Leave Eagle Feather behind and bring Melody here. It has to do with Cade."

"What about Cade? Has something happened?" Melody looked at her wrist unit. "That witch terminated the connection." She contacted Jace. "This is Eagle Feather. I need to meet with Nizhoni. Can you send me a ride?"

Jace said, "A flitter will be there in ten minutes." He grinned at the efficiency of Nizhoni as he contacted Conner to arrange the flitter.

Within an hour, Melody entered Nizhoni's private chambers. She saw Nizhoni sitting behind her desk.

Nizhoni smiled and said, "Please have a seat."

Melody sat across from Nizhoni. "What did you need to tell me about Cade?"

Nizhoni sighed. "First, I have to tell you that Jace and I have been lying to you."

"What? Lying about what?"

"Melody, please be patient. This is complicated, so hold your questions until I'm finished. Before I get to the reason for my call, I need to tell you about my relationship with Cade. Before I met him, I was lost and insecure. I didn't think I could go on living. Just meeting him for the first time, and experiencing his kindness, I decided to lean on him. I stuck to him like glue. I even slept with him for two weeks."

Melody rose from her seat. "You slept with him? That Casanova! He had me convinced of his love for me."

"If he had you convinced, why did you leave? It's obvious you love him too. We slept fully clothed. I asked him to do that. He told me you were his only love, and I told him about my fiancé. We didn't sleep together for intimacy. It was for us to comfort one another with our presence. I finally was able to step out from under his wings. After that, we were able to sleep without a security blanket. I hope you believe me, because it will probably come up at some point, and the truth will be distorted.

Melody settled back into her seat. "I actually believe you. It sounds just like something Cade would do."

When you rejected Cade's love, and told him not to follow you to New Terra. He decided to ignore your wishes and came here to help restore you to your former life."

"He came to New Terra? Why didn't I…" She fell silent.

"I know about the connection between the two of you and the animals. You should have felt his presence, right?"

Melody nodded her head but remained silent.

Nizhoni reached into a desk drawer and pulled out her Sparrow Hawk mask. She slid it across the desk to Melody. That is the mask I wore when Red Arrow and I carried out our mission here. That mask contains a woven shield of special metal that blocks brain waves."

Melody picked up the mask and looked at it. "If you were Sparrow Hawk, then Red Arrow was Cade?" She suddenly stood. "You said the Red Arrow died from his wounds."

"Another lie of convenience. Cade was adamant that you should never know he had been here. That's why we both wore these special masks. He came here for you, but you weren't supposed to find out."

Melody settled back into her chair. "Why tell me now? I would have done anything he asked, if I had known what he did for my people and me."

"That is the reason. He said you would go against your heart and accept his love out of gratitude. He didn't want to do that to you. He loves you too much to force you into a relationship you didn't want."

Melody held the mask up to her face and began to sob. "I lied to him. I thought my past would slowly dissolve his love, and I convinced myself that my leaving would be the best thing for him. My gratitude would have been only a small part of my willingness to accept his love. My love for him is the greatest part, and now, he won't believe me if I go to him and profess my true feelings."

"I'm afraid you must go to him, and soon." Nizhoni paused. "We did not lie about his serious wound. His body has been put back together, but he refuses rehab. There is great pain involved, but he should be able to endure what needs to be done. He refuses to do the work, and Sarah believes you are the only one who can force him to do it. She pointed out that your constant presence by his side helped him recover from his previous injury."

"He will probably reject my help because he will believe I'm forcing myself to do it."

Nizhoni grinned. "I've been talking to Melody, but I believe this task requires someone more along the lines of Eagle Feather. He needs some tough love, that you can give him, but he doesn't have to know it's you." She pointed at the mask. "I believe we can remove the largest part of the mask itself, and modify the skull part so that it fits under a white…, no, a black outfit. You will wear a black nurse's uniform and a black head covering like some medical people wear. Perhaps plain glass lensed glasses to change your appearance."

Melody laughed. I get the idea. I will push, pull, shove, and force him to move. I will pick him up as need be and I will definitely ignore his protests. I'll make him angry enough that he will rehab without thinking about it."

Nizhoni said, "If you can tolerate his moaning and crying, and you truly love him, keep this in mind. When he completes his rehab, we will have a reveal, and you will tell him that you have paid him back for helping your people. That will remove gratitude from the table as a reason for the two of you to be apart."

"We need a back story to explain my presence."

Nizhoni laughed. "I have a hilarious idea. I believe his mother would go along with us. Cade's mother will tell him that Helga is a candidate for bonding and is Navajo, as well as a rehab specialist. That will cause him to be receptive to your help."

Melody sobered. "We may have some fun, but the main thing is that we get him better. It is possible he will hate me when he discovers I tricked him."

"Let's get him better before we cross that bridge. What can you tell your parents that will help them accept an off-world trip?"

"I think I have that covered. I have been talking to my parents about Cade and how I want to see him again. I could tell them that he asked me to meet with him on Faroe."

"That should do it. When you return home after this meeting, tell them about his request and see if they're receptive to the idea. Let me know. I'll let Jace know, and have him find some black uniforms."

Fourteen hours later, a Patrol scout landed near Cade's cabin. Melody left the ship, wearing a hat to cover the cap created by Nizhoni. Sarah was waiting for her at the end of the gangplank.

"Melody, I'm so happy to see you again. I have your uniforms in the cabin." They entered the cabin, and Sarah said, "I have a uniform laid out for you in the bedroom. Since he isn't leaving his bed, you can stay in the cabin when not working with Cade." She turned to leave but stopped at the door. "When do you want to start?"

"Helga doesn't believe in delays. I will be there as soon as I'm dressed."

Sarah smiled. "I like your style." She left the cabin and returned to the prefab. She entered Cade's room to find him staring at the ceiling. "I have good news. Helga just arrived and is preparing to meet you."

Cade turned his face toward Sarah. "Helga? Who is Helga?"

"Helga is the Navajo woman your mother sent to look after you. Remember what your mother said, about knowing a woman who would make you a great wife."

"I told her not to shop for a wife to bond me with. I can't believe she actually sent someone for me to meet."

"Well, she's not just any woman. She's a respected physical therapist who's offered to get you on your feet."

Cade returned his gaze to the ceiling. "This Helga has wasted her time coming here. By the way, I think I'll need the bedpan." A loud voice invaded his peace.

"Mr. Storm! We do not like bedpans, do we?"

Cade looked toward the door. A woman entered the room wearing all black, including a black nurse's hat perched on her head. She peered at him through horn-rimmed glasses. She walked over to a spot near the wall on the side of the room he was facing, and turned to look at him.

"Look, Helga, my mother has wasted your time sending you here. I know you're probably an excellent therapist, but I'm not moving until this leg stops hurting." She continued to stand, unmoving and silent. He looked at Sarah standing next to his bed, and whispered, "What is she doing? Did she pass out while standing?" He almost jumped when the silence was broken.

"I will not permit laziness on my watch. There will be no bedpan, and you will clean your own sheets."

Cade lifted his head and glared at Helga. "You're not listening to me." He looked at Sarah. "She can't talk to me that way. It's poor bedside manner. Say something to her."

Sarah walked over to the therapist. "Good luck, Helga. Call me if you need me." She turned and left the room.

"Wait, Sarah. About that bedpan." A movement caught his attention as he saw Helga walking slowly toward him. He noticed she was wearing black painted nails. "I am not getting out of this bed. You're making my leg hurt worse by not leaving."

She broke her silence. "Your mother told me you were a strong and brave man. Helga doesn't see it."

"Why do you keep referring to yourself as…"

"Silence." She threw his blanket off the bed.

"Hey. That wasn't funny. Put that blanket back; this gown is drafty."

She suddenly stooped, wrapped her arms around him, and slung him over her shoulder in one motion.

Cade screamed, tears running down his face. "You're killing me. Are you nuts? Put me down."

She took two steps from the bed and leaned to lower his feet to the floor.

"No. Put me back on the bed."

"Mr. Storm. We are two steps from the bed, with no bedpan, and two steps from that wheelchair, and a ride to the bathroom."

"You are evil, and you won't get away with this bullying." He looked at the wheelchair, slowly took a step, and turned shakily away from her. She continued to hold him by his right arm. He staggered and yelled in pain, but managed to flop into the chair.

"That was a good start, Mr. Storm." She knelt to flip down the footrest on the right side. "Now lift your foot and put it on the rest."

Cade groaned, with the pain running up and down his leg as he lifted his foot to the pad. He wanted to scream, but he refused to give his tormenter the satisfaction of knowing how much pain he was in.

She lowered the left-hand footrest, and gently lifted his good leg into place. "That wasn't so bad, was it?" She pushed him out of the room and down the hall to the fresher. She opened the door and asked, "Do you want me to roll you inside, or would you rather do it yourself?"

He noticed a handrail system had been placed in the room. Two handrails, wide enough apart to accommodate his wheelchair, started just past the sink and curved to bracket the commode. "When did this stuff get installed?"

"I believe Sarah told the Patrol engineers what was needed, so they installed them for you."

He wheeled himself to the handrails and said, "Close the door. I'll do this myself."

She closed the door, but stood near enough to hear him cry out with every step. Tears ran down her cheeks.

Sarah came to stand by her. "I was watching through the one-way. You're doing great."

She wiped at her tears. "I nearly threw off my mask. I wanted to hold him and take away the pain. This takes more strength than facing a warrior in battle." She removed her glasses and wiped at her eyes with a tissue. "I don't know how much longer I can continue a mean attitude."

"From what I witnessed, he will push himself more, and you will be able to back off some. I don't think it will take long for him to graduate from needing Helga." They both heard Cade yell out. It was obvious he was returning to the wheelchair, as he groaned with every step. Sarah handed her a pair of walking shorts. "Getting these on him should make for good therapy." She turned to go. "Keep up the good work."

Melody put the glasses on and got herself into Helga mode as she waited for her patient. She heard water running in the sink. "Are you ready for the door to be opened?"

"Yeah, I'm decent."

She opened the door and found he was standing at the sink, washing his hands. He had pushed the chair out of the railing path and into the open area in front of the sink. "I see you tied your gown. At least I won't see your bottom again." She held out the shorts to him. "Do you want my help getting these on?"

"I think I can handle it." He grimaced and moaned as he turned to settle into the wheelchair. He took the shorts from her and cried out as he lifted his foot. "I guess it would help if you get them started, when I raise my feet.

Carefully turning the chair so he faced her, she knelt in front of him and focused on his right foot as he lifted it. His foot was shaking, but he managed to raise it high enough for her to slip the leg of the shorts over his foot. He groaned the whole time, but waited for her to say, "Okay, now the other side."

He eased his foot to the floor, and sighed in relief.

She slid the shorts above his knees. "Can you stand and pull them up?"

"Push me between the handrails."

She moved him by grasping the arms of the chair. She backed between the railings so she could remain in front of him. He was facing her as he lifted himself from the chair. He steadied himself and pulled the pants the rest of the way, under his gown, to his waist. He smiled at her and carefully returned to the chair.

"You have accomplished a lot, today, Mr. Storm. Do you want to return to your room now, or go to the galley for a cup of caff?"

"Actually, I've worked up an appetite. Let's go to the galley and get some food. You can tell my mother that I took you on a date."

"Mr. Storm, you have a sense of humor. I can't stand funny people."

He began wheeling himself toward the galley. "I've got to tell my parents that a sense of humor is necessary in any crackpot they intend to send my way."

Melody almost laughed when she heard him, but caught herself. "You go to the table, and I'll pull our meals."

He rolled his chair to the table and waited for her.

She set two cups of caff on the table. One with cream, she sat in front of him. She set a cup without cream, across from him. She went to the counter and returned with two steaming plates of food. She sat one plate, with utensils, in front of him, and carried the other around the table and set it by her caff. She looked across the table and saw he was staring, sadly, at the plate.

"Are you okay? Did I select a food you don't like?"

"No, it isn't that. You happened to select my favorite foods. This plate of food has brought back memories of the best of times."

Melody realized her mistake. She drew the foods he preferred without thinking. "What kind of memories? Perhaps a favorite restaurant where you enjoyed this same food?"

"It isn't that either." He hesitated to say more, but his heart was aching with the pain of holding everything inside. "Helga, my mother shouldn't have sent you here. She means well, but I hold someone else in my heart."

"I understand. Your mother told me about someone, but I can't remember her name. Don't worry, I will get you well and leave."

"Melody. Her name is Melody. At least that is the name I will always remember."

"Mr. Storm. You don't have to tell me anything. I'm here to help you get better." Melody felt like she was going to collapse. Her heart ached for him.

"She's the reason I considered giving up. She didn't love me and told me not to follow her. But I wanted to do one last thing to help her. To give her what she really wanted in life. A life that doesn't include me. Without her ever knowing, I've managed to bring her happiness."

"Mr. Storm. Please stop. You're causing me to be emotional." She hurriedly left the table and ran out of the building.

Cade watched her leave. "What's with her? I'm the one with an injured leg and a broken heart."

Sarah entered the room. "What happened to Helga? I saw her run from the building like it was on fire. Did you say something mean to her?"

"No. I thought she was a psychopath when I first met her, but I thought we were starting to hit it off." He paused for a moment. "I started telling her about Melody, and she got emotional. That's when she ran out."

"Cade, do you think you're the only person in the universe with a broken heart? She may have experienced the same kind of loss that you have known."

Cade hung his head. "I hadn't thought of that." He turned to Sarah. "Go bring her back. Tell her she is needed to get me back in bed." He hesitated a moment. "Tell her I'll try not to be funny, and I won't eat until she returns."

Sarah laughed. "Okay, I'll find her." She left the prefab and went to the cabin. She found Melody sitting in the living room, with Maska lying in her usual spot. "Has Maska recognized you?"

"She doesn't have to access my mind to recognize me."

"Do you think she will tell Cade?"

"No, we had girl talk."

"Did you remove your head cover? Cade may have detected you?"

"No, she understands human speech. It's only natural since Cade and I touch their minds using our language."

"Cade sent me to find you. He said he wouldn't be funny anymore if you came back."

Melody laughed. "Now that is funny." She stood. "Helga is still on the clock. Let's go torment my patient some more." They returned to the prefab and entered to find Cade waiting at the table.

Helga picked up the plates and carried them to the processor.

Cade said, "Hey. We haven't eaten yet."

"That food was cold. I'm drawing us fresh plates." She carried them to the table. "Are you going to eat with us, Sarah?"

"I have a report to finish. I'll look in on you later." She left the room.

"Helga, I'm sorry about earlier. I won't bring up any more personal stuff."

"That's all right. You didn't know that my heart yearns for one who is beyond my reach."

Cade swallowed a bite of food and pointed to her plate. "Go ahead and start eating before it gets cold again." He watched her take a bite of food. "If you ever need to talk to someone, I'm right here."

Helga looked up from her plate. "Are you this caring with everyone?" She hesitated. "You are burdened, and yet you would take time to listen to a stranger."

He picked up his cup and took a drink. "You're not a stranger. I've known you for at least four hours."

Helga laughed. "I thought you promised not to be funny."

"Your laugh is beautiful. You should do it more often by developing your sense of humor."

When they were finished eating, Helga said, "You've done well for your first day. Do you want to go back to bed? You could sleep in the regular bed in the corner of the room."

"I think it would be better to go back to the medical bed. I'll try to use the mechanical leg manipulators."

Sarah entered the galley. "I heard what you said. I'll be glad to help you onto the table and get it started."

"Thanks, but my official tormentor can help me." He turned to Helga. "Let's return to the torture chamber."

Melody smiled as she returned him to the medical suite. She stopped about three feet from the bed and locked the brakes. Moving to the front of the chair, she stooped to help him.

"Don't help. Let me try on my own."

She straightened and backed away.

Lifting his right leg, he groaned and grunted as he moved it clear of the footrest. He moved his foot slightly under the footrest and slowly lifted it until it was stowed. He repeated the process with his left foot.

"I am impressed, Mr. Storm. You did that quite nicely."

Grasping the arms of the chair, he tried to push himself up, but he couldn't quite do it. "Let me hold on to your arm."

She moved close to his injured side, and stood a little in front of the chair, facing him. She leaned forward and held the chair's right armrest. "Go ahead and pull yourself up."

He grasped her arm between her elbow and shoulder. "You have small arms. How did you ever manage to throw me over your shoulder?" He managed to stand. He released her arm and reached for, and grasped her hand. He stood still and closed his eyes. Her hand felt like Melody's. He inhaled a deep breath and a shock went through him. Her scent gave her away. He realized he was holding the hand of the woman he loved. A tear streaked his face.

"Are you okay, Mr. Storm?"

He cleared his throat and brushed away the tear. He noticed she was looking at his face. "I just felt a stabbing pain, but I'm okay now." He moved to the bed with her holding his hand. He placed his hands on the bed.

"Mr. Storm, it would be less painful if you turn your back to the bed and allow me to assist by lifting as you lift with your arms."

"Helga, have you lost your thirst for torture? I'm going to climb onto this table. I may scream a little, or maybe a lot, but I'm going to do it." Raising his good leg, he was able to settle it atop the bed. The right leg hurt worse than ever as his weight rested on it. Reaching across the bed and digging his fingers in as he moved ahead, his body raised higher as his left upper leg became perpendicular to the bed. Yelling loudly as he began bending the knee of his right leg, he lifted it high enough to rest next to his left knee. The pain was excruciating as he knelt there, but he was determined not to scream. He moved his upper body toward the head of the bed and eased his right hip and leg against the surface. He rolled so that he was face up. He ended up being close to the edge of the bed.

Helga went to that side of the bed and moved him toward the middle as gently as she could. "I could see you were in a terrible amount of pain. Why didn't you let me help you?"

He saw a tear trickle down her left cheek. He reached up with his right hand and gently brushed it away. "I'm fine. Don't be upset because I did it myself. If I had damaged myself, the blame would be on me."

"I'm not familiar with the controls on this table. I'll go get Sarah."

Sarah was watching through the one-way as Melody left. She watched as Cade brought his right hand near his face. He kissed the side of his finger. *Her tears! He knows who she is.* She slid the concealing cover into place and went to the great room. Melody was drinking a cup of caff. "I was watching you work with him. I believe you would be a great physical therapist."

"I'm good with him because I love him." She took another sip of caff. "He is so stubborn. If I weren't wearing this cap, I would have heard screams inside his head."

Sarah sighed. "I'll go in and start the knee manipulator. He might punch me out." She went into the room and moved to the side where the controls were located. Checking to make sure his legs were in the right position, she asked, "Are you ready for more pain?"

He took a deep breath. "Bring it on."

She started it on the lowest setting. She watched his face as his knees and hips were being worked. He didn't make a sound, but his face told a different story. "Let me know when you want to take a break."

He tersely asked, "How long should it run for best results?"

She realized he was forcing his words past the pain. "As long as possible. Usually, until a person wants to take a break from the worst pain."

"So, I could use this all night long?"

"Yes, but there is no need. You have already made great progress today, and actual walking is much better for your legs."

"How long before sunset?"

"About an hour, why do you ask?"

"We'll stop the machine in an hour, and I'll sleep in the other bed tonight. Helga can assist me."

"You seem to have adapted to her methods in a short time. Out of medical curiosity, why did you decide to work with her?"

"Mostly, it was because she reminded me of a drill sergeant. I didn't like her methods, but they were effective. I got so angry at her that the pain seemed less. I guess when telling me that others had broken hearts, you opened my eyes, and I sympathized with her."

"Why did you insist upon climbing on the table without assistance? Was it because of your sympathy for her?"

"When she helped me out of the chair, and held my hand." He didn't say anything for a minute. "I guess it dawned on me that under the drill sergeant façade, was a woman that I needed to respect." He hoped his near admission of his knowledge of her true identity, was smoothed over by his quick change of track.

"Helga is taking a break, but she will return at bedtime. If the pain gets too much, call me. We can always shut the machine down earlier."

"I've got this, Doc. Take a break." When she was gone, he closed his eyes and focused on his memories of Melody. The pain was gone as he visualized her face and pretty smile. He couldn't help but smile as he lay there in peace.

Sarah watched him through the one-way. "He has such a serene face with a wide smile stretched across his lips. Does she have this much effect on him?"

An hour later, Sarah entered the room, accompanied by Melody. Melody looked at his peaceful face with the broad smile still glowing. Melody whispered, "What could he be dreaming about?"

"I'm not sleeping. I'm remembering happy moments when I was with…" He opened his eyes. "I was thinking about my team."

Sarah turned off the machine. "I don't believe Helga knows about the team."

"Cade's mother told me about them. She said that Cade, a woman named Nizhoni, a panther, and an eagle all worked together, played together, and slept together."

Cade lifted his head and said, "Wait just a minute. That's misleading. The woman and I didn't sleep together in the sense of being intimate."

Helga shrugged. "Don't worry. Why should you worry about what I think?"

Cade sighed and lay back on the pillow. "You're right. What does it matter?"

Helga smiled. "If it makes you feel any better, I believe you."

"Why would you believe me?"

"I haven't known you long, but I recognize an honorable and trustworthy man when I see one. And you are one."

Cade grinned. "That sounds good, but I barely trust myself." He rolled onto his stomach and swung his legs over the edge. He slid over the edge, and his legs held his weight. "It's easier to get off than it was to climb on."

"Do you want me to bring the chair closer?"

"I believe I can walk to the other bed, if you hold my hand like you did earlier."

Helga took his hand. "Are you certain you are stable enough to walk without support?"

He looked at her and smiled. "I'm practically walking on air." He took one short step after another to begin with. At about the halfway point, he took longer steps and flexed his joints to a greater degree than necessary for the length of the step. When he reached the bed, he turned around and sat, with his feet resting on the floor.

Sarah patted him on the shoulder. "It looks like we found the best therapist to work with you."

Helga blushed noticeably. "I really did very little. He's doing all the work."

He gazed at her face. "I disagree. If not for you, I would have simply faded away."

She glanced at Sarah and then looked him in the eye. "Don't ever do that. Don't fade away. I've been told that you have a world full of people who adore you, the people of Faroe."

"If I ever feel like I'm fading away, I'll get my mother to send you to me."

"Sarah and I need to let you get some sleep. We'll work hard again tomorrow." They turned and left the room, dimming the lights down low as they went.

They stopped in the galley, and Sarah drew two cups of green tea. They sat in silence as they sipped the tea. Finally, Melody said, "This has been the longest day of my life. My energy is completely gone."

"I'm not surprised. Cade has covered light years today. When you showed up and pushed him, he began to push himself. Since his body is healed, I don't believe he can overdo it, but his pace may wear you down. Tomorrow, we need to slow him down a bit. In less than twelve hours today, he went from no motion to climbing on a bed. I've never seen anything like it." Sarah stood and stretched. "You need to get a good night's sleep tonight if you're going to keep pace with him tomorrow."

"I'll head over to the cabin. Even if I weren't this tired, I always slept well over there. See you in the morning."

Sarah watched her leave and started down the hall. She heard a sound and stopped. She realized the sound came from the medical suite. She returned to the galley and sat at the table. She pulled the monitor from her pocket and selected the cameras in the medical suite. "I guess he doesn't need much sleep after being in an induced coma for nearly four weeks." She watched as Cade made several laps around the suite, using the wheelchair like a walker. "He wears me out just watching him." After a few minutes, he left the room and turned in the direction of the fresher. She went to the hall entryway and saw him enter the fresher and close the door. She hurried down the hall to get in her room before he came out.

Chapter 25

Cade left his room and walked to the galley on the morning of his third day of rehab. Helga was sitting at the table drinking caff, and Sarah was sitting across from her. Cade selected his breakfast and carried it to the table with his cup of caff. He sat next to Helga. "Good morning. What are we going to do for rehab today?"

Sarah said, "Since you are walking without a limp or any support equipment, I thought you and Helga should walk around the property. The ground is not perfectly flat like these floors, so it will be beneficial for you to experience the outdoors on your last day of rehab."

"The last day? But I thought Helga would be here for another week or two."

Helga smiled. "I'm not leaving tomorrow. I want to enjoy the warm weather for a few days. Back home, it is early winter, and cold."

"Great. I'd like to show you around the area, if you like?" He took a bite of breakfast and followed it with a sip of caff.

Sarah said, "Take your time eating. Helga and I are going to Jace's ship for a few minutes. His ship came into port this morning, and he brought me something I requested."

"Okay. I'll be here, waiting."

When they were aboard the Hermes, Sarah led Melody to an empty berth. "We can talk in here." Sarah closed the door behind them. "This is my berth when traveling aboard the Hermes."

"Why the secrecy? What's going on?"

"I debated whether or not to tell you, but you should know. Remember your first day, when you helped Cade out of the wheelchair to get him on the table?"

"Yes, it's hard to forget him climbing onto the table. What of it?"

Sarah pulled the monitor out of her pocket. "Watch this." She ran the video to where he took her hand, and then stopped it. "Cade took your hand, and suddenly became still. The pain didn't move him or cause him to sway. He stood there."

"I don't understand."

"Watch this split screen. His back is to the camera on the left, and his face and chest are on the right. What do you see?"

"While he's standing still, he inhales a deep breath. But I still don't understand."

"This last segment will make it clear."

"He wiped my tears away and then kissed his hand. He recognized me. But how? Has the voice modulator in the mask stopped working?"

"It still alters your voice." She paused. "It's clear to me, but it doesn't seem logical. When he touched your hand, he recognized it was you. You don't wear a ring, and I can't see any defects that would be obvious to the touch. He takes in the breath right after touching your hand. I believe he can detect a scent that only he recognizes. I haven't noticed any cologne or anything that you wear to produce odors." She paused. "The main thing is that he knows, but he's playing along."

"Why would he do that?"

"Because he enjoys your company and knows you will be leaving soon. He's probably afraid you would leave sooner if he revealed his knowledge of your true identity."

"What should I do?"

"I understood that you were going to reveal your identity to him and proclaim your debt of gratitude to be repaid in kind. If that is the case, you should go ahead and do that today."

"That is what I planned to do, but I can't."

"Damn. I don't understand you two. There is no reason to remain apart, and this is the perfect opportunity for the two of you."

"I know you don't understand, but I will leave him a letter explaining how I feel. It's already written." She paused. "I would like for you to read it, so you can tell me what you think. Would you do that for me?"

Sarah nodded her head.

Melody pulled a folded paper from a pocket inside her medical jacket and handed it to her.

Sarah read the letter and glanced up at Melody with tears in her eyes. It's a very good letter. Don't change a thing." She took out a tissue and blew her nose. "This is the better way to let him know of your love." She dried her tears. "I think you should continue being Helga until you've left for home. Let's return to the prefab."

Cade was waiting at the door. He took Helga's hand and said, "Let me show you my favorite spot." They walked around the cabin and soon stood looking out over the lake."

Melody looked out into the water, and remembered Cade embracing her when she was sad. She smiled. "I bet it's a nice place for swimming. And look at those mountains in the distance. You can't find a view like that on many planets."

Cade stared out over the lake. "I think this would be a good place to settle down, but I will probably go wherever my possible future bride would want to live."

She looked at him. "You would really give this up for some woman?"

"If we love each other, why not? It's not about where we are, but where our hearts are." He paused, "If you don't mind a long walk, I'd like to show you the village. We could ride the horses if you like?"

"As your therapist, I opt for the walk."

"Okay. Do you mind if I hold your hand?"

"Well, I guess it would be okay."

He reached for her hand and gently grasped it as they walked. The people are very good neighbors. A strong woman warrior, joined another warrior in defeating an evil slaver who terrorized the town."

"You're being too modest. Your mother told me how you and a female beast master teamed up to free the people."

"Melody is the one who freed them, and the townspeople love her. They actually thought Nizhoni was Melody."

"Isn't Nizhoni the other team member your mother mentioned?"

"Yes, but all that is in the past. Now I'm where I was back on Arzor. Alone."

"You're not alone. I envy you because of all the friends you've made."

They were entering the village and people began to gather. Some of them were saying, "That's Melody. She's back." Cade glanced at her and saw a smile on her face. "Here's my favorite café; let's go in."

Irving met them when they entered. "I have not seen you in a long while, Mr. Storm. And you have the beautiful Melody with you today. Would you like some pie with your coffee?"

"That would be great." Cade noticed the crowd was growing inside the café. He leaned toward Helga and said softly, "They will inevitably believe you to be Melody. Just play along, and they will be happy."

Melody smiled. "What if you brought a blond woman here for a date? Would they still think her to be Melody?"

"Oh, no. They would threaten to tell Melody that I was unfaithful. They like her a lot more than they do me."

A little girl came over to Melody with a paper in her hand. "Miss Melody, I drew a picture of you shooting the metal man. Please take it."

Melody took the drawing and smiled. "I never looked that good. You are an artist." She folded the paper and put it in her pocket. "Thank you for the gift." She watched the little girl as she joined her mother in the crowd. "Is it always like this when you come to town?"

"No, sometimes the crowds are much larger."

Irving returned with the coffee and pie. He set them on the table. "Enjoy."

Melody took a bite of the pie and smiled. "This is really good, and coffee is a little smoother than caff. I would probably eat pie at least once a week if I lived here."

When they finished, Irving refused to be paid as he ushered them to the door. They moved through a large crowd as they began their walk up the hill. Cade asked, "Do you think you'll ever be back this way?"

"I don't know. I would like to, but it depends on how things work out. You know, if I find the love of my life and settle down, I'll probably never see this place again, unless my love happens to live here."

Cade's mind was spinning. He didn't want her to go. Just being near her brought him so much happiness. Cade's thoughts were interrupted by a wrist com request alert. He accepted the connection.

"Cade, this is Jace. I need to see you aboard my ship, priority red one."

"On my way." He turned to Helga. "I've got to report. You'll be safe walking back to the prefab." He broke into a run without waiting for her to reply.

"I'm going with you." Helga was running beside him. "I need to monitor the effect of stress you're putting on your leg by running."

Cade didn't reply, but maintained a pace that would not gas him. He reached the ship and slowed to a walk as he went up the gangplank.

Jace met him in the cargo bay, and glanced at Melody. "We have a level one emergency. Come with me to the conference room."

Cade fell in beside Jace, and noticed Helga was tagging along. "Helga, you can wait for me in the prefab. This is probably Patrol business."

"I am making it my business." She continued to follow them.

Jace stopped at the conference room door and looked at Helga.

"Jace, I told her to go back, but she didn't listen to me."

The lieutenant started to say something, but remained silent for a moment. He was looking at Helga's face. *I see a fire in her eyes, Melody's in Eagle Feather mode.* "She can come in, too." They entered the room and Jace motioned them to sit. "We have a situation." He pressed a button on his wrist, and the image of a planet appeared on a wall-mounted screen. "This is an extremely primitive planet and was only recently discovered and added to star charts." He displayed a second image. "This is one of the few images we have of the people living there. As you can see, they are brandishing crude metal swords and knives. Other images show they have bows and arrows as well."

Cade examined the scene. "They appear to be a reptilian race. Since the planet is a recent discovery, I guess we don't have much history."

Turning his attention from the screen, Jace looked at Cade. "You know about the Nautilus, but I didn't tell you about her sister ship, Discoverer. She was completed six months ago, and is now studying this planet which they named Desonia." He paused. "We have hours of video taken by Discoverer, and it is being studied."

Cade sighed. "The discovery of this planet can't be the reason you contacted me."

"Cade, because of your injury and recovery, I haven't been able to update you concerning the plot you uncovered during your time on New Terra. The Military has used the information from the captured computers to eradicate a big part of the war preparations being made by the rebels." He sighed. "But there is still a significant number of pirates roaming the lanes." After a short pause. "Six days ago, a pirate vessel attacked a transport owned by Central Control. The president of the Central Council and his daughter were on the transport. The ship was damaged and believed to be close to implosion, so the two were ejected in a life pod. A Patrol cruiser arrived at the scene and destroyed the pirate, and the transport was saved from destruction."

"So, the president and his daughter are somewhere on Desonia." Cade looked up at the ceiling as he began considering the small amount of information.

"Yes, but we know where they are, and it's not good." He brought up another image on the screen.

Cade stood and moved closer to the screen. A roughly made cage was suspended over a wide, circular opening in the ground. Two people were in the cage.

"The Discoverer scanned the pit, and found it to be three hundred feet in depth. There is liquid at the bottom that spectrometers show to be brackish water with a high alkali content."

"Jace, why don't you just stun the whole bunch and retrieve the prisoners?"

"We did a test run to see how the natives would be affected. We landed a scout some distance from the pit, and marines fired stunners at natives who attacked them. They are not affected by stunners. We considered blasting our way, sacrificing many of the inhabitants against our own laws. Even though they are hostile, they are not responsible for the presence of the prisoners. They are essentially innocent, and carrying out some kind of ritual or ceremony that they practice. There is another reason that becomes apparent with close scrutiny of the system securing the cage."

Cade examined it for a moment. "It's a primitive dead man switch." If anything happens to this guy…" Cade pointed to a Desonian seated with a loop of rope in his hand. "The rope will retract into a hole in the rock, and the cage will drop." Cade looked intently at the mechanism. "How did they drill a hole in the rock and rout a rope through there? It is very complicated for such a primitive race."

Jace sighed, "The jailor at the switch is relieved every ninety minutes. It seems they don't want a tired hand controlling the rope."

Cade forgot about Melody sitting in the seat next to the one he vacated. "If I had Nizhoni, I believe I've found a way to render the dead man inoperable."

"Why do you need Nizhoni? I'll go with you on this mission."

Cade turned and looked at Helga and saw her standing with her fists clenched. "I can't put you in that kind of danger."

"Drop the charade. You know who I am." She removed her hat and the mask under it, in one motion.

Cade inhaled and closed his eyes as he heard her in his head. He opened his eyes and saw she wasn't speaking, but communicated only by thought. He silently answered her, *This, has nothing to do with you, and you should go.*

I will not go. I'm as much a part of the team as Nizhoni.

Melody, your people need you, and you don't owe me anything. Follow your heart back to your world.

Don't try to tell me where my heart is, and I'm no longer Melody.

Jace broke into their argument. "Cade, I see you and Eagle Feather are having a lover's quarrel. Can't that wait until some other time? The two of you are creeping me out with this silent verbal warfare, and Eagle Feather looks like she's going to punch a hole in my ship. Respect me enough to use verbal communication."

Eagle Feather unclenched her fists and demurely said, "I'm sorry, Jace. Cade and I will settle this on our way to Desonia."

"We are not settling anything because you are not going."

"Cade, don't let your misplaced feelings for me cause you to be so blind. It will take both of us and the animals to accomplish this mission." As soon as the words were out of her mouth, she regretted them. *By wanting to go along, to protect him, I've just pushed him further away.*

"Me and my feelings are capable…"

Jace interrupted them again. "You two are driving me crazy. I'd tell you to get married, but you already act like you are. Enough is enough. Focus on the task at hand, and Eagle Feather will be part of the team."

Melody looked at Cade. Flashing a smug smile, she said, "Huh!"

Cade shook his head. "How childish." He turned to Jace. "Show us the scenes with the natives again." Cade studied the scene carefully as Melody moved beside him. He looked at her. "What do you see, Melody?" He couldn't bring himself to call her Eagle Feather. Melody was the name she carried when he fell in love with her. She was near enough that he detected the scent he was so familiar with.

She pointed to a statue resting on a ledge some distance in the background. "Can that be magnified?"

Jace magnified the image and said, "Well, I'll be."

"Where's my ship, Searcher, located?" Cade lifted his left hand to cup his chin as he considered the apparent idol sitting on the ledge.

Jace was in the process of closing a communication over his wrist communicator. "The Searcher is actually on the way. Zina says they will arrive in less than an hour." He looked up from his wrist com device.

Cade started to communicate with Melody through mind touch, but remembered Jace's request. "Melody, do you have your other clothing?"

Jace answered, "Her kit is still in her berth aboard this ship."

This time, he used mind touch, *Summon the team, and show them what we face. I've always been hesitant to put them in harm's way, so let them know it is dangerous and the decision to stay or go, is theirs to make. I need to gather my kit.*

You can depend on me. She turned and left the room.

Jace asked, "Are you going to ask Zina for help?"

"You saw the idol. It was a Zacathian female. If she's willing, I think she can provide a diversion while Melody and I save the president and his daughter. There is still a lot to work out, but it will be best to do it while we travel. Time may be short."

Jace smiled. "It's good to see you and scary woman back on the same team."

"I agree. I wish it could be permanent, but we have different goals."

Jace patted him on the shoulder. "Those differences are invisible or non-existent in my view. The problem is that neither of you will give in to your heart."

Cade headed for the door. "I need to get my stuff while we wait for the Searcher." Stopping short of the door, he pulled a folded paper from his pocket and walked back to Jace. "I almost forgot this. Please file it for me at your earliest convenience."

Jace opened it and read the contents before looking at Cade. "You're sure you want to give the Searcher to Zina?"

"I would have done it sooner, but she wasn't ready. The ship belongs with her."

"What do you mean when you say she wasn't ready?"

"She's no longer estranged from her family and her world, and her independent life is no longer necessary. She discovered Zacathia had changed. Instead of her being an aberration, she is now the norm. I'm happy for her."

Jace grinned. "I'll file the change of ownership for you."

Chapter 26

Cade and Melody watched as the Searcher gently settled next to the scout. Maska and Aeolus waited expectantly nearby. Zina appeared at the top of the ramp with Zangari standing next to her.

Zina hurried down the ramp, ahead of Zangari, and wrapped Cade in a tight hug. "I've missed you." She released him, turned to Melody, and embraced her. "I'm so happy to see you here, with Cade."

Cade said, "We're together because she's here as a member of the team. We have a mission, and need your help."

She released Melody and took a step back, but gently grasped the woman's right hand. "I'm so sorry. I was hoping the two of you had come to your senses."

Melody said, "Don't worry about us, Zina; it's a long story."

Releasing her hand, Zina said, "I'll continue to hope there will be much more added to your story in the years ahead."

Listening to them, Cade felt a deep sadness as he realized how brief his remaining time with Melody really was. He noticed two more Zacathians standing at the top of the ramp. "Who are your friends, Zina?"

Zina laughed. "I guess they are my friends, but they are also my parents." She motioned for her parents to join them. "Come down and meet my adopted children." They came down the ramp and stood beside Zina."

"Cade and Melody, this is my father, Zartol, and my mother, Allia."

Cade bowed his head. "I'm honored to meet the parents of Zina."

Allia smiled. "Zina has told us so many things about the warrior, Cade, and the beautiful Melody."

Melody blushed. "I'm afraid Zina exaggerated concerning me. I will always hold her in my heart like a sister."

Cade held up an electronic storage unit. "I have video files that will be of special interest to our Zacathian friends, and it has to do with a mission that will involve Zina."

"I get to participate? Let's see what's on that storage unit." She turned and led them to her science laboratory, where she took the device and connected it to her computer. She selected the first image."

Zartol leaned toward the screen. "Can that be a Zacathian statue?"

Allia was leaning in to look. "Zina, put that image on the big screen." A larger display appeared on the wall to their right. Allia moved closer and said, "Magnify the rock to the right of the statue." The view zoomed in on the rock. Allia turned and looked at her husband with amazement showing on her reptilian face, neck frills were fully extended and were a luminescent blue. "Tizala! Her name is chiseled into the face of the rock."

Zina said, "Wait, I thought she wasn't a real person, only a myth."

Melody asked, "Who is Tizala?"

Cade interrupted, "We will have time to talk about this on the way, time is of the essence."

Zartol asked, "Are we going to the place on the screen?"

Cade replied, "We're going there, and I need our pilot and navigator on the bridge. We need to secure for lift."

Melody focused her mind on the team. "The team is settled in their area, and Maska reports they are ready."

Zina and Zangari exited the lab with Cade. Cade said, "I'm going to bring the scout aboard before we secure for launch. Zina, contact Jace when you get to the bridge. Tell him to transmit the route coordinates for Desonia."

Zina headed for the lift.

"Cade turned to Melody, you and I will square away the cargo bay for the scout."

Thirty minutes later, Cade and Melody were strapping into jump seats on the bridge.

Zina announced, "All departments secured, external ventilation secured and hatches dogged."

Zangari thumbed the com unit. "Faroe Space Port Control, this is Searcher requesting launch clearance."

"Searcher, you are cleared, no traffic within thirty thousand miles."

Cade felt the characteristic slight vibration as the magnetic flux field generators lifted the ship through the atmosphere.

Zina checked her navigation readouts. "We will reach the transition point in one hour and fifteen minutes. Hyper corridor transition will be six hours and ten minutes."

Cade released his restraints. "Zina, let's go to the galley so I can give you a quick overview. You should have your parents meet us there." He started to leave the bridge and noticed Melody wore a frown and wasn't making a move to follow him. "Aren't you coming too?"

Her face brightened. "I didn't think you wanted me there." She released her restraints.

"You're part of the team. Let's go."

Cade entered the galley and drew two cups of caff. He settled in a chair and set Melody's cup at the place next to him.

Melody took her seat and lifted her cup to take a sip. She sighed as she set the cup in front of her and stared into the liquid.

Cade turned his head to look at her. He resisted the urge to reach for her hand, as he had done with Helga. "What are you thinking about?"

"The first time I sat in this galley and drank a cup of caff. I've been in here so many times, but it's coming to an end. It felt like family with Zina, and being part of the team."

Cade struggled to honor his promise to her. His vow that he wouldn't bother her with declarations of his love, held his heart in a self-imposed prison.

Zina and her parents entered the galley, allowing Cade to turn his thoughts away from his love. Zina grabbed a cup of caff, and her parents did the same. She sat across from Cade. "What do you want me to do when we arrive in Desonia?"

"There may be an element of danger, but we are tasked with saving a man and his daughter, being held prisoner by the natives. It has already been proven that stunners do not affect the inhabitants, and we don't want to use lethal force unless there is no other way."

Zartol sat down and placed his cup on the table. "Since you invited my wife and me, I assume you expect our opinions."

Cade nodded his head. "Since there is risk involved, I believe family should be a part of the decisions that need to be made."

"I think I know what you have in mind. Zina will approach the natives with the hope that they will respect her, providing a diversion while you rescue the captives."

"That is the basic plan, but if Zina or her parents, are not willing to do it, we'll find another way."

Allia cleared her throat. "May I say something?"

Cade smiled. "That's why we're here. Every opinion matters."

"I believe there may actually be no danger to us. Think about it. The captives are still alive when they could have easily been killed. And the cage system where the two are held, seems to be more of a deterrent to prevent unwelcomed visitors, than a means of making sacrifices." Allia took a drink of her caff and waited for someone else to speak.

Cade nodded his head as he considered the evidence. "I believe you're right. It may be enough for Zina to approach them in peace."

Zartol raised his left hand and scratched behind his right ear flap as if considering the information. "I think it would be best if Allia and I approach them instead. We are older, and will be closer in appearance to the aged Tizala."

Zina asked, "Father, are you sure about this?"

Allia answered her. "I agree with your father. We will approach them without weapons."

Melody was deep in thought. "I, too, believe it will work. What if the natives will be excited to meet you, and the fellow holding the rope lets it go if he gets excited."

Zangari's voice came over the com system, interrupting the meeting. "Zina, we have ten minutes to transition."

Zina stood. "We'll have time to discuss this further after we enter hyperspace." She left for the bridge.

Zartol left his seat and held Allia's hand as she stood. "We're going to our berth and rest. Wake us if needed."

Cade nodded, and remained seated.

Melody held the cup with both hands, turning it round and round as she stared into it. "Are you going to stay in the galley during the transition?"

"Yes. The transitions are so smooth, there is no need to strap in."

She continued to look at the cup. "Is it okay if I ask Zina to take me home after the mission?"

He wanted to say no, as he turned his head slightly to look at her hands holding the cup. "Yes. I'm sure she will be happy to make the trip. She thinks of us as her children."

"Did you load the Scout because you're planning on taking it back to Faroe, after we've rescued the captives?" She continued to twirl the cup between her hands.

"No, I'm going to stay with the Searcher." He watched her stop turning the cup, and she rested her hands on either side of it.

Her voice was soft as she asked, "Why will you stay, when you could be home a lot sooner?"

He sighed and turned in his chair to face her. "Last time you left, I didn't tell you goodbye. I felt bad about that. Though you don't feel the same as I do, we have been through a lot together. We are at least friends, and friends have to say goodbye when the time comes."

"Cade, I've lied to you about my feelings." She reached out to grasp his right hand. "I have strong…"

He interrupted her, pulling his hand away. "Don't say it, Melody. I refuse to let you commit to me out of gratitude, and a sense of obligation. Sometimes, I let selfishness take control of me. I convince myself to accept you even if you wind up hating me, but I can't do it. During our briefing, you said my feelings were misplaced." He stood. "I no longer hold you so dear, and have moved on. We need to focus on the mission. This is the last one we'll do together." The Star Hyper Drive began its hum as he left the galley.

Melody remained seated at the table, rotating the cup between her hands as she quietly murmured, "I did too good a job of convincing him that I didn't love him."

Zina entered the galley. "Mind if I join you for a cup?"

Melody smiled. "I need to ask a big favor of you anyway."

The Zacathian took a seat across from her. "What kind of favor?"

Clearing her throat, she began to feel the impact of her conversation with Cade. Trying to stifle her tears, she managed to choke out her request. "Can you take me to New Terra after the mission?" Sobbing louder, she wiped at her tears.

"Why are you so upset? It's no problem; I'll take you home." Leaving her seat, Zina went around the table to sit next to the weeping girl and hugged her. "I don't think it's the ride home that's upsetting you. Is it Cade?"

She freed herself from Zina's arms. "No. It's me. I spent so much time lying to Cade, pushing him away from me, that he doesn't believe me when I try to confess my love for him. He thinks I feel gratitude and an obligation to stay with him, because of all he has done."

"Should I talk to him? I've recognized, along with everyone else, that you two are in love."

"No, don't talk to him about this. I've written a letter telling him how he can find out the truth of my love for him." She pulled an envelope from within her blouse and laid it on the table. "I have one other favor to ask of you. Will you give this letter to him after you return to Faroe?"

"Why not now?"

"If he reads the letter, and comes for me all the way from there, I will know he is willing to accept a major flaw I have, and that he believes in my love for him."

Zina was curious. "What flaw would that be?"

"The one that has caused me to push him away." She looked at her hands resting on the table. "Because of the things I had to endure, I hated all men and shuddered at the thought of ever being intimate with any man. When I met Cade, I discovered my ability to feel love still existed. I didn't cringe at his touch, but welcomed it. I fear this limited way of showing my love for him, is all the affection I'll be able to share, a touch and a warm embrace. I believe Cade will not consider being with me if I can't…" She fell into silence, wringing her hands in frustration. "I've discovered that I need more than my opinion about whether he can love me, and stay with me. My heart belongs to him, and I don't want to live the rest of my life wondering what might have been. If he comes for me, I will have my answer."

Zina rested her right hand on Melody's entwined, trembling hands. "I was bonded with a human for more than twenty-five years. Even though it was physically impossible for us to be intimate in that way, we loved each other dearly. I slept in his arms every night, even on the last days when he was near death. I believe Cade will love you even if you can't give your entire self to him." She picked up the envelope and placed it inside her tunic.

"My entire self? That's right! I hadn't considered that."

Zina looked puzzled. "What did you not consider?"

"The entirety of who I am. Thank you, Zina. You've exposed an element I had not thought about."

"I did? I must be a really good counselor, because I have no idea what you're talking about."

"If things work out, I'll explain it another time. Right now, I need to get some rest." She left the galley.

Zina rose from her seat and went to her berth. Removing the letter from her tunic, she opened a drawer and lay the letter inside. She left her quarters and returned to the bridge.

Cade entered the bridge, after four hours in hyper-space, settling into the jump seat behind Zangari. "Zina, how long before emergence?"

"One hour and fifty minutes."

"Announce a crew meeting in ten minutes, in the galley. Zangari can hold down the fort for you. Make sure to ask your parents to attend." As Zina made the announcement over the com, Cade left the seat and headed to the galley. Entering, he found Zartol and Allia already seated, drinking caff. He drew a cup and moved to sit across from them. Zina entered, and Melody followed, accompanied by Riley, who was having a conversation with her. Cade waited for everyone to be seated as Riley settled next to him.

Cade looked to Allia and asked, "What can you tell us about Tizala?"

"I have been studying the archive information stored in Zina's laboratory computer, and added to my limited knowledge. Tizala was in the last octet of her expected life cycle, when she announced that she and her mate were leaving for a planet they had stumbled upon some fifty years earlier. She said they were going to study forerunner ruins on the planet, and provide help for the primitive inhabitants of that world, which she did not identify. The ruling scientific council protested her intentions, stating she would be needlessly interfering with the native population's development." Allia paused as she glanced at Zina. "Tizala chose to ignore the protests on the grounds that she was performing an act of humanitarian aid, and that the natives were stalled in their natural development."

Melody said, "I thought the Central Council had laws against interference."

Zartol smiled as he responded, "The Central Council did not yet exist. After Tizala left, Zacathia instituted the noninterference laws, which were adopted fifty years later by the newly formed alliance, called Central Control."

Taking a drink of caff, Cade set the cup down and sighed. I have been studying the video, trying to find a way to secure the cage without the natives spotting me. There is no access that will allow an undetected attempt on the cage device." He paused. "After considering our earlier meeting, I believe our only recourse is to approach the natives openly. It seems they hold Tizala in great respect. Here's what I think. We land some distance from the prison. Zina and Zangari will carry two chairs out and set them up, side by side. Zartol and Allia will exit and sit on the two chairs. I will escort Zartol, with Aeolus on my shoulder perch. Melody, with Maska by her side, will accompany Allia to her seat. When I was in the military, I took x-tee training concerning dealing with primitive races. Since these natives are somewhat primitive, they will be curious because of their superstitions. We will need to establish communication of some sort for any of this to work. If we can gain their trust and cooperation, Allia can direct them to take me to the prisoners for their release. There's a lot of unknowns, but I believe Tizala had a good relationship with the natives."

Zartol smiled. "I like the plan. I assume we will go without weapons."

Looking at the faces around the table, Cade replied, "Since the Patrol has shown aggression by testing their stunners, the natives will recognize any weapons and consider us invaders." He looked around the table. "If anyone has a better idea, I'm willing to listen."

Allia smiled. "We Zacathians always seek peace. Tizala would have approached them without weapons, and their reverence of her testifies to their acceptance of her. I believe in the plan."

No one else had anything to add, so Cade said, "Let's all be ready to play our parts. Melody will go down to the hold and present the plan to the animals. If anyone comes up with something I've missed, feel free to let me know. That's all for now." As everyone filed out, Cade said, "Zina, I need to meet with you for a minute."

Zina settled in the seat next to him and asked, "Is anything wrong?"

He placed his left hand on her right hand. "The Searcher is yours."

Surprise shown on her face. "What do you mean?"

"I no longer need the ship, and it really belongs to you anyway, and I won't listen to any arguments. I've already transferred ownership to you."

Tears flowed down her cheeks. "I was going to ask about leasing the Searcher. My mother and father want to seek knowledge with me, and Zangari has asked me to bond with him."

"I am happy for you. I could tell Zangari was smitten from the first time he saw you." He leaned close enough to give her a hug. "It looks like things are falling in place for you, and it couldn't happen to a finer person."

"Are you sure giving the Searcher away is good for you?"

"I still have the scout, and Jace says the Patrol is keeping an eye open for a freighter for me to use for my horse ranch." He stood and said, "Let's have another cup of caff to celebrate the new owner of the Searcher." He drew two cups and returned to sit beside her. "Just remember one thing. You'll need to keep in touch." They both took a drink and sat for a while, as Zina told him about plans to pay another visit to the artificial world created by the forerunners.

Chapter 27

The Searcher settled quietly in a large clearing. Zina looked at her biosensor data as Allia entered the bridge to stand next to her. Zina said, "We have a very large audience within the tree line. Let's hope they're not trigger-happy." She paused for a moment. "External audio sensors have recorded some chatter between the natives."

Allia smiled. "They are speaking a broken form of northern Zacathian. We should be able to interact with them. Let's go, daughter, it's showtime." With the ship secured for planet-side operations, Zangari joined them as they made their way to the cargo hold.

Dressed in his leather, native clothes, Cade stood in the cargo bay, with the Yoris hide shoulder perch covering his left shoulder. Melody stood next to him wearing the leather clothing Cade had sent to her by Nizhoni back on New Terra. She wore her hair in a long braid with the tiara Cade had given her, encircling her head and resting against the headband, an inch above her eyes.

He looked at her and resisted the urge to tell her how beautiful she looked. "I've never seen you wear Eagle Feather's costume and tiara." He thought about how he had them designed for her restoration act.

"These weren't the clothes I wore as Eagle Feather. I value them because they were a gift from Red Arrow, and I like them."

Hoping Nizhoni had not broken her promise, Cade asked, "Who's the Red Arrow?"

"He was the warrior, along with Nizhoni, who made my restoration possible." She did not reveal her knowledge of the Red Arrows true identity. Cade already believed her feelings for him were merely out of appreciation.

"Jace told me you were restored to your former position and life. I'm happy for you."

The four Zacathians joined them. Zina and Zangari each carried a chair.

Cade asked, "Are you ready to begin?"

As she activated the hatch, Zina said, "Ready as we'll ever be." The ramp rolled out and rested on purple-colored grass. Zina and Zangari walked out slowly, side by side. They stopped about twenty feet from the ramp, and after testing the firmness of the surface, set the chairs on the ground. They each took a position behind the chair they had carried.

Allia exited the ship with Melody following close behind. Maska slinked alongside. Maska issued a satisfactory growl that elicited excited chatter from within the trees and undergrowth. Allia settled in one of the chairs, and Melody halted alongside Zina, so the three females and Maska were on one side.

Zartol exited next, followed by Cade with Aeolus perched on his shoulder. Zartol took the other seat, with Cade settling next to Zangari.

Raising her voice, Allia said, "We come in peace, as did our sister, Tizala." The chatter from within the forest quieted. After five minutes passed, one of the natives emerged timidly from its concealment within the purple undergrowth of the forest.

The native was reptilian, and resembled the Zacathians, with differences. He did not have hair on his head, whereas the Zacathians had varying color iridescent hair. There were no ear flaps but small openings served as his hearing organs, with neck frills which were larger than those of the Zacathians. Standing about five feet in height, with a very slender build, he wore rough clothing and sandal-like footwear. "I greet you on behalf of the Aikeery people. I am Amil, leader of my tribe." He bowed for a moment and then straightened. "How may we be of service to those who are kin to Tizala, our honored teacher?"

Allia smiled. "We, of Tizala's world, only recently discovered your existence." She paused. "We were fortunate to find you because two of our friends made an emergency landing on your world. Their transport went through difficulty, causing them to come here. We know that you feared them and have them in a cage."

Amil sank to his knees as he said, "My apologies. We did not intend harm to them."

"Do not worry. We understand." She raised her arm, and, pointing toward Cade, she said, "Please escort my servant, Cade, to our friends so that we may bring them here."

Amil rose to his feet and beckoned for another native to leave the concealment of the trees. A female, slightly shorter than Amil, approached. She wore similar clothing, but her slender body was obviously female. Her head was covered with thin strips or ridges of red and green in color. The ridges ran from forehead to the back of her head, giving the appearance of hair, but was more like the flesh of her neck frills. Both natives had very human-appearing eyes and mouths, but their noses were flattened with two horizontal slits. Amil said, "This is Kareel, my mate. She will guide Cade to those you seek."

Cade moved to stand slightly in front of Zartol. He sent Aeolus skyward. "I will follow Kareel."

The female wore a surprised look. "You speak our language too?"

Cade smiled and nodded his head. The girl turned and he followed her into a path cutting through the forest. The natives were losing their initial fear and were slowly moving into the open, giving in to their curiosity. As Kareel led him along the pathway, signalers among the natives voiced whistling sounds that were repeated by others further ahead, announcing Cade's approach to the cage area. The vegetation was a riot of purple, red and yellow. Looking upward, Cade saw a lavender sky with white puffy clouds drifting across its expanse. They finally entered the clearing where the cage was located. He noticed the cage had already been swung away from its previous position, and now rested on solid ground.

The male captive said, "Thank the creator! You're a welcomed sight."

Cade opened the cage. "Mr. President, I'm Cade Storm of the Space Patrol. We have a ship waiting to transport you home."

The president left the cage. "My daughter has an injured ankle and needs assistance."

Cade looked at the injured woman. Her clothes were torn and filthy. Even though the dirt was crusted on her face and arms, with her hair tangled and full of dirt, her beauty shown through. He stepped into the cage and said, "If you will allow, I'll carry you to the ship."

She smiled through the dirt. "I regret being seen in this condition. You may carry me."

He knelt next to the woman where she sat, and carefully slipped his left arm under her legs, and his right behind her back, under her left arm. "If you can, put your arm around my neck." He noticed her right ankle was swollen and purple. He lifted her and backed out of the cage.

Kareel led him and the president back to the clearing where the Searcher was, and Cade was surprised to see the Hermes sitting nearby in the clearing. Zartol and Allia were still in their seats, facing a multitude of natives sitting on the ground in front of them. The two Zacathians were engaging in conversation with the natives. He saw Sarah rush toward him as she exited the Hermes.

He stopped as Sarah looked at the injured ankle, while Jace exited the Hermes and moved to help the president into the ship.

"Cade, bring her into the Hermes, and I'll treat that injury."

Cade carried her into the decontamination chamber of the medico.

Sarah said, "Sit her on that chair. I'll remove her filthy clothes, and she will be showered and decontaminated."

Cade turned to leave, and the woman said, "I'm Lillia, Cade. Do not leave; I'll need your help to enter the medico."

Cade nodded, stepped out of the decontamination room, and stood with his back to the glass enclosure until Sarah said, "You can carry her to the knitter."

Cade turned to see her clad in a white gown. He went in and lifted her as he did earlier. Moving to the knitter, he carefully lowered her onto the table. He turned to leave.

"Please stay for a while." Lillia's voice had a musical quality.

He turned to see Sarah adjusting the knitter arm assembly over the ankle.

She looked up and said to Cade, "It's a severe sprain, no broken bones. It should only take an hour to repair the tissue." She stepped away from the knitter. "I'm going to check on the president's condition, so it will be helpful if you stay here, with the patient." As she left, Cade moved to stand next to the bed.

"Do you have much pain?"

She smiled. Her face and hair, though not brushed, were clean, and there was a radiance about her. "No, it doesn't hurt when I don't walk on it." She hesitated before saying more. "I appreciate you carrying me so far. Forgive my boldness, but I am from Arcturus Three. Are you bonded to a mate?"

He tried to maintain a passive expression. "No, I'm not bonded."

"Then you must have a girlfriend."

"I don't have a girlfriend either."

Lillia smiled. "I think you and I should get to know one another."

Cade said, "I'm sure your father would not appreciate me taking any interest in his daughter. After all, you are an Arcturian, and that race sees the rest of us as inferior."

"You are correct concerning Arcturian racist ideas, but my family does not ascribe to those attitudes."

"I don't think it's a good idea for us to be anything other than friends. Even if you and your father are open to the idea, your colleagues on Arcturus, would probably make your lives miserable."

"I'm not giving up on you. You saved my life and stirred my heart."

"Lillia, you know nothing about me, and only known of my existence for an hour. You should never allow yourself to seek a close relationship that quickly."

"You are aware that my race can see into the minds of others. With your permission, I can know all about you in a few minutes."

"No, I don't want you probing around in my head. I know some Arcturians can control others with their minds. That would definitely cause me to dislike you."

"I am only level one and cannot control people. It hurts that you would think that of me."

Cade noticed the president had entered the room.

He approached Cade. "I am Colmus, and Jace told me you are Cade, the man who prevented a systems war."

"I'm pleased to meet you, Mr. President. Jace has overstated my part. There were a lot of people involved in bringing down the plotters."

Smiling, he said, "It will give me great pleasure if you will use my name from now on." He looked at his daughter. "How are you doing, my dear?"

"I'm doing very well, with Cade taking time to talk with me."

Colmus smiled as he rested his hand on her shoulder. "We will soon travel home aboard this ship." He turned from her and said to Cade, "Let's step outside for a moment."

They left the medico, but remained in the cargo hold. "Cade, I heard my daughter's conversation with you. I find it very interesting, because she has never warmed up to a man the way she has with you."

"I apologize if I've done anything that she may have misconstrued."

"I know you aren't responsible for her being infatuated. She sees you as the one who saved her from death." He paused. "If you should ever develop feelings for her, I'm fine with that."

Cade said, "My grandfather used to tell me that a knight has shining armor only as long as he stays on his horse. Let him fall, and the armor loses its luster. You have a beautiful daughter, but I must confess I lost my heart to someone who is no longer here. I may never be free of her memory."

Colmus sighed. "I know how you feel. Lillia's mother died shortly after giving birth to her. I have never been interested in another woman. I hope you can eventually leave those memories in the past, something I have been unable to do."

"I'm sorry about your wife. You're fortunate to have Lillia to love." He paused. "I should probably return to the Searcher for debriefing the crew." He shook hands with Colmus and left for the Searcher.

As soon as he left the Hermes, he saw Zartol and Allia were still interacting with the natives. He boarded the Searcher and went up to the galley to find a very animated Zina talking to Zangari and Melody. He asked, "What has gotten you so excited?"

Zina said, "We've contacted the Ministry of Science and Exploration on our home planet. We requested permission to study the inhabitants of this world and aid them with education and other needs. We will also explore the forerunner ruins that Tizala was studying before she died."

"Looks like I will need to find another ride."

"No. I'm going to take Melody home, and then return you to Faroe. Mother and father are going to remain here. Jace is leaving a scout for them to use for living quarters and meals while we are gone."

Riley's voice came over the ship's internal com system. "Cade, you have a visitor. Can I bring her up?"

"It'll be okay." Cade drew a cup of caff as he considered what he wanted to eat. It had been a long time since the last meal.

"Hi, Cade, it's me. I was wondering if you would dine with me before our ship leaves."

He turned to see Lillia's smiling face. Her hair was neatly brushed, and was the color of burnished copper. "Sure, I was just deciding what I wanted."

"I actually used the galley on the Hermes and made selections for a picnic. If we were on Arcturus, I would prepare the meal for you myself."

He glanced at Melody and saw an odd look on her face. *Perhaps she won't be so intent on comforting me because of obligation. She will see that I'm okay, and know that I've put my feelings aside.* "Sounds great, let's go on a picnic. Hopefully, there are no ants in the area." He disposed of his caff and joined her at the door. She reached out and took his hand as they walked toward the lift.

Melody watched, emotionlessly, as they departed. *I realize my hopes have been in vain. He can obviously move ahead without me in his life. Now, I have to find a way to live without him.*

Cade enjoyed the time spent with Lillia. She was extremely intelligent and had a very strong sense of humor. They talked and laughed until they heard the Hermes' klaxon sound recall. He stood and gave her a hand. "It's time for you to go aboard the Hermes."

She picked up the container Jace had given her for the food. "Father told me about your heartache. If you ever need a willing ear to listen, you know how to find me."

He walked her to the Hermes ramp. She suddenly dropped the container and threw her arms around his neck, and her lips met his. He was almost thrown off balance and grasped her waist to steady them both. It was a long, sweet kiss, and Cade finally had to push her gently away.

She looked down at the ground and said, "I just couldn't go without a kiss. I'll never forget you, Cade." She retrieved the container and went up the ramp.

Melody stood just inside the cargo bay of the Searcher. She witnessed the kiss, which caused her even more heartache than she thought. *We were so close and never shared a kiss in all that time. I am such a fool.* She turned and went up to her berth and settled onto her bunk. She didn't shed any tears as she tried to push him from her mind.

One hour and thirty minutes after entering Hyper Space, Cade couldn't sleep. He lay on his bunk, staring up at the overhead plating, but seeing Melody's face staring back at him. He closed his eyes, but found himself gazing into her deep, dark eyes. He turned on his right side and imagined her scent. He sat up abruptly. Resting his elbows on his knees, he cradled his face with his hands. He said to himself, "How can I forget her? The only solution is to find someone I love more than her, but that isn't possible. There's not enough of my heart left to ever find that much love." Rising from the bunk, he paced back and forth across the length of his cabin. Deciding to visit the animals in the cargo hold, he left the room and soon stepped off the lift in the hold. Melody was sitting on the straw, stroking Maska's back. Aeolus nestled in the hay next to the woman, turning her raptor head to look at Melody's face.

Clearing his throat to announce his presence, he approached them. Putting on a smile, he pushed sadness to the back of his mind. "I see you had the same idea as me."

She looked up at him. "I guess so. I thought to spend some time with the team before…, before I have to leave them."

He sat on the hay, a few feet on the other side of Maska. "You'll probably see them many times in the future. I'm sure to be visiting New Terra when I have stock to sell."

She looked away from him. "I have grown accustomed to mind talk. I took it for granted, but realize I will never have that experience again." She looked at him. "I know you will probably visit the people on New Terra. Do not plan on seeing me. This journey home, is the last time we will meet.”

Cade’s heart burned like fire as he heard her words. The air left his lungs, suffocating him. Struggling to maintain control, he said, “There’s no reason why we can’t be friends.”

She stood and brushed straw from the long skirt she wore. “I can’t be your friend.” She turned away from him and walked to the lift.

As she rode up and out of sight, he felt like chasing after her. He suddenly realized the animals were silent. They usually made mind talk when they were together. He turned his mind to Maska. *“Why no talk?”* The cat stared at him and then stretched out on the hay, ignoring him. Cade realized the animals were giving him the silent treatment. Rising from the hay, he went to the galley. He drew a cold drink and sat at the table, drinking slowly as he thought about the times he spent with Melody. Lowering his head to his arm, where it rested on the table. He fell asleep, thinking of her.

A sound woke him. Zina’s voice sounded over the ship’s com system. “Emergence in two minutes.”

Cade got up and carried his glass to the receptacle. He drew a cup of caff and settled in his chair at the table. *We’re about an hour and a half away from goodbye. I knew the time was coming, but it is a time I’d rather not face.”*

Chapter 28

The Searcher settled on New Terra, within sight of the Sioux fortress. Cade was waiting in the cargo bay for Melody. She descended on the lift, with her kit in one hand and a duffel in the other.

Cade opened the cargo bay hatch and deployed the ramp. She approached him and walked on past, stepping onto the ramp. He said, "Goodbye, Melody. I hope you find true happiness."

Her back to him, she halted and said, "I wish you all the happiness you seek." She continued down the ramp and proceeded to walk toward the fortress gate.

Cade watched until the gate opened to allow her entrance. She never looked back. He retracted the ramp and sealed the hatch. He keyed his com unit. "Cargo bay secure. Ready for lift."

Zina acknowledged his transmission as he settled on the hay next to Maska. They were soon out of the atmosphere, making the one hour and fifteen-minute trip to the Hyper Space entry transition. He went up to his bunk and lay deep in thought until he heard the ship's alert chime, and Zina's voice announce, "Two minutes to transition." He closed his eyes and fell asleep.

He awoke and was aware of the hyperdrive hum as he left the bunk. He went to the galley and found Zina seated at the table, drinking caff.

"I see you finally decided to wake up."

"How much longer will we be in hyperspace?"

"You slept through the first six hours, so we have two hours left." She took a sip of caff and watched as he drew a cup, before settling next to her."

She set her cup in front of her and said, "After we left, Faroe, Melody gave me a letter and asked that I give it to you after we return to Faroe."

"She did? Where is the letter?"

Zina picked up her cup and took a sip. She remained silent for a couple of minutes. "After she saw you plant a passionate kiss on Lillia, she told me to destroy the letter. She was crying at the time."

"I didn't kiss Lillia. She surprised me by practically jumping on me." He paused. "So, you destroyed the letter?"

Zina pulled the letter from her pocket, but did not hand it to him.

"If that's the letter, let me see it."

She sighed. "You have been so thick-headed, that I don't know what good it will do to allow you to read this precious document."

"You read it?"

"Yes, she asked me to read it." She handed the letter to him.

He opened the letter, and read it to himself. *Dearest Cade, I know you won't believe me, but I fell in love with you between the time you found me in the tree on Thane, and the time I spent with you in the Scout during our journey to the Searcher. I couldn't tell you then, because I was afraid. Because of the evil I endured at the hands of men during captivity, I did not believe I could ever accept the love of a man. But meeting you, I felt your kindness toward me, and yes, I felt your love. The reason I pushed you away, was my fear that even though I loved you deeply, I would never be able to endure the intimate love that binds a man and woman together. I still fear that you won't want a woman who cherishes your touch, and embrace, but may never be capable of consummating a marriage with you. I know you love me, but can that love endure with the possibility that I may never be able to fulfill the responsibility of a loving wife? I have written this letter so that you will know the truth, and because I do not want to walk through life with the knowledge, that I didn't give you the chance to decide. No matter your decision, I will always love only you. If you can love a damaged woman, I wait for your return to me. The evidence that I loved you before I could have felt any obligation to you, should be on the security video of the Scout. Look for the night we spent alone on the Scout before our struggle with the battle droid. Love forever, Melody.*

He looked at Zina, and stood. "Thank you for saving the letter. I'll be in the Scout if I'm needed. He went down to the cargo bay and entered the Scout. Sitting at the auxiliary computer, he soon found what he was looking for. As he slept on one of the bunks, Melody reached across the aisle and lifted his hand to her lips. Tears came to him as she kissed his hand and said, "I'll love you forever." He wanted to turn the ship around, but it would not be possible until emergence from hyperspace. Leaving the scout, he made his way to the galley and found Zina still there. She was pacing the floor as he entered, her cheeks damp with tears.

Zina wiped her damp cheeks with a napkin. "I see on your face, that you've come to a decision."

He cleared his throat and held his emotions in check. "I know you need to return to your parents, and get on with your life. When we drop out of HyperSpace, I'll take the scout and return to Melody."

"I've been thinking, Cade. I made a mistake showing you the letter. I let my emotions get the best of me."

He raised a brow as he processed her words. "Why do you think it was a mistake?"

"She put her heart on paper, before you sent a dagger through her breast and further damaged her ability to trust or even love another person. You must realize that when she said goodbye, she was embracing the emptiness she had long feared. You will probably be rejected outright, and not allowed a chance to redeem yourself in her heart.

"Redeem myself?" He paused before saying, "Ironic, isn't it? I put so much of myself into restoring Melody to her people, and now, making the same effort to restore her love, may not be possible. But I must try."

"You won't return to New Terra in the scout. I'll take you back there, because I need to see what path you will find yourself traveling through life." She smiled and said, "I'm hungry. Let's have something to eat, so you can puzzle over what to say to her, over a full stomach."

Zangari's voice came over the com unit. "Zina, four minutes until emergence."

"We'll eat after I turn this ship around. That Zangari is a good pilot and beau, but his timing is always off. I better hurry. After all, I need to lay in the course for our return." She hustled out of the galley.

It proved to be the longest nine-hour journey Cade had ever made. He stood on the bridge and watched New Terra grow larger as the planetary drive pushed the Searcher at top speed.

Zina said, "I received acknowledgement from New Terra approach control, allowing us to sit down near the Sioux Fortress. They coordinated the request with Chief Natahay." She paused. "Space Patrol has sent landing coordinates for the non-standard landing request. I have them laid in."

Zangari said, "Course recognized. Hold on to your hats."

The ship settled quietly, cushioned by the magnetic flux drive. Cade made his way to the cargo bay and opened the hatch. He stepped out and found it to be late morning. He didn't carry any weapons as he walked toward the fortress.

As he approached, Chief Natahay looked out, over the wall and then turned his attention to Eagle Feather. She rested on one knee, so she wouldn't be seen by Cade.

"My daughter, after you told me and your mother all about this man, it was obvious to us that you love him. Why do you want me to turn him away? He obviously doesn't care if you can't fill the wedding bed as a bride is supposed to do."

"Father, I put that in a letter that Zina destroyed. He doesn't know my reasons for rejecting him in the past. Just send him away."

Cade halted ten feet from the wall and looked upward at the face of Chief Natahay. "I request a meeting with Chief Natahay and his wife."

Natahay looked at his daughter. "Since he didn't ask for you, I can't turn him away. After all, Nizhoni told me about the great deeds he did for us in the guise of Red Arrow."

"But, father."

"I have made my decision." He called down to Cade, "Your request has been accepted."

The gate opened, and Cade saw a woman waiting for him to approach. He halted about three feet from her. He saw the tiara resting on her brow and realized she was the Queen Mother. He went to one knee and bowed his head in respect. "Your Majesty, I am humbled by your presence."

She said, "Rise and accompany me to our chambers."

He rose to his feet, but followed custom by waiting for her to speak.

She reached out and grasped his right hand with her left. "I am Aiukli, Eagle Feather's mother."

He smiled and bowed his head slightly. "It is an honor to meet you."

She released his hand and said, "Come with me. We will meet in our private chambers." She led him through the great hall, and passed through the throne room to enter a door a short distance past the throne. Chief Natahay was waiting for them inside.

The chief said, "You are welcome here, and there will be no need for honorifics. I am Natahay, and this lovely woman is Aiukli. Please address us as such while in our quarters."

Cade looked around, but Melody was not in the room.

Natahay said, "Let's go sit around the table and visit over a cup of coffee." They followed Aiukli through an arched doorway and entered a kitchen area. Natahay took a seat and motioned Cade to sit across from him, while Aiukli carried three cups to the table and set them next to the urn. She poured the cups and asked Cade if he wanted milk.

He nodded and said, "Thank you, Aiukli." He watched her take the chair next to her husband.

Natahay said, "Tell us why you're here."

Melody was standing in the pantry, out of sight, as she listened.

"I came to ask permission to speak with Melody; I meant to say, Eagle Feather."

Aiukli asked, "Why did you call her by the name of Melody?"

He smiled. "It was the name she chose to give me when we first met. It is the name I knew her by when I fell in love with her, and it will probably be the name I will remember her by, for the rest of my life."

Melody squeezed her eyes shut as she tried to maintain a stony heart. She heard her father say, "Our daughter has told us everything about your time spent with her. She said she wrote a letter explaining the reason for her rejection of you, but she had that letter destroyed."

"Our friend didn't destroy the letter, but gave it to me when we were nearly back to Faroe. The words she wrote, reflect my own love for her."

Aiukli looked earnestly into Cade's eyes, trying to see his heart. "Our daughter was quite candid with us and shared very personal reasons to doubt your ability to love her. It is hard for me to ask this of you." She hesitated. "Are you able to love her unconditionally, as she loves you, with the knowledge that her deep affections may not include the possibility of the greatest intimacy?"

Melody resisted her impulse to enter the room and stop her parents from saying more. *What is she thinking? I told her I was over him.*

Cade didn't hesitate. "My love for her was never based on sex. I loved her smile, her voice, and even her scent is familiar to me. I even accepted her mean treatment of me, when she was rejecting me, as a challenge to be overcome. My life was brighter when she was in it. I found joy when she held my hand. I dared to embrace her on two occasions in an effort to comfort her, and those were times when I found comfort as well."

Melody burst out of the pantry, tears flowing down her cheeks. She stopped before reaching the table. "Why didn't you tell me?

Why didn't you ever try to kiss me, the way you kissed Lillia? Why didn't you hold me, and not let me go?"

He left his chair and moved to stand in front of her. "I wanted to do all of that, but I gradually believed your rejections to be real. It seems we were both trying to protect the other. I didn't kiss Lillia. She did that. It wasn't the kiss I wanted or yearned for. That one is still upon your lips." He took her in his arms, as their lips and hearts met at last.

Aiukli, tears in her eyes, said to Natahay as she rose from her seat, "Let's give them some space." They left the room with Cade and Melody still locked in a tender embrace.

Melody gently released her hold on him and reluctantly moved her lips from his. "We should sit at the table and talk." She held his left hand in her right and guided him to their seats. They sat next to each other, still holding hands, resting them on the table between them.

She turned her face to him, and they gazed into one another's eyes. She asked, "What should we do now?"

"I want to take you as my wife, this very day." He paused. "Where we live and how we show our love to each other, will be according to what makes you happy. If you're happy with me, then I will be satisfied."

"Since you read my letter, and my mother blabbed my deepest concerns to you, are you willing to have the kind of wedding night that doesn't allow complete fulfillment?"

Cade sighed. "Laying by your side every night for the rest of my life, knowing you love me, will be enough."

She smiled. "Like you did with Nizhoni for several weeks?"

"Like that, but not in the same way. My heart did not belong to her, and she was not my lover."

"What are you waiting for? Ask me?"

Cade felt a little sheepish. He cleared his throat. "I need to ask your parents' permission first."

Melody threw back her head and laughed. "The fact that they left us here while we kissed, was affirmation they approved of you."

Natahay and Aiukli reentered the room. Natahay said, "You have our blessings. There is no way we could stand in the way of our daughter's true love. Your parents should be here for the bonding ceremony. As you know, both our nations see marriages as a close family event, without everyone being invited. You will have to wait for their arrival, and I already sent word to your ship to contact Jace. He says they will be here tomorrow afternoon. In the meantime, you need to decide on what your plans are for after the wedding night."

"Father, since I heard Cade tell you that it is up to me, I already know what I want. After our wedding night, spent in my cabin, we will go to our home on Faroe."

Cade asked, "You really mean it? What about your responsibility here?"

"It probably never came up, but I have a younger, annoying, brother. He can replace me quite easily." She turned to her father. "If that is permitted by his father."

Natahay smiled. "The young prince still has much to learn, so he may need occasional guidance from the princess. He will make a good chief when it is time."

"I'm excited that you want to live on Faroe." Cade squeezed her hand.

"It's not just for you. Most of my memories of being with you are in the cabin."

Aiukli said, "It seems like all that is left is for the two of you to prepare for tomorrow. I will arrange the ceremony. I understand that a ship's captain has the authority to carry out a wedding. Perhaps Jace could do that."

Melody said, "He's a good choice, but I'd rather have Zina do it. She is from another world and looks much different than us, but she has a heart of gold, and is my friend."

Her mother said, "That helps, as I won't have to arrange for someone to conduct the wedding."

The afternoon of the next day, Cade, dressed in his white native clothing, watched the Hermes descend from the sky. Zina was in the great hall, going over her part in the ceremony. Cade approached the Hermes and saw his mother and father come down the ramp as they hurried toward him. They were dressed in their best native costumes, yet both wore items that were more a part of later traditions, established on Arzor. Mother wore a corsage and his father wore a boutonniere on the left side of his white vest. Both were dressed in leather-stained white.

Anna hugged her son with tears dampening her cheeks. "I was so happy to hear the news. I am getting the daughter-in-law that I wanted." She handed him a yoris hide pouch. "These belonged to your grandparents."

Cade opened the pouch and found two rings. They were silver with turquoise stones set in them. There were also two silver necklaces with heart-shaped pendants of silver with red coral and turquoise stones. "These are beautiful, mother. Thank you. Let's go inside."

When they entered the great hall, Melody was waiting inside the doorway. She wore all white, with her only jewelry being the tiara Cade had given her. He took one of the necklaces out of the pouch and fastened it around her neck. Handing the second one to her, he waited as she placed it around his neck.

"These are beautiful. Are they from your parents?"

"Yes. They belonged to my grandparents." He handed her his ring. "I hope these fit; we may have to fake it." He turned toward the altar, and saw his parents had taken their places after being greeted by Melody's parents. He smiled as he looked into her eyes. "It's time." He stood on the right and reached with his left hand to grasp her right hand. They walked slowly toward the Altar. They came to a halt in front of Zina, and stood between the two sets of parents. Between Zina and the others, were three candles on separate stands. The candles were unlit. Natahay handed a long, lighted match to Melody, and Curt handed one to Cade. They both reached forward and lit the candle in front of them, leaving the center candle unlit.

Zina said, "Just as Cade and Melody were born into this life, the light of each candle represents the years they lived before this day."

Cade held up her ring and said, "This ring symbolizes the love I have for you. It is a circle and bears witness to the fact that my love, while having a beginning, will never have an end." He placed the ring on her finger and was pleased to see that it fit her. "I pledge that every breath I take from this moment will be for you."

He saw a tear trickle down her left cheek as she raised his ring. "This ring, too, symbolizes my love for you. I didn't have any idea what love was all about, until those first moments we spent together. Though our love didn't start out perfect, I believe it has reached perfection, and will never end as symbolized by this circle of silver." She placed the ring on his left ring finger. "With this ring, I promise to give you all of me. My entirety belongs to you."

They turned to face the unlit candle as they were both handed new matches. Each of them lighted their match from their respective candles and together, combined their flames to light the middle candle.

Zina said, "This candle represents the combining of their lives, lived apart, into one that they will live together. They will love one another and cherish their times together. There will be rough times, and smooth times. There will be times of great joy, and of great sorrow. They face these challenges together while in this life." She paused. "You may face each other."

Cade and Melody turned to face each other.

Cade said, "I, Cade Hosteen Storm, take you as my forever wife."

Melody grinned at his unscripted pledge. "I, Melody Eagle Feather, accept proudly your surname and love. I will forever be Melody Eagle Feather Storm."

He grinned and mouthed, "Melody?"

"Why not? You said it was the name you knew me by. I don't want you to forget me."

Zina said, "By the power granted me by Central Control, and the Creator, I now name you as husband and wife. Cade, you may kiss your bride."

Melody quickly wrapped her arms around his neck and met him with a passionate kiss. He pulled his face away and grinned. "I was supposed to kiss you, not the other way around."

"You were taking too long."

Zina said, "Let me be the first to introduce Cade and Melody Storm."

They walked down the aisle, and the small crowd of invitees followed them to the banquet hall. Nizhoni and Chayton approached, and Nizhoni hugged his neck and then turned to hug

Melody. "My brother came through by giving me a sister. I'm so happy for both of you, and the ceremony was the most beautiful I have ever attended."

Melody gave her a kiss on the cheek. "I'm proud to have you as a sister."

Cade met Melody's little brother and noticed that his parents and Melody were hitting it off. It was a very good day as they enjoyed the food and festivities. A small band with a drummer and a couple of guitarists played music suitable for dancing. As darkness began to fall, Natahay announced it was time to let the newlyweds begin their marriage with some privacy.

Melody took Cade by the hand. "Shall we go to my cabin?" She paused. "I mean, our home away from home. Father said it is a wedding gift for us."

"I'm ready to spend alone time with you, but we need to do something first."

"What is it?"

"Since you left, the animals are ignoring me. I guess they're unhappy about you leaving. Would you mind a quick visit to the Searcher?"

Melody laughed. "It's probably my fault. I unloaded my problems on them, and I wasn't very kind to you during that conversation. I'm going to the cabin while you beg for Maska's forgiveness." He watched her go into the cabin before continuing to the Searcher, where he found Maska sitting on her haunches, doing her impersonation of a feline goddess.

He heard Maska in his head. *"Good, I see the team is back together. Now go, and allow me to rest."*

Cade thought. *"Thank you, Maska. We are a team, and Melody is back."*

"She already told me. She said you need to hurry home."

"We haven't been married half a day, and she's already ordering me around. I love it." He left the ship and hurried to the cabin. He opened the door and found it to be very dark inside.

"Cade, come to bed."

"I haven't changed into night clothes yet."

"Just remove your outer clothes and get under the covers, it's chilly in here."

He stripped down to his shorts and eased under the blankets. He felt her hand and grasped it as he felt extremely happy to be lying beside her."

"No. I want you to cuddle with me."

"Are you sure? I thought you wanted me to love you without getting too close."

"I'm sure. Let's snuggle against this cold night."

"I want to go on record as saying this may not be the best thing for you." He rolled toward her and moved his arm to hold her. He started to pull his arm back, but she held it tight to her. You aren't dressed."

"I know, since I happened to be the one who undressed me. I wanted to surprise you. I had my doubts until Zina said something during a conversation, I had with her. She said, "I understand that you cannot give your entire self to him. I realized at that moment, that what I thought was crucial to who I am, that part that was stolen by evil, was not who I am. I am the one who can choose to give all of me to you. That's what I'm doing tonight. All of me is yours, just as all of you is mine."

He pulled her tightly against him. "Zina is a wise woman."

Melody giggled at his touch. "Did you lock the door?"